AC

The journey to publication is a long and often arduous one best taken in good company.

My deepest gratitude goes out to my fabulous critique partner, Dana Delamar. Without you, Dana, this book would have remained a draft. Your constant support and enthusiasm for my story dragged me through the valleys and helped me over the peaks. I couldn't have dreamed of a better companion for this journey.

Overwhelming thanks to the CherryPlotters, a team where the sum of the parts far exceeds the whole. Carol, Cherry, Christina, Ciara, Dragon, Heather, Julia, Kelli, Laurie, Rebecca, and Shelli, this story would not even have made it to draft status were it not for all of you.

Special thanks to Dawn, Josefin, Karen, Marianne, and Sherri for having the courage to wade through the first draft of this story. Your writing experience and expertise served me well. I can only hope that, in some small way, I've returned the favor.

To Edith, beta reader extraordinaire. Thank you for the time you spent reading the first of my many final versions. Your insightful comments helped make this book much better than it would have been without you.

Finally, thank you to my family for putting up with the endless hours I spend at the computer and at writing meetings. You know why I do it. And someday, you may even appreciate it. Love you!

CHAPTER 1

Don't forget Nic—you belong to me. If you stray, she'll pay.

The darkened theater closed around Nic Lamoureux like a cave, filled with unknown, unseen dangers. How had the stalker gotten his private number? Clenching the cell phone in his fist, he glanced at his *Bad Days* co-star, Jane Carver, sitting on his right, then at his agent, Vivian Carmichael, on his left. Which woman was the message targeting? With a flick of his thumb, he brought up the text again. Sweat beaded on his back, making his silk shirt cling to his skin.

Jane leaned in close and smiled, oblivious. "You were great in this scene. Oscar-worthy." He studied her face. Why would anyone want to hurt her? Jane was beautiful, intelligent, and absolutely unavailable. During one of their late nights working on the next day's scenes, he'd discovered her secret engagement to the film's director. If anything happened to Jane because of one of his crazy fans, her fiancé would have his balls.

As Jane settled back in her seat, a woman in the next row turned around to face him. Light from the screen reflected off something in her hand. On instinct, he twisted sideways to protect Jane. Blood pounded in his ears, drowning out the sound of gunfire blasting from speakers all around the theater. After snapping a photo with her camera phone, the woman gave him a thumbs-up and returned to watch the movie.

Vivian patted his arm as he sat back and shot him a questioning look. After flashing her what he hoped was an easy smile, he caught his bodyguard's eye. Kaden leaned across Vivian's seat. "Everything okay, sir?"

Tucking the phone in his hand, he reached over, resting his arm on Vivian's shoulders, and slipped Kaden the phone. His bodyguard barely glanced at the message before standing up, his mouth a thin line. "Sir, we need to leave." Nic started to tell him to sit down, that the movie was almost over, but the words died on his lips. Kaden's hand hovered above his gun as his eyes raked the crowd. "You're too exposed." He signaled to Jane's bodyguard. "Get her out of here."

Kaden was right. The sender could be any one of the hundreds of people crowding the screening room. Nic grabbed Vivian's hand. "Let's go."

"But—"

"Now." Nic jerked his head in Kaden's direction. She nodded, eyes wide. Kaden rushed them outside, calling out to the festival security guards to back him up as they ran to their limo. Nic glanced behind to make sure Jane was taken care of. Seeing her bodyguard secure her in a limo, he relaxed. A bit. He still had Vivian to worry about.

When they reached their limo, he opened the door and pushed Vivian inside as Kaden climbed into the driver's seat and started the engine. They slammed the doors shut and took off, tires squealing.

"Darling," Vivian said after fastening her seatbelt and straightening her skirt. "What the hell was that about? Taking off in the middle of your own premiere? How do you expect me to spin this with the press?"

He shot her a flirty grin. "Tell them I had a hot date."

"A booty call? That's your excuse?" Vivian sighed and brushed a loose strand of auburn hair from her cheek. "Tell me the truth. What's going on?"

Trying not to scare her, he shrugged. "I was being watched."

Vivian stared at him for a moment, then dropped her head against the seat and laughed. "Of course you were. Do you think people came to the premiere tonight to see your movie? No, they came to see Nic The Lover."

"This felt different."

You belong to me. Just thinking about it made his stomach roll. He stretched his shoulders to relieve the tension. When that didn't work, he watched the streets of downtown D.C. zip by his window.

"Is this about the Internet postings by NicsBitch, darling?" When he didn't respond, she continued. "Trust me. All celebrities have fans who follow them around and post about them online. Ninety-nine percent of the time, they're harmless."

"And what about the other one percent?" If the poster had followed him from L.A. to D.C., they weren't dealing with a harmless fan. "Someone sent me a text tonight. I think it was NicsBitch."

"A text? How did she get your number? It's unlisted."

He held up his hands. "Don't look at me."

"Anyways, she's been keeping tabs on you for months. And nothing bad's come of it."

"Yet." He handed Vivian the phone. "Read the message. I think you and Jane were in danger." As soon as the words were out of his mouth, he regretted them. Vivian was such a mother hen, she'd ignore any danger to herself and focus on him.

She bit her lip and frowned. "Maybe Kaden should room with you tonight."

Shit. Nic shook his head. "If anything, he should stay with you."

"Don't be silly," she said, offering him a shaky smile. "I'll be fine."

Heavy silence accompanied them the rest of the way. Nic watched Vivian, his agent, mentor, and friend of ten years, fidget in her seat. Vivian never fidgeted. If anything were to happen to her because of him, he wouldn't need an enraged fiancé to rip his balls off—he'd do the honors himself.

At the hotel, he and Kaden escorted Vivian to her door. As she was unlocking it, she turned back to Nic. "I'll see you at ten?"

"Ten?"

"You have a photo shoot with Rafael, remember?"

"Damn. I completely forgot." He rubbed his stiff neck. "I was looking forward to going back home."

Vivian pursed her lips. "I can reschedule it."

He shook his head. "I'll be there." The GI Film Festival, which celebrated the American Armed Forces, had chosen to premiere *Bad Days* because the organizers believed in the film's message as much as he did. The photos from the shoot would garner additional sponsors and publicity. He couldn't let them down.

Once Vivian was in her room, safe behind a locked door, Kaden crossed the hall and opened Nic's door. After a quick inspection, he gave the all clear. Nic walked into the living area and dropped onto the couch, propping his feet up on the coffee table. "Do you think NicsBitch sent the message?"

"Probably." Kaden took the armchair across from the couch.

Nic yawned and glanced at his watch. "You can't stay though."

"I can't?"

"Isn't tomorrow your girlfriend's birthday?" Kaden's relationship was already strained enough without adding a missed birthday to Beth's list of grievances.

Kaden winced. "Shit."

Seeing his bodyguard's expression, Nic laughed. "Go. As soon as I'm done with the photo shoot, I'll hop a plane back to L.A."

Kaden narrowed his eyes. "No can do. This situation has gone way beyond some celebrity sightings and even a few stalkerish postings. This is serious. How the fuck can I do my job if I'm not here?"

It was bad enough having a babysitter at public events—he didn't want or need one dogging his every step. "I'm a big boy. I can take care of myself. Besides, the stalker isn't targeting me."

"Just any woman near you. I'm staying. Beth will have to understand."

"And if she doesn't?"

"Then we're done."

The words shook him. Life wasn't perfect, but he had great friends. No way was the stalker going to dictate his actions or theirs. And nothing was going to happen to Vivian. He wouldn't let it. "If I show fear, start acting like a victim, then she's already won. I need to do this. On my own."

"If the stalker comes after you or Vivian, what's your plan to stop her?"

Nic tugged on his tie, loosening it. Did everyone think he was a weenie? "I can shoot just as well as you can."

Kaden looked around, searching the hotel room with his eyes, before arching a sarcastic brow. "Yeah? Where's your gun, hotshot?"

Nic's gaze sharpened. Kaden knew exactly where his gun was—at home, locked in his safe. D.C. was one of the few places that had denied him a permit to carry. "The whole thing won't take more than a couple hours. I'll be home before dinner. Nothing's going to happen to me, or anyone else."

After finally convincing Kaden to return to L.A., Nic changed into his favorite jeans and a loose T-shirt, and grabbed a Coke from the mini-fridge. Popping open the can, he made himself comfortable on the couch and settled in for a long night of mind-numbing TV.

Anything to forget someone out there was watching him, following him. Obsessing.

Where was the best place to shoot Nic "The Lover" Lamoureux? The king-size bed or the beige club chair?

Lauren James scanned the hotel room through the lens of her Nikon D700. She adjusted the intensity of the lights and the angle of the umbrellas around the bed. With her foot, she moved the chair an inch to the left, then after a moment's consideration, nudged it an inch to the right. She glanced at her watch for the tenth time in as many minutes, confirming what she already knew. He was late. Everything she needed to get the cleanest shot possible was already in place, *except* her target.

She hoped he hadn't turned into one of those Hollywood diva types who'd blow off a contracted photo shoot to go party with some fangirls. This was a huge opportunity for her and he'd better not ruin it.

Oh, who was she kidding? In minutes, she'd be seeing Nic in the flesh, once again. For years, he'd been her own personal porn star, playing the male lead in her nightly fantasies. Her hands flew to her cheeks and she bit back a giddy laugh. If he walked in and read the thoughts on her face, she'd die.

The door opened. Her heart rate spiked. Nic entered the room followed by a pretty redhead she didn't recognize. They made a perfectly matched, elegant couple.

As Lauren stood rooted to the spot, gaping at the most beautiful man she'd ever seen, he crossed the room, stopping directly in front of her, and smiled. "You don't look like Rafael...."

Oh, God. His voice still held a hint of the sexy Québécois accent he kept hidden in his movies and public appearances. With considerable effort and concentration, she fought to close her mouth and struggled against the need to slowly peruse his amazing body. After surreptitiously wiping off her sweaty palm, she met his gaze and held out her hand. "I'm Lauren James."

"*Enchanté*." Nic raised her fingers to his lips and lightly kissed her knuckles. She watched, mesmerized, as the expression in his eyes turned inquisitive. "Have we met?"

A sharp pang of disappointment stabbed her chest. He didn't remember her.

Before she could answer his question, the redhead joined them. She had a certain ageless quality Lauren admired. Although ten or fifteen years older, the tall, slim woman with her flawless skin, gorgeous hair, and tailored clothes could turn the heads of men still in their twenties. Based on Rafael's description, she could be none other than Vivian Carmichael, Nic's very demanding and very protective agent.

The woman leaned forward. "Where's Rafael?"

"He's feeling under the weather today so he asked me to handle the photo shoot on my own." Lauren turned to Nic. "I hope that's okay?"

"Of course it's—"

"Not okay!" Vivian interrupted, pointing a perfectly manicured finger at Lauren. "I only agreed to this arrangement if Rafael were here to direct and supervise."

Nic frowned. "What's the big deal? We agreed to do a photo shoot after the *Bad Days* premiere. Let's get on with it."

Vivian grasped his forearm while making a dismissive gesture toward Lauren. "This woman isn't a professional photographer, darling. She works in a two-bit Seattle department store taking snapshots of snot-nosed babies."

"Why's she working with Rafael then?"

Vivian glared at Lauren. "Somehow she managed to win a contest, and you were the prize."

He turned to Lauren, looking impossibly sexy with one black eyebrow raised. "I'm the prize?"

"Not exactly." Heat crept up her neck and her cheeks burned. "I won a *photography* contest organized by the GI Film Festival. The prize was to assist on a photo shoot with you."

Vivian insinuated herself between them, draped her arm around Nic's shoulder and whispered in a loud stage voice, "I can't let you do this. My God, she works in a *department* store. Think of your reputation. You need someone with experience and talent."

Lauren gritted her teeth. All she needed was a chance to prove herself.

"Come on, Viv. She did *win* the contest."

When he'd shown up late for the photo shoot, Lauren had been prepared to write Nic off as just another smooth talking, self-indulgent Hollywood celeb, but here he was, standing up for her.

Vivian patted his arm. "All right, darling. But I'm staying to supervise, and I will personally approve any shots before they are released." She stared pointedly at Lauren. "Is that understood, Lorna?"

"Her name's Lauren."

Vivian smiled tightly but remained silent, apparently waiting for her response.

Sighing with relief, Lauren readily agreed. As long as she got to work with Nic, she'd deal with any conditions Vivian imposed on her. This photo shoot could be the key to jump-starting her career.

Lauren waved toward a room service tray on the ottoman in the hotel room's sitting area. "I ordered a pot of coffee and pastries in case anyone wants some refreshments. Please help yourselves." Nic loved coffee and éclairs, or so she'd read in *Star* magazine. *God, let them be right.* She couldn't afford for anything else to go wrong today.

She closed the heavy curtains that covered the room's single window and asked Vivian to take a seat in the sitting area so she wouldn't interfere with the lighting equipment. After sucking in a somewhat shaky breath, she pasted on a bright smile and faced Nic.

"Okay, let's get started." She thumped the back of the club chair, surrounded by lighting equipment. "Please remove your jacket and tie, then sit here. I'll take a few test shots."

"The chair? Not the bed?"

Her breath caught at the sheer sensuality in the curve of his lips. The same perfectly shaped lips she'd imagined kissing hundreds of times. She absolutely *had* to capture that look.

"We'll use the bed later," she mumbled, lowering her head to retest the light.

"Promise?"

Startled, she looked up, her face flushed. Why couldn't she flirt back like any normal woman, like Vivian?

With his gaze locked on Lauren's, Nic undid the top buttons of his shirt. He lowered himself into the club chair, lounged back and stretched out his long, lean frame.

The man exuded sex.

Nic's eyes, fixed on hers, penetrated her mind, seeing far more than she wanted him to see. None of the photos she'd seen did justice to his overwhelming animal magnetism. If she succeeded in fully capturing his allure, her career would definitely take off.

The dark slacks he wore outlined his muscular thighs as he crossed one foot over the opposite knee while the white dress shirt highlighted the broad expanse of his chest and shoulders. With one elbow on the armrest, he cradled his chin in the palm of his hand. A Cheshire cat grin spread across his handsome features. "Like this?"

Perfect. "You've obviously done this a few hundred times." Lauren smiled and raised the camera to eye level. "Now lace your hands on your stomach and lean your head back with your eyes closed. Open your eyes slowly… excellent."

She talked him through a few more basic poses, making minor lighting adjustments to maximize the contrasts, emphasizing his deep blue eyes, making them the focal point of the shot.

"No, no," Vivian scoffed. "These colors make Nic look bland." *As if.* Nothing in the world could make Nic The Lover look anything less than spectacular.

Nic laughed. "Vivian, let the woman do her job."

Lauren turned away and coughed to hide her grin. "We'll start with something suave and sexy. Think James Bond."

She instructed Nic to twist in the chair so he could swing his left leg over the armrest and crook his left elbow over the back of the chair. He looked delectable, but his right leg and arm were still not positioned exactly how she wanted.

Deciding it would be more effective to show than explain, she risked a glance in Vivian's direction. Seeing the woman busy serving herself a cup of coffee, she quietly approached Nic.

With a trembling hand, she applied a slight pressure on the back of his knee to keep it bent as she grasped his calf with her other hand, pulling it toward her to extend his leg. As the well-defined muscles shifted beneath her palm, shivers of pleasure rolled up and down her spine. Shocked, she let go and backed away. She'd dreamed of touching his smooth tanned skin, but now that she had the opportunity….

"Please put your right hand on your thigh." God, if she weren't such a coward, she could have the pleasure of putting it there herself. "Now for the finishing touch." She extracted a large silver gun from the pocket of her cargo pants. "Don't worry, it's fake," she added, when she saw Vivian open her mouth.

She placed the prop in his left hand so it dangled from his fingertips. "Now relax and smile like you're seeing the sexiest woman in the world."

Lauren stared, mesmerized as Nic's expression transformed from one of subtle amusement to one of smoldering sexual intent. His lips curved ever so slightly and a light flush colored his cheekbones. His eyelids slanted and his pupils dilated. The heat of his intense gaze was enough to melt her camera lens.

My God, the man could act. What would it be like to have him look at her that way and mean it? His gaze filled with such lust, her stomach clenched and tumbled. This was the shot she'd been seeking. The shot that would drive women wild.

The shot that would propel her career into the upper stratosphere.

Quickly, she moved around him, capturing photo after photo. When she'd exhausted all the different angles, she put down her camera and eyed Nic from the tips of his black leather shoes to his silk-clad shoulders. He'd need to change his clothes for what she had in mind. She handed him a black gym bag. "Here's your outfit for the next pose. We're going for a dark, sexy soldier look. Give me a shout if you need help getting it on."

Nic burst out laughing.

Her head jerked up. "What?"

"Nothing." Still chuckling, he took the bag and walked into the bathroom.

Getting it on. The double-entendre finally dawned on her. Heat baked her face. Jeez, as if Nic The Lover would ever need help in that department. Grateful he wasn't in the room to see her blush, she concentrated on her camera, making adjustments for the next series of shots, ignoring Vivian, who roamed around the room, examining all the equipment.

"I couldn't find a shirt in the bag," Nic said, reentering the room a few minutes later, slowly swinging the shoulder holster around his finger. "Do you want me to put this on?"

"Not yet," she muttered as she ducked her head. *Holy crap!* Bare-chested, in a pair of low-slung fatigues and combat boots, Nic personified rugged hotness. How could he look even better in person?

She handed him a small bottle of oil. "Rub this on your chest and arms."

"Wanna help?" he asked, grinning.

Vivian raced forward and snatched the bottle from Nic's hand. "I'll do it." She poured some of the fragrant oil into her palms and, after warming it up, began sliding her hands all over Nic's smooth chest, his arms, and then down to his sculpted eight-pack. Judging by her expression, she enjoyed her task, perhaps a little too much.

On the other hand, Nic didn't seem to be affected in the least by Vivian's ministrations. As Lauren raised her eyes to his face, she found his hungry gaze focused on her, and almost groaned. Where she'd expected to see cool amusement, she saw something hot and dark that set her skin on fire. He didn't look away and neither did she. Blood thundered in her ears, her vision narrowed, and she became blind to everything else.

"Nic, darling. Your pocket's ringing," Vivian interrupted as she finished with the oil. The mournful sounds of Daughtry's *Home* finally penetrated Lauren's trance-like state, and she tore her gaze away from him.

Frowning, he pulled a cell phone out of his back pocket. "Sorry. I need to take this."

Nic sat on the bed to take the call. She didn't mean to eavesdrop, but the room wasn't very big. It didn't matter of course, because although she could hear what he was saying, she couldn't understand much of it. The sometimes gruff, sometimes flowing tones of Nic speaking his native language washed over her, stirring something deep inside her.

Maybe he'd interrupted her work to talk to a *girlfriend,* who was perhaps also the reason he'd arrived late in the first place. But she didn't remember hearing anything about Nic having a steady girlfriend. In fact, in the magazine photos, he always had a different woman wrapped around him. Whenever he saw a reporter with a camera, he'd grab the nearest woman and kiss her. The press even had a name for these women—Paparazzi Girls.

Nice. He'd better not try that with her.

Nic ended the call and pressed the base of his hand between his eyes where a headache was growing. As if the stalker wasn't enough, now he had Rachel to worry about too.

Vivian settled next to him on the bed, her hand rubbing comforting circles on his back. "Trouble at home?" she asked.

He shot her a narrowed glance. Vivian knew better than to bring up his private life in front of strangers. His gaze swung to the stranger in question. Concern and irritation warred in Lauren's pretty eyes. Eyes that read right through him. Eyes that seemed to know him. Lauren opened her mouth to speak, but Vivian cut her off.

"You look like you could use a break." Vivian offered him the steaming mug she'd prepared earlier. "Have some coffee. One sugar, one cream. Just the way you like it, darling."

"Thanks, Viv. You always know what I need." He smiled crookedly. "What about you, Lauren?"

Her curls swung wildly as she shook her head. "I'm fine, but while you're having your coffee, I can do your make-up." She turned to Vivian, holding up a small face-paint kit. "He needs camo paint. Do you want to apply that too?"

Vivian grimaced. "I'll spare my manicure. But you go ahead, Lorna dear. From the looks of things, a manicure is the least of your concerns."

With a wink for Lauren, he leaned in close to Vivian's ear. "Her name's Lauren."

Her eyes focused on the various shades of green and brown she was mixing, Lauren approached the bed to stand between his legs. "I don't want to obscure your features, so I won't use quite the same pattern the military does." Her fingers shook as she drew thin lines diagonally across his eyelids and brows, horizontally across his nose, and vertically across his mouth.

As she worked, Nic checked out his cute little photographer. A tan v-neck T-shirt molded her full breasts, and baggy cargo pants accentuated the roundness of her hips. The large pockets on her thighs bulged with an endless supply of gadgets she pulled out as needed. So cute, like a grown up Girl Guide.

Her curly hair was a beautiful light brown, what he'd call *châtain* in French, and her eyes were a rare blue-green. Wrapped in his arms, the top of her head would tuck under his chin. Nic felt a stirring in his BDUs. Damn, he loved short, curvy women.

She stepped away from him, the heat of her eyes on his face, his chest, his legs. "Rough, dangerous. Perfect," she said, her voice husky. He imagined it would sound exactly like that if he had her underneath him. His cock hardened and he was suddenly very thankful to be sitting down.

He cleared his throat. "Okay, what do I do now?"

Kiss me. Had she said that? Or was that just his wishful thinking?

"Put on the shoulder holster," she said, destroying his fantasy.

The experience he'd gained with military gear while working on *Bad Days* served him well. She watched as he expertly slipped into the holster, bolstering his flagging ego. No, he wasn't some weenie who needed a bodyguard 24/7.

"You'll need these, too." She lifted a set of military issue dog tags from around her neck.

After reading the imprinted name, he raised an eyebrow. "Todd James. A relative of yours?"

She nodded. "My husband. He died in Afghanistan five years ago."

Christ. He'd never been married, but he could imagine the pain she'd gone through. Losing a spouse at such a young age had to be devastating. He tried to hand the dog tags back to her. "I'm sorry for your loss," he said, the words sounding inadequate.

A shadow flitted across her face, but she waved his hand away. "Thank you. Now put them on."

He'd done a lot of acting, but this was the first time he'd felt like an impostor. He was no hero, not like her husband, a man who'd died for his country. But the brittleness in Lauren's eyes warned him not to fight her. He slipped the tags on. They were warm from her skin.

She smiled, but it seemed forced. "Lie down on the bed and lean against the pillows."

Nic hated the tension that had settled over Lauren. He wanted a real smile from her this time. Crossing the room in a couple long steps, he threw himself onto the bed. He wiggled around for a few seconds before settling down. Right on cue, Lauren laughed.

Success. "What? This isn't good?" he asked, feigning confusion.

"You look great, and if I was going for a cross between GI Joe and Fabio on Barbie's bed, this would be the perfect shot." Amusement lit her eyes, making them glitter like topaz stones. The delight on her face kindled a fire in his chest. Seeing her smile was a better reward than a mantel full of Oscars.

He stood while she tore the salmon-colored bedspread off. After pulling back the top sheet, she showed him where to sit and adjusted the pillows behind his back. She covered the leg that was in the middle of the bed, twisting the sheet so it snaked over his leg, leaving his black combat boot exposed.

"Lift up your outside knee and anchor your leg with your foot," she instructed, rushing to check the scene through the camera lens. She came back and adjusted the position of his raised knee, angling it toward the edge of the bed.

Although her touch was light, his skin burned where her hand wrapped around his knee and he wanted her to slowly slide her fingers higher and higher and higher….

He blew out a long breath. *Rein it in, lover boy.* His attraction to Lauren was explosive and he'd love nothing better than to explore it to the utmost limits. But with the stalker breathing down his neck, jealous of the women around him, the timing couldn't be worse. He wanted to get to know Lauren, not get her killed.

Oblivious to her effect on him, Lauren backed away and nodded. "Perfect. Now raise your right arm and grab the headboard." She reached into one of her big cargo pockets. "I'm going to hand you a knife. Hold it in your left hand and place the blade flat on your left thigh."

"Lorna dear, is that really necessary?" Vivian asked, her voice coated with high-fructose corn syrup.

Lauren made a face and gritted her teeth. "The shot won't work without the knife."

Nic glanced at Vivian and frowned. "Lauren knows what she's doing. She's a professional."

Vivian flashed him a broad smile, then turned to Lauren. "Of course she is, darling." Sarcasm dripped from her voice like venom from a viper's fangs.

"Viv, play nice." She wanted the best for him, but if she didn't tone it down a bit, she'd ruin the shoot.

Lauren shrugged off the interruption and the insult. She unsheathed a long silver bayonet and handed it to him. As he followed her instructions, she checked the composition of the shot through her camera viewfinder. A frown marred her forehead.

"I'm not getting this right, am I?" he asked.

"Almost. But the knife needs to be higher." As she leaned over his shoulder, she very slowly slid her hand along his leg, pulling his hand higher until the blade lay diagonally along his upper thigh, pointing to his groin. He sucked in a breath. His muscles quivered under the warmth of her hand, so close to where he wanted it to be. "I won't hurt you," she said in her low sexy voice.

"Too late for that, *ma chère.*" He groaned at the thought of her hand on his cock.

Her face coloring, she snatched her hand back and returned to her camera. "Perfect," she said, taking shots from different angles. All of a sudden, a wave of exhaustion crashed over him. He yawned widely and his eyelids drooped. "Hey, Nic. You okay?"

"Just tired. Vivian, could you get me some more coffee?"

"Whatever you need, darling," Vivian said as she went to refill his cup in the sitting area. "How much longer will this take, Lorna?

Rolling her eyes, Lauren turned to Nic. "Just a few more shots, then we're done."

Lauren picked up her camera and walked around the bed. "Lie on your side, please."

Grinning, he scooted his butt down, then grabbed the pillow and placed it under his head as if settling down for the night. Now that was an idea. He was so damn tired.

"Maybe you could rest your elbow on the pillow and hold your head up?"

Trying to get some more hands-on action, he placed his hand behind his neck, crooking his head back at an awkward angle. Her eyebrows pulled together and she shook her head. Nic swallowed a laugh. She set her camera on the nightstand and tugged on his shoulder to pull it forward. He resisted and, when she let go, rolled onto his back. Eyes closed, he lay there, waiting.

Lauren shook his shoulder. "Nic."

He opened his eyes and met her concerned gaze. What the hell was wrong with him? He'd spent most of the night watching TV, but still…

He'd *never* fallen asleep on the job.

A loud commotion in the hallway startled him. Heart pounding, he jack-knifed in the bed. The door flew open and slammed against the wall. Without waiting to see who it was, he jumped up and pulled a frozen Lauren back. With the bed between her and the door, he pushed her to the floor. If the assailant had a gun, she'd be safe. Feet apart, fists clenched, he turned to face the intruder.

CHAPTER 2

Relief crashed over Nic when he recognized several members of the paparazzi squeezing through the door of the hotel room. He turned and helped Lauren to her feet. Her eyes were glazed with confusion. Coming here without a bodyguard had been more than stupid; it had been irresponsible. The reporters would wonder why he'd reacted so aggressively, and he absolutely didn't want them to catch wind of his troubles with the stalker. He owed it to Vivian to turn this near fiasco into a photo op.

There was only one solution. With a resigned sigh, he pulled Lauren close, crushing her breasts against his chest.

"Oh no, you don't," she hissed. "I'm not one of your Paparazzi Girls."

She wasn't happy, but what could he do? Nic The Lover *always* found a Paparazzi Girl when cameras were around. His gaze darted between her and the photographers standing less than ten feet away. He arched a brow.

She rolled her eyes. "Fine. Do it."

He bent down and brushed his lips against hers. For the first few seconds, she didn't kiss him back, but she didn't push him away, either. Then, on a sigh, she leaned into him and her arms locked around his neck. His tongue darted out to taste her bottom lip. Mmm… cherry—his new favorite flavor. When her mouth opened, he didn't hesitate.

He dove in. And drowned.

He'd meant this to be a quick kiss, only now he just couldn't stop. His lips traced a path to her throat. Cupping her bottom with his hands, he lifted her up, grinding against her. She moaned. It was a beautiful sound, one he definitely wanted to hear again.

A loud noise pierced the fog of his lust. He raised his head from where he'd been nuzzling Lauren's apple-scented neck to tell whoever it was to fuck off, but as the sexual haze cleared, he swallowed the words. The paparazzi had gathered around, applauding and calling out crude encouragements. Some snapped photos while others rolled film. *Shit.* He'd pay for this fuck-up and so would she.

His arm still around Lauren's waist, he turned her toward the flashing lights and whispered, "Smile for the cameras, *chérie.*"

She tried to struggle out of his grasp, but he held her firmly. After forcing his lips into what he hoped was a sexy half smile, he made a show of winking at her.

"Hey Nic, who's the new girl?" shouted one of the male reporters.

"Lauren James is an up-and-coming photographer from Seattle."

"Looks like she's not the only one who's up and coming," snickered someone in the back of the group. Laughter erupted.

He ground his teeth and pasted on a cocky smile. It took only one glance in Lauren's direction to gauge her reaction. With camo paint smeared on her neck and across her beautiful face, she appeared feral.

"Nice makeup, Lauren," one of the women called out.

The paparazzi had to go. Now.

He searched the room for Vivian. She stood, her back to the window, observing the scene with a wide smile. Agents loved this sort of publicity.

"Vivian," he snapped, jerking his chin toward the door.

She stepped forward. "Ladies and gentlemen. Please follow me. I'm happy to answer any questions you have about Nic and the brilliant success of his new action film *Bad Days.* As you may know, *Bad Days* premiered here at the GI Film Festival last evening. By all accounts, it's yet another Nic The Lover blockbuster. There's even talk of an Oscar…"

Nic's tension drained out as she led the paparazzi into the hall and closed the door. With both palms, he rubbed his weary eyes. Too late, he remembered the camo paint. *Great.* Eyes burning, he turned to Lauren and gently grasped her shoulders. "Are you okay?"

She nodded stiffly. Unsure whether *he* was okay, he dropped into the nearest chair and closed his eyes. His legs felt heavy, like he'd run a marathon.

"Did you set this up?"

His eyes snapped open. Lauren stood in front of him, fists on hips, eyes sparking, lush lips pulled back in a fierce grimace. *Oh, yeah.* Even spitting mad, she looked absolutely gorgeous. If only he weren't so damn tired…

"I have no idea how they found me. Sorry you had to deal with that."

"With what?" Lauren asked, her eyes blazing. "Being made into another one of your Paparazzi Girls or being the butt of their jokes?"

He was the worst kind of shit. What had started out as a simple kiss for the camera had snowballed into so much more, because he'd enjoyed it.

Because he'd enjoyed her.

Because he'd wanted it to go on forever.

Too bad getting involved with him could get her killed.

~ ~

Gazing at the photo in her hand, she caressed Nic's strong jaw. This beautiful man was the only one for her. The only one who measured up. The only real man left in the world.

Other men were weak imitations. The people in Hollywood knew it, too. And that's why they tailor-made movies for him, showcasing the dark, dangerous man and the tender, sensuous lover. Like every alpha male, he needed an alpha female to keep him in line, and she was the perfect woman for the job.

Nic was such a naughty boy. She ran her fingertip along his full lower lip and smiled. She'd have to keep punishing her bad boy until he learned his lesson. If sightings, texts, and surprise visits from the paparazzi didn't work, she had no qualms about escalating the punishments, until he got her message. After all, she'd do anything—*everything*—for him.

She laid the photograph down on the table, cocking her head to the side as she examined it from a different angle. She could hardly wait to have him all to herself, to have him wrap his strong arms around her and lose control. Sex with Nic The Lover would be wild and rough, just the way she liked it. All his fans wanted him, but only she could have him. She was his perfect match.

Her lips curled into a tight smile. Yes, she would have him. One way or another. And anyone who got in her way? Her lips flattened and she slammed her fist onto the photograph. They'd live to regret it.

Or not.

~ ~

Nic was nothing like Lauren had imagined. He wasn't anything like she remembered either. He'd been cute in high school, but now he took her breath away.

Lauren placed the photos she'd been reviewing on the side table and sank into the overstuffed wingback chair. Sighing with pleasure, she kicked off her shoes and stretched her legs out on the matching ottoman. The prize package of the photography contest included this elegantly appointed room that was easily as large as her entire apartment.

Despite the warm weather, Lauren had lit the gas fireplace facing the king bed. The large picture window reflected the dancing flames and the lights of downtown D.C. It made an intriguing backdrop to the writing desk where she'd set up her laptop and portable photo printer. *Returned*, one of Nic's movies, played with the volume turned low on a flat-screen television that put to shame the old set she had at home.

She watched the movie for a few minutes, smiling as she recalled the first time she'd seen it. Several years after Todd died, her friends Sandra and Julie decided she needed a little adult time and invited her out for dinner. They'd extended the evening with a movie, and ended up seeing *Returned*. Her instant and fierce attraction to the film's lead had scared and thrilled her. For the first time since Todd's death, her body was responding to a man. She didn't realize until later that Nicolas Lamoureux was the same Nic she'd gone to high school with. The same Nic she'd crushed on.

The same Nic she still wanted.

Seeing Todd's dog tags around Nic's neck had felt strange, but Todd was long dead. How many more years could she keep her life on hold for a man who'd never hold her again?

Lauren picked up the first photo from the pile next to her and took note of the differences between today's Nic and the Nic she'd known in eleventh grade. Even though they'd never exchanged more than a quick "hi" or "excuse me" as they'd crossed paths in the halls, she'd been shocked and confused by his family's unexplained departure from the Chicago area.

But that sweet, funny, slightly clumsy, seventeen-year-old was gone. The photo in her hand showed the successful, confident man he'd become. She ran her finger along the curve of his jaw, then across his full lips. Although she was upset with Nic, she was angrier that she'd let herself get carried away. The kiss had been everything she'd wanted, but like her fantasies, it hadn't been real. Her face grew hot at the memory of raking her fingers through his silky hair as his mouth captured hers. She'd never taste cherry again without thinking of him. And it wasn't like she needed any more reminders; he was in her dreams almost every night.

She'd had no problems coming up with poses for Nic because she'd photographed him hundreds of times in her mind, clothed… and not. It didn't matter that she'd never seen him naked, she had no trouble filling in the blanks to her satisfaction. Her stomach clenched and her fingers curled just thinking about how those dreams invariably ended.

Eyes closed, she let the image form in her mind. Reinforced by the time she'd spent with him today, the fantasy was so vivid she could feel his hands slipping under her shirt. The heat emanating from him burned her as his hands skimmed up her stomach, cupping her breasts, rolling her nipples between his thumbs and forefingers.

A shiver shook her shoulders. His hands drifted down her back, over her hips, tugging at her pajama bottoms and panties until she sat naked. He nudged her knees apart, slowly opening her up to his eyes. Her legs trembled and her belly quivered. When she dragged her eyes to his face and saw the desire, the lust, sharpening his features, she cried out. He leaned forward, and her hips rose to meet his mouth. As his warm, wet tongue plunged deep, his groan vibrated throughout her body.

The phone on the nightstand rang, jarring her out of the fantasy. *Jesus!* Heart pounding, she tried to catch her breath. She pushed a lock of hair off her damp forehead and saw her hand was shaking. The throbbing between her legs and the feeling of emptiness shocked her. None of her previous fantasies had been this realistic. A quick downward glance confirmed that at least she was still wearing her pajama bottoms.

Rising on quivering legs, she stumbled to answer the phone. With the three-hour time difference, it would only be eight back in Seattle. Jason was probably calling to wish her good night. She let out a deep breath, desperate to slow her rushing heart. Picking up the receiver, she prayed her voice sounded normal. "All ready for bed, honey?"

"Absolutely," replied a familiar voice.

It was *him.* Her pulse accelerated and she hoped he couldn't hear her panting. "I thought you were my son. Are you feeling better? You seemed to have no energy by the end of the shoot."

"I couldn't keep my eyes open, even missed my flight back to L.A." He paused and cleared his throat. "I acted like an asshole today, and I'd like to make it up to you. Can you have dinner with me tomorrow night?"

Should she accept? He had acted like an ass. A really cute, really hot ass.

When she didn't answer, he continued. "The proofs you sent me are fantastic. Completely different from anything I've seen before. I'd like to discuss doing another photo shoot."

Giddiness bubbled in her chest at the compliment. He'd given her enough to fulfill the terms of the contract, but additional shots could be exactly what her career needed. "And the Paparazzi Kiss?"

"Won't happen again."

"Good, because I'm a photographer, not a fangirl." Even as she said the words, Lauren rolled her eyes. *Liar.*

They agreed to meet in the lobby around seven, which would give her plenty of time to post-edit today's shots before their date... uh… *meeting.* She really needed to get a grip and forget her fantasies. Her career was on the line.

Besides, Nic The Lover wasn't interested in her. Even though she'd never forgotten him, he didn't remember her. Obviously, she'd never starred in any of *his* fantasies. And she never would.

Lauren was exactly the type of woman Nic had always liked, always wanted, but had never allowed himself to have. He rolled onto his back in the bed and stared at the hotel room ceiling. Working with Lauren yesterday had been fun. Kissing her had been amazing. But more than the feel of her generous curves flush against his body, the intelligence radiating from her eyes and her no-nonsense attitude had piqued his interest. When she'd leaned over him to adjust the knife, he'd wanted to roll her underneath him.

Could he risk a relationship with Lauren? He usually dated tall, willowy women who looked good on camera. The less they had going on in the brains department the better. That way he could keep things light. Any relationship with Lauren would be serious.

Someone knocked, but before he could call out, he heard the sound of the door opening. *Damn.* He must have forgotten to put the security lock on when he'd stumbled in yesterday. If the maid hoped to catch him naked—he glanced down and smirked—today was her lucky day.

"Good morning, darling. Or, should I say good afternoon?"

Shit. At the sound of Vivian's voice, he lunged for the sheets that had drifted down during the night. "Did I forget another appointment?"

When she'd checked him in, she must have gotten a key for herself. He'd called her on this many times, but she insisted that having a key to his room was the only way she could keep him on schedule. Still, he didn't like it.

He barely had time to scoot back against the headboard and tuck the sheets around himself before she rounded the corner and came into view. He slammed a pillow onto his lap and smiled tightly. Her gaze roamed over him and settled on the strategically placed pillow. Her lips curled. "You're looking rather *pained* today."

"Ha-ha, very funny."

"Here, this should cheer you up. You made the front page of almost every tabloid in America." She held out a newspaper. His knuckles grew white as he stared at the photo of him and Lauren in an impassioned embrace. He hadn't realized how out of control he'd been.

His eyes widened in disbelief as he skimmed the article. The reporter speculated that Lauren James, department store photographer, would do anything to further her career, including using Nic The Lover to get to the top. *Christ.* He'd used her, not the other way around. Everyone in Hollywood used someone and was used by someone.

And he was no different.

Like a stupid teenager, fueled by hormones and adrenaline, he'd let himself get carried away without a single thought to the consequences for her. Everyone expected the Paparazzi Kiss stunt, and women all over the country fought for the chance.

But Lauren was different.

She hadn't wanted it. This kind of press could kill her career before it even began. Nic glared at Vivian. "Who tipped off the paparazzi?"

"They picked it up from CelebrityStalker.com."

He rose from the bed, wrapping the sheet around his waist as he stepped through the French doors to the sitting area. "I'll see who posted the information." He sat on the couch and powered up his laptop.

"Calm down, darling. I already checked."

"It was NicsBitch, wasn't it?"

Vivian sat beside him. "Yes, but that doesn't tell us much. A lot of people knew about the photo shoot, including Rafael, Lauren, the festival organizers, and some hotel staff. Any one of them could have leaked the information. Anyways, no harm was done."

Was she for real? Didn't she get the seriousness of the situation? The idea that this person had followed him, clear across the country, from L.A. to D.C., worried him, *a lot.*

His skepticism must have shown on his face because she added, "Until this settles down, get Kaden to accompany you when you're out in public. And we'll keep a tight lid on your location to identify the source of any leaks."

"You're in more danger than I am."

"I'll be fine." After patting his knee, she stood up. "Keep doing what I tell you and everything will be all right."

Huh? She was treating him like a fucking child. Nic gritted his teeth and stood to face her. "What the hell does that mean?"

She glared at him. "It means you do the acting. I do everything else. I'll handle this."

"I'm not the lost teenager you knew ten years ago."

"I'm aware of that." Vivian's voice was barely above a whisper.

Nic raked a hand through his hair and scrubbed at the stubble on his cheeks. Why was he yelling at her? She'd been like a mother to him, and she was only trying to help. "Sorry. This situation's getting to me."

"You'll be fine once you're back home."

"About that. I need a break." He tightened the sheet around his waist.

Vivian peered at him, concern etched in her features. "A vacation? What a fabulous idea. I'll book us a couple rooms at this wonderful little resort I know in Acapulco."

Shit. His gut cramped and he rubbed his stomach. "I'm still not fully recovered from whatever hit me yesterday. I just want to stay here for a few days and relax. Maybe grab a beer with some buddies."

"I'll make the arrangements. Now get some rest." She patted his cheek, before turning to leave. "I'll drop by later this evening."

When the door closed behind her, Nic fell back onto the couch and let out a tired sigh. If he could, he'd leave all this behind and go home to the ranch and Rachel. Every time he had to fake smiles for the paparazzi, he felt like grabbing their cameras and smashing them on the ground.

But even though he was sick of Hollywood and the madness surrounding the movie industry, he needed to make movies, big blockbuster movies so he could make loads of money. He was an actor, wasn't he? Every damn minute of every damn day.

Nic The Lover Lamoureux didn't make movies for the love of acting. He did it to secure the ranch and ensure Rachel's future. For her he'd sacrificed everything.

Even his own happiness.

Tonight, he'd have dinner with Lauren to discuss business. Tomorrow, they'd finish the photo shoot. Then he'd fly back to L.A. And never see Lauren again. Excellent plan. Yeah. It was great. So why did he feel like shit?

CHAPTER 3

Lauren couldn't tear her eyes from the front-page photo of her and Nic locked in a heated embrace. As she read the accompanying article, her cheeks burned and anger replaced shock. Her dreams of a better future for her son flashed before her eyes.

No matter how much she wanted to slink home with her tail between her legs, she had to grow a spine. Jason deserved better than what she could give him with her small pension and meager salary.

She had to hope that when Vivian released the photos Lauren had taken of Nic, people would recognize her talent. Her fresh and riveting poses captured the essence of the dark, brooding, sexy hero. She needed someone to give her a break, to give her a chance to show what she was capable of doing. The article couldn't be further from the truth. She hadn't even kissed another man since Todd died.

Except for Nic.

And, although he had rocked her world, it was hardly front-page news. The doorbell rang, making her heart race. Were the paparazzi here to hound her?

Get a grip. You're a department store photographer, not a movie star.

The photo had made the news because of Nic, not her. The paparazzi were probably camped in front of his door right now.

"Flower delivery for Lauren James."

Who would send her flowers? After a glance through the peephole, she opened the door. A delivery man juggled a pad and a large bouquet of apple blossoms and miniature yellow roses, barely managing to hold onto both. "Are you sure this isn't a mistake?"

He handed her a delivery slip and pointed to her name. After signing the receipt, she handed him a few dollars tip. The door banged shut as she read the card she'd plucked from the buds.

Ma chère Lauren,

By now, you've seen the photo in the papers. Please believe I never meant to hurt you. I hope you aren't too angry to have dinner with me this evening.

They had to share the blame for this fiasco. Although maybe it *was* his fault for being such a damn good kisser. Her chest tightened as she finished reading the note.

Give me a chance to make it up to you. I'll be waiting in the lobby.

Nic

Like her, all he wanted was a chance. How could she refuse to hear him out? After a third reading of the note, the sweet scent of apple blossoms distracted her. She pulled a sprig out of the bouquet, gently cupped the fragile blooms in her hand, and inhaled deeply. How had Nic discovered her love of apple blossoms? Even after years of marriage, Todd hadn't.

Nic was more like the boy she'd known in high school than he let on. The note showed sensitivity and an endearing vulnerability that drew her to him now as it had drawn her to him then. *Did anyone really get over their first crush?*

Her spirits buoyed by the note and flowers, Lauren turned on the radio and danced her way to the closet. She changed into a light gray business suit and pink sleeveless turtleneck sweater. Julie had dragged her to a boutique, insisting that if she wanted to be taken seriously as a photographer and a business woman, she needed to look the part. And Julie had been right. The feminine cut of the jacket molded Lauren's curves beautifully and defined the indent of her waist, resulting in a perfect mix of professionalism and sophistication. Her mood lightened even further as she sprayed on some DKNY perfume.

Her feet, however, needed work. As Lauren stood in her stockings, she contemplated her choices: her sturdy iron gray pumps or the black leather stiletto boots Sandra had coerced her into purchasing along with a matching long coat. She slipped on the stilettos. After all, she was meeting Nic The Lover, not Nic The Accountant.

Not normally a wearer of make-up, Lauren fiddled with the blush she'd bought for this trip, alternately sucking her cheeks in and puffing them out again. The instructions stated that if applied properly, the three colors would make her appear to have actual cheekbones. She shook her head and sighed. Clearly, she needed more practice.

But lip gloss, now *that* she could handle. Her lips curled into a girlish smile as she spread it on. The taste of her cherry gloss on Nic's perfect lips—soft yet firm on top, full and plump on the bottom—had driven her wild. Maybe she'd get another taste tonight. At the thought, she shivered and felt a sudden dampness between her legs. Laughing at her own naughtiness, she air-kissed her reflection. *Get over yourself Lauren. This is a meeting, not a date.*

A man leaning against the check-in counter, speaking with a pretty young hotel employee, caught Lauren's attention as she entered the lobby. The man, whose back was toward her, wore faded blue jeans and heavy black biker boots. His wide shoulders filled a black leather bomber jacket. If his front looked even half as good as his back, he'd be some serious eye candy.

The man turned around and she stopped breathing. Although Nic looked fantastic whatever he wore, this look, straight out of *Darkness Rising,* was her favorite. As Sandra liked to say, it revved her engine. Several moments later, she managed to suck in some air and get her feet moving again.

He didn't say a word or move from his spot at the check-in counter as she approached, but his intense eyes followed her. When she reached him, a wide grin spread across his face and he pushed himself off the counter. "*Bonsoir, chérie.* You look breathtaking." He lifted her hand to his lips and placed a soft kiss on her knuckles.

As it had the day before, the old-fashioned gesture caused her cheeks to flush with pleasure. "You don't look so bad yourself." If understatements were dollars, this one would make her very rich.

He pulled her into his arms and kissed her on each cheek. She breathed in the fragrance of his cologne, combined with his own masculine scent. Something deep inside her awakened, and she barely resisted the urge to hold his cheeks in her hands and kiss him senseless. This was a *business* meeting after all.

They said good night to the desk clerk, and Nic escorted her out of the hotel. He stopped beside a sleek black motorcycle with Triumph written on the side and handed her a helmet.

"Oh, no." Lauren shook her head. "I may be wearing leather, but I'm not a biker chick."

"Come on, *chérie.* It's a great night for a ride. Where's your sense of adventure?"

"Don't you have a car? It doesn't have to be a Porsche; even a Prius would be okay."

His smile faded. "I should have asked you first. Let me call a taxi."

Feeling like she'd kicked a puppy, she took the helmet from his hands. "Promise you'll go slow?"

"*Chérie*, I'll go as slow as you need." The heat in his eyes when he spoke curled her toes.

Oh, God. She was really going to have to do this. But what could be hotter than Nic on a motorcycle? She climbed on behind him and fastened the helmet.

"The only thing you need to do is lean when I lean," he advised her over his shoulder. When she nodded stiffly, he smiled. "Relax and hold onto my waist."

No problem. She wound her arms around him.

Nic coughed and then chuckled. "Maybe not so tight…"

Lauren groaned and snatched her hands back. Instead of impressing Nic The Lover with her sexy sophistication, she'd turned into a freaking boa constrictor. Why was she doing this again? Ah, yes. Because she couldn't deny him anything.

Reaching back, he took her hands and laid them across his stomach. Lauren could feel the hardness of his muscles even through his jacket. With a small pat, he let go and started up the bike.

True to his word, he drove slowly down the busy city streets. But even then, each time he turned a corner, she had to muffle her screams against the back of his leather coat. He'd told her the restaurant was nearby, but instead of staying on the local streets, he drove up a ramp onto the Beltway. She tensed and clutched at him as their speed increased. After a few miles, she realized that while the Beltway meant going faster, it also meant no more turns. Relaxing, she leaned against him and began to enjoy the ride.

Pink, orange, and mauve colored the sky as the sun began its descent. A few times, she'd risen early enough to photograph from her living room window the sun rising over the Cascade Mountains, but had remained a mere observer to the overwhelming beauty of nature. Tonight, as they sped along the Beltway surrounded by the colors and the descending night, she felt at one with the beauty of the sunset. No longer was she simply viewing the world through a camera lens. She was out in it, part of it. All too soon, the lights on the streets and in the houses turned on, one by one, twinkling like tiny stars in the darkness.

Nic took the next exit and stopped at a traffic light at the bottom of the ramp. "I'm going to head back to town so we can go eat. Having fun?" She gave him a quick squeeze, and Nic drove across the overpass.

Todd had been the wild one, the adrenaline junkie, not her. She never drove past the speed limit, never rode motorcycles, and definitely never hugged a gorgeous man on the back of a bike as they sped along a highway. But she was loving the ride. Closing her eyes, she marveled at the sensation of her breasts pressed against Nic's back, her hands on his stomach, his butt against her thighs, the vibrations of the powerful bike between her legs.

Sometime during the ride, her hands had worked their way under the edge of his jacket, but they were still a little cold. Without thinking, she unclasped her hands and slowly scrunched up his shirt until she touched his bare skin. Nic sucked in a breath as she spread her frosty hands across his abdomen. His hard muscles rippled, and she shivered.

What was wrong with her? Maybe it was the vibrations, or the handsome man in her arms, or the feel of his hot skin, or the vivid fantasy from last night. She shouldn't be touching him like this, but no amount of self-recriminations could get her to move her hands. Gone was the sophisticated professional. Five years of celibacy had turned her into a slut.

If they didn't get to the restaurant soon, she'd come on the back of Nic's motorcycle.

The tight knot in Nic's gut began to relax at the sight of the Thailand Delight restaurant. Thank God the ride was over. Another few minutes of *that* and he would have disgraced himself. What was wrong with him? He was Nic The Lover, not some overeager teenager. He pulled into a parking spot in the small strip mall, turned off the motor and kicked out the stand. Sighing deeply, he braced himself on the handlebars and hung his head.

Even though they were no longer moving, Lauren was still plastered against him. Her breasts and stomach warmed his back while her thighs cupped his butt. Her arms remained around his waist, and her hands… Her hands had not stopped massaging and caressing his stomach. Nic shivered in pleasure as one hand began a downward path.

A slow sensual swirl of a finger around the sensitive rim of his navel sent waves of sensation rippling up his spine. Her hand hovered mere inches above the bulge in his jeans, but then she pulled back. Although his cock was practically begging for her touch, her reaction pleased him. Too many women felt that because he was a public figure, they somehow had a right to his body.

"Ready, *chérie*?"

Her body stiffened and she jerked her arms away, losing her balance. Nic twisted around and steadied her as she scrambled off the bike.

"I'm so, so sorry about… that!" Blushing furiously, she indicated his chest with a wave of her hand. "Maybe I should go back to the hotel." She averted her gaze.

Nic couldn't help but be flattered. "Hey, it's okay. I'm not offended. What man wouldn't want the touch of a lovely woman on a night like this?"

She shrugged and wrapped her arms around herself before looking up at the night sky. "I never imagined a motorcycle ride could be so magical, so exhilarating."

After removing her helmet, he removed his own. With his feet firmly planted on the ground to maintain the bike's balance, he reached for her arm and pulled her beside him. "Twilight is my favorite time to ride. I'm glad I got to share it with you."

He imagined lifting her up to straddle him on the bike, leaning her back over the handlebars then kissing her deeply and suckling on her peaked nipples. Heat rushed to his groin and he hardened even more. Going by the look on her face, the lovely Lauren was as affected by their ride as he was. "Let's go inside."

When she stepped back and turned toward the restaurant, he pocketed the keys and adjusted himself. He certainly didn't want a repeat of yesterday. Although he hadn't spotted any paparazzi as he'd driven into the parking lot, these days, everyone had a camera at the ready. The last thing he needed was more front-page photos of himself sporting a hard-on.

He climbed off the bike and stowed both helmets away in the saddle bags. When he slipped on a pair of black-framed Oakleys, she gaped. "You wear glasses?"

"No. But for some reason, when I wear these, people don't recognize me."

"Like Clark Kent?"

Nic nodded. Although he was no Superman. If he could make time go backwards and change the past, he certainly would have used the ability back in eleventh grade.

The wonderful spicy scents of oyster sauce and fried noodles teased his senses as they stepped inside the Thai restaurant. Lauren closed her eyes and inhaled, a small smile tugging at the corner of her lips.

"Look at the beautiful pergola." She pointed to the ornately decorated wooden structure in the center of the room. Nic was amused. He'd had no idea what the thing was called, but he had to admit it did add to the garden-like atmosphere of the restaurant.

Nic led Lauren to a table in a back corner, separated from the others by a low wooden wall. Several colorfully decorated pots of exotic flowers and leafy green plants lined the top of the partition. From his seat, he had a perfect view of the door and the large windows, but was well hidden if any paparazzi showed up.

The hostess handed them menus and took their drink orders. A few minutes later, a waitress arrived with an MGD for him and a chardonnay for Lauren. They placed their orders: two-star cashew nut chicken for him and five-star pad thai for her. Another delicious surprise; he loved women who liked it spicy.

Lauren took a sip of her wine. "I want to ask you something, but maybe it's not appropriate."

Nic grinned as her cheeks colored. "The inappropriate questions are always the best."

"At the photo shoot, didn't it bother you when Vivian oiled you up?"

Laughter rumbled in his chest. "I keep forgetting you haven't been tainted by Hollywood yet. On set and for most photo shoots, there're people who do my hair and makeup. If the costumes are complicated, they dress me. If I have to be bare-chested, I get waxed, painted, and oiled. And I won't even mention the fans. Anyway, to make a long story short, wherever I go, people touch me."

"If I ever get somewhere as a freelancer, I'll keep that in mind. I want my clients to feel respected, not molested."

"Not if, when."

She smiled. "I've been wondering, why Nic The Lover?"

"I earned it."

She blinked. He laughed. "It's the English translation of my name. Lamoureux means The Lover."

"So it's not a reflection of your abilities… on screen… or off?"

"The name stuck because I acquired a certain reputation with the ladies… on screen… and off." He loved teasing her but kept it gentle. She seemed somehow fragile and innocent, even when she was trying to get in his pants.

The waitress arrived with their entrées. As Lauren ate, he watched her. She was nothing like the women he usually dated. Okay, so this wasn't a date. Whatever. She was intelligent and funny, reserved yet unpredictable. The sparkle in her ever-changing eyes made him smile, and he wanted to kiss the small heart-shaped freckle below her right ear.

What he'd grown up around and what attracted him were petite curvy women, women like Lauren. But his life was the opposite of hers. Whereas hers was simple and safe, his was chaotic and, now, dangerous. Even if she could see beyond the ugliness of his past, who knew what the stalker would do if they got into a serious relationship? He couldn't afford to get involved with her.

Even so, it wouldn't hurt to know more about the beautiful Lauren. "Did you grow up in Seattle?"

"I moved there when I got a scholarship to study photography at the Art Institute of Seattle." She leaned back in her chair and took a sip of her wine. "You're from Montréal, right?"

Nic watched her lick a stray drop off her lips. He stared as she swallowed. He wanted to kiss her lips and lick the long expanse of her throat. *Christ.* He spread his legs a little wider under the table, easing the pressure against his fly. What had she asked him? He shook his head and tried to focus.

Her eyebrows flew up. "You're not? Every article I've ever read about you said you were from Montréal."

Nic slugged back his beer and forced himself to concentrate on her words and not on her mouth. "No. I am from Montréal."

"Do you go back there often?"

He grimaced. "Whenever I can, which isn't often enough. Vivian keeps me pretty busy."

"Don't you miss your family? I've only been here a few days, and I miss my son already."

How could he answer her question without revealing anything? She leaned over the table and placed her hand on his. "That's too personal. Please forget I asked."

Great. She probably thought he was hiding something. Which he was, but he didn't want her to know that. "There's nothing to talk about. Hollywood is my only family."

Using a redirection technique he'd picked up from Kaden, he changed the subject. "Tell me about your son."

"Jason is eight going on eighteen." Her face shone with pride, making his heart ache. He missed seeing that look on his own mother. "I think he's your youngest fan. He's seen all your kid-friendly movies and knows the dialogue by heart."

"What's his favorite?"

"He has two." She counted them off on her beautifully shaped fingers. "One is *Lost Treasure.* He loves all the action. Last Halloween, he dressed up as your Jonathan Buckley character." Her eyes twinkled as she laughed at the memory.

Leaning back in his chair, he took another sip of his beer and stretched his legs out under the table. "What's the second?"

Nic admired the view as Lauren crossed her legs. His heart thudded in his chest when he saw her feet again. The thought of Lauren in nothing but those black leather stiletto boots and a smile was enough to kill him.

"His second favorite is also my favorite." She raised her eyebrows.

Still slightly dazed, he mentally shook himself and accepted her challenge. "*Days of Fire.*"

She snorted. "Not even close." When he frowned, she added, "But I liked that one too."

He was very proud of the work he'd done on that film. "Okay, so which one is it?"

"*Small Town Blues.*"

"Why?" In *Small Town Blues*, he played a father in a rural town whose farm is bought out by a large dairy corporation, prompting the family to move to the big city to start a new life. It was a musical with lots of singing and dancing, and since he wasn't particularly talented at either, the movie had bombed in theaters and gone straight to DVD.

She picked up her napkin and started twisting it between her fingers. "The situation of the family in the film is like ours. They're starting a new life too, and it brings him hope that someday we'll be happy."

He pulled his feet in and leaned forward to ask in a low voice, "When you lent me the dog tags, yesterday, you mentioned your husband..."

"...died five years ago," she finished, lowering her eyes. "Todd worked on a medevac team in Afghanistan, rescuing downed soldiers. Until insurgents with RPGs shot down their helicopter. There were no survivors."

Her husband had died a hero, protecting his country, whereas Nic had destroyed his family. She would be disgusted if she ever found out.

Nic took her hand in his. "I'm sorry. Too many good men are dying in that war. It must have been very difficult."

She nodded. "Jason was only three and didn't really understand. Each time he asked me, 'When's Daddy coming home?' in his little baby voice, my heart broke all over again." Her expression suddenly brightened, and she looked up, a hint of a smile playing on her lips. "But whenever we watch *Small Town Blues,* he's happy again."

He answered with a smile of his own. It always surprised him how much his movies affected people, people he didn't even know.

Mick Jagger's *She's the Boss* blared out, startling both of them. Grinning sheepishly, he pulled his cell phone out of his pocket. "Sorry, it's Vivian." He answered the call.

"Darling. I'm here, in your room, and you are not."

Uh-oh. He knew that tone very well. "I went out to get some dinner."

"When we spoke this afternoon, I told you I'd see you tonight."

"Hey, sorry about the mix-up. I'll make it up to you."

"Never mind, we have something more important to discuss. Fifteen minutes ago, our friend posted another sighting on CelebrityStalker. It says you're at… what was it? Here it is. Thailand Delight on Stanley Street. Is that where you are?"

Nic met Lauren's gaze. "Yes, but I didn't tell anyone." A sudden pinch in his palm made him relax his death grip on the phone.

How did NicsBitch know where he was?

To protect Lauren from the paparazzi, he'd kept his plans for the evening secret from everyone, including Vivian. The bike belonged to a friend and couldn't be traced back to him. The clothes he wore were pretty much the opposite of his usual Nic The Lover style. And, with the helmets, he and Lauren should have been incognito. He leaned forward so he could see around Lauren and checked the entrance to the restaurant, including what he could see of the parking lot through the front windows.

"I'd suggest you get your dinner to go and leave as quickly as possible. Let me know when you're back in your room."

"Thanks for the warning." He flipped his phone closed and put it back in his pocket. This was bad. If the paparazzi showed up, Lauren would be angry. But he didn't want to leave before they had a chance to discuss the photo shoot. Could he risk staying a while longer?

Lauren's brows furrowed. "Do we need to leave?"

"It's nothing." He'd keep an eye out for the paparazzi and sneak her out through the kitchen if they showed up.

"I have an idea for a photo shoot," she began as he picked up his fork and took another bite of chicken. "I read somewhere that you like hockey."

He put down his fork and wiped his mouth with a napkin. "I have season tickets for the Los Angeles Kings, and I catch as many Montréal Canadiens games on TV as I can." He'd also been on the high-school hockey team back in Chicago. Even though he'd only been a junior at the time, the college scouts had already started showing an interest in him. And the school newspaper often printed funny action shots of him—preparing a slap shot, celebrating a goal, taking a tumble.

He'd had such a crush on the cute photographer from the school paper. Chuckling ruefully, he remembered how many times he'd purposely taken a fall so she'd take a picture of him. He seemed to have a thing for cute photographers named Lauren.

Just as he was about to ask Lauren where she'd gone to high school, a glint in the parking lot caught his attention. He leaned sideways to get a better view. Only a few people remained in the restaurant and the parking lot stood nearly empty. Shaking his head at his overactive imagination, he returned his attention to Lauren.

She turned to look over her shoulder. "Is something wrong?"

"I thought I saw something outside." He slumped back against his chair. At this point, he couldn't decide what would be worse—a single stalker showing up or an entire army of paparazzi. Both had the potential to ruin his night. "So, what's your idea?"

"I want do the next part of the shoot at an arena." She took a deep breath before continuing. "We'd do a few outfit changes and get some shots of you in and out of the goal. Yesterday's shoot was posed and serious. With the arena shots, I want to capture your joy and spontaneity."

She picked up the paper napkin beside her plate and proceeded to shred it into tiny pieces. He reached forward and clasped her wrist. "*Chérie*, don't be nervous. I trust your instincts. The results will be perfect."

"I'm worried Vivian will reject hockey photos because they aren't sexy."

Captivated, Nic watched her nibble her lower lip and had to stifle a groan as heat arrowed straight to his groin.

Lauren looked up. "She said the shots had to be sexy, not artistic. Magazines want photos that will get women to pick up their latest issue at the checkout counter in local grocery stores. I think the hockey photos could be both artistic and sexy, and women would want to buy the magazines so they could take the photos home and enjoy them in privacy."

Hundreds, perhaps thousands of women lovingly gazing at his photos, tracing their fingers over his jaw, his neck, his chest, his stomach, his… The image of Lauren doing just that flashed through his mind, arousing him further. Nic shifted uncomfortably. Next time he saw Lauren, he'd have to wear looser pants.

"Why does that make you smile?" she asked as she took a sip of her wine.

"You have passion and talent." A frown continued to mar her otherwise smooth forehead, so he tried another angle. "Yesterday, during the photo shoot, could you envision how the photos would turn out?" She nodded. "And they turned out great, didn't they?"

She acknowledged his words with a quick jerk of her head. "I need to trust myself." Lauren cleared her throat and ducked her head. "Sorry. I didn't mean to have a meltdown."

Was she embarrassed to share her concerns because of who he was?

Celebrities were no one special. He should know. "You should have seen me the first time I went on stage. I had the role of Joseph in the school Christmas play. Half-way through, my nerves got the better of me. I ran offstage and threw up in the boys' bathroom. Poor Mary had to deal with the three wise men alone."

The oddly erotic sight of Lauren politely trying to stifle her laughter with her hands pleased him. Soon, they were both laughing so hard the other restaurant patrons turned to stare at them.

Nic met her gaze and his laughter evaporated. With her glittering eyes and pink cheeks, she was beautiful. His own face heated as he pictured her naked and flushed, her sweet moans singing in his ears. Averting his eyes, he took several deep breaths before he could return to their conversation. "When do you want to do this?

"Do this?"

Her bewildered tone brought his eyes back to her. The beautiful Lauren appeared a bit dazed, as though her thoughts had been along the same lines as his. "The hockey thing."

"Right. If you're available tomorrow, I can try to book the Pepsi Center for a couple hours. The Avalanche are away for the next few days."

"Perfect." Good thing he'd already arranged for a few days off. "Do you want any coffee or tea, or some dessert?"

She glanced at her watch and shook her head. "It's late. I'm sure these poor people can't wait for us to leave, and I should get to bed."

After settling the bill, Nic looked out the windows. When he was sure no paparazzi were hiding in the parking lot, he took Lauren's arm and led her outside. He considered driving in circles around the hotel to extend the ride so he could feel her heat against his back and her cold hands on his chest again. He coughed into his hand to hide his grin.

After a short ride back to the hotel, he parked the bike. As they crossed the lobby toward the elevators, she said, "I know you don't like to be out in public, so you don't have to walk me to my room."

Nic had to grin at her naïveté where the press was concerned. Odds were high that the paparazzi had staked out her room rather than his because hers was booked under her real name.

"But maybe I want to," he said.

As she was removing her coat, Nic pressed the button for the eighteenth floor. Lauren raised an eyebrow. "You know my room number?"

He relaxed against the elevator wall and caught the reflection of her backside in the mirrored doors. "Sorry?" She had a perfect round butt, beautifully outlined by her tailored pants. He barely stopped himself from reaching out.

"How did you get my room number?"

With effort, he pulled his eyes away from the entrancing sight to focus on her face. "The hotel operator gave it to me when I called your room yesterday."

"A woman?"

He grinned. "Of course."

"She wasn't supposed to do that."

"No, but I'm hard to resist." When the elevator doors opened, he stepped out and scanned the hall for any waiting paparazzi. It was empty.

At her door, he pulled her close and kissed her on each cheek. The feel and taste of her tempted him. Behind her door, a nice big bed waited for them. One word from her and she'd be underneath him. Reluctantly, he released her and stepped back. The paparazzi could arrive at any time, and he couldn't risk exposing her again.

He walked back to the elevator, his steps slow. If he turned around, she'd probably welcome him with open arms. When the elevator doors closed, he let out a relieved sigh. A war raged inside him, and he'd almost lost the battle.

He had *to stay away from her.*

As he stepped out onto his floor, his phone rang. Not recognizing the ringtone, he read the caller ID: 514, the area code for Montréal.

"Mr. Lamoureux. This is Dr. Marseau at the CHUM." Why was The University of Montréal Hospital Centre calling him? He glanced left and right to make sure the halls were empty. The last thing he needed was for some reporter to overhear this conversation.

"Do you know a Rachel Lamoureux?" the doctor asked. "Her medical file lists you as next of kin."

The air rushed out of Nic's lungs. "What's going on?" he croaked as he raced to his room where he could talk freely. Rachel didn't deserve to have her life splashed on the front page of the newspapers.

"We admitted her an hour ago. She was kicked by a horse and sustained multiple fractures of the left tibia. Because of her condition, this is very serious. The break is messy and she's running a fever. If the fever persists overnight, we'll need to operate."

Jesus. He hoped Rémi was with her. After letting the doctor know he'd be there as soon as possible, Nic ended the call.

"That sounded serious."

"Jesus Christ!" *What the fuck was she doing in his room again?* Nic glared at Vivian. "You scared the shit out of me."

"Darling, what's wrong? Did you get bad news?"

He rubbed the back of his neck as he tried to figure out what to do. "Rachel's been hurt. If I leave right now, I can be in Montréal by morning."

"Do you need me to get you a rental car?"

"I've got a friend's motorcycle."

"Nonsense. A ten-hour drive on a motorcycle at night would be very uncomfortable, not to mention dangerous. A rental car will be waiting for you in front of the lobby in fifteen minutes."

He kissed her cheek. Maybe he had been too hard on her lately. After all, she'd proven over and over that he could count on her. "I almost forgot. Lauren is setting up a photo shoot tomorrow. Let her know I had an emergency."

She pulled a cell phone out of her purse and began dialing. "Darling, start packing."

Nic raced to gather his belongings. *Please God. Let her be okay.* How much more could Rachel take? She'd already suffered enough. Nothing he could do would erase all the pain he'd caused her. But he could show her how much he loved her, how much she meant to him, how sorry he really was.

As he'd done a million times since the accident, he wished he could switch places with his sister.

CHAPTER 4

Another yawn threatened to crack Nic's jaw, despite the gallons of caffeine he'd slugged back during the long drive through the high peaks, deep valleys, and breathless turns of the Adirondack Northway. During the day, it was a sight to behold. At night? A roller-coaster ride in unrelenting darkness. But as he drove over the Jacques-Cartier Bridge onto the island of Montréal, the Saint Lawrence rushing underneath sparkling in the morning sun, his heart felt a little lighter. He was home.

At the end of the bridge, Nic followed Rémi's directions to the visitor parking lot of the CHUM's Notre-Dame Hospital pavilion. He cut the engine and took a moment to prepare for the scene inside. Even if Rachel didn't need surgery, her injury was still very serious, and Nic had to be ready for anything the doctor might tell them. He had to be her rock. He white-knuckled the steering wheel and gritted his teeth. For Rachel, he'd deliver an Oscar-winning performance and be a regular ray of sunshine.

In the hospital lobby, he detoured into the gift shop. He laughed out loud when he spotted a bear dressed like a nurse in blue scrubs. Rachel would love it. He also chose a box of Turtles and a bouquet of wildflowers.

The flowers reminded him of Lauren, of the smell of her perfume and her expression as she described the apple blossom bouquet he'd had delivered to her in D.C. He regretted having to postpone the photo shoot, but Rachel had to come first.

Nic paused outside the door to Rachel's room. Taking a deep breath, he pasted on a happy face. One step into the room, a shudder tore through him, almost making him drop the gifts he held in his arms. His sister looked frail and vulnerable, her face drawn and pale, surrounded by a multitude of tubes and machines, her injured leg suspended in a hammock with ropes and pulleys. When she pushed her long dark hair behind her ears, her slender fingers trembled. Quickly, he rearranged his features to hide his shock, his remorse, and his shame.

Rachel's eyes widened, and a smile spread across her face as he approached. "You're here!"

Unable to speak, Nic placed his purchases on a table at the foot of her bed and pulled her into his arms. He buried his face in her hair as tears threatened to escape and his chest ached with emotions he couldn't show. Nic swallowed hard and blinked several times, fighting to regain control.

"I can't believe you came all this way to see me."

"Family sticks together in times of need, *ma chouette*."

Rachel leaned around him and winked at Rémi, sprawled in the room's only chair. "Did you teach him that one?"

Rémi held up his hands in surrender and grinned. "No way. He came up with that fortune cookie bullshit on his own. Iroquois expressions are much more eloquent."

Nic shot his friend a playfully stern look, then turned back to Rachel with a crooked smile. Rémi had obviously been working overtime to keep her spirits up.

"How're you feeling?" Nic asked softly.

She lifted a shoulder and shrugged. "I didn't get a fever, which was the doctor's biggest concern."

"I can't tell you how happy I am to hear that."

"Oh, I think I know." She grinned impishly as she eyed the table where he'd set his purchases. "Anything in that pile for me, or are all those gifts for the nurses?"

Nic laughed. God, he'd missed his sister. He got up and handed her the flowers.

Rachel inhaled the heady fragrance, pleasure evident on her face. "I love them! They smell like the meadows on the ranch."

Rémi fetched a water pitcher and with great fanfare arranged the flowers, amusing Rachel with his antics. He was the best friend a man could have. When he was done, Rémi turned to Nic and waved to the pile. "Don't stop now, my friend."

Nic presented her the box of Turtles.

"Aren't you going to open them? I have to try at *least* one."

Since he shared her addiction to chocolate, Nic couldn't deny her plea. He slit open the box, but before she could take one, Rémi's hand was already there. Nic pulled the box away. "Ladies first."

"Age before beauty," Rémi retorted.

Nic raised a haughty eyebrow. "Fairies before fiends."

"You snooze—you lose."

Rachel's laughter rang out. "Guys, enough, please. My sides are sore from laughing so much."

Rémi shot Nic a triumphant grin, and the two of them cracked up.

"Okay, you win. This time," Nic conceded. He placed the box on Rachel's lap and held out his final package.

Rachel grinned when she pulled the nurse bear out of the bag.

"Oh, look," Rémi said. "He came *bear*ing gifts."

"She's adorable! I didn't have a nurse in my collection."

Nic's heart constricted. Rachel had always been so easy to please. "She's the only nurse cute enough to bring home," he joked.

"I've got to disagree with you there, man." Rémi shook his head. "The little night nurse was f—"

"Hey! Watch your mouth. There's a girl in the room." Nic cuffed his friend on the arm, but his heart was bursting.

Rachel's eyes twinkled with amusement. "I'm twenty-two, you twit."

"Speaking of women who are no longer children." Rémi picked up the magazine on the nightstand. "Tell us about the bodacious brunette."

Rachel grinned. "We want all the details."

Nic groaned and scrubbed his face. On the cover was the photo of him and Lauren caught in the throes of their Paparazzi Kiss. Did he want to explain how he'd felt sparks in the air when he'd walked into that hotel room in D.C.? How his lips had burned when he'd kissed her knuckles? How he'd lost total control at the first touch of her lips?

He really didn't. But he had to tell them something. "Lauren's a photographer from Seattle. We did a photo shoot together last Friday."

"Looks like you did a little more than shoot a few photos," Rémi teased.

"Things got a little out of hand."

"I'd say things got a little *in* hand…"

"Rémi! I think he really likes this woman." When Nic didn't respond, she prodded, "Don't you?"

No matter how much he might want to at this moment, he couldn't lie outright to his sister. "She's just starting out, and I want to help her, if I can. But it's strictly professional. I'm not interested in a relationship right now."

Rachel considered this. "I can't imagine that photo and article did her career any good. She'll need some good solid work to live this down."

Ouch. As usual, Rachel's assessment was spot on. He hadn't been thinking—at least not with the head on his shoulders. But he wouldn't let his thoughtlessness ruin Lauren's life the way it had his sister's.

"Her photos are incredibly creative. We discussed some of her ideas last night, and once we're done with this next photo shoot, magazine editors will be beating down her door."

Rachel and Rémi smiled, a little too smug for his taste.

He narrowed his eyes at them. "What?"

"Sounds to me like you want to be the one beating down her door," Rachel said.

"Nah, he doesn't want to beat down her door. He wants to bang—"

Rémi was interrupted by a knock on the door. The doctor entered the room. "I received your lab results. There doesn't seem to be any infection, but we'll continue the antibiotics to be safe. However, you do have multiple fractures, which will take some time to heal."

"Am I going to have a cast?" Hearing a quaver in her voice, Nic sat down beside Rachel and held her hand.

"Yes. But because you don't have much sensation in that leg, we'll use a bivalve cast. It's open and will allow us to see the skin and ensure no further damage occurs."

"Will I be able to walk on it?"

The doctor shook his head. "The risk of re-injury is too high. You'll need to use a wheelchair until the fractures heal."

Rachel's eyes filled with tears, and she made a small sound that tore Nic's heart to shreds. His own eyes watering, he wrapped her in his arms and smoothed her hair. When she'd first been injured, the doctors had warned them of the severe bone loss that caused almost a third of paraplegics to suffer fractures within ten years. Why hadn't he hired more ranch hands to help her? Damn it! She should never have been anywhere near a birthing mare.

"Will she," Nic started, then cleared his throat. "When her leg heals, will Rachel be able to walk with crutches again?"

"Possibly." The doubt in the doctor's voice made Nic's stomach drop. "But I have to warn you, there's a very difficult road ahead. We'll immediately start physical therapy on the uninjured leg to avoid loss of strength and range of motion. Then, after the injured leg is healed, it's going to take many more months of therapy to regain the previous level of mobility."

Rachel's face drained of color; her eyes filled with fear. He'd give everything he had to change places with her, to make her whole, to see her dance again. He caressed her cheek. "Round-the-clock care, on-site physical therapy—we'll get whatever you need, Rachel. I promise."

The doctor nodded. "A technician will be in shortly to make your cast. You should be all set to leave in a few hours. Mr. Lamoureux, may I speak with you for a moment?"

Nic followed the doctor into the hall. As soon as they were alone, the doctor said, "Depression in situations like these is common. Since you don't live with Ms. Lamoureux, is there someone, family or friend, who can keep an eye on her?"

"My friend, Rémi, owns the ranch next door. He can make regular visits and tell me if he notices any problems."

"Perfect." The doctor handed him a business card. "Call me if you have any questions or concerns."

As soon as the doctor left, Rémi joined Nic in the hall. "How're you holding up?"

Nic shook his head. "Rachel's barely had time to get over losing our mother, and now this? The doctor warned me to be on the lookout for depression." He met his friend's gaze. "I'm really worried about her."

Rémi clasped his shoulder. "She's young and strong, and she has us. I'll run the ranch until she's able to take over again. We'll get her through this."

Nic slapped his forehead. "The kids! She'll be devastated if she has to cancel the horse therapy sessions."

"I'm sure I can find some teens on the rez who'd love to help out."

"Thanks, man. I'm counting on you to be my eyes. If she seems even a little unhappy, I want to hear about it."

"I'm on it, brother." Rémi pulled Nic into a big bear hug. "Our little sister will be so sick of me hanging around, she'll beg you to kick me off the ranch."

Nic snorted. *As if.* Without Rémi, he and Rachel would both be lost.

At the end of a very busy week of making modifications to the house and hiring help for Rachel, he had to fly back to L.A. He hated to leave her. "I love you, Rachel."

The sweet loving way she looked at him made Nic's throat constrict until he could hardly breathe.

"I love you too. Now go, or you'll miss your plane."

With the bitter taste of guilt in his mouth, Nic drove the rental car to the Montréal-Trudeau International Airport and flew back to his life as Nic The Lover.

Nic struggled to make a graceful knot in his tie, as he stood in front of his bedroom mirror getting ready for the footprint ceremony to be held in his honor at Grauman's Chinese Theatre. He glanced at his Movado dress watch, a gift Vivian had insisted on giving him when he'd refused to buy a $25,000 Jaeger-LeCoultre. He had enough time to check on Rachel. Sitting on the edge of the bed, he placed the call.

"How did your visit with the doctor go?"

"He said things are progressing nicely, and if I'm very careful to let the leg heal properly and follow up with intensive physical therapy, he's optimistic that I'll walk again."

Nic let out the breath he'd been holding. Her voice sounded stronger than it had since she'd been injured. "Make sure you follow the doctor's recommendations to the letter. How are things going with the nurse?"

"Marie-Soleil's fabulous and funny. Hey, who are you taking to the footprint ceremony tonight? Rémi's coming over to watch it with me."

"Vivian set me up with someone." Without having even met his date, he knew the wanna-be starlet would be tall, blonde, and none too bright. But hey, they'd look great together on camera; Vivian's setups always did.

"Another blind date! Why aren't you taking Lauren?"

"Our relationship is strictly professional." Nic could hardly believe the words coming out of his mouth. There was nothing *strictly professional* about his attraction to Lauren.

Rachel laughed, clearly seeing through his smoke and mirrors. "Have you at least talked to her since you got back?"

With a sigh, Nic fell back on to the bed. "No."

Although he'd considered asking Lauren to accompany him tonight, he hadn't heard from her in the ten days since they'd had dinner. Several times he'd asked Vivian if Lauren had called or sent proofs. But there'd been no sign of her. Maybe she'd decided he wasn't worth the trouble. It was probably better this way.

"Why do you keep doing that to yourself?"

"Doing what?" Letting Vivian set him up?

"Pretending. I know you have an image but, once in a while, you could let yourself get close to someone you might actually like."

"Trust me, Rachel. It's for the best."

"Best for who? Certainly not you."

"Best for everyone. I live in a fishbowl. How could I ask a woman like Lauren to put up with that?" He sat up and looked at his watch again. "I'm going to be late."

"This conversation isn't over. Anyways, congratulations again."

Nic cleared his throat. "It's all for you, Rachel."

"For once, I'd like it to be for you."

So would I. But it was never going to be that way.

"Mom! Come quick."

At Jason's frantic call, Lauren ran into the living room still wearing the rubber gloves she'd put on to clean the bathroom.

"What is it, honey?"

"Nic Lamoro's going to be on TV."

She grinned. Jason's mispronunciation of Nic's last name made it all too clear why he and Vivian had decided to go with the much easier Nic The Lover. Pulling off the gloves, she sat down on the couch beside her son and braced herself against the impact of seeing Nic again. She'd been trying so hard not to think about him since he'd stood her up ten days ago that she'd managed to forget tonight was his footprint ceremony.

As she watched, Nic climbed out of a limo in front of Grauman's. While he turned to wave to the enthusiastic fans, a large blond man she assumed to be his bodyguard helped a woman out of the car. The TV camera panned to the south side of Hollywood Boulevard, capturing the thousands of people who had turned out for the star-studded event.

"That's Nic!" shouted Jason as he pointed to the television screen. "Why's he all dressed up and who's that woman?"

Lauren bit her lip. That woman, who looked like a supermodel in her black stripper heels and little black dress, emphasis on *little,* was exactly Nic The Lover's type—tall, thin, and blonde. Black stilettos notwithstanding, Lauren was the polar opposite of this woman—short, brunette, and with more than a few pounds to lose. How could she have thought he was even the slightest bit attracted to her? Trying to hide her irritation, she answered, "I think she's his date." Jason looked at her askance but didn't say anything more. He wasn't buying her act at all. Hmm, maybe she should have taken some acting lessons from Nic.

Together they listened to the on-site reporter. "Ladies and gentlemen, welcome to Entertainment Buzz's coverage of Nic The Lover's footprint ceremony at Grauman's Chinese Theatre. Here's a tidbit for all you movie buffs. Silent film star Norma Talmadge started this tradition in 1927 when she accidently stepped in wet cement at the premiere of *King of Kings*. Since then, less than two hundred actors have placed their footprints, handprints, and autographs in cement tiles in the famous forecourt of this landmark theater."

"Did you hear that, Mom? Nic must be really special."

Lauren fought against the ache in her throat. "He's certainly something, all right." Her gut twisted as she noticed Vivian hanging off Nic's arm. At least his date had stayed in the main red carpet area.

A huge roar rose from the crowd when the reporter announced, "Folks, Nic The Lover is heading across the boulevard to greet his fans."

"Do you think someday I'll get to meet Nic?" Jason asked.

If he'd asked her while she'd still been in D.C., she probably would have replied, "Sure, someday." But now? "I don't think so, honey."

Security guards spread out along the row of barriers as Nic walked along the fence, shaking hands and talking with his fans. The crowd constantly surged forward and back as people tried to get closer. A few had signs or pictures for him to autograph. When one lady handed him a Sharpie and asked him to sign her shoulder, he laughed but complied.

At one point, he reached over the barrier to wipe the tears from a young girl's face. When he kissed her check, Jason made a face like he'd swallowed a bug. "That's just gross. Who'd want to kiss a girl?" His eyes opened wide as he realized what he'd said. "Oops. Sorry, Mom. You don't count." Lauren smiled and ruffled her son's hair.

In that moment between Nic and the young girl, she'd caught a glimpse of the sweet, caring boy she'd known in high school. But Nic wasn't that boy anymore. He was a man who could capture a woman's heart with a simple grin, just as he'd captured hers. Her heart ached, knowing she'd never again get to run her fingers through his dark hair or kiss his smooth lips.

But the reality was that while she'd been making herself sick worrying about him, he'd probably been living it up somewhere with the blonde.

He was, after all, Nic The Lover.

~

"Socialize, be polite, talk to the reporters. I got it." To take some of the bite out of his words, Nic smiled at Vivian.

She gently rapped his arm, but she was smiling too. "You're impossible. Now go enjoy yourselves."

Nic took his date by the arm and started to mingle. Almost immediately, he was waylaid by reporters milling around the red carpet area. "Good evening, Nic," called out the reporter from Entertainment Buzz. Kaden stood back for the interview, vigilant but out of camera range.

"Good evening, Tammy."

"Ladies and gentlemen, our honored guest this evening, Mr. Nic Lamoureux or, as he's better known, Nic The Lover. Nic plays Blake Winters in the highly acclaimed *Bad Days,* recently premiered at the GI Film Festival in Washington D.C. Nic, how did you like working with Jane Carver?"

Nic smiled and turned toward the camera with the flashing red light atop it. "Jane was wonderful as Emma Sanders. It was a pleasure to work with such a talented leading lady. In fact, the entire cast and crew were tremendous."

"One last question, Nic. Everyone's dying to know." She glanced around with a wide, knowing grin. Then she turned back and looked pointedly at him. "Where's your girlfriend?"

Nic blinked. *What girlfriend?*

The reporter raised an eyebrow. "The photographer. From the festival."

"Tammy, this is—" Hoping she'd get the hint, he pulled his date forward by the arm, and widened his eyes at her. What the fuck was her name?

"Summer. Summer Rayne. I'm an actress. Nice to meet you, Tammy."

Nic barely resisted rolling his eyes. Jesus Christ. Where did Viv find these women? With a smile for Tammy, he placed his hand on Summer's lower back and guided her deeper into the crowd of assembled celebrities.

His step faltered when he overheard Tammy say, "Well, there you have it. Ladies of America, rejoice. Playboy Nic The Lover could not be captured by the wily single mom photographer from Seattle. The staff here at Entertainment Buzz are placing bets on how long Nic will play in the *Summer Rayne.* Who'll be next? Tune in tomorrow night and we'll let you know." Laughing, she moved on to her next interview.

Nic ground his teeth. Vivian planned to tone down his image in a few years but insisted he had to stick with the sex symbol act for now. Nic couldn't wait to have a normal life again.

And Lauren? What did she want?

Stop right there, idiot.

By all appearances, she'd dropped him like a box office bomb. If he were smart, he'd leave things at that. With the stalker on his tail, it wasn't safe to get involved.

Glancing at the woman beside him, he saw Summer smiling brightly, unfazed by the insinuation that she'd be only a one-night stand. Then again, she didn't need to care. She'd gotten what she wanted: her name mentioned on national television twice. That was the Hollywood way—use and be used.

They made their way through the crowd. With Summer's help, he side-stepped countless questions and comments from the press regarding his relationship with Lauren. He couldn't understand the press's fascination with her. Okay, maybe he could.

Lauren's sincerity and innocence were rare in Hollywood, where even the young were jaded and cynical. And his fans could relate to her, a single mom trying to raise her kid the best she could, because she was like them.

As they walked through the crowd, Summer flashed him a seductive smile. "When we're done here, maybe we could hang out at your place for a while."

Like hell. He never went out with the same woman more than twice, and he never took them home. The loft was his sanctuary, the only place he could take off his movie star mask and just be himself. Summer stepped in front of him and wrapped her arms around his neck. "Or we could go to my place." She nibbled his earlobe.

"That could work." He disentangled himself from her arms and surreptitiously checked his watch. Fifteen minutes to go.

Summer pressed a hand to her chest. "Oh Nic! My chest is starting to feel tight, and I forgot my purse with my inhaler in the car."

The crowd roared as more celebrities arrived. *Shit.* It wouldn't be safe to leave the red carpet area. "Kaden, can you get Summer's purse from the car?"

"I'll get the head of security to assign a guard to cover you." Kaden walked over to a burly man about thirty yards away.

Nic spotted some acquaintances and led Summer over to make introductions. When a commotion arose behind him, he glanced over his shoulder. Bodies parted like the Red Sea to reveal a woman walking with a determined step in his direction. He did a double take and spun around to stare at the approaching Anna Nicole Smith look-alike.

The woman was very tall in her red stiletto heels. Curly blonde hair hung halfway down her back. Her curvaceous body was crammed into a very tight, very short crimson dress, the bodice of which left absolutely nothing to the imagination. Her smile, enhanced by the matching lipstick, resembled the grin a lioness might make upon spying her prey.

All he could do was take a step back before she launched herself at him. He let out a strangled "Ooof!" as Anna Nicole tackled him to the ground.

CHAPTER 5

Was he being punked?

Nic landed hard on his back, the woman draped across his chest. Wrapping her arms around his neck, she smothered his face in a pair of double D's. He wasn't able to drag in a lungful of air until she scooted down to kiss his forehead, nose and cheeks. The situation was kind of funny. He'd even been on the verge of laughing—until she started talking.

"Oh Nic, I'm so sorry I was late and you had to come here with that bimbo. Why, she's just using you to get on TV," she told him in a southern accent. "I knew you weren't really interested in that photographer either. Don't you know, sugar, I'm the only one for you?" And with that, she kissed him long and hard on the mouth.

What the fuck? Was this woman NicsBitch? Her dress looked poured on, but she could have a knife hidden beneath those mammoth breasts. *Christ*, she was an octopus, all eight of her hands groping him in places he preferred to have groped only in private.

He had to get her *off*. She was attached to his face and he couldn't *breathe*.

Arching his back, he pulled his knees up to get some leverage, placed his hands on her shoulders and, pushing as hard as he could, heaved her to the side. Her weight and the momentum caused them to roll over until he was on top of her.

Gently but firmly, he extricated himself from the tentacles of her arms. He managed to get on his knees before she blocked him by wrapping her mighty thighs around his waist and locking her ankles at the small of his back.

Kaden arrived at a dead run. He grabbed the woman under her arms and wrenched her away. Boots stomped on the ground behind him and in a rush, a group of shouting security guards arrived. As they hauled the woman to her feet, Nic remained kneeling, sucking in air.

Cameras flashed furiously, illuminating him and his zealous fan as the guards led her away. She was crying and calling out to him, begging him for help. What she'd said too closely echoed NicsBitch. Until the police confirmed she was harmless, he wasn't stepping one foot closer to her, tears or no tears.

Summer knelt beside him and pressed his hand to her chest while Kaden spoke with the security guards. "Oh Nic. That was so awful. The nerve of that cow pretending to be your girlfriend."

Nic stared at her. She couldn't be more wrong. He didn't give a shit about the woman's weight. In fact, he preferred his women with a little more meat.

The security guards established a perimeter around him, with everyone but Summer and a disconcerted looking Kaden on the other side. "Are you hurt, sir?"

Nic shook his head, feeling pretty disconcerted himself. "Just winded." When he moved to stand up, Kaden rushed forward. Exasperated and embarrassed, Nic waved him off. "I'm fine."

Instantly, he regretted his harsh tone. The man was only doing his job, after all. He forced himself to sound calm. "Have the guards identified the woman?"

One of the security guards said, "Her driver's license says she's Abby Clanwell from Hartsville, South Carolina." He peered at Nic, one eyebrow raised in speculation. "I take it you don't know her? She says she's your girlfriend."

Another girlfriend? He sure was fucking popular tonight. "Never saw her before."

"We didn't find any weapons on her. She's probably just an over-excited fan. We aren't sure how she got through the perimeter, but we'll be reviewing the security tapes to find out."

The guard left and Kaden turned to him, chagrin on his face. "Sir, this shouldn't have happened on my watch. If you want to get a new bodyguard, I'll understand."

Nic gripped his shoulder. "Relax, man. Even you can't be in two places at once. Besides, this area was supposed to be secure."

Kaden exhaled sharply. "Christ. She could be NicsBitch."

"Believe me, it's crossed my mind. But you know, if this had happened at any other time, we'd both be laughing."

"Maybe so. But from now on, I'm sticking to you like glue."

When the security guards gave up the perimeter, people flocked to his side. Turning to the fans across the street, Nic waved to reassure them. Then, he addressed the reporters gathered around him. "Thank you all for your concern but, really, I'm okay. I have truly wonderful fans, even the ones that get a little over-excited, and I'm honored by their love and devotion."

"Now, if they could only stay behind the barriers," Kaden muttered.

Everyone laughed, and just like that, the tension evaporated.

❧ 🎭 ❧

Lauren couldn't believe her eyes. The woman had appeared out of nowhere and thrown herself at Nic. Where were the security guards? And for that matter, where was his blond bodyguard? Even Vivian was nowhere to be seen.

Lauren couldn't help but smile when the bodyguard leaned down to help Nic stand up and Nic shoved his hand away. People often acted like she was fragile, weak, and she hated it. She could well imagine how Nic would feel about being treated like he was made of glass.

When the paparazzi had busted in on the photo shoot, he'd been so warrior-like. She got chills remembering how he'd jumped off the bed, landing between her and the door of the hotel room. A man like Nic would resent the need to have someone guard him.

His life had to be difficult. He had no privacy, no time to himself, and no freedom to *be* himself. Nic always had to be on his game, always had to be over the top. Always had to be Nic The Lover.

Lauren looked down at Jason, asleep in her arms. She didn't need glitz and glamour to be happy. Nic may have discarded her like yesterday's pizza box, but he didn't have what she did. His life was empty. Hers was full.

And someday, she'd meet a stable family man and fall in love. Until then, she had her friends, her family. And her fantasies.

❧ 🎭 ❧

Nic stepped out of the limo in front of Summer's apartment building, then turned to assist her. Kaden stood stone-faced, holding the passenger door open. "Can I have a private word, sir?"

Nic pulled Summer to his side. "Wait for me in the lobby."

She rubbed against him and giggled. "Hurry, okay?"

After she entered the building, Nic caught Kaden rolling his eyes. He grinned. "She's not so bad." Besides, all he wanted right now was to get his mind off Lauren. Maybe Summer was the answer.

"Not so bad if you like them without a brain." Nic shrugged. "What about the photographer, Lauren?"

"She's got a brain."

"What the fuck's wrong with you? Do you *want* to blow it with her?"

Nic sighed. Everyone insisted on reminding him of Lauren. "I like Lauren. I like her a lot. I'm just not the right guy for her."

"Based on the photo I saw, she might not agree."

"You know what this life does to people." He thrust his hands in his pockets and stared at his shoes. "I could never ask her to deal with all the shit that goes on in this business. Anyways, I haven't heard from her since D.C., and neither has Vivian." He raised his eyes to meet Kaden's gaze. "If she wants to work with me, she needs to let me know."

"So, it's just business?"

"It has to be."

Kaden raised his eyebrows. "But why Summer?"

"She's Nic The Lover's type."

"I see," he said although it was clear from his expression that he didn't. "You want me to wait?"

Nic shook his head. "I'll walk home."

"The woman's a barracuda. What if you need to make a quick escape?"

Nic laughed and clapped Kaden on the back. "I can handle her." He waited while Kaden drove away, then jogged up the steps to the lobby where Summer waited for him.

She led him to her apartment and ushered him inside. "My roommate's out of town, so we have the place to ourselves."

Nic smiled. Sex was definitely on the agenda. And exactly what he needed to get Lauren off his mind.

"The living room's right through there. Why don't you make yourself comfortable while I get us a drink?" The living room wasn't large, but she'd made the most of it. A couch and an armchair crowded around a mid-size flat screen TV hanging on the wall. He was easing into the armchair when Summer handed him a beer. "I hope you like German."

Nic eyed the bottle appreciatively. The woman knew her beer. "Love it, thanks."

She held her bottle up to his. "Cheers!"

"Cheers." He slugged back the fine German brew and watched her wander over to a stereo on a shelf. Her skimpy dress exposed long lean thighs and slim calves. Summer was beautiful, and like any man, he could appreciate her beauty, even if she wasn't his type. Now, if *Lauren* were here, wearing that dress, well, she wouldn't be wearing it for long.

After thumbing through a few CDs, Summer inserted one into the player. Moments later, Nic heard the opening notes of Bob Seger's *Old Time Rock and Roll*. He raised a brow. Did she want to dance with him?

Summer started swaying her hips, but it wasn't until she began undoing the zipper along the back of her dress that he understood. She wanted to dance *for* him. Hooboy! Relaxing into the comfortable armchair, he prepared to enjoy the show.

With her eyes on him, she shimmied and let the dress slowly drift down the length of her body to pool at her feet. She stood before him in a black lace bra and panties. The matching stripper heels were a welcome bonus.

She retrieved her beer from the shelf and ran the rim of the bottle against her lips, the condensation making them glisten. Nic stared as she stretched her neck and slid the bottle down the valley between her large breasts, leaving a wet path behind. A path that begged to be licked.

Turning her back to him, she bent over to place her drink on the low coffee table. Her hips rolled and she flipped her long hair from side to side. Nic's mouth went dry and a sheen of sweat covered his forehead. *Christ.* Summer looked like she was being fucked from behind.

After a final saucy lick of her lips, she straightened and started dancing, her body flowing and undulating in time with the music. She pressed her hands to her stomach and trailed them up to cup her tits, squeezing them together. Nic gulped and had to loosen his tie so he could breathe. Normally, he didn't go for this kind of thing, since women tended to be uncomfortable with it, but in this case, it all looked rather *professional.* He had no difficulty seeing the imaginary pole she was grinding against.

Like a cat, she slinked her way over to him, took the bottle from his hand and set it on the table beside his chair. Carefully, she placed one knee on either side of his legs, straddling him. With each beat, she swayed forward so his roughened jaw slid across her belly.

The song changed to something sultrier, more soulful. Arching her back, she undid the clasp of her bra and her tits spilled out. She settled on his lap and took his hands, pressing them to her chest. "Don't be shy."

Nic smiled. He'd have to be made of stone not to be a little turned on. She overflowed his large hands. Unfortunately, her implants felt like twin rocks.

Suddenly, he remembered touching Lauren's soft breasts, and had to close his eyes against the wave of lust that swamped him. When he'd cupped her during their Paparazzi Kiss gone wrong, she'd filled his hand. Not too much, not too little—just right.

What the hell was he doing here?

He gripped Summer's hips to guide her off his lap, but she placed her hands on his shoulders and began to ride him, grinding against his cock. A cock that was hard and aching. She moaned and rubbed her chest against his in a sinuous motion. Her tongue darted out to lick his lips and then sought entrance to his mouth.

Lust fogging his brain, he wrapped her long hair around his hand as he took control of the kiss. He plunged deep into her mouth, his tongue tangling with hers. She leaned into him, and he felt hard lumps pressing against his chest instead of Lauren's plush mounds.

Fuck!

This wasn't working. He had to get out of here. He shoved Summer off his lap and stood up.

"What's wrong? Didn't you like it?"

He smiled to soften the blow. "Nothing's wrong, sweetheart." *You just aren't Lauren.* "But I've got to go. I have an early interview in the morning."

She narrowed her eyes at him, clearly not buying his bullshit. "Oh, I get it. I'm not good enough for Nic The Lover."

Christ. How did he get into these situations? Oh, yeah. Because he thought with his dick. Time for some damage control. "That's not true," he said, glancing at the bulge in his pants. "You know I enjoyed it."

She looked down, then ran her hand along his cock. "So, why don't you stay? I can take care of this for you." Meeting his gaze, she ran her tongue along the edge of her lips.

An image of Lauren licking a drop of chardonnay off her lip at the restaurant popped into his mind and he had to take a deep breath before he could talk. Why the fuck hadn't he listened to Kaden?

"I really need to go. If I don't show up bright-eyed and bushy-tailed for this interview, Vivian will have my balls in a sling."

"I could have your balls in my mouth." Nic almost swallowed his tongue.

Fuck, fuck, fuck.

He had to get out of the apartment, now. "As nice as that sounds, I can't."

Mick Jagger's *She's the Boss* started playing. He pulled out his cell phone and said a quick thanks to God for over-protective agents. After an apologetic glance at Summer, he answered the phone. "Hey, Viv. What's up?"

"Darling, I hope you aren't still at the after-party. You have an interview with Good Morning, L.A. at six."

"Funny. I was just telling Summer about the interview."

He heard Vivian snort. "Let me guess. She doesn't believe you?"

"I'm sure she does now."

She laughed. "Glad I could be of service."

Nic hung up and, looking as earnest as he could, said, "Maybe we can do this again, sometime." Then he opened the door and high-tailed it out of Summer's apartment.

At three in the morning, Nic stumbled into the loft. Going to Summer's place had been a huge mistake. The girl had *moves*. But even she couldn't keep his mind off Lauren for more than thirty seconds at a time. Night after night, and half the day, he fantasized about having sex with Lauren, leaving him horny as hell, and the encounter with Summer hadn't helped.

He slumped onto the couch with his feet on the coffee table and turned on the television. Entertainment Buzz was playing clips of the footprint ceremony and the incident with the zealous fan. The news reporter went on to discuss last month's premiere of *Bad Days*.

When they showed the photo of him and Lauren kissing, Nic closed his eyes. The woman had imprinted on his mind. He saw her everywhere, whether his eyes were open or not. He saw her smile when she'd photographed him, her shock when their Paparazzi Kiss had gotten out of hand, her confusion when he'd kissed her goodnight on the cheek outside her hotel room.

Lauren was definitely the kind of woman he could get serious about. But he understood how she might not want to get involved with him and have to deal with the constant intrusions into her personal life. What he couldn't understand, though, was how she could give up this opportunity to jump start her career.

His phone sat on the coffee table, taunting him, daring him to call her. Okay. He'd give her a call and see how she was doing, maybe find out why she'd changed her mind about the photo shoot. And, even though Vivian had called her to cancel, he did owe her an apology for skipping out on their appointment at the Pepsi Center. Yeah, a personal call wouldn't hurt. He dialed 411.

Ten seconds later, he heard the phone ringing and had to wipe his sweaty palms on his pants. He was definitely crazy. Crazy about her.

"Hello?"

At the sound of her sleepy voice, his heart started pounding and his stomach did a weird little flip. Nic checked his watch. *Shit.* He'd been so focused on calling her he'd forgotten all about the time. "*Chérie.* I didn't realize how late it is. I should let you get back to sleep." His gut twisting, he waited a few tense moments for her reply.

"Jason and I watched the ceremony on TV, and we saw that woman attack you. Are you okay?"

Interesting. Not only had she watched the footprint ceremony, she'd also been worried about him. "All I lost was my breath and my dignity. She was just an excited fan, but she'd make any hockey team an excellent defenseman, though."

Lauren laughed. "The way she body-checked you, she'd give Lidstrom a run for his money."

A feeling of warmth spread across his chest. She shared his passion for hockey. "Yeah, she kicked my ass."

"I'm surprised you called me." Lauren didn't sound sleepy anymore; she sounded upset.

"Why's that?"

"Well, for starters you stood me up. I called Vivian and left her a voice mail with the time for you to meet me at the Pepsi Center. I waited there for over an hour and called her several times, but she never answered. In fact, she never returned any of my calls."

Nic frowned. He clearly remembered asking Vivian to let Lauren know he couldn't make the photo shoot. "I had to leave town on an emergency. She was supposed to call you to reschedule."

"An emergency? I hope everything is okay."

"It will be." Determination thickened his voice. After clearing his throat, he continued. "So, let me get this straight. Vivian never contacted you?"

"Even the proofs I sent her came back unopened."

"There has to be a mistake." If Vivian had wanted to reject the photos, she would have taken great pleasure in telling Lauren and certainly wouldn't have resorted to returning them unopened.

He heard Lauren sigh. "It wasn't a mistake. She thinks I'm not good enough for you… that I'm not a good enough photographer, I mean."

"You're very talented."

"This has nothing to do with my photography skills." She sounded a little frustrated. "Anyway, talk to her, and if you still want to finish the photo shoot, let me know."

Nic shook his head. The woman clearly had no idea what she did to him. Suddenly, an image of Lauren straddling him on the motorcycle flashed in front of his eyes. Molten lava flowed in his veins at the mere thought of touching her. His cock hardened, and he had to stand up or risk emasculation.

"We're doing this, *chérie*. I'll call you tomorrow." Being with her and knowing he couldn't take their relationship beyond a professional level would be torture. But still, he wanted the pleasure of hanging out with her, of being treated like a normal man for a few short days, of seeing her again, one last time.

Lauren lay back on the pillows and watched the shadows dance on her bedroom ceiling. The last thing she'd expected tonight was a call from Nic. As far as she could tell, the only person standing in the way of Nic helping launch her career was Vivian. If Vivian didn't release the photos of Nic, Lauren's career would be dead before it even started. She grinned, remembering how he'd sweet-talked his agent into getting his way in D.C. If anyone could get around Vivian, it was Nic.

God, she missed him. She *did* want another chance to finish shooting Nic, but even more, she wanted another chance to spend time with him. The ride they'd taken together on the motorcycle had been exciting; *Nic* was exciting. And despite his superb acting skills, she was sure his interest in her had been genuine. She smiled. Certainly, the bulge in his pants had been genuine.

Closing her eyes, she gave in to the desire, the need to feel him near, and drifted into one of her favorite fantasies. She wasn't normally an exhibitionist, not even close, but in her fantasies, she could explore situations she'd never dare to in real life…

She's in some sort of Midwestern redneck bar wearing a peasant blouse, a long loose skirt, cowboy boots and nothing else. The lights are low and a band plays loudly in the corner. She leans against a tall wooden table, watching people dance in front of her. She closes her eyes, letting the music sweep through her, setting her hips to swaying.

Hands slip under the edge of her shirt, searing her skin as a warm mouth nips the sensitive flesh of her neck just below her ear. His touch and his smell tell her this man is

Nic. With a smile, she turns her head to kiss him. She traces the seam of his lips until they part, the taste of the Guinness he's been drinking thick on his tongue. His strong arm around her waist pulls her tightly against his groin, where he is hot, hard, and ready. His hands skim up her ribcage, smoothing their way to her breasts, which he cups and kneads. She gasps. Her back arches in pleasure, her peaked nipples poking his palms, begging for attention. Gently, he rolls them between his thumbs and forefingers, creating a pleasurable friction. Then he increases the pressure and adds a tugging motion that ratchets up her need, making her want more.

She squirms and pushes her bottom against his erection until his length is eased between the cheeks of her butt. The only thing separating her flesh from his is the thin material of her skirt. Reaching back, she grasps him in her hand, her mind reeling at the feel of him, the strength, the heat, the long hardness. Looking over her shoulder into his eyes, she whispers, "I need you inside me, now."

"Your wish is my command." He grins as he tugs the back of her skirt up. "Face forward." His voice is breathless, urgent like her own.

Beyond all sanity and desperate to have him where she needs him, she complies but loops an arm around his neck, pulling his head down so his beard-roughened cheek rests against her shoulder. The blunt head of his erection presses against her opening but doesn't go farther. Unable to wait, she pushes back, but he grips her hips with his hands, holding her in place. When she grumbles, he lightly bites her neck, then soothes it with a swirl of his tongue.

"Please," she begs.

She can't see his triumphant grin but she can feel it as his lips curve against her sensitive skin. She is rewarded when he begins to stretch her, filling the emptiness in her body, in her heart.

As the tempo of the music increases, Nic speeds up his strokes to match. Together they are dancing, pressed tightly, swaying to the beat of the music along with the crowd. One of Nic's hands returns to a breast to tweak and tug at her nipple while the other slips under her skirt and one long finger finds her nub. With slow circular motions in time with his strokes, he brings her higher and higher. She writhes against him. Her arms thrash, her legs shake. As the music reaches its crescendo…

A powerful orgasm roared through Lauren's body, igniting every nerve ending in its path. Until finally, spent, shaking, her breath coming in rapid gasps, she descended from the peak.

As a figment of her imagination, Nic The Lover was beyond compare. Would she ever find out if the real Nic could live up to the fantasy?

❧ ❧

She paced back and forth, her angry steps wearing a path in the carpet. If that crazy fan were within arm's reach, she'd gladly strangle her. The nerve of that woman, attacking Nic. She'd actually knocked him to the ground!

Poor Nic was so shaken up, she'd permitted him to take a small measure of comfort from the stupid blonde who'd accompanied him to the footprint ceremony. Since Nic didn't like stupid blondes, she had no reason to be jealous. He'd taken the bimbo because she fit Nic The Lover's image. A smile curved her lips. She understood the need for a good front. She wouldn't need to punish him for that.

Yet.

As for the short, fat photographer, if he saw her in anything but a professional capacity, Nic's punishment would be severe. She'd be watching. And she'd know. He'd learn how creative she could be.

Soon, the money would be safely offshore and they would be the owners of a small island far, far away from everyone. She'd have him all to herself.

Soon, she'd take him from Hollywood and he could finally drop his Nic The Lover act. He'd owe her for setting him free.

Soon, he'd realize how much he needed her and how perfect things were with just the two of them. She'd be his and he'd be hers.

Soon.

Early the next morning, Nic stormed into Vivian's office, completely ignoring Margo, who called out to him that Vivian was on the phone. He didn't care. Vivian needed to explain the situation with Lauren.

At the sound of his voice, Vivian looked up. After making a quick excuse to her caller, she hung up. "Darling, how lovely to see you. Please have a seat."

The warm greeting on her face faded when Nic remained standing. "I spoke with Lauren last night. You never called her to cancel the photo shoot when I left for Montréal."

With irritating precision, Vivian relaxed in her seat and crossed her legs. "As I recall, you told me Lauren would call me *if* she found a location, and that I should let her know you had an emergency. She didn't call, so there was no reason for me to contact her. You were very agitated that night, maybe that's why you don't remember?"

Was it possible? He *had* been frantic with worry about Rachel. "What about the voice mail she left you, and the proofs she sent for your approval? They were returned, unopened."

Vivian's brow furrowed as she tapped a finger on her lip. "Maybe she called the wrong number? As for the proofs, Margo keeps a log of all sent and received mail. Let's take a look." She pressed the intercom button on her phone. "Margo, please bring in the correspondence log."

Nic sank into one of Vivian's rather uncomfortable straight backed guest chairs. Seconds later, Margo arrived with the log book, handed it to Vivian and left.

After scanning through a few pages, Vivian tapped a line with her nail. "Here it is. May 28, 11:00am, a FEDEX delivery from L. James. Did Lauren say when it was returned?"

Nic shook his head.

After flipping through a few more pages, she read, "May 31, 3:00pm FEDEX pickup. Envelope for L. James."

"So you received it and then sent it back, like Lauren said."

Vivian leaned back in her chair, swinging her foot. All of a sudden, she slapped her hands on the desk. "I bet I know what happened. Margo received the FEDEX, opened it and accidentally placed the envelope from Lauren in the outbox instead of the inbox."

Nic rested his elbows on his knees and scrubbed his cheeks. Could the answer be so simple?

"I'm terribly sorry. Margo will be reprimanded, and I assure you such an incident will never occur again."

"It was an honest mix-up, Vivian. Don't be too hard on her."

"Is Lauren very upset?"

He nodded. "She thought I'd blown her off. I'll need to convince her this was all a big mistake."

Vivian met his gaze and raised her eyebrows. "Convince her? Darling, I think she needs to apologize to you for overreacting. You can work with any photographer you want, yet you choose to work with her. She should be grateful."

"Nah, we're the lucky ones." He looked up and smiled. "It's too bad you haven't seen the proofs yet because then you'd understand. And this next shoot she has planned, it'll be even better than the last one."

Vivian didn't return his smile. "You seem very certain."

"She wants to do this part on location in a skating arena. It's going to be fantastic."

"An arena, Nic? Do you think the magazines will want photos of Nic The Lover on ice?" She grimaced.

Anger trailed a burning path up his neck. Lauren had pegged this perfectly. He didn't give a shit if Vivian liked Lauren's ideas. He loved them. Standing up, he placed his hands on the edge of the desk and leaned over until his nose almost touched hers. "Listen to me, Vivian. Whether you like it or not, I'm doing this photo shoot."

"Of course. I didn't mean to imply otherwise." She smiled sweetly and held his cheeks in the palms of her hands. "Have Lauren send me the proofs again and I'll review them. I only want the best for you, darling."

Nic pulled her hands away from his face and took a few steps back. "But sometimes, I'm the only one who knows what that is."

Lauren stared at the phone on the kitchen wall, willing it to ring. All day, she'd struggled against the urge to pick it up and dial Nic's number instead of waiting for him to call. Only she couldn't do that because he hadn't exactly given her his number. He just hadn't blocked his caller ID last night.

She had to stop acting like a lovesick teenager. Grabbing the mailbox key, she headed outside, locking the door behind her. That's when the phone rang.

As she fumbled the key into the lock, Lauren wanted to scream. She dashed across the living room and snatched the phone off the hook. The rush of adrenaline made her sound breathless. Great. Nic probably thought he'd reached some singles hotline.

"*Bonjour, chérie.* Did I catch you at a bad time?"

"Not at all. I was folding laundry." Lauren wanted to die. Did she have to sound so domestic?

"I spoke with Vivian." Nic explained how Vivian had misunderstood his instructions when he'd had to leave D.C. and how there'd been some confusion with the proofs. Vivian's explanation stank of coincidences.

"Why don't you give me her number again? If I need to call her about the photos, we'll be sure I have the right one."

Nic gave her the number and she checked it against Vivian's contact entry in her phone. They matched. Vivian was lying. *What a bitch.* She'd let it go this time. But she wouldn't be so forgiving if it happened again.

"Now that everything's been cleared up, let's schedule the rest of the photo shoot. I want to do it as soon as possible."

Lauren barely managed to suppress a squeal. "Great. Let me check my schedule." She forced her voice to sound casual as she flipped the pages of the calendar hanging on the inside of the pantry door. How was she going to fit in a trip to L.A.? "Between work and taking care of Jason, it's hard for me to get away. Can you come to Seattle? If so, maybe we can do it this week?"

"Not a problem."

Wow. He hadn't even hesitated. "Don't you have to check with Vivian?"

"She can postpone anything she has planned. What's a good day for you?"

Lauren could hardly believe her ears. A tingle of excitement sizzled through her body and pooled low in her belly. "Can you make it out here Friday evening or Saturday morning?"

"I'll check the flights and let you know. Can you book some arena time Saturday afternoon or evening?"

"I'll get right on it." Her hands started to tremble. Was this all too good to be true?

"Let me give you my cell phone number in case you need to reach me."

Lauren leaned against the wall as her heart threatened to pound a hole through her chest. Nic The Lover wanted to give her his *personal* cell number. Not that she didn't already have it, but now she'd actually be able to use it. She held the receiver away from her mouth and took a deep calming breath, then asked, "Don't you want me to call Vivian and have her contact you?"

"No. I'd like to avoid any more mix-ups where you're concerned." He gave her the number. "Call me, anytime."

Was she imagining the huskiness in his voice? She grinned and couldn't help wondering what ringtone he'd assigned her contact entry. In her fantasies, he'd pick something like Savage Garden's *Truly Madly Deeply*, but he'd probably chosen something more along the lines of Depeche Mode's *Photographic.*

"By the way, my son has a sleepover planned for the weekend so maybe you could, um, stay here instead of going to a hotel." Lauren closed her eyes and sighed. So much for being professional; she sounded like she was propositioning him. "I mean… I have two bedrooms…" *Even worse.*

Nic laughed. "*Chérie*, I accept your gracious offer."

She groaned. Everything she said to him seemed to have a double meaning. Maybe it was her subconscious, or rather not so subconscious, desires bubbling to the surface.

After ending the call, Lauren stood staring out of her patio door with the phone clutched to her chest. *Nic The Lover was coming here.*

She looked around the apartment. What would he think? Small and plain and surely nothing like his L.A. loft, the apartment was perfect for her and Jason. Nic could use her room since she was pretty sure he wouldn't fit in Jason's twin bed. The image of Nic lying in the small bed with his feet hanging off the end made her to smile.

Although, she preferred to imagine him sprawled across her own bed, with his head on her favorite pillow, the sheets twisted around his hips. She laughed and fanned her face. That image was sure to fuel a few fantasies. This weekend could be the closest she'd ever get to having Nic The Lover in her bed for real.

Too bad she wouldn't be in it with him.

CHAPTER 6

Lauren glanced at the kitchen wall clock for what must have been the hundredth time. Late last night, Nic had called. There'd been some problem with his flight and he was driving in from San Francisco.

Knowing he was alone on the road, she'd tossed and turned, unable to sleep. By dawn, she'd already showered and dressed. Of course, she'd spent a little of that extra time on her hair and makeup. Why not? It wasn't every day a girl had a movie star coming to her home.

The table was set, the coffee was brewing, and everything was ready for the omelet she planned to make for breakfast. Back and forth, she paced the length of the living room. As she passed the patio door, she spotted a large black SUV pulling into a parking space in front of her apartment.

Oh God, he was here. Her heart slammed in her chest, and she had to force herself to breathe. It wouldn't do to answer the door panting like an excited puppy. Resisting the urge to rush out and meet him in the parking lot, she ripped off her apron and sat down. Knees bouncing, hands tapping, she waited. When the bell finally rang, she vaulted off the couch and threw open the front door.

Lauren's stomach did a slow roll as she took in the vision before her. Leaning against the jamb, duffle bag thrown over a muscled shoulder, baseball cap pulled low over sunglass-covered eyes, stood a grinning Nic. "Good morning, *chérie*. Aren't you a sight for sore eyes."

Lauren blushed at the compliment. But as far as she was concerned, he was the one who was a sight for sore eyes. God the man was gorgeous. Too bad she didn't have her camera on hand. The ladies would go crazy for a photo of Nic standing in a doorway, looking all sexy and triumphant. "Come in. I thought you'd never get here."

"I was beginning to think the same thing." He leaned down to kiss her on both cheeks, and Lauren had to swallow a disappointed sigh. She shouldn't want more from him. But she did.

"Here, have a seat. Tell me about your trip."

"Ah, that feels great," he said, flopping onto the couch and tugging her down next to him. "It was pretty crazy. Nothing worked out as I'd planned. I told Vivian I needed to be free by 1:30 yesterday, but I didn't tell her why."

She felt a small thrill at his words. "You didn't tell her you were coming here?"

Nic shook his head. "And because she was ticked her off that I wouldn't tell her my plans, she filled my schedule like I was going away for a month. I had a radio interview followed by guest appearances on two morning talk shows, an early lunch meeting with Vivian, and then a magazine interview."

"You must have been exhausted."

"But that's when the fun started." He paused and his lips curved on one side. "Lunch ran late and the interview was delayed. I rushed through it, then raced home to grab my bag. I waited fifteen minutes for the limo service before calling them, only to be told someone had cancelled my pickup request."

"Oh no!" Lauren wouldn't have been surprised to learn Vivian was responsible. "Has this ever happened before?"

"Never. They offered to send another car, but by then it was too late. I went to get my car. And one of the tires was flat."

"Are you serious?"

"As a Stanley Cup playoff game." Nic rubbed a hand along the nape of his neck and then rested his arm on the back of the couch. "I tried to catch a cab. Only, my street was blocked off because of an accident. I ran the mile to Gordon street and finally managed to hail a cab."

"But you still missed your flight."

He nodded. "I rebooked with a stop in San Francisco, but I should have taken the later direct flight to Seattle. My connecting flight was cancelled because of some mechanical problem and no other planes were available."

"This sounds like one of your action movies. I'm amazed you didn't turn around and go back home. It's almost like someone was trying to tell you something."

Playfully, he tugged at one of her curls. "Maybe, but the only thing I wanted to hear was you saying hello as you opened your front door."

When his flirting made her blush, he grinned and brushed his knuckles against her warm cheeks. He'd gone through hell to come to Seattle, to her home, to work with her on a photo shoot. It had to mean *something* to him.

As if confirming her thoughts, he added, "But, I'm here now and very excited about the photo shoot." He toed his duffle bag. "Where should I put this?"

She led him into the master bedroom. "You can leave your things here."

He dropped the bag on the floor and laid his jacket, cap, and sunglasses on the freshly made bed. "I'm putting you out of your room."

"It's no problem, really. Besides, Jason's bed is too short for you."

"Maybe you'll join me?" When she blushed again, he grinned and started laughing.

"Mom? Who's here?" Jason called out in a sleepy voice.

"Or maybe not," Nic whispered, grinning even more.

"One minute, honey," she said, then turned to Nic. "I hope you don't mind. Jason's sleepover was cancelled."

"Hey, no worries. This is your son's home and he shouldn't have to leave because I'm here."

By the seriousness of his expression, he meant every word. A movie star *and* he didn't expect special treatment? Nic The Lover was definitely in the running for the World's Most Perfect Man. "I didn't tell him you were coming. Want to walk out first and surprise him?"

If the mischievous glint in his eyes was anything to go by, Nic must have loved pulling pranks as a child.

"Give me a minute to get my video camera." She reached for a case on her closet shelf and pulled out a small camcorder. After turning it on and fiddling with a few settings, she shot him a smile. "All set."

Nic put his finger to his lips and tiptoed through the door, hugging the wall. He paused, tilting his head as if listening to the television. Then he walked into the living room. "Hey Jason, buddy. How did you know SpongeBob Square Pants was my favorite show?"

While Jason continued to stare at him wide-eyed, Nic joined him on the couch. After making himself comfortable with a lot of wiggling and stretching, he turned to Jason, who by this time was holding back a fit of giggling. As Lauren filmed the scene from the doorway to her bedroom, she also tried in vain to hold back her own laughter. Nic was quite the comedian.

"SpongeBob's the best. Hey, is this the Bad Neighbors episode?"

"Uh, yeah." Jason's gaze darted left and right, like he was searching for someone. Lauren smiled. He still hadn't spotted her.

"What's your favorite episode?" Nic asked Jason. "Mine's the Truth or Square one. It's so funny when everyone gets locked in the freezer and SpongeBob starts making up all these wacky stories." Lauren's heart melted at his boyish expression. She'd better step in before Jason started getting worried.

"Mine is the one where SpongeBob and Patrick try to break Mrs. Puff out of jail," she said, leaving her hiding place.

"Uh, Mom…?" Jason indicated Nic with wide eyes and a jerk of his head. He was practically jumping up and down on the couch.

"Yes, honey?" She regarded him innocently.

"Look!" he whispered loudly, pointing at Nic. "It's Nic Lamoro! Can't you see him, Mom? Can't you see?"

Nic burst out in a fit of laughter. Tears streaming from his eyes, he rolled onto the floor, clutching his stomach.

"Mom, did I miss something?" Jason's confused expression was so adorable, Lauren couldn't hold back her own laughter anymore. His eyes continued to reflect his bewilderment at the whole scene, but he soon joined them in their laughter. She took Nic's place on the couch and hugged her son tightly. It was so good to see Jason having fun. After taking a few deep breaths and wiping the tears from her eyes, she was able to speak again.

She gestured to Nic, who'd managed to calm down enough to sit up. "Nic will be visiting us this weekend. But you can't tell anyone until after he leaves. Nic doesn't want any reporters to bother us."

Jason turned to Nic and shook his head. "I won't tell anyone. I promise."

Nic got up on his knees and shook Jason's hand, man to man. "I appreciate your help, buddy." Then he winked, adding, "Between the two of us, I'm sure we can keep the reporters away."

"You bet!" Jason jumped off the couch and shouted over his shoulder as he ran to his room, "What's for breakfast, Mom? I'm starving."

"It's good to know the shock hasn't affected his appetite," Lauren said, her tone wry. "Come have some coffee while I make breakfast. Do you like omelets?"

He took the cup she handed him. "Love 'em."

"There's cream and sugar on the table. Please help yourself."

Nic doctored his drink then tasted it. "Mmm… this is really good." He took another sip. Lauren practically drooled. With his eyes closed like that, his expression was almost orgasmic. She'd make sure to have fresh, hot coffee on hand all weekend.

Nic opened his eyes and caught her staring. Lauren turned away to hide her heated cheeks. "This will take another twenty minutes or so. Do you want to take a shower or a nap? You must be exhausted."

"I'd love a quick shower." He wrinkled his nose. "I'm more than overdue."

His expression stirred something low in her belly. He seemed so unspoiled, so happy, so much like the boy she remembered. "Take your time. There are clean towels in the cabinet in the bathroom. And there's soap and shampoo in there, too. Shout if you need anything."

Soon, she heard the sound of water running. As she mixed up the ingredients for the omelet, her mind drifted to images of Nic in the shower, water sluicing down his beautiful face, between his exquisitely sculpted pectorals, into his belly button, over his flat stomach, separating into two flows around his hard… She gasped as cold liquid splashed her arm. *Damn*, she'd just poured milk all over the counter.

Nic pushed his empty plate to the side and patted his full stomach. Warmth spread throughout his body as his gaze locked with Lauren's. What was that bubbly feeling in his stomach?

He felt comfortable here, in this small apartment with its cooking smells, childish artwork decorating the walls, and family photos on every available surface except in her bedroom. Even if at least half the photos were of a man who, judging by the uniform he wore, could be none other than Todd James, Lauren's dead husband.

Had he been selfish in coming here? He didn't know how far the stalker was willing to go. Still, he'd wanted to be here with Lauren and Jason, enjoying himself, rolling around the floor, laughing his head off.

Lauren must have sensed the mix of pleasure and worry roiling around inside him because she leaned over and rubbed her finger along his eyebrows, then cradled his cheek in her palm. Today, her beautiful eyes were a soft Mediterranean green. He wanted to dive in their deep waters and stay there all day.

Not wanting her to know the turn his thoughts had taken, he smiled and asked, "What's on the schedule for today?"

She dropped her hand and sat back in her chair. "The arena is booked from 7:00 to 9:00 tonight, but other than that, we can do anything you want."

He gave her a cocky grin. "*Anything?*"

She blushed and cleared her throat. "Anything G-rated."

His grin widened. "Is there some place you and Jason like to go? Something you like to do on weekends?"

"I know, I know," Jason shouted as he raced around the corner from his room. "Let's go bowling. Please, please!" he insisted, seeing his mother's dubious look.

Nic shrugged. "Fine with me. But I should warn you, I was the city champion in my youth." He raised an eyebrow, including Lauren in his challenge. "Are you up for it?"

Lauren winked at her son, a half smile curving her lips. "I think we'll manage. Isn't that right, Jason?"

Eyes twinkling, Jason pressed his lips together tightly as if trying to keep them from spilling some huge secret.

Unable to maintain his haughty expression, Nic grinned at Jason and initiated a complex series of knuckle-bumps. When he caught Lauren's wistful expression, his smile faded. Before he could ask what was wrong, she smiled brightly and ordered them to be at the door, ready to leave in exactly five minutes.

Jason grabbed Nic's hand and began dragging him toward his room. "Whoa there, little man. What's up?"

"I got your disguise," he said, his expression earnest as he held out a black knit cap and goggles. "We'll be twins, see? People won't recognize you."

Nic dropped to his knees, putting them at eye level. He took the offered items and put them on. "You know what this means, don't you?"

Eyes round, lips pursed, Jason shook his head. Nic fisted his right hand and pounded it sharply against his left shoulder. When Jason's eyes widened even more, Nic forced his expression to remain serious. "We're brothers, little man. Brothers in arms, and this is our first mission. Our mission has three objectives." He ticked them off on his fingers. "One, we must protect our secret. Two, we must beat your mom at bowling. Three, we must…" He winked. "Have fun!"

Childish squeals filled the room as he flipped the startled boy over his shoulder and swung him around in circles. He loved children. Loved their innocence and craftiness. Loved their resilience and determination.

After agreeing to surprise Lauren with their disguises, Nic dashed off to his room to change into a pair of black jeans and a black long sleeved T-shirt. Black biker boots completed the outfit. He checked himself out in the full length mirror behind Lauren's door and laughed out loud. Oh, man. Vivian would kill him if she ever found out about this. But Jason was right. People would stare but no one would recognize him. At least he hoped not. He really didn't want any pictures of himself in this get-up hitting the front page.

Hearing a soft knock on the door, he turned the knob and peered down at the little boy. "All set?"

"Roger that."

Nic flashed him a quick grin. "Let's roll."

With military precision, they marched to the front door. Seeing them, Lauren's jaw dropped and her eyes darted between the two. "Wha…What?" she stuttered as they stopped abruptly in front of her, saluting with a smart snap of their right hands and a hard stomp of one foot.

Jason managed to hold onto his salute for all of five seconds before jumping up and down, clapping his hands. "Do you like our disguises?"

Biting her upper lip, she looked up at Nic. "Absolutely perfect." Something in her eyes made him believe she wasn't talking about their outfits.

They'd decided to take her car to the bowling alley because any determined paparazzi could trace the rented SUV to him, but he stopped short when Lauren unlocked the doors of a blue Mini Cooper convertible. How the hell would he fit into such a puny car?

Angling his head, he examined the vehicle from all directions, considering the possibilities. If he pushed the seat all the way back, and if he pulled his knees up to his chin, and if he hunched his back, and if he held his breath, he just might be able to squeeze in.

"Are you sure you don't want to take the SUV?" she asked as he began easing into the passenger seat. When he bumped his head on the roof, Lauren smirked. "I'll open the roof so you don't get a cramp."

"How kind." Little Miss Lauren was definitely getting a kick out of this.

Maybe they should have taken the SUV. If only to save his manly pride.

"You know, this could work for you," she teased, eyeing him up and down, focusing first on his head, then on his knees tucked under his chin. "This car, with those goggles, everyone will think you're Austin Powers. Except he's really short and you're, well, not." She grinned.

Smartass.

Nic grinned back. He was having a blast. Everything from the small apartment to the tiny car and his outrageous outfit was so different from his regular life. But the biggest difference was the laughter. Nic The Lover smiled a lot for the camera, even laughed on cue. But Nic the man? Until he'd met Lauren, he'd had too few reasons to laugh.

Letting go of the past, letting go of the mask he perpetually wore, at least for a few hours, felt so unbelievably good. And every time Lauren gazed into his eyes, the connection between them grew stronger, and he had to resist the urge to open the door wider and let her into his life.

For a moment, when his cell phone started blasting "She's the Boss," he considered not answering it; he'd told Vivian he'd be off the grid for the weekend. But she wasn't the type to call simply to chat.

Lauren raised her eyebrows. "Aren't you going to answer? It's Vivian, isn't it?"

"Yeah." He leaned to the side so he could inch the phone out of his pocket. "What's up, Viv?"

"Hello, darling. I have some news. NicsBitch has been a busy bee. Another sighting on CelebrityStalker put you in San Francisco last night. Since you neglected to tell me where you'd be this weekend, I didn't know if it was a real sighting or not. Should we be worried?"

"I'm not in San Francisco." Nic tried to hide his concern but his adrenaline spiked and sweat broke out on his forehead. How did NicsBitch know he'd been in San Francisco?

"Good. I'd hate for the paparazzi to ruin your weekend. I know things have been difficult lately."

Nic relaxed as best he could in the tight space, leaning against the headrest and letting the wind cool his heated skin. "Thanks Viv. You're a good friend."

"Anything for you, darling."

Nic finished the call and looked over at Lauren. She was focused on the road, but her lips were stretched in a tight line.

"Is everything okay?" she asked. "You seem a little tense."

"Someone posted a sighting of me in San Francisco last night." He shrugged casually, hoping to keep things light. "It's no big deal."

"On the Internet? You mean on one of those websites that specialize in tracking celebrities?"

"CelebrityStalker.com in this case. Fans who spot a celebrity can go there and post the location of the sighting, the date, even a photo if they have one."

"I've heard some of these sites even show maps of all the places where a particular celebrity was spotted." She glanced at him furtively and nibbled her lips. "I've often wondered about people who do things like that. I'm sure some are random sightings by excited fans. But it wouldn't surprise if some of these so-called fans are actually stalkers."

Nic's jaw clenched. *Stay calm.* She'd put into words everything he'd been thinking. Before telling her more, he checked the backseat to make sure Jason wasn't listening. "One of them is a repeat poster. Vivian checks regularly and lets me know if she finds anything about me. There've been several in the last month."

"That's creepy. It's good you have someone like Vivian watching your back. Has she been your agent a long time?"

"Since I first came to Hollywood. She and her husband signed me as a client, and within two months, I had my first movie contract. She's a terrific agent."

Lauren pulled the car into a spot in the bowling alley parking lot and cut off the engine. Turning in her seat, she snapped her fingers. "Hey! Didn't I read something about you giving her husband a bone-marrow transplant when he got sick?"

It made Nic uncomfortable when people knew things he hadn't shared with them. Unfortunately, that was life in Hollywood. The paparazzi made certain of it. Nic nodded. "David had leukemia. I got tested and found out I was a donor match."

"So how is he now? It was several years ago, wasn't it?"

"Two years. The transplant didn't take and he died."

"Oh, I hadn't heard. Vivian must have been devastated."

Nic closed his eyes for a moment. The last two years had been extremely hard for both of them. Vivian had lost David, and he'd lost his mother. "It's been difficult. The agency lost most of David's clients, so she's had to deal both with losing her husband and struggling to keep the agency going."

"But you stayed on," she said softly.

He smiled. "She's helped me with some personal issues as well as with my career. I owe her a lot."

"Even so, don't you think she can be a bit much sometimes?"

"Absolutely." He grinned. No one knew that better than he did. "I think she's just been really lonely since David died. And she's immersed herself in her work. Her focus is one hundred percent on rebuilding the agency."

"Hey, are we going in or what?" Nic looked behind them to see Jason, elbows hooked over the two front seats, his irritated gaze darting between him and Lauren.

"That depends. Are you ready to get your butt whipped?"

Jason grinned. "The question is, are you?"

Staying back to reassess her plan, she watched Nic go into the bowling alley and had to laugh at his ridiculous outfit. She jotted down one last note in her journal before stowing it in her purse.

The sight of her phone reminded her of her luck in finding Tony. Last year, while searching the Internet, she'd come across repeated sightings of Nic. Using some clues in the postings and some online messages, she tracked the postings to Tony Spagnoli, a stage hand during the filming of *Bad Days*. He had a huge crush on Nic, but when Nic told him he didn't swing that way, Tony snuck into his dressing room and installed spy software on Nic's phone. He didn't want to hurt Nic, but he did want to rattle him and teach him a lesson. In turn, she'd decided to teach Tony a lesson.

When she revealed what she knew, Tony had explained where he'd gotten the tracking software, how he'd set up the account, and how he'd obtained a stolen credit card so he could remain anonymous. If he hadn't been working on the set, she'd never have caught him.

Armed with that information, she let Tony go with the threat that if he ever posted about Nic again, or came anywhere near Nic, she'd turn all the information she had on him over to the police. Tony would be arrested for stalking, and given Nic's status, Tony's ass would be in prison until he could no longer even feel it. Someday, she grinned, she'd have to thank Tony for the education.

A few months ago, she'd used what she'd learned to buy a stolen credit card, which she'd used to pay for the tracking software, and she'd created NicsBitch. Even if someday Nic discovered the tracking app on his phone, no one would be able to trace it back to her.

When she'd seen the flashing light on her phone that indicated Nic's GPS position moving from San Francisco International Airport to Seattle, she hadn't known whether to wring Nic's neck for being so foolhardy or be proud of his resourcefulness. And that was one of the things she loved best about him. He kept her on her toes, slightly off kilter, surprising her at every turn. He added spice and excitement to her life. And that, along with his smile, his caring words, and his innate tenderness had brought her out of the depression that had gripped her heart.

When her world had been torn to pieces, he'd stepped in and helped her. He'd saved her life. And you know what they say—when you save someone's life, that person becomes your responsibility. Nic had saved her, and so now, she was his. Only, he didn't know that yet. She was making arrangements so they could be together forever.

He had sexual needs she couldn't take care of yet, and she understood that. She wouldn't punish him if he satisfied those needs with women who only took his body, but she would be very angry if he let any woman take his heart.

His heart belonged to her, and only her.

Picking up her camera, she got out of the car and followed her heart into the bowling alley where she could keep a close eye on it.

CHAPTER 7

Three hours later, Lauren couldn't keep the smile off her face as she, Jason, and Nic tramped back into her small apartment carrying a pizza box and a six-pack of Coke. Bowling had never been so much fun. She and Jason had neglected to inform Nic they were state champions in the parent-child bowling league. He'd been a really good sport about losing to an eight-year-old.

"That was the most unfair game in the history of bowling," Nic grumbled as he ruffled Jason's hair.

"We sure whipped your butt. No city champion can beat us."

Lauren watched Jason trudge off to the bathroom to wash up for dinner. "I haven't seen him so happy in years,"

"He's a great kid." Nic took off the knit cap but forgot the goggles.

Moving in close, she removed them, revealing his raccoon-ringed eyes. "Does this hurt?" she asked, rubbing the indents with her fingers. He caught her gaze. Her heart stuttered at the lust swirling in the blue depths of his eyes.

His arms snaked around her waist, and she couldn't resist pulling his head down, bringing his mouth close to hers. Close but not touching. His warm breath feathered her lips, making her shiver. Was she imagining the heat in his eyes?

An emotion she couldn't name crossed his face. He released her, as if he'd touched fire, and she stumbled.

"Sorry." He caught her arm.

Jason ran into the room and took his place at the table. Nic sat in a chair next to him and handed Jason a slice of pizza. Taking his cue, she handed out the drinks.

While Nic and Jason discussed the finer points of hockey, Lauren's mind wandered to what Nic had told her in the car. Todd had led a dangerous life, but it had been clear who the enemy was, and he'd felt safe on American soil. How awful it must feel to always have people digging into your life, tracking your every move. Having Googled Nic many times, she knew how much private information about him was out there. Later, she'd have to check out this CelebrityStalker site.

Refocusing on Nic and Jason, her chest tightened. Jason's little face was flushed, his eyes bright with excitement. He was thoroughly caught up in a friendly argument about proper hand placement when executing a slap shot.

Todd had loved hockey, and except for the few photos scattered around the apartment, it was all Jason had left of his father. Blinking rapidly, she cleared the moisture from her eyes before either man or boy noticed. When Jason got up to put his dishes away, she smiled brightly at Nic and whispered, "Thank you for talking guy stuff with him."

Nic frowned in mock astonishment. "What? You don't talk guy stuff with him?"

She put on her best pout and shook her head. "I've been watching hockey for years with him, but…" She looked up and batted her eyelashes. "I'm at a total loss when it comes to discussing things like jock itch and the art of the chest bump."

Nic's expression morphed into a grin. "Oh, you're good. But you can't mock the great sport of hockey and get away with it. You may have beat me at bowling, but let's see how you do on the ice."

When she remained silent, his grin faded. "Don't tell me you were an Olympic figure skater?"

"Okay." She laughed. "I won't."

After finishing dinner, they went to a near-by skating rink. While Lauren and Jason set up the props, Nic changed into the tuxedo pants and Montréal Canadiens jersey he'd brought. In high school, he'd often imagined skating victory laps with the Stanley Cup firmly clutched in his hands, high above his head, wearing this jersey. But when Rachel had gotten hurt, he'd given up his NHL dreams.

Nic laced up his skates and charged onto the ice, ready to warm up. At the sight of Lauren executing a perfect double toe loop, he caught himself on the boards to keep from falling. Was there anything the woman couldn't do?

She finished her circuit of the ice with a few more jumps and spins, ending in front of him, flushed and pleased. At the same time, Jason completed his own circuit with a magnificent hockey stop, covering Nic in a twinkling shower of ice.

"Gotcha!" they teased.

Blinking the ice from his lashes, Nic pretended to glower. "You think so?" He maintained his expression until they started to fidget, then let go of his pent-up laughter. "Well, you'd be right." With Jason's giggling in his ears, Nic grabbed a shrieking Lauren around the waist, lifting her off the ice, the momentum carrying them forward. "You're good at keeping secrets, aren't you?" he whispered in her ear.

The pretty blush spreading across her face told him he was right. Something stirred deep inside him. Maybe she was the kind of woman he could trust with his secrets. He lowered her to the ice, gently pushing on her hips, separating them. "We'd better get to work."

"Can you and Jason start shooting some pucks to get warmed up while I set up my equipment?"

While Lauren got ready, Nic played goalie, and Jason shot puck after puck at him. Thank God Lauren had borrowed goalie pads from the arena equipment locker. The kid sure had a wrist on him.

Lauren circled them, her blades silent as she snapped shot after shot. "Anything special you want me to do?" he asked.

"Keep playing and ignore me."

Yeah, as if. Awareness ripped through him each time he caught a glimpse of her. Her elegance and ease was a thing of beauty as she executed flawless forward and backward crossovers and cutbacks.

A few minutes later, Lauren instructed him to take off his jersey and helmet. As he bared his chest, he turned to Jason. "Don't you dare laugh." Obviously, the child had no sense of self-preservation; he laughed so hard he tipped over onto his back, a helpless turtle.

Nic skated up behind Lauren, not stopping until her bottom pressed snuggly against him. He breathed in her sweet apple scent. He should let go before she realized how much he enjoyed holding her this way. Instead, he gave a few pushes with his feet, turning them so his back was to Jason, who had a row of pucks lined up and was busy shooting at the goal.

Lauren looked at him over her shoulder and he twisted her around. Face to face, her breath warmed his lips. For the length of a few heartbeats, she remained silent, her eyes fixed on his mouth. Nic's breath caught in his chest, the pressure so strong he almost exploded like a B-list actor's career after an Oscar win. He had to kiss her. Had to taste her one last time. As they continued to glide, he pressed his lips to hers, sealing them in a sweet soft kiss. Where their first kiss had felt like an end, this one felt like a beginning.

Tentative. Tender.

Damn. What was he doing? A tremor coursed through her body before she finally met his gaze. Reluctantly, he released her. "Let me take a few pictures of you." Even to his own ears, his voice sounded rough.

She handed him the camera. "Please don't fall. I really wanted the D3S, but this was the best I could afford."

Sweet. That was a good word to describe her. Most people he knew in Hollywood would have been praying for him to fall and break their camera so he'd have to buy them a new one.

He took some photos of Lauren executing a few twirls and jumps, then he shot some of her playing with Jason. They made a beautiful family, like the one he'd always dreamed of having.

Lauren took the camera back and asked him to change into the hockey pants. "Do you know how to do a Lacrosse shot?"

"Of course."

"Don't sound so insulted." She laughed. "We'll finish up with you taking some laps around the rink. We'll need some speed on those. I'll adjust the aperture so you're in focus, but the boards and seats will be blurred."

After changing, Nic paused to watch Lauren shoot some pucks with Jason. Damn, she was good at that too. When he joined her on the ice, Lauren started chafing his goosebump-covered arms. "You're cold."

Was that the only reason she was touching him? "Thank you for your concern, *chérie*. But I can't feel the cold at all right now." Nic flicked his gaze to her hands rubbing his biceps, and smiled. Lauren yanked her hands from his skin and turned away.

After shooting some goals, Nic started taking some laps. Cool air surrounded him and wind blew on his face, tugging at his hair as he flew around the hockey rink. Swooping in, he scooped Jason up, sideways above his head. Jason's laughter echoed as Nic lived his NHL victory dream, using the boy as his Stanley Cup. He pumped his arms up and down a few times facing the seats.

"Excellent, Nic. Keep going," Lauren encouraged as she skated alongside them.

Suddenly, the lights went out, plunging them into complete darkness. Jason screamed. Concerned about slamming into the boards, Nic executed a quick stop and lowered Jason to the ice. "It's okay, buddy. I've got you. Lauren?"

"Over here."

Jason hugged his leg and whimpered in fear. "Your mom's coming. Call out to her so she knows where we are."

"Mom," he croaked. Then louder, "Mom!"

"I'm coming, honey."

Although he was braced for her to arrive from any direction, the force of her banging into his back knocked him over and he fell to the ice, taking Jason down with him.

"Jason! Are you all right?" Lauren called.

Jason was crying so hard, Nic couldn't understand what he was saying. He'd tried to twist when they fell so he wouldn't land on the boy, but maybe he'd gotten hurt.

The generator kicked in and a few scattered emergency lights came on. Jason lay face down in his arms. "Hey, little man. Everything's okay. Let me take a look at you." Gently, he rolled Jason onto his back.

Oh God! Blood. Everywhere.

"Jason's bleeding," he called out to Lauren. He could barely watch as she crawled through the blood splattered all over the ice. *Fuck. Fuck. Fuck. Not now.* Nic swallowed hard, fighting to keep a steady head.

Reaching into her pocket, Lauren pulled out a travel pack of tissues and pressed a wad of them to Jason's nose. Together they pulled him into a sitting position so his head was bent forward. After a few minutes and almost the entire pack of tissues, Jason's sobbing quieted and the bleeding stopped.

Nic tilted Jason's chin up and gently felt the boy's nose. "It's a bit swollen but not broken. The girls will think you're even cuter now. They love us tough guys." He winked.

"Girls are gross." Then, after shooting a quick look at Lauren, he added, "But you don't count, you're a mom."

Relieved that Jason was okay, Nic pushed to his knees. Blood was splattered on the ice, dripping from his hands, *on his bare chest.* The ice shimmered into a white leather car seat, smeared with great splashes of blood. Legs in pink tights were crushed against the dashboard. Rachel's body, torn, twisted around, hung halfway out the broken window. The rink began to spin and droplets of blood swirled in front of him. Then everything went dark.

The first thing he saw when he opened his eyes was Lauren's beautiful face, and the first thing he heard was Jason's relieved voice. "He's back, Mom."

"Are you okay? You were out cold."

No kidding. He'd fucking *passed out.* Nic turned away and pretended not to have heard.

"Nic. Are you all right?"

"I'm fine." With his naked back against the ice, he should be frozen. But the heat from his full body blush warmed him up fast. At least his complete and utter embarrassment served a purpose.

Shit. Why hadn't he been able to control the flashback? He'd learned to breathe through them. Then again, he hadn't seen a child bleed like that since the accident. Very few people knew about his little problem. Only three. Five now.

"You fainted." She smiled, gently. "I was imagining the media circus if I had to take you to the hospital."

He forced his lips into a cocky grin. "Nah, I was just resting."

"Mmmhmm."

"Come on. Let's get Jason home. He'll feel better once he's clean and warm. I'm sure he's looking forward to snuggling on the couch and relaxing with the *Mighty Ducks.*"

As he changed into his street clothes, his phone beeped. Opening the message, he saw a photo of himself wearing tuxedo pants and no shirt, kissing

Lauren. A bolt of fear shot through him. Whoever sent it had been in the arena, was perhaps still here now.

He scrolled down to see if there was anything else.

You've been naughty. Lose the bitch.

Who the hell sent this? Was it NicsBitch?

"Lauren, we need to leave, right now." Her eyes widened as she caught the urgency in his voice. They hurried out to her car. "Drive to the nearest police station."

With shaking hands, she started the motor. "What's going on? Is this about the message you got?"

He indicated Jason in the back seat, and without saying a word, handed her his phone. "Oh my God! This photo was taken tonight."

He met her gaze. "Scroll down."

When the blood drained from her face, he knew she'd read the text. "Do you think this is from the person who cut the power?"

"I'm sure of it."

Lauren handed him the phone and started driving. He stared at her hands tightly gripping the steering wheel. He shouldn't have come here.

When the car stopped in front of the police station, Jason asked in a small voice, "Mom? Why're we here?"

"Nic wants to tell the police about the lights going out."

In the police station, Lauren sat on a bench with Jason while Nic approached the front desk. "Good evening, officer."

"What can I do for you?"

Nic knew from experience the police rarely did anything with stalking cases unless there was clear evidence of an imminent threat. Taking a deep breath, he prepared to make his case as best he could. "I'm Nic Lamoureux. And I'm being stalked."

The officer squinted at him for a moment, then nodded. "Thought I recognized you. Why do you think you're being stalked?"

Nic told the officer about the postings on the Internet, and the text he received at the premiere of *Bad Days*. "I was in the middle of a photo shoot at a local arena tonight when the lights went out. A few minutes later, I got this." Taking out his phone, he showed him the latest message. "That photo was taken during the photo shoot. It proves the sender was in the arena."

The officer peered around Nic's shoulder and indicated Lauren with a jerk of his chin. "That the woman in the photo?"

"Yes. She's the photographer."

"What happened to the kid? He looks a little banged up."

"He fell when the lights went out and got a nosebleed."

"I can send a unit to check out the arena. But there really isn't much else we can do. The language in the message is harsh, but there's no real threat."

Nic leaned on the counter, taking the man-to-man tack. "Look, you and I, we're used to this kind of thing. But the lady, here? She's scared. Tomorrow I have to go back to L.A. I don't want to lead some crazy person back to her apartment."

"What do you want us to do?"

Your fucking job.

He pasted on a genial smile. "Maybe you could send a unit to watch her apartment."

Apparently, tonight's performance wouldn't be winning any Oscars. The cop bristled. "This ain't L.A. We don't have the resources to post a car at her door *in case*."

"Come on, man. Help me out here. What am I supposed to do? This stalker has followed me all over the country."

The officer sighed and grabbed a sheet from a pile on the desk and began filling it out. "If this person's been following you, they probably already know where you're staying. But give me her address, and I'll send a patrol every hour until tomorrow afternoon. She should be safe after you go."

As they were getting in the car, Lauren asked, "Everything okay?"

Jaw clenched, he nodded. "But take the long way home."

They drove in silence while Nic kept an eye on the back window. As far as he could tell, they weren't being followed. But as the nice officer had so kindly pointed out, the stalker probably already knew where Lauren lived. *Jesus Christ.*

When they got back to the apartment, Lauren marched Jason to the bathroom. "Have a shower, you'll feel much better after." She planted a kiss on his head.

Nic was close enough to hear Jason say, "Please tell him it wasn't his fault. We fell, that's all."

Eyes burning, Nic turned and went back into the living room. Seconds later, Lauren's small hands encircled his waist, reminding him of their motorcycle ride in D.C.

"What did the police say?"

The warmth of her breath on his back sent shivers up his spine. "Pretty much what I expected. They can't do much without an overt threat. But a unit will drive by every hour until tomorrow afternoon."

"That's something."

"I've put you and Jason in danger. I should leave."

She grabbed his elbow and spun him around. "And do what, Nic? Your flight doesn't leave until tomorrow afternoon."

"I could go to a hotel or the airport and try to get on the first flight out in the morning."

"No." She crossed her arms under her breasts.

Despite the seriousness of the situation, her show of fire turned him on. She was so cute, so passionate. So goddamn perfect for him.

"You're not leaving." She opened her arms and gestured with her hands. "What if you leave and this person decides to pay me a visit during one of the fifty-nine minutes each hour the police aren't driving by?"

Good point. The stalker would probably follow him if he left, but what if he were wrong?

She pinned him with her eyes. "You're staying here tonight. You can take your scheduled flight tomorrow."

Tonight, he'd stay and make sure they were all right.

Tomorrow, he'd leave and never see her again.

But, right now? Right now, he *needed* to get this fucking blood off his chest.

Standing across the parking lot from the photographer's apartment, she burned, her hands clenching into fists. She could see Nic with the woman and her kid, cuddled together on the couch. A television screen flickered and she heard laughter through an open window.

Why was he doing this to her? She'd been willing to permit the photo shoot, to overlook that he'd spent the day with the photographer and her kid, even though it sickened her.

But she could not accept and would not forgive the kiss.

Didn't he know how much she loved him? Didn't he understand he was hurting her? God! She didn't want to punish him anymore. She just wanted him to see her, to love her, the way she loved him.

Maybe she could give him one more chance, one more warning.

She climbed into her car and picked up the camera on the passenger seat.

The events at the ice rink had certainly shaken him up. Nic was, after all, hemophobic. She'd learned about his troubles a few years ago, quite by accident. Smiling, she clicked her way through the photos she'd taken. She'd set the ASA high, so she could take photos while the lights were out. Her finger paused. There it was: the perfect shot. Nic lying on the cold ice, blood splattered on his naked chest. As though he'd been shot. The image saddened her, repulsed her even. It would be a very powerful warning to him should he ever do anything hurtful to her again. It showed how vulnerable he really was, bodyguard or not. Had she been holding a gun instead of a camera, he'd be dead.

But she didn't want to kill Nic. She was the only one for him. And he was hers. It was her duty, even her right, to protect him from himself, no matter the cost.

She found her journal and opened it to her last entry. Using her favorite pen, she traced the outline of a body on the opposite blank page and wrote "<< insert photo here >>." Grinning at her own hilarity, she brushed her finger along the lines of the male body she'd drawn.

The whole episode had been perfect. The anxiety in Nic's voice after he'd received the message had said it all. Now all she had to do was wait. He'd come to her on his own. That's the way it had to be.

But just to be sure, she'd send him another warning. One he couldn't ignore.

Sunlight streamed in through the unshuttered bedroom window, painting Nic's exposed chest with a soft golden light. Awakened at her regular six AM time by the family of birds nesting in the tree outside her apartment, Lauren hadn't been able to resist peeking in to observe Nic as he slept in her bed.

A wave of tenderness washed over her as she took in his face relaxed in sleep, relieved of the previous day's stresses. He looked so much like the boy she remembered from high school. Except he wasn't a boy anymore, was he? No. Nic Lamoureux was definitely a man.

Nic shifted in his sleep, the sheet sliding low on his hips and revealing a tantalizing glimpse of sculpted muscles and jutting hip bones. A scattering of dark hair arrowed down his stomach to disappear under the sheet. Her fingers curled around the doorknob. How she wanted to lift that sheet. Heat suffused her cheeks. Scolding herself, she backed out of the room and closed the door.

Coffee. She needed some very strong coffee. As she took out the ground beans and filter, her thoughts drifted back to the previous evening and the message Nic had received.

Lose the bitch.

She shuddered. The picture had been taken when Nic kissed her. Was she being threatened or was Nic? If they got involved, what would the stalker do?

Although she'd convinced him to stay the night, it was probably safer if they didn't see each other again until this person was caught. She had to put Jason's safety first. And, really, they had no reason to see each other again. No reason at all. Unless that kiss last night meant as much to him as it did to her.

The rich aroma of brewing coffee filled the air. Inhaling deeply, she sighed and poured herself a cup. Sitting at the table, she booted up her laptop. When the browser window opened, she typed Nic's name in the Google search bar. Immediately, several sites came up, including CelebrityStalker. When the site finished loading, she gasped. Nic had been spotted at a bowling alley in Kirkland, WA. Quickly, she scanned the page for any mention of the arena. Nothing. Was that good or bad? She didn't know.

A warm hand landed on her shoulder, making her jump.

"Easy there." Nic squeezed her shoulder gently before taking a seat across from her. Despite the racing of her heart, she had to smile at his ruffled hair and the bed crease across his cheek. He reminded her of Jason when he first woke up in the morning. His boyish grin revved up her pulse even more, but for an entirely different reason.

Lauren poured him a cup of coffee, adding one cream and one sugar. When she handed it to him, she repeated Vivian's words, "Just the way you like it, darling."

He grinned, catching her joke. She watched, anticipation curling in her stomach as he raised the cup to his lips. After taking a sip, he pointed to her computer. "Don't let me interrupt you."

"I was done." Because she sounded annoyingly breathless, she inhaled deeply before adding, "Someone posted a sighting of you at the bowling alley yesterday." When he blanched, she squeezed his hand. "I didn't see any mention of the arena."

Several minutes passed, during which neither of them spoke. Unable to stand the silence, Lauren said, "Forget it. Let's relax, eat breakfast, and catch up on the news." She got up and walked to the front door. "The paper should be here by now." The newspaper lay on the mat as usual. Beside it sat a white box with a pretty pink bow. "Did you order something?"

"No. Why?"

There was no return address on the package. Lauren's heart started to pound. "I think the stalker left us a gift."

His mouth dry, Nic reached the landing in a few long strides and crouched down beside Lauren to examine the box. No name, address, or any other markings. *Fuck.* "Do you want me to open it?"

"Be careful."

He teased the bow open and pried up one corner of the lid. The box was filled with white tissue paper. Setting the lid aside, he pulled back the tissue paper to expose the interior of the box.

"I see something." Lauren pointed to a bit of brown peeking through the almost translucent paper.

He moved the tissue. "It's hair."

She gasped and slapped a hand to her mouth. "Maybe we should call the police."

He had to see what was in the box. "Get behind me." He positioned himself to block her view, then tore off the remaining paper. Inside lay a Barbie doll with long brown curly hair.

Lauren leaned over his shoulder. "Is that supposed to be me?"

Something hung from the doll's neck. Dog tags. The blood in Nic's veins turned to ice. He forced himself to breathe. Whoever had sent this knew Lauren, and more importantly, knew she wore Todd's dog tags. *Fucking bitch!* Yeah, he was pretty certain the stalker was a woman.

When Nic lifted the doll out of the box, the head separated from the body. *Christ.* Could this get any worse? A small square of pink paper was tucked under Barbie's body. Nic pulled it out and read the message printed in block letters.

I TOLD YOU TO LOSE THE BITCH. IF YOU DON'T DO IT, I'LL DO IT FOR YOU.

He threw the note and the doll back in the box and slammed the cover down. *Goddamn!* He couldn't live like this. He had to find this fucking stalker.

Lauren's legs buckled as she stood up. Nic wrapped an arm around her waist and placed the other behind her knees. In one motion, he lifted her against his chest, then took her inside and sat on the couch cradling her in his lap. "I'm so sorry, *chérie.* I never meant to put you or Jason in danger."

"I know."

He'd let his attraction to Lauren override his common sense. And look where it had gotten him. This woman he held in his arms, this woman who was so perfect for him, was now quivering with fear. He should never have come here, should never have tried to act normal. He wasn't normal. His life was a fucking Hollywood nightmare.

"Lauren." His voice was thick. "This woman, whoever she is, wants me to leave."

Lauren nodded, her eyes bright with tears.

His chest contracted painfully. He didn't want to end things this way. "Once I'm back in L.A., she'll leave you and Jason alone."

Lauren buried her face in his chest. "I don't want you to leave."

He spoke past the lump in his throat. "I don't want to either."

"Will I see you again?"

He closed his eyes. This weekend had been a dream realized. For the first time in a long time, he'd been a part of something, part of a family. He wanted this, wanted a family.

Could he stand by and let Fate take another part of his life away, take another choice away? No. But to protect her, he had to make the stalker think he'd given her up.

"Maybe, but it's too dangerous right now. I need to know that both you and Jason are safe."

Lauren wiped her eyes and looked up at him. "Can we talk on the phone at least?"

Fucking shit. She was shredding his heart. Nic cleared his throat to ease the tightness. "You can always call me if there's an emergency. But for business, it's probably better to go through Vivian."

She sobbed once, a truly heartbreaking sound he never wanted to hear again.

He sighed. "I'll get my things and leave. Tell Jason how much fun I had with him this weekend." He nearly choked on his next words. "Tell him I had to go on a new mission, but we'll always be brothers in arms."

Her smile was bittersweet. "I will."

He moved her off his lap, grabbed the package, and collected his things in the bedroom. He emerged a few minutes later with his duffle bag thrown over his shoulder, holding up the knit cap and goggles Jason had lent him. "Do you think Jason would mind if I kept these?"

"He'd be pleased."

Without taking his eyes from hers, he fumbled with the zipper of his bag and stuffed the disguise inside.

She held his gaze, despite the tears making tracks down her cheeks. "I wish things didn't have to be this way."

"Meeting you is the best thing to ever happen to me. If things were different…" He shook his head. "But they aren't."

Her lips trembled and she hiccupped back a sob. "Maybe someday when this is all over..."

He leaned down and brushed his lips against hers. "Maybe someday."

CHAPTER 8

Nic tried to read the script of *At Last,* but the words kept running together. He'd come outside on the balcony, hoping the change of scenery would inspire him. That it would get his mind off Lauren so he could get some work done. Shooting for the romantic comedy started in two weeks, and Nic The Lover always arrived on set prepared. He rubbed his eyes and tried again. After several more attempts, he set the script aside and walked back inside the loft.

Light from the setting sun poured through the large windows covering the west wall, creating a kaleidoscope of color as it reflected throughout the living room. The beauty of it made him feel worse. Lauren would have loved to see the sunset from this vantage point. He sank onto the couch and threw an arm over his eyes, blocking the view.

The only good news was that there'd been no text messages, no photos, no sightings, no postings, and no strange packages since his return. He'd told Lauren to call if she received anything else from the stalker but so far, no calls. He'd been right; as long as he stayed away from her, the stalker was happy.

Lucky stalker.

The past weekend had been both the best and the worst he'd had in years. His mind kept flashing back to images of Lauren and Jason, images of normalcy. Like an unending reel, the life he could have had—the life he still wanted—replayed in his mind, over and over. But, until and unless he caught the stalker, he would have no happily ever after. He should forget about them.

He launched himself off the couch. What was wrong with him? He was a survivor. Always had been. He needed a plan, and the solution was a phone call away. Pulling out his phone, he dialed Kaden's number.

"You free tomorrow?" he asked when his bodyguard answered.

"Sure. What's up?"

"I went to Seattle. To see Lauren."

"Alone?" Kaden asked, his voice like ice.

Nic blew out a breath. "I know you're pissed. And you're right. I should've had you come with me."

"Why didn't you?"

"I wanted to feel normal for once." He leaned against the window. "What a fucking joke. My life is so far from normal it's not even funny."

"What happened?"

"The stalker's going after Lauren. We need to put an end to this."

"So it's not just *business* anymore?"

Nic closed his eyes and sighed. "Life would be so much easier if it was." He pushed off the window and started pacing. "We can't let anything happen to her."

"What about the cops? What are they doing?"

"The investigation's pretty much stalled."

Kaden scoffed. "Figures."

Nic told Kaden about the package and the broken Barbie. "The techs weren't able to lift any prints. And they couldn't determine a point of sale. That doll is sold in every Walmart, Target, and Toys"R"Us in the country, not to mention all the online stores."

"What about the message? Can't they figure out who sent it?"

"Apparently, with a few mouse clicks, anyone with access to the Internet can send virtually untraceable text messages."

After a brief pause, Kaden said, "I'll think about it tonight and we'll talk tomorrow. Don't worry."

Soon after Nic ended the call, his phone started blasting *Maneater* from Hall and Oates, Summer's ringtone. Listening to the lyrics, he wanted to laugh. Since their last date, he knew exactly how well the song suited her.

"Summer. How are you?" he asked cautiously. She hadn't been very happy with him when he'd left her place. Of course, he'd practically been running at the time.

"I'm doing good. What about you? I haven't heard from you since the footprint ceremony."

He squirmed in his seat and searched for something to say. He couldn't tell her he'd been in Seattle having the best time of his life. "Been busy with work."

"Do you have a new movie lined up?"

"You know Vivian. She's a slave driver."

"I wish my agent was more like her. But"—her voice brightened—"I'm being considered for a pretty important role. Anyway, are you busy tonight? I was hoping you'd join me at Taylors."

Nic scratched his jaw. Taylors was a popular club frequented by stars and the paparazzi. Maybe he could use this to deflect the stalker's attention from Lauren.

Just as he was about to answer, she added, "The callbacks are this week. I was hoping you could give me some pointers."

Even better. She'd help him and he'd help her. "Sure, what time?"

"Around ten?"

"Pick you up at your place?"

"Let's meet there."

Nic hung up the phone. He'd put on a show for the cameras. Nic The Lover would flirt and dance, and maybe there'd be a Paparazzi Kiss or two. So what if Nic the man couldn't stand the idea of kissing anyone but Lauren right now? Nic The Lover didn't wallow when things got bad. He did what was necessary to protect those he cared about.

A few minutes before ten, Nic walked into Taylors and slipped into character. As he waited at the entrance for the club patrons to notice his arrival, he scanned the bar, marking a few Paparazzi Kiss candidates. Summer hadn't arrived yet.

"Ladies, we have a special treat for you tonight. Mr. Lover's in the house!" Nic grinned when he heard the D.J's announcement and his unofficial theme song, Shaggy's *Luv Me, Luv Me,* started playing.

Women always loved his Nic The Lover get-ups, and tonight was no exception. They swarmed around him and dragged him onto the dance floor. Several copped a feel of his leather clad ass as they slithered around him, gyrating to the music's sexy beat. One wrapped an arm around his neck and tried to unbutton his silk shirt. "I could be your Paparazzi Girl," she suggested through permanently pouting collagen-filled lips.

He winked and patted her ass. "Maybe later, sweetheart." When the song finished, he ordered a beer at the bar, then wove his way to an empty table at the back of the room. As he dropped into a chair, hands covered his eyes.

Had NicsBitch come out of the shadows? Adrenaline surged through his body. Hands balled into fists, heart slamming against his ribs, he jerked around, ready to face his stalker.

"Guess who?" Summer asked.

Christ. Nic slumped back in the chair. He had to get himself under control before he hurt someone. While Summer settled into the chair beside him, Nic took a sip of beer and forced a smile. She leaned over and kissed him on the mouth. He resisted the urge to roll his eyes. Whatever. This would fit right in with his plan. "Can I get you a drink?"

"A strawberry daiquiri would be good."

He might have guessed she'd want something fruity and frilly like her orange dress. The color probably had a fancy name like burnished copper or autumnal auburn, but to him it was still orange.

He threaded through the crowd to the bar and caught the attention of the female bartender. She took her time eyeing him up and down before taking his order.

"I can't imagine this drink is for you," she said, handing him the daiquiri.

Nic laughed. "Wouldn't be caught dead drinking that girly stuff."

"If you need a Paparazzi Girl, you know where to find me."

He winked. "I'll keep it in mind."

"That was quick," Summer said when he returned to the table. "I bet women never keep you waiting."

Despite her smile, she had an odd look in her eyes. Was she still upset over what had happened at her apartment? "Listen, Summer. About the other night—"

"No, no." She pressed a finger to his lips. "I'm the one who should apologize."

"What for?" She'd been honest enough to let him know she was attracted to him. Nothing wrong with that.

"Maybe I came on a little too strong, too quick. It's just that I feel like I've known you a long time." He got that a lot. People saw him on the screen and thought they knew him, when all they knew was a character.

Raising his glass, he arched a brow. "To new beginnings?"

She clinked her glass against his bottle, and they drank to the toast. "To new friends," she said, raising her glass again. After they'd finished their drinks, Nic asked Summer to dance. He led her through the throng to the dance floor. The rock music was fast and the rhythm strong. People flowed around him and more than a few hands brushed his body. When a slow song began to play, he started for their table, but Summer held onto his arm. "One more?"

From the corner of his eye, he saw several members of the paparazzi lift up their cameras. Time to give them what they wanted. He pulled her into the circle of his arms, and together, they swayed to the beat.

Vivian had been right; they did look good together. By tomorrow morning, they'd be number one on the Hottest Hollywood Couples list. What would the entertainment shows call them? Nummer? Sumic? Sic? He buried his face in her hair to hide his snicker. They were definitely not a match made in heaven.

Nauren? Nic The Lauren? Lic? Now *that* had possibilities.

Summer must have thought he was nuzzling her neck because she slapped her hand on his ass and yanked his hips against hers so they were pressed together, from shoulder to thigh. Placing one arm at her waist and a hand behind her neck, he twisted her body, arching her over his arm. Then he swooped in for a camera-perfect Paparazzi Kiss. Right before their lips touched, something gleamed in her eyes. Happiness? Triumph?

The crowd whooped and cheered, and lights flashed from a multitude of cameras. His job here was done. With a flourish, he pulled her up and kissed the knuckles of her hand before leading her back to their table. "I'll get us some refills," he said when she sat down.

She nodded and pulled a cell phone out of her purse.

The idiot was supposed to have reported in twenty minutes ago. When the phone on her desk finally rang, she snatched it up. "Where are you? What's happening?"

"I did what you asked."

"Did the paparazzi get photos?"

"Sort of."

"Remember what I said. Keep it simple, keep it clean. If you play this right, I'll get you what you want."

"The female lead in *Alone No More?*"

She fought to keep from laughing. The only starring role a no-talent bitch like her could ever get would be in some porn flick named *Summer of Sixty-Nine*. "Absolutely. You get the job done and it's yours."

"Awesome. I've got the perfect plan."

She stiffened. "What are you up to?"

"He's coming. I've got to go."

"Summer!" The phone clicked in her ear. After slamming the receiver down, she shot out of her seat and began to pace the room. All she'd asked Summer to do was get Nic to go out with her a few times and have the paparazzi take some photos so everyone would forget about the stupid photographer. How hard could it be?

If the crazy bitch fucked this up, she'd die.

When Nic returned, Summer was still on the phone. He set the drinks down and signaled to her that he was going to the restroom. He was hot and sweaty, and the cool air of the back hall was a welcome relief. After using the facilities, he headed back to join Summer and have his second and last beer. Since an embarrassing high school incident when he'd mooned the cute girl from the school paper, he maintained a strict two-drink limit.

Summer had finished her call and sat sipping her daiquiri.

"Having fun?"

She smiled. "Yeah. You?"

Strangely, in some ways, he was. At least here, Lauren intruded on his thoughts only every three minutes instead of every two. He curved his lips into a half smile. "This was a good idea."

All the dancing and the heat in the crowded room had left him parched. He downed half his beer in one swallow. "When you called me, you mentioned you were up for a role?"

At his words, her face brightened and her eyes sparkled. "I'm being considered for a part in *Alone No More*."

"I've read the script and it sounds like a hit. What part are you up for?"

"The lead—Shauna."

Nic choked on his beer. "Shauna?" No fucking way. The role was difficult. Unless he was way off base, Summer could never land such a part.

She nodded. "Hey, didn't I hear you were offered the male lead—Jamie?"

"Yeah." But he'd turn it down flat if she was playing Shauna.

"Maybe we'll be working together." Nic hid his grimace behind the lip of his beer bottle. Summer practically vibrated with enthusiasm. He, on the other hand, felt slightly nauseated.

Desperate to get off the subject of *Alone No More*, he asked what other roles she'd had. He hadn't met a starlet yet not thrilled to regale him with her full pedigree.

"A little of this and that."

Nic blinked. She believed she was going to get the lead in a hit movie and she couldn't name even one prior part? He angled his head and took a good look at her—was she a porn star? She had the body—and the name—for it. He resisted the urge to laugh. Wouldn't it be priceless if Vivian, so eager to protect his image, had set him up with a porn star?

After some time, a hand shook his shoulder. What was with him? He'd just been sitting here, staring, unmoving. Shrugging, he tried to get rid of the underwater feeling. *Christ.* He couldn't be drunk on only two beers. "What the hell is in these drinks?"

Summer blinked. "You're probably just tired."

"Maybe." But he didn't think so. Using all his concentration, he reached into his back pocket to get his phone.

"What are you doing?"

"Ima call Viv."

She grabbed his hand. "No." He tried to cock his eyebrow, but it wouldn't obey. And his eyes wouldn't stay focused. "I'll drive you home, but first…" She scooted her chair closer to his and wrapped her arm around his neck. "For the callback, I have to do a romantic scene."

"A womance scene?" What the fuck? He sounded like Elmer Fudd. He rolled his shoulders a few times to relax. Or rather, he tried.

"Shauna seduces Jamie." She cradled his cheek and looked into his eyes. "Tell me if this works." Then she pressed her lips against his, thrusting her tongue in his mouth. As she deepened the kiss, he tried to push her off. But all he managed to do was hold onto her arms. He felt disconnected, as if he were watching himself being kissed on screen or in a dream.

She slipped off her chair and swung her leg over his thighs, straddling him. "Put your arms around me," she whispered, positioning his hands at her back.

Why was he going along with this? He didn't want to, but his body wasn't responding to his directions. Something was wrong. Seriously wrong.

"This is a Paparazzi Kiss," she said. "See the cameras? After they take a few pictures, I'll take you home, okay?" He hated the professional way she undulated on his lap and rubbed her hard breasts against his chest. He wanted to push her away, to get away. But he couldn't. At least the paparazzi were getting an eyeful, and there'd be another fabulous front-page photo of him.

The stalker would be happy.

And Lauren would be hurt.

Nic woke to a world of pain. Shards of glass stabbed his eyeballs with each pulsing throb of a headache that blotted out all else.

Christ, kill me now.

Just as the pounding reached unbearable proportions, it stopped. Maybe he'd feel more human with a few extra hours of sleep. He drifted back into oblivion.

Bang, bang, bang!

What the fuck was making so much noise?

He tried to grab the pillow to bury his face in it, but his arms refused to obey. Had he fallen asleep on them, and they'd gone numb? Someone was calling his name. He managed to crack open one eye and was relieved to find himself in his bedroom.

Until the room began to spin.

When he heard a loud crash, a spike threatened to pierce his skull and split it in two. The overwhelming pain induced a nausea so immediate he barely managed to turn his head before vomiting. He groaned and remained with his head angled over the edge of the bed.

The mattress dipped, jostling him. He opened his mouth to speak, but nothing came out.

"Poor darling. What have you done to yourself?" Out of the corner of his eye, he saw Vivian grab something off the floor. With a gentle hand, she turned his head. "Darling, I'm going to wipe you off a bit." Something soft rubbed against his bare chest. Strange. He didn't remember getting undressed. Hell, he didn't even remember coming home.

Vivian left, but within moments, she returned and began cleaning his face with something wet. His tongue seemed to fill the entire cavern of his mouth, but at least he wasn't covered in puke anymore. What the fuck had he done last night?

A glass pressed against his parched lips. "Only a little," she said softly.

Unfortunately, even the small sip he took unsettled his stomach. The coolness of the towel on his forehead and short rapid breaths helped keep the nausea down, but nothing helped make sense of what was happening. He forced his eyes open and focused on Vivian's face.

Oh God. He shouldn't have done that.

Her head was whipping from side to side like some sort of video loopback. Over and over and over… His stomach revolted. As he began heaving, Vivian rolled him onto his side.

"I'm calling 911."

He tried to listen as Vivian made the call. But images raced through his mind and even with his eyes closed, his head swam.

Suddenly, the swirling memories cleared and what remained was an image of Lauren. They were in his room and he was seeing her from below as if she were straddling him. Her hair covered the tops of her breasts and he reached up to push it over her shoulders.

His hands slid down to cradle her breasts, bringing them together in an offering to his mouth. He moaned and called out, "Oh God. Lauren."

The images began to swirl again, an endless vortex. Memories of Vivian interspersed with snapshots of Lauren in his bed and Summer at the bar.

God help him, he was losing his mind.

"It's okay, darling. I'm here," a voice said. It was Vivian, not Lauren. Yes, Vivian was here; Lauren was safe at home in Seattle.

Vivian pressed against his back, her arm around his waist as she ran a comforting hand through his hair. "The EMTs are on their way."

Several minutes later, there was more pounding. Nic moaned.

Vivian called out, "We're in here."

He felt her move away as she murmured, "The EMTs are here now."

Thank God. If they could make the god-awful pounding in his head go away, maybe he'd stop throwing up. Heavy boots clumped on the wood floors. A man's voice rang in his ear, then a warm hand touched his neck.

"His pulse is fast. How long's he been vomiting, ma'am?" Too sick to care, too weak to look, Nic could only imagine the mess that had prompted the EMT's question.

"I'm not sure. But he's thrown up twice since I got here. What's wrong with him?" Even in his current state, he heard the distress in her voice. What had he done?

"Let's have a look." As the lethargy began to pull him under once more, strong hands gripped his shoulders and, with surprising gentleness, rolled him onto his back. Through the slits of his half-open eyes, he made out the blurry face of a large black man. Something slid around his arm and squeezed it. "Blood pressure's low. I smell beer on your breath, sir. Have you been drinking? Taking any drugs?"

He licked his lips and tried to answer, "Ownwwee twoooo."

"Nic doesn't do drugs and he has a strict two-drink limit," Vivian said. He wanted to say thank you or smile at her, but doing either would take more energy than he had.

The EMT gripped his chin and shined a strong light in his eyes. "Speech is heavily slurred and pupils are dilated."

The flash of light caused Nic's stomach to heave. "Easy there." The EMT rolled him onto his side yet again. A cool metal trash can pressed against his cheek.

"Jenn, let's bring him in." The EMT must have been talking to his partner.

Nic heard her say, "Dispatch, this is unit twelve. We have a white male, about 6'3", 200 lbs. Pupils are dilated, pressure's low, rapid breathing, awake but unresponsive, repeated vomiting."

"What's your ETA, unit twelve?"

"Fourteen minutes."

The EMTs lifted Nic onto a hard flat surface and wheeled him out of the room. He heard Vivian telling him he'd be okay. Then everything went dark.

Lauren loved to start her day watching Entertainment Buzz. She got a kick out of all the silly Hollywood news. And of course, she eagerly ate up any tidbit on Nic.

But not today. Today, she sat frozen as a picture of Nic flashed onto the TV screen again, and the reporter from Entertainment Buzz rehashed their top story.

"Nic The Lover Lamoureux has been admitted in serious condition to Cedars-Sinai Medical Center, where he arrived by ambulance. There are reports that he was seen last evening at a local celebrity hangout with starlet Summer Rayne, who also accompanied him to his Grauman's footprint ceremony last week. In photos taken last night, Mr. Lamoureux appeared intoxicated and out of control. Is this yet another drug overdose by a Hollywood actor in his prime? We'll continue to update you as this story unfolds."

Nic was intoxicated?

That couldn't be right. He wouldn't risk his career, his life, for the temporary euphoria of drugs or alcohol. None of this made any sense. Could it be another Paparazzi Kiss that got out of hand? The press had a way of making things seem worse than they really were. She knew that.

Her phone rang. When she saw Nic's caller ID, a mix of hope and adrenaline shot through her body. Maybe there'd been a mistake. Her heart pounding in her ears, she grabbed the phone. "Nic?"

"Hello?" a gruff male voice said at the same time. Definitely not Nic. "Ms. James, I'm Kaden Christiansen, Mr. Lamoureux's bodyguard."

"How is he? I heard he'd overdosed, but I don't believe it."

"He's still unconscious. Listen, Ms. James—"

"Lauren, please."

"Lauren, I'm sorry to call you out of the blue like this. But I know some things happened when Nic was in Seattle. I think it would help the case if you came and talked with the police." He paused. "I don't know what's going on between you and Nic or how serious it is, but last night when Nic and I spoke, he seemed very worried about you. At least if you were here, I could keep an eye on you. And it would reassure him to have you nearby."

Tears burned her eyes and she had to swallow past the ache in her throat before she could speak. "I'll be there for him." Even though Nic had asked her to stay away.

After finishing the call, Lauren started packing. Jason came to sit on the bed. Fear etched his little face. His bottom lip trembled and his eyes were shiny with tears. "Mom, is Nic going to die?"

She swallowed her own panic. Jason deserved honesty. "He's very sick right now, sweetheart. But he's strong, and as soon as the doctors figure out what's wrong, they'll make him better."

Sniffing back tears, she hugged him tightly. Even though Jason had been only three when Todd died, he still had occasional nightmares about it. Her own nightmares had stopped only when they'd been replaced by dreams of Nic. She couldn't bear something happening to him, too.

The time she and Jason had spent with him last weekend had been magical. She'd gotten to know the real Nic a little, and she'd give anything to spend more time with him. Her fantasies wouldn't be enough anymore—she needed the real man.

Five hours later, Lauren stepped out, sticky and sweaty, of what had to be the only taxi in L.A. without air conditioning. Standing on the sidewalk in front of Cedars-Sinai, doubt took hold. Had she been stupid coming all the way to L.A.?

"Ms. James, Lauren?"

She turned to see the tall blond bodyguard from the footprint ceremony. Obviously, he recognized her from the Paparazzi Kiss photo. At least it had been good for something. A blush colored her cheeks. "Kaden, right?"

After shaking his hand, she asked the question foremost on her mind. "Any change?"

"Nic's still out of it. The doctors are running more tests. They've eliminated alcohol poisoning and street drugs." His jaw flexed. "Idiots. I told them they wouldn't find anything."

Cameras flashed as a group of reporters rushed up and surrounded them. "Ms. James, are you and Nic involved?" asked one reporter, pushing his microphone in Lauren's face.

Kaden didn't allow her to answer. "No comment." He took her elbow and started for the entrance.

Lauren hesitated. "Will the hospital personnel even let me in?" She gestured at the throng gathering out front. "I mean, how am I any different from all his other fans?"

Kaden looked at her, a bemused expression on his face. Then he shook his head. "It won't be a problem. Let's go. Nic will want to see you when he wakes up."

Would he? Lauren wasn't so certain.

CHAPTER 9

Something soft caressing her cheek brought Lauren awake. She jerked her head off Nic's hospital bed and froze. Despite the haggardness of his features and the paleness of his cheeks, his glorious smile brought tears to her eyes. Swallowing to ease the tightness in her throat, she smiled tremulously. "You're awake. Thank God."

"How..." He cleared his throat and tried to speak again. "Water..." he managed to rasp.

She poured him a glass of water from the pitcher on the bedside table and brought the straw to his mouth.

He took a sip. "How long was I out?"

Although his voice was still rough, it was the most beautiful sound Lauren had ever heard. The tears she'd been holding back spilled out. Without saying a word, he slowly opened his arms.

Careful not to disturb the IV, she embraced him. As his warmth enveloped her, her tears turned to sobs.

"*Ça va, chérie,*" he whispered in her ear as he held her tight and ran a hand through her hair. "I'm okay."

Oh God. He was the one lying in a hospital bed, and he was comforting *her*. As she'd sat in vigil by his bedside, she'd been so worried, so scared. She'd prayed to God and every saint she'd ever heard of. And this time, her prayers had been answered. She could have stayed like this forever, wrapped in the circle of his arms, her head tucked under his chin. It didn't matter if it was dangerous for her to be here. It only mattered that he was alive.

Pulling back to see his beautiful blue eyes, she smiled and kissed his cheek. "You really had me scared."

Nic gazed into her eyes, kissing first one tear-stained cheek, then the other before pressing his lips to hers in a sweet, tender kiss. Then, a small smile curving his lips, he lay back against the pillow and drifted to sleep.

For several minutes, Lauren didn't dare move for fear of shattering the moment. She was exactly where she wanted to be. But he needed his rest. She kissed his cheek again and maneuvered out of his hold, trying not disturb him or the multitude of equipment that surrounded him.

She sank onto her chair, utterly drained, and leaned her head against the seat back. She'd rest while Nic slept. But as soon her eyes closed, the events of the past few hours raced through her thoughts.

Vivian had urged the police to investigate. While Nic's behavior last night may have been business as usual for most movie stars, it had definitely been out of character for him. Vivian had fought for him when he'd been unable to fight for himself. Nic had been right about her; she was a good friend. Lauren felt a pinching in her chest. She had no right to envy Vivian's relationship with Nic, but she did.

"Lorna, dear. You really should go to the hotel and get some rest. Nic will be scared out of his wits if he sees you like this."

Startled by Vivian's abrupt entrance, Lauren scrambled to sit up. Vivian cared about Nic, but it wasn't enough to make Lauren like her, and this was a perfect example of why.

"Nic did wake up." She smiled victoriously. "And he didn't look at all frightened."

"What? When?" Vivian raced across the room to Nic's bed. She ran a finger under his chin and traced the outline of the bandage above his eye. "Was he awake long?"

Unable to stomach Vivian's tender expression and the familiar way she combed a dark lock of hair off his forehead, Lauren turned away before answering. "A couple minutes." Remembering the staff's instructions to let them know of any change, Lauren rose from her seat. "I need to alert the nurses." She practically ran from the room.

Why did she let Vivian get to her? From everything Nic had said, Vivian had some driving need to protect his image, almost to the point of obsession. But Vivian's need went beyond protecting his image. Lauren got the impression Vivian thought she needed to protect Nic from her. And how ridiculous was that? Brusquely wiping away the tears slipping down her cheeks, she walked to the nurse's station.

After speaking with the head nurse, she bought a coffee from the vending machine at the end of the hall. The hot liquid soothed her dry throat. The orgasmic expression on Nic's face when he'd taken his first few tastes of coffee in her small kitchen flashed through her mind. Smiling, she took another sip. He'd been pleased to see her when he'd woken up. She'd done the right thing in coming.

When Lauren returned, Dr. Jacob was examining Nic's chart while two men stood to the side talking with Vivian. They introduced themselves as

Detectives Anderson and Becker.

Becker addressed Dr. Jacob. "Doctor, we have additional details concerning Mr. Lamoureux's activities last night. Eyewitnesses say Ms. Rayne joined Mr. Lamoureux at 9:45 PM. They danced, he ordered more drinks, and then he left to use the restroom. At the time, he appeared sober. The only event of note was a so-called Paparazzi Kiss during the dance."

He checked his notes before continuing. "Fifteen minutes after he returned from the restroom, the couple was behaving in an overtly sexual manner. When they left the bar at 11:00 PM, Mr. Lamoureux was unable to walk unassisted."

Anderson took over. "Given the eyewitness accounts and the results of previous testing showing no excessive alcohol or recreational drug use, doctor, we would like Mr. Lamoureux to be tested for predator drugs."

Vivian's eyebrows shot up. "Predator drugs? What are those?"

"They're drugs used by sexual predators to render their victims passive and unable to resist or assert themselves," Becker explained.

Lauren nodded. "Date-rape drugs." She'd heard about them on the news.

"Exactly," Anderson confirmed. "We believe this woman, Summer Rayne, slipped one of these drugs into Mr. Lamoureux's beer."

Vivian paled. If the police were correct, Vivian had introduced Nic to the woman who'd drugged him. Of course, it wasn't Vivian's fault, but guilt had to be eating at her.

Dr. Jacob considered the detective's request. "The use of such a drug would be consistent with many of the symptoms Mr. Lamoureux has been experiencing: excessive sedation, impairment of balance and speech, respiratory depression, low blood pressure, and stomach disturbances."

"It's not too late to run the tests?" Vivian asked.

"These drugs stay in the blood for about 24 hours and in urine up to 36 hours, sometimes longer. I suspect flunitrazepam, but I'll order tests for gamma hydroxy butyrate and ketamine hydrochloride as well. Once we know what he took, we can give him an antidote."

Lauren looked at Nic's sleeping form and then turned to Dr. Jacob. "Flunitra—?"

"Flunitrazepam," the doctor finished. "You may know it as Rohypnol, or by its street name roofies."

The doctor left to order the tests, and Vivian stepped into the hall to confer with the detectives regarding the statement she would release to the press.

Lauren sat on the edge of Nic's bed, studying his face as she stroked his stubbled cheek. When Todd would awaken from nightmares of his time in combat, she'd hug him until he went back to sleep. Looking at Nic now, she longed to stretch out beside him and hold him tightly.

With the tip of her finger, she traced the dark circles under his eyes and sighed. Nic had been right. His life was dangerous. Could she deal with the reality of Nic's life on a daily basis?

Terror had gripped her when Nic opened the package containing the doll with the broken neck. Fear for him and for herself. But mostly for Jason. And it was out of fear that she'd agreed with Nic's decision to not see each other. She didn't agree anymore. He wanted to protect her, to keep her safe. But there were other ways.

Violence had stolen Todd from her, but it wouldn't steal Nic.

Life was too damn short.

Moonlight streamed in through the window, illuminating the center of the room with a silvery glow, but leaving the edges in darkness. The excruciating nausea-inducing pain in his skull had lessened to a dull throbbing. Careful not to jar his head, he looked around.

An IV tube stuck out of his arm. Machines beeped somewhere behind him. Why was he in the hospital?

He'd gone to Taylor's to meet Summer. Vague memories circled in his mind. Eyes closed, he concentrated until one crystallized. Vivian had found him puking his guts out, unable to move or call for help. *Shit.*

What had he done to make himself so sick?

Suddenly a vision of making love to Lauren surfaced. Lauren? Focusing, he tried to identify where they'd been. His room. Was the memory real?

He groaned as a wave of dizziness caused the room to spin and bile to rise in his throat. A shadow stirred in the chair. His blood ran cold. Swallowing, he pushed the nausea down and managed to turn his head toward the movement.

Someone was in the room.

Was it the stalker? Summer? His chest tight, he struggled to breathe. He fumbled around, trying to locate the call button. If he could alert the nurses…

The shape grew, looming above him in the murky moonlight.

"Who… who's there?" he croaked. Christ, he sounded like an owl. He forced back an insane urge to laugh. He had to calm down. The last time he'd felt this vulnerable, Rachel had been hurt, bleeding.

No. Damn it. He wouldn't think about that now.

The shadowy figure moved closer. The pounding of his heart matched the pounding in his head.

"Darling. You're awake."

Vivian perched on the side of his bed and turned on the personal reading light above his head. Relief washed over him, draining the tension from his body. As her soft hand cradled his cheek, he felt a sudden sense of déjà vu. His view of Vivian was overlaid with a vision of Lauren, cradling his cheek in much the same way. His eyebrows beetled in confusion as he heard Lauren's voice say, "You're awake. Thank God."

His heart began to race and he panted, unable to catch his breath. Vivian—or was it Lauren?—placed a hand on his shoulder. "Relax, Nic. It's over."

Eyes closed, he breathed deeply, and then blinked several times to clear his vision. Lauren faded away, leaving Vivian sitting on his bed. Wow, fucking weird. He could have sworn Lauren had been right here, that she'd spoken. But it wasn't possible. She was safe at home where he'd left her. Nic pushed a hand against his chest to ease the pain. He'd been going crazy with the need to see her, to hear her voice.

He'd done the right thing. But it still hurt like hell.

Concern in her eyes, Vivian smoothed his hair off his forehead. "Let me get the doctor. He's been waiting for you to wake up again."

Again?

Nic watched her leave. He balled his fists. Dammit! Why couldn't he remember?

A few minutes later, Vivian returned, accompanied by a short balding man wearing a lab coat over black trousers. "Hello, Mr. Lamoureux. I'm Dr. Jacob. It's good to see you awake. How do you feel?"

"Not so good," he grunted. "Tired, nauseous. What day is it?"

"Friday evening. You've been here since early this morning."

Nic stared at the doctor in shock.

"Do you remember anything?"

"Not much. I went to Taylors last night to meet Summer Rayne. The next thing I remember is Vivian finding me."

"Your test results show you ingested Rohypnol along with some alcohol."

Nic narrowed his eyes at the doctor. "Rohypnol? The date-rape drug?"

The doctor maintained a serene expression. "The police suspect Ms. Rayne gave it to you without you knowing."

Nic's breath caught in his throat. *Fucking bitch!*

Vivian put her hand on his shoulder. "Darling, do you remember what happened at the bar?"

A muscle jumped in his jaw. "Everything's a big jumble." He closed his eyes as a hazy memory began to surface. "I bought us some drinks and we danced." He paused. "We talked for a while but I don't remember what we talked about. The rest is a blank until Vivian found me."

Dr. Jacob nodded. "Rohypnol, especially when mixed with alcohol, is known to cause anterograde amnesia. Your memory may return, but it is also entirely possible that you may never remember what happened."

"Have the police questioned Summer? Are they sure she's the one who did this?"

Vivian answered this time. "I spoke with the detectives assigned to your case. Summer hasn't been located yet. But they retrieved packets of Rohypnol from her apartment." She sat on his bed and held his hand in her lap.

Nic turned away. He didn't want pity; he wanted to rip Summer's fucking head off. Adrenaline surged and his heart started to pump like a locomotive. He bolted upright, yanked his hand out of Vivian's grip, and swung his legs off the side of the bed.

The fucking bitch had drugged him!

The doctor rushed forward, pushing a hand against his chest. "Mr. Lamoureux, I know you're angry. You have every right to be, but you need to calm down."

Nic's molars ground together, and he spoke through clenched teeth. "With all due respect, doctor. Get out of my fucking way."

"Darling! Please." Vivian shot an apologetic look at the doctor, pissing Nic off even more. "Lie down. You'll hurt yourself."

"What? You mean I might pull out my IV?" He grabbed hold of the tube on his forearm and yanked out the needle. "Like this?" *Fu-u-u-ck!* Maybe he should've thought that through.

Vivian gasped. Dr. Jacob pulled a square package out of a drawer and ripped it open as he approached the bed. "We need to stop the bleeding."

Nic straightened to his full height, towering over the smaller man, and snarled. "Don't fucking touch me."

Dr. Jacob bristled and threw the gauze into the trash beside the bed. "Let me know when you get yourself under control." As the doctor stormed out of the room, Nic heard him mutter something about Hollywood divas.

Vivian pointed to the tube sticking out from under his hospital gown and arched a brow. "Are you going to pull the catheter out too? I hear it's quite painful."

Nic looked down at his crotch and sighed. Pulling a tube out of his arm was one thing, but pulling one out of his *dick* was something else entirely. He needed to switch tactics. "Get the doctor to release me. I want to go home. Tonight. And where's my phone? I have to call Kaden." He needed someone on his side.

"Here." She handed him her phone. "Kaden has yours. I'll talk to the doctor, but I really think you should stay here, at least until morning."

"Why?"

"Thousands of your fans are holding a vigil for you right outside this hospital. How do you think they'll feel if you sneak out and go home?"

He shrugged. "I can speak to them first."

"I understand how you feel. I hate hospitals, too." She laughed bitterly. "Here's the thing. If you stay tonight, we'll get you released properly, have a press conference, and then you go home. Everyone will leave you alone to recuperate. If you sneak out now, the media and the fans will follow you and stake out your loft. Is that what you want?"

He blew out a breath and fell back against the bed. *Christ.* Vivian was right.

"I'll play this your way, but come morning, I'm out of here. Make sure the doctor knows."

"Of course, darling."

"And get a nurse in here. I want this fucking catheter out. I refuse to be tethered to this place by my dick."

She smiled, then leaned in close and whispered in his ear, "Don't worry, darling. Everything will be all right. I'll make sure of it." After patting his hand, she left the room.

Nic smashed his fist into the mattress. He didn't need Vivian to clean up this mess. As soon as he got out, he'd find Summer, he'd find the stalker, and he'd find out what the hell was going on.

And then he'd put an end to this fucking nightmare.

From the doorway of an empty room, Lauren watched Vivian walk toward the elevators. She didn't want to deal with her tonight. She simply wanted to sit by Nic's bed and hold his hand while he slept away the last lingering effects of the Rohypnol.

When she entered Nic's room, she had to catch her breath. Even with mussed hair and a sallow complexion, he was still the most beautiful man she'd ever laid eyes on. And he was awake! More than awake. He stood, staring out the window in his hospital gown. She could hear his fans calling out to him.

When he leaned forward to wave to the crowd, the back opening of his gown shifted, revealing a tantalizing glimpse of a muscular, perfectly curved butt cheek. Using all her willpower, she forced her eyes to move up his body. When her gaze landed on the new bandage around his arm, she gasped.

He spun around, his intense gaze fixed on her. "You *are* here," he said, disbelief evident in his voice. Lauren froze. Why was he acting so surprised?

His face darkened and his eyes narrowed. His voice sounded cold, harsh even. "Why the hell aren't you in Seattle?" She could practically hear his teeth grinding. "I thought I made it clear we couldn't see each other again."

Lauren's stomach plummeted to the tiled floor. Nic continued to watch her, lips pressed into a tight line. They came from different worlds, and nothing lasting could come of their attraction for each other. She got that. But she'd honestly thought that they were becoming friends, that he'd want her here.

"My mistake," she said, heading for the door.

"Lauren… wait."

Keeping her back turned to hide the tears that threatened to spill, she massaged the pain in her chest with her hand. "I don't think there's anything else to say." She was so stupid. He didn't need her. He had Vivian.

"I'm handling this badly. Come, sit for a minute."

Irritated with herself, she wiped the corners of her eyes before turning around. Nic sat on his bed and motioned to the chair in front of him. Slowly, she walked over and perched on the edge of the seat, staring at her hands folded in her lap.

"Lauren. Please, look at me." Hearing the ache in his voice, she lifted her gaze but kept her mouth clamped shut. He'd have to do the talking.

"I was caught off-guard and my head hurts like a motherfu—" He stopped himself and swallowed before continuing. "But that's no excuse. I'm sorry. I shouldn't have spoken to you that way."

She nodded but remained silent. He'd apologized for the way he'd spoken to her but not for what he'd said.

"When did you get here?"

"This afternoon."

"Why?"

"Kaden called and told me what was going on. He thought I could help. So, I jumped on a plane and came here." *Fool that I was.*

When he raised a hand to scratch his cheek, she again saw the bandage. "What happened to your IV tube?"

"I pulled it out."

"What? Why?"

He shrugged. "I wanted to leave. *Christ.* I still want to leave, and I would if it weren't for all my fans outside. I don't know if this mess with Summer is connected to the stalker, but I'm going to find out."

"Shouldn't you let the police handle this?"

He snorted. "You saw how much help they were last weekend."

"But it's different now. The detectives were the ones to push for the predator drug testing."

"Yeah, well. I bet that's only because it's a crime to sell Rohypnol, and they want to know where Summer got it."

"I don't think you realize how much pressure is on them from the press and your fans to solve this."

Nic turned to her. "Listen, *chérie*, I appreciate you wanting to help." He paused and she was struck by the regret in his eyes. "But it would literally kill me if anything happened to you or Jason."

Lauren's heart stalled. "Do you really think he's in danger?"

"Anyone associated with me is in danger."

She didn't agree with him but she could at least reassure him about Jason's safety. "Jason's fine. School lets out tomorrow, and then he'll be with my parents for a few weeks. My father's a former policeman on Chicago's South Side. Believe me, Jason couldn't be any safer. My dad won't let anything happen to his grandson."

Visibly relieved, Nic let out a long sigh. Hope sparked deep in Lauren's chest. Maybe she'd misread his reaction to seeing her?

Looking at her as if puzzled by something, Nic asked, "You said you arrived this afternoon? Have you been in my room before now?"

Where was this going? "I was here when you woke up earlier."

"Did I see you?"

"For a few minutes, yes." Oh God. A thought hit her like a punch to the gut. What if he'd been acting affectionate because he'd still been under the influence of the Rohypnol? She was such an idiot.

"And you weren't here last night, right?"

Nic's question took her by surprise. Did he think she had something to do with his being drugged? "What's this about, Nic?"

"Nothing." He turned away quickly.

How she wished she could read his thoughts. "Come on, you can tell me."

"Everything's all confused in my head. I don't know what's a memory and what's a hallucination."

"If you tell me what you think you remember about me, I can tell you if it really happened."

He stared out into the dark expanse of the room's single window for a full minute. Afraid to spook him, she remained silent, her expression carefully blank. He turned and peered at her.

Lauren sank into the blue of his eyes, metal to his magnet. The doubt and confusion on his face compelled her to press her hand on top of his where it lay on the mattress.

Turning his hand up so they were palm to palm, he held her fingers and raised them to his lips. While maintaining her gaze and his hold on her hand, he murmured, "In my mind, I see us making love."

Lauren blushed as her fantasies rushed through her mind. At the same time, she felt ridiculously pleased.

Nic *was* attracted to her.

His earlier words were a lie. He'd been putting on an act to protect her. Excitement thrummed in her veins. "In my mind, I've seen us making love many times."

Nic's eyes widened and a grin spread across his face. Then all too quickly, his expression turned serious again. "But then, what? Was it a dream? A hallucination? Or did I actually…?" He shook his head and clamped his mouth shut.

Reaching over, she cupped their entwined hands and raised them to her own lips. "It doesn't matter. Just think about tomorrow, think about going home." Nic groaned and pulled his hand from hers, leaving Lauren disappointed. "What is it?"

"My loft. It's going to smell like someone died in there. I'm not sure I can deal with that yet. Maybe I'll stay with Vivian until I can get a service to clean the place up."

The thought of Nic staying with Vivian, even for a few days, made Lauren squirm. Vivian may have saved his life, and she was his best friend. But Lauren definitely wanted Nic for herself.

"Don't worry. I already cleaned it."

Nic's brow wrinkled. "How did you get in? How did you even know where I live?"

Uh-oh. Those weren't exclamations of joy. "I suggested it to Kaden, and he went with me. I wanted to surprise you."

A flurry of expressions flashed across Nic's face. Was his address some kind of state secret? For a few dollars you could get a tour passing by movie stars' homes. Then again, his definitely hadn't been the luxury Beverly Hills mansion she'd been expecting. Although large and well appointed, Nic's loft was actually in one of the more industrial parts of town and probably not a stop on any tour.

He let out a long ragged breath. "No one's ever been to my home except Vivian and Kaden, and now… you." And no doubt Summer had been there too, but Lauren wasn't going to bring it up. Nic would come to that conclusion on his own, when he was ready to accept what had happened.

Nic yawned and Lauren chuckled at his little-boy-well-past-his-bedtime look. "Why don't you get some sleep?" She smiled and turned to leave.

"Stay." He held out his hand. "Until I fall asleep…" When she moved to sit down in the chair, he tugged on her fingers, pulling her to the bed. "Not there. Here."

Lauren wrapped her arm around his waist, holding him tight. The beat of his heart and the sound of his steady breathing soothed her. Once again, she was exactly where she wanted to be, where she needed to be.

Even though their defiance put her in the stalker's sights. Dead center.

❧ ❧ ❧

"Here's your breakfast, Mr. Lamoureux." The nurse set his tray on the bedside table. "Don't you look handsome this morning."

"I always dress up for a pretty lady." Nic winked at the round-faced, fifty-something nurse whose lips seemed permanently curved into a smile.

Her cheeks colored. "My, my. What a charmer." Nic chuckled when she added an extra bit of swing to her walk as she left the room. Over her shoulder, she added, "The doctor will be here in a few minutes to sign your release papers."

Thanks to Lauren, he could go straight home after the press conference. A smile tugged at his lips. He'd fallen asleep with her in his arms. Her warm body pressed against his and her head on his heart had felt right. Unbelievably right.

Taking a sip of the bitter hospital coffee, he grimaced and remembered the strong, rich taste of the coffee he'd shared with Lauren. Was it only last weekend? Although he hadn't known her long, he felt a sense of peace when she was around, a sense of belonging, as if he'd known her forever. He wanted to find out where this connection between them would lead.

Fuck the stalker.

Fuck the fear.

Lauren had taken the first step; she'd come to L.A. despite the stalker's threats. Now the puck was in his offensive zone. Since Jason was with his grandparents, maybe Lauren could stay with him for a few weeks. Between the two of them, he and Kaden could protect her. And they could finally spend some time together.

Just then the object of his thoughts sauntered into the room, a cup of take-out coffee in each hand.

"Tell me that's Starbucks."

She smiled, turning the cup to show him the logo. "As a self-respecting Seattleite, I couldn't let you start the day without a grande house blend, one sugar, one cream."

With one hand, he pushed away the hospital tray and with the other, eagerly reached for the coffee. And caught her eyeing his bottom half.

"Like the pants?"

She grinned. "Oh, yeah."

He grinned back. She'd like what was under the leather even better. But that would have to wait.

Eyes closed, he inhaled the aroma of the full-bodied coffee, and took a sip. "This is so good." When he opened his eyes, Lauren was staring at his face. Her eyes had gone soft, and the lust in her expression almost drove him to his knees. "I can't wait to get out of here," he groaned.

She swallowed visibly then dropped into the chair beside his bed. He set his cup on the table and slid his gaze to her. "I was wondering. How long are you planning on staying in L.A.?"

When she frowned, he rushed to add, "I was thinking if you were planning to stay a while… hotels are pretty expensive… and… umm… maybe you could stay with me?" *Christ*, could he sound like more of a moron?

Lauren tilted her head to the side, her brow slightly puckered. "Didn't you tell me last night you liked to keep your place private?"

"Yes, but you've already been there."

"I see," she said, although it was clear she didn't.

"It'll be easier to protect you if you're staying with me. I can ask Kaden to watch us full time and…" He trailed off with a frustrated sigh. Leaning his head against the pillows, he closed his eyes and tried again. "What I'm trying to say is that I'd like you to stay with me for a few weeks. I do think it would be safer for you, but it's not just that. I want to spend some time with you." He opened his eyes. Something he'd said must have sounded good because she was smiling at him again.

"I'll stay. But only for a week. That's all the vacation time I've got."

Good enough. With a wide grin, he tugged on her hand until she leaned over him. When their lips were almost touching, he looked deep into her gorgeous blue-green eyes and whispered, "I really like you."

He threaded the fingers of his free hand through her silky hair to cradle the back of her neck and closed the gap. Their lips met in a soft kiss. He yearned for more, so much more. A moan rose from deep in his chest as he let go of her hand to grasp her waist, pulling her completely on top of him. At last. This is where he wanted her to be, covering him, like a warm blanket.

With a sigh of her own, Lauren began nibbling on his earlobe. Oh God, that felt so good. A quiver ran up his spine and his toes curled. He spread his thighs and pulled up his knees, pressing her more intimately against his cock, now almost painfully hard. Her hands, running through his hair and caressing his neck and shoulders, drove him crazy with want. She swirled her tongue around the folds of his ear, making him groan.

Unable to stand the torture, he pulled her head back to his mouth and licked her lips. She opened up and their tongues met, dancing and curling around each other. His head was going to explode. Her jeans had to come off and she had to be under him. *Now.* He reached for her zipper as someone coughed in the doorway.

Shit. Whenever he managed to get Lauren in his arms, the rest of the world faded away. He rested his forehead against hers, pleased she was breathing as hard as he was. After a final small kiss, he whispered against her ear, "We'll continue this later."

He turned his head to see Detectives Anderson and Becker. "Sorry to interrupt, Mr. Lamoureux." With an incline of his head toward Lauren, Anderson added, "Ms. James." Nic laughed as she scampered off the bed, quickly adjusting her clothing. But his laughter died when the detectives' grim expressions registered.

Once they were all settled, Becker asked, "Have you seen the morning news?"

Their poker faces revealed nothing. "What's this about, Detective?"

Becker reached into his sports jacket, pulled out a rolled up newspaper, and handed it to Nic. "This photograph was posted on CelebrityStalker late last night and then picked up by every rag in the country. All the entertainment channels are running it ad nauseum. You're a very hot topic today, Mr. Lamoureux."

Nic laid the paper on his lap so Lauren could see it too. When he got a good look, he swore and slapped his hand over it. He appeared to be naked with Summer, in all her nude glory, straddling his lap.

"It's all right, Nic." She nudged his hand out of the way. "Let me see."

When he reluctantly removed his hand, she gasped. "You shouldn't have to see this," he said.

"No, no." She waved away his apology. "Look at it. Your forehead's bleeding, your eyes are closed, and she's holding your hands." She rubbed his shoulder. "This was taken while you were drugged."

Anderson nodded and put together the pieces for them. "Based on the evidence, she managed to get you home before you passed out. We found traces of blood on the headboard where you probably hit your forehead falling onto the bed. We believe she used a camera with a timer."

Looking at the photograph again, Nic replaced Summer's face with Lauren's. A sickening jolt hit him in the stomach. The picture matched the image he'd had of him and Lauren making love. He touched his forehead where the cut was almost healed. Had he hallucinated making love with Lauren while having sex with Summer? *Christ.* "Did I have sex with her?"

"We can't be certain, but we haven't found any evidence of it. We lifted prints in your room, which we've identified as belonging to you, to Ms. Carmichael, and a third pair we expect will belong to Ms. Rayne, but we can't confirm that until we find her."

Nic risked a glance at Lauren. She took his hand and sent him a small, shaky smile before turning to the detectives. "Don't you think that's odd? I mean, where is she?"

He squeezed her hand, grateful for the support. "And who posted the picture?" he asked. Maybe Summer and NicsBitch *were* the same person.

Anderson shook his head. "We don't have all the answers yet. But let me assure you, we're doing everything we can to find her and to track down the person who posted the photograph."

Becker took a notepad out of his pocket and flipped it open. "Mr. Lamoureux, are you in a relationship with Ms. Rayne? We know she accompanied you to the footprint ceremony."

Nic met the man's gaze. "Vivian arranges dates for me when I need to go to publicity events. I'd never met Summer before that night."

"And since then?"

"Nothing other than meeting her at Taylors."

"Can you think of any reason why she might have done this?" Anderson asked.

Nic shot a surreptitious glance at Lauren and cupped her hand in his. Despite the paleness of her face and the tension around her mouth and eyes, she was still sitting in the chair. Most of the women he'd dated, the Hollywood starlets, would have run out of the room by now, afraid to be tainted by this scandal. But Lauren, single mom, department store photographer, remained by his side, even defending him. He owed it to her to be honest.

"After the footprint ceremony, Summer made me an offer and I turned her down."

"What kind of offer, Mr. Lamoureux?" Becker pressed.

Nic took a deep breath. "Sex." Becker raised his eyebrows but didn't otherwise react.

"Did Ms. Rayne seem upset?" Anderson asked.

"When I turned her down, she was pissed. But at Taylors, she seemed surprisingly friendly, now that I think about it." He snorted in disgust. *Christ,* he'd been naïve. "I should have suspected she was up to something."

Lauren scoffed. "Why? You're a good person Nic, and good people don't go around expecting other people to do bad things."

Nic squirmed as doubt wormed up his spine. If she found out what had happened to Rachel, she wouldn't think he was such a good person. Could he ever tell her what he'd done?

The detectives stood, jolting him from his thoughts. After shaking hands with both him and Lauren, they left.

A smile lit up Lauren's face. "Cheer up. You're going home."

Images of what he would do with her flashed in front of his eyes. He answered her smile with a wide grin. "And you're coming with me."

Once he had her alone and naked, they'd both be coming.

CHAPTER 10

Nic smiled as he spoke into the phone. "Rachel, I'm fine. The drugs have completely worn off."

"So, you're going home today?"

"After the press conference."

"You won't be alone, will you?"

"No." Lauren was coming home with him. He almost couldn't believe it. Since she'd agreed, his mind had been swirling—them in his bed, against the wall, in the shower...

"Nic?"

"Yes?"

"You sound strangely happy for someone who was drugged against his will."

"Let's just say, I got a visit from a friend."

"Oh! *Lauren* came to see you."

He couldn't keep the joy from his voice. "She's staying in L.A. for a week."

"I have a good feeling about her."

Just then Vivian stormed in. "Rachel, I've got to go. I'll call you tonight."

When he hung up, Vivian slapped a newspaper with the photo of him and Summer onto the bed. "Why are you so happy? Did you see this?"

His good mood evaporated like ice on a hot day. "Unfortunately. The detectives were here earlier to discuss it."

She grabbed the paper up and tore it in two. After dropping the pieces in the trash, she crossed her arms and turned to face him. "The nerve of that woman! I can't believe she did this to us… to you, I mean."

Nic ignored the slip. Vivian was hurting too. "She won't get away with it."

"The police will find her."

"The police don't give a shit. I'm going to find her, before things get any worse."

"Darling, I don't think that's safe."

"Why the fuck not? I can handle her." Vivian arched a brow. "I won't let my guard down again."

"The woman's obviously crazy. Who knows what she'll do next."

He shook his head. "There won't be a next time."

She patted his arm. "At least make sure Kaden is with you."

He bit back a retort but couldn't resist shrugging her hand off him. Did she think he was a freaking pansy? "He's already agreed to stay at my place until we find Summer."

"Good. I'm glad you won't be alone."

An image of Lauren sprawled across his bed came to mind. Nic barely suppressed a smile. "So," he said, changing the subject. "What's the plan for this press conference?" Answering questions about being drugged sounded like torture.

"We're going to present our side. People expect sex from you, but they don't expect drugs. We need to make it clear *she* drugged *you*, and you're not just some Hollywood celebrity indulging in a bit of sex, drugs, and rock and roll."

Message received. The press would be on him like rats on cheese if he didn't give them something to chew on. He pointed to a garment bag draped across one of the guest chairs. "Is that a change of clothes? I can't go to the conference in leather pants."

"You know I think of everything." He grabbed the bag, and as he passed by her, she stopped him with a touch. "Everything will be fine, darling."

A glance in the bathroom mirror told him his appearance was not up to Nic The Lover standards. Quickly, he shaved, showered and dressed in his favorite Hugo Boss suit. Somehow Vivian had intuited this was the one he'd want to wear to the press conference. How well she knew him.

Shoving his things back into the dopp kit, he spotted the bottle of Armani. Lauren had burrowed her nose in his neck when he'd hugged her last night. Grinning widely, he spritzed the cologne below each ear, eager to see if she could resist the double dose of Hugo Boss and Armani. He shot his cuffs. *Now* he was ready to face the world. The bathroom door clanged shut behind him.

As Vivian flicked a speck of lint off his shoulder, Kaden popped his head into the room. "Hospital security called, sir. The press is assembled. We're ready to start."

When Vivian threaded her arm through his, Nic shook his head. "Lauren isn't here yet."

"Darling, we can't keep the press waiting."

"I need to call her." This wasn't like Lauren. He pulled out the phone

Kaden had returned earlier and dialed her number. After several rings, the call went to voice mail. Odd. He left a message telling her to call Kaden or Vivian if she couldn't reach him, and hung up. He pinned Vivian with a stare. "If she calls you, answer."

Vivian blinked innocently. "Of course, darling." Nic almost rolled his eyes.

What was keeping Lauren?

Unease slithered up his spine and made the short hairs on the back of his neck stand up. He tried to shrug it off. He'd feel so much better when they were both inside his home with Kaden guarding the door.

When they reached the lobby, a hospital security guard ushered them into a large conference room already filled to capacity. Flashes of light and a barrage of questions assaulted Nic. He pasted on a smile. Kaden and the guard made a path for him to a table at the front of the room where Dr. Jacob and the detectives were already seated. He took a seat beside Vivian.

Scanning the room, he spotted many familiar faces among the reporters. But he didn't see Lauren. He should have insisted Kaden accompany her to the hotel.

A few minutes later, Vivian stood up to read their statement. "Good morning, ladies and gentlemen. Thank you for being here. We will take some questions at the end and will be limiting our comments to only the things we know for sure so as not to taint the ongoing investigation."

She gave a short account of what had happened and concluded by saying, "Mr. Lamoureux will be taking a well-deserved break until shooting of his new romantic comedy *At Last* begins in two weeks. We fully expect him to be on set and ready for work. At this time, we will take questions." She pointed to a reporter in the second row. "Mr. Jones, please go ahead."

"Ms. Carmichael's statements imply that foul play is suspected. Detectives, can you elaborate?"

Becker took the microphone. "Eyewitnesses place Mr. Lamoureux in the company of a woman in a bar on Thursday night. We have reason to suspect she deposited a drug in his drink without his knowledge."

Another reporter called out, "What was the drug?"

"Rohypnol."

"What are the side effects?"

Dr. Jacob shot Nic an apologetic look before answering. As he listened to the doctor discuss memory impairment, lack of judgment and sexual disinhibition, Nic tensed. This was the worst part of Hollywood, having your life discussed in such a cold, unemotional way. He'd been *drugged* for fuck's sake. And then to have photos of his humiliation plastered all over the papers....

"Nic, is this how you're spinning the photo of you having sex with Summer Rayne?"

Jesus Christ. These people were sharks. He was a person, not some fucking fictional character.

Before he could tamp down his anger and put together a response, Dr. Jacob continued. "Mr. Lamoureux has no memory of the events that took place, and there's no medical evidence anything of a sexual nature occurred."

Excited by the scent of scandal, the reporters fired off questions faster than they could be answered.

"Doesn't the photo prove sex took place?"

"Did Ms. Rayne give Nic the drugs?"

"Is Ms. Rayne a suspect?"

Anderson held up his hands. "We cannot comment on an ongoing investigation. However, I will confirm that Ms. Rayne is a person of interest in this case."

"Nic, do you know why Ms. Rayne would do this to you?" How many times had he asked himself this same question? All he knew for sure was she had to be one sick bitch.

As he opened his mouth to respond, Anderson spoke. "I'm advising Mr. Lamoureux not to respond to that question. Ms. Rayne has not been charged with anything, and it would be speculation on his part." With a nod, Nic acknowledged the detective's statement.

"Since the premiere of *Bad Days*, there've been many sightings of you posted to CelebrityStalker by someone calling themselves NicsBitch. Is this person stalking you?"

It had finally come. The question Nic had been dreading. How could he answer? Having the press involved could only make matters worse. He glanced toward the detectives. Becker shook his head, the slight movement indicating he'd field this question. Nic held his breath as he waited.

"No comment."

Fuck. Becker flinched under the weight of Nic's glare. Everyone knew that when a cop said *no comment*, that meant yes. Judging by the buzz in the room, the press knew it too.

Vivian stood up and ended the press conference. As Nic left, he ignored the questions the reporters continued to throw at him. Kaden led them to the limo parked outside.

A large crowd had gathered behind the security fences erected by the police. The stalker could be hiding here in plain sight. A shudder arrowed up his spine.

Nic looked around at the smiling faces surrounding him. These people, his fans, made his life bearable. Yesterday, as they'd waited for news of his condition, they'd held candles, and today, they shouted encouragement and held signs wishing him a speedy recovery. Without their support over the years, he'd have turned tail and gone back home. He couldn't let fear take this moment away.

Buoyed by the cheers, he smiled and waved. "Thank you, everyone, for your kindness. As you may know, I will be attending a charity fundraiser for the Make-A-Wish Foundation in two days. To show my appreciation of your support and to share it with others, I'll match any private donations made to Make-A-Wish through my website within the next week. I'm blessed to have the best, most loyal fans in the world. Thank you!"

After one last wave for the crowd, he turned to Kaden, who opened the car door and winked at him. What the hell? While Vivian exchanged a few final words with members of the press, he climbed into the limo, scooting over to the far side to leave room on the seat for her. When he encountered a warm body, he lurched away, startled.

"Gotcha." Lauren chuckled.

He relaxed against the seat back. "Where've you been?" he asked, pulling her into his arms. "I was getting worried."

She shrugged. "I must have gotten the start time of the press conference mixed up. When I got here, it was already under way. Kaden suggested I wait in the car so as not to rile up the paparazzi."

"How very thoughtful of him." The man deserved a raise. His gaze slid along Lauren's lush body and his hand followed. She'd changed into a white sleeveless blouse and a loose fitting blue skirt with little red flowers. "You look fantastic." He couldn't imagine her in the austere business suits Vivian favored.

"So do you." She smoothed her hands along his shoulders then pressed her nose to his neck. "And, you smell delicious."

Victory.

"A little late, are we?"

At the sound of Vivian's voice, Nic released Lauren and she sank down beside him. After Vivian settled in the seat across from them, Lauren spoke. "I thought you said the press conference started at ten fifteen."

Vivian shook her head. "My dear, I said ten. If you have any hope of making it in this business, you need to keep better track of your appointments."

Nic almost laughed when Lauren turned to him and did an exaggerated eye roll. Clearly, she wasn't accepting any responsibility for this latest *mixup*.

"Are we dropping you off at the airport, dear?"

Lauren's pretty face turned puzzled. To avoid a confrontation, he hadn't told Vivian. That had worked out real well. *Not.* "I've invited Lauren to stay in L.A. for a while."

Vivian leaned forward and patted Lauren's knee. "Perhaps we can employ your services to take some photos to go along with the press release. What hotel shall I instruct Kaden to drop you off at?"

Nic removed Vivian's hand from Lauren's knee and held it. "Lauren's staying with me."

Although Vivian snatched her hand back, her expression remained impassive. "Is that wise, darling? I know how you value your privacy."

Nic struggled to keep his tone neutral. "It's what I want."

"Of course it is." She pressed the call button to tell Kaden to take her to the office.

He smiled. Vivian would get used to the idea. He wrapped his arm around Lauren's shoulders. Her beautiful blue-green eyes danced with happiness and her full pink lips curved in a sexy grin. All the blood in his body rushed south.

He wanted her. Now.

Everything paled in comparison to Lauren. She'd seen him, if not at his worst, certainly at a very low point, and still she wanted to stay. Maybe she could see beyond his past, see beyond his mistakes, see beyond the mask, and accept him, warts and all. He was tired of being alone.

Lauren leaned her head on his shoulder. He nuzzled her hair and inhaled the sweet scent of apple blossoms.

Need tore through him.

Oh, God. Could he wait two more blocks? All he could think of was pressing Lauren down onto the seat and—

Shit. Kaden had better hurry the fuck up if he wanted that raise.

As soon as the car door closed behind Vivian, Lauren let out a relieved breath. "*That* was uncomfortable."

Nic's gaze locked on hers, shooting her pulse into overdrive. "Who cares what Vivian thinks? I meant what I said. This is what I want."

Oh, my. The fire in his eyes scorched her skin. She couldn't breathe, couldn't think, couldn't look away. Her body overheated, lost in the swirling flames.

"I hope it's what you want, too," he added, tugging on one of her curls. "But no pressure. I do have a guest room…." One corner of his mouth curved up.

As she stared into the bluest eyes she'd ever seen, she wondered who was this man sitting beside her, telling her all the things she wanted to hear? Leaning forward until she could feel his breath on her lips, she whispered, "It's what I want, too." She brushed her mouth against his.

When she pulled back, Nic caught her off-guard, lifting her onto his lap. Laughing, she clutched his shoulders to steady herself. "Are you sure we should be doing this?"

"I assure you, *chérie*, I'm fully recovered." He yanked her tight against him.

She moaned at the contact. "I can tell." There was indeed no residual sedation. All of Nic's body parts were in full working order. She motioned her head toward the front of the car. "Can he see us?"

"I raised the privacy window. Kaden can't see or hear us. Although…" He hesitated playfully. "I'm pretty sure he can guess what we're up to."

"Oh? Do you do this often?" Blushing furiously, she pressed her fingers to his lips. "Don't answer." *Be careful what you ask. You might not like what you hear.* She'd read enough articles to know Nic The Lover had definitely earned his reputation as the ultimate Hollywood womanizer.

"*Chérie*, I've entertained women in my limo before, but I've never brought any of them home. I want you to know that." Her heart melted at the sincerity in his voice. But could she trust it? After all, he was an Oscar-winning actor.

The limo stopped in front of the old warehouse where Nic lived. Although it wasn't in one of the more sought-after zip codes in the Los Angeles area, the neighborhood had a lot of character. Rather like the man himself.

As they rode the key-controlled elevator up to Nic's floor, he explained how he'd bought the three-story building and converted it into two lofts, keeping the top two floors for himself. Entrance to the building, lofts, and elevator all required a key and a code. Outside his door, Nic typed a code on the security keypad on the wall and inserted his key into the deadbolt.

Kaden put his hand on Nic's arm, stopping him from opening the door. "Something wrong?" Nic asked.

"How did Summer get you in the building?"

Nic's eyes hardened. "She had to have the key and the code."

"And if she made a copy of the key, she can get in anytime she wants," Lauren added.

"Stay here, sir. I'll take a look around." Kaden pulled a revolver from the holster under his arm and pushed open the door. A few minutes later, he returned. By the tightness of his jaw, Lauren knew he had bad news. "I found something in your bathroom." He gestured for them to follow.

Nic entered the bathroom first, and stopped so abruptly Lauren ran into his back. "What is it?" she asked. When he didn't reply, she moved around him and saw a message written on the mirror.

You're mine, only mine.

Nic turned to Kaden. "Is that…?"

"Yes, sir. I believe it is."

What were they were talking about? "Is it what?"

"Looks like blood to me, ma'am."

Nic inhaled sharply and gripped the countertop, his face ashen. *The blood.* "Let's get him out of here," she said to Kaden.

"I'm fine. Was there anything about this in the police report?"

"No sir."

Nic closed his eyes, took a deep breath and expelled it slowly, as if fighting off a dizzy spell. He then opened his eyes and turned to the mirror. What was he doing? Why was he forcing himself to look at the blood?

After staring at the message for almost a minute, Nic pulled his arm back and smashed his fist into the mirror. "Fucking bitch!" She jumped back as he continued to hit the glass, shattering it into hundreds of small pieces.

When he was done, he turned to her. "Sorry," he muttered.

She raised her brows. "Feel better?"

"Yeah." He grinned. "I do."

Kaden laughed.

"Good." She grabbed a towel and wound it around Nic's hand before he could see the blood dripping from it. "Do you have a first aid kit somewhere?"

Kaden nodded. While he jogged off to get the kit, Nic and Lauren walked downstairs to the living room. When he flopped onto the couch, Lauren took a seat beside him and rubbed his shoulders. "Are you all right?"

His cheeks darkened and he turned his face.

"Don't be embarrassed. Even big tough guys are allowed to have their quirks."

"I bet Todd didn't have any."

"Are you kidding?" She laughed. "Todd was terrified of wasps. One time he actually jumped out of the car when one flew in. Good thing I was the one driving."

Nic's eyebrows shot up. "Was he hurt?"

"Nah, we were in a parking lot so I was going slow. But I'm almost sure he would have jumped even if I'd been going fast, or if he'd been driving."

He shook his head. "I doubt he would have let you or Jason get hurt. He would've fought off his fears."

"Like you did today." She kept her tone soft and even. Nic smiled crookedly.

Kaden returned with the kit and handed it to her.

Nic grimaced. "I didn't leave much evidence, but call the detectives. And run a check of the security system."

Kaden nodded. "I'll get right on it, sir."

"And Kaden?"

"Sir?"

"Stop calling me sir." Kaden opened his eyes wide and angled his head in her direction. Nic laughed. "It's okay. Lauren's one of us now."

Kaden grinned. "Glad to hear it."

"Later today, I want the three of us to discuss a plan to find Summer."

When Kaden left, she took Nic's hand. "Lean back while I clean this." He closed his eyes. Small stress lines had begun to curve around the edges of his mouth and between his eyebrows. Poor guy.

After everything that had happened to him in the last few weeks, it was a wonder he could still function. She'd have been a hysterical wreck by now. Quickly, she wiped off the blood and disinfected the cuts. Thank goodness none needed stitches. Even the hounds of hell snapping at his heels couldn't have forced Nic back to the hospital.

As she put the kit on the coffee table, Nic opened his eyes. "You're very good at this."

She chuckled. "Jason has a tendency to leap before he looks."

"Sounds like me." He grinned.

Scooting over to the end of the couch, she patted her thighs. "Come here and relax for a bit." Nic removed his tie and loosened the collar of his shirt before lying down with his head in her lap. As she began to massage his temples, he moaned and closed his eyes.

Fifteen minutes later, she shook Nic's shoulder. He peered at her through one eye. "The cops are here."

He rubbed his face with both hands, then sat up. While Kaden opened the door, letting Anderson and Becker in, Nic got up to greet them, and she followed.

"We were hoping not to see you again so soon," Anderson said. "Your bodyguard mentioned something about a message?"

"Yes, but unfortunately, there was a problem with the evidence."

"Does this problem have anything to do with your new accessory?" he asked, eyeing the bandage wrapped around Nic's hand.

Kaden turned away from the detectives and smirked. "Sir, I'll take care of this. Detectives, this way, please."

After examining the bathroom, Anderson and Becker returned downstairs. Anderson took out his phone. "I'm going to get CSI over here to take some samples. I found a larger piece with some writing on it. Based on the smell, I'm certain it's blood. We'll run the DNA through our database and the team will dust for prints. I can confirm there was no message on the mirror when we searched your house yesterday."

"Can you give us a list of the people who've had access since Thursday?" Becker asked.

Nic nodded. "Vivian Carmichael came here today to pick up my clothes, and Lauren was here last night with Kaden." Turning to Kaden, he asked, "Can you pull the records from the security system so we know when it was enabled and disabled?"

"Already done, sir." He picked a sheet of paper off the table. "The system was disabled Thursday evening at 11:35 PM, reset two hours later. It was disabled and reset on Friday morning and Friday night as expected. Unexpectedly though, it was disabled and reset twice this morning."

Anderson pulled out his notepad. "The Thursday night hours match up with the eyewitness accounts of when you left the bar with Ms. Rayne. We imagine she used your key and you gave her the code to get in."

"Then she made a copy and let herself in again this morning," Nic said. Lauren took his hand and squeezed it.

"Ms. James, what did you do while you were here?" Anderson asked.

Her eyes flicked to Nic. "I cleaned up Nic's room." She arched a brow. "Then I tidied up the mess left by the police."

Anderson cleared his throat. "Sorry about that, ma'am. The CSI guys are focused on collecting evidence. Did you see anything unusual?"

She pictured the message dripping with blood and shuddered. "There certainly wasn't anything written on the bathroom mirror."

Becker questioned her, then Kaden regarding their whereabouts during the past twenty-four hours. "Ms. James, you had a window of opportunity between leaving the hospital this morning and your return during the press conference. The timing matches when the security system was disabled."

"But I don't know the code."

"You could have seen Mr. Christiansen enter it last night."

Kaden crossed his arms and frowned at the detectives. "That didn't happen. And even if it did, how would she get a key?"

Nic stepped up behind her and pulled her into the comforting circle of his arms. "What's this about, Detectives? Why are you hassling Lauren?"

Becker didn't bat an eye. "Everyone is a suspect… until they aren't."

"What happened to innocent until proven guilty?" Nic snarled.

"Only in court. During an investigation, it works the other way."

Nic walked to the door and opened it. "You don't want to solve this case. You just want to close it."

Anderson shot Lauren an apologetic look, then turned to Nic. "Mr. Lamoureux, we don't want to offend anyone, but we do need to be thorough. We haven't ruled out that the stalker is someone close to you." Nic paled and shut the door.

An hour later, after the detectives and the CSI team left, Nic joined Lauren in the living room. He paced between the large picture window and the stone fireplace, his frustration visible in the tight lines around his mouth and in the stiffness of his shoulders.

If it were winter, she could light a fire, put on some soft music and offer him a glass of wine. She wanted to help him relax, but didn't know him well enough to know what to do. Vivian would know. Her stomach twisted with jealousy. She pushed those thoughts away. Vivian might be Nic's best friend, but she wasn't the one he'd brought home.

She hugged his waist from behind. "It's going to be all right. We'll find Summer soon."

Turning until they were face to face, he wrapped her in his arms. Her hands roamed his back, massaging the tight muscles while he nuzzled her neck. "Summer might not be the stalker. The text messages and the sightings began before I even met her."

Lost in the pleasure of exploring his strong back, Lauren didn't hear him at first. Then his words sank in. She pulled back to see his face. "You think there's more than one person involved?"

His lips thinned and a tic appeared in the sharp line of his jaw. "It's a definite possibility."

Nothing she could say would make it all better. She rubbed his eyebrows with her thumbs, smoothing out his frown, and kissed his lips. "You don't deserve this."

"How can you be so sure?"

"What do you mean?"

"For all you know, I could be a very bad person."

A smile curved her lips as her eyes roamed his gorgeous, distraught face. "You may not know me very well, but I've known you for years. No one in your position can keep deep dark secrets for long. If you had done anything worthy of making you a bad person, everyone would know about it by now."

Somehow, instead of reassuring him, her words had the opposite effect. He kissed her on the nose. "I have to make some calls."

Lauren followed him with her eyes as he headed up the stairs to his office. This was the second time she'd described him as a good person, and both times he'd become uncomfortable.

What skeletons were rattling around Nic The Lover's closet?

⁂

She trembled with rage at what had been done to her Nic. Anger sat on her chest like a heavy weight. The fear of losing him had literally driven her to her knees. There could be no life for her without Nic.

And there would be no life for that stupid, conniving bitch who'd drugged him.

It was all over the news. The awful photo had gone viral on the Internet. The police claimed Summer wanted everyone to think Nic was *her* boyfriend. But she knew the truth. He'd never willingly have sex with the porn star. Drugging him was the only way she'd ever get near his bed.

Summer was only supposed to dance with him, get one or two Paparazzi Kisses. The photos would have drawn the media's attention from the photographer. Instead, the slut had played her; she'd had her own plan all along! And to make matters worse, the paparazzi had photos of the fucking photographer at the hospital.

Her fingers curled around the pen she held in her hand, breaking it.

The press was calling her a stalker. But it wasn't true. Didn't they know that Nic was hers? That he would only ever be hers?

Nic was a lucky boy, even if he didn't know it yet. As the red ink from the broken pen dripped down her arm, she smiled. She would take care of Summer. The bitch would never hurt Nic again.

And she'd take care of the photographer, too. Very soon.

Her blood thrummed with excitement. Nic would be thrilled with her for taking care of his problem, taking care of him. After this, he'd understand she'd do anything for him. Even crawl through broken glass.

Grabbing the newspaper, she rubbed her hand across the photograph, leaving a red smear of ink over the whore's face. She'd take away anything, anyone that caused him pain. For him, she'd wash her hands in blood.

CHAPTER 11

Nic paused at the top of the steps, hearing the muted voices in the living room. He stretched his shoulders, trying to relieve the tension building in his chest. His life was such a fucking mess. He sucked air deep into his lungs as he descended the stairs and entered the living room. "Kaden, can I have a word with you?"

Lauren jumped up. "I'll get some drinks while you two talk. Pop okay?"

"Thank you, *chérie*." Nic followed her with his eyes, enjoying the sway of her hips as she walked to the kitchen. She was probably confused about his behavior, but he'd make it up to her later, when they were alone.

Hearing Kaden chuckle, Nic dragged his gaze to his bodyguard's knowing grin. He shrugged and grinned back. He'd been so excited to come home and spend time with Lauren, he'd all but forgotten Summer was still on the loose, and even worse, she had his keys and the code to the alarm system. Were he and Lauren safe here? He had to be sure. "Get a locksmith to change the locks. And after doing a full inspection of the security system, change the codes. I don't want anyone but you and me to have access to this place."

"I'm already on it."

"One more thing, can you work for me full time until this situation is resolved? You can have the spare bedroom."

"Absolutely." Kaden nodded.

"Is Beth going to hate me for this?"

Kaden threw his head back and laughed. "No. She's a huge fan."

Nic smiled. "Is there anything I can do to thank her?"

When Kaden hesitated, Nic made a get-on-with-it motion with his hand. "She'd love an autographed photo."

"The ones I have on hand are all pretty racy. Can you handle the competition?" Nic teased.

"You might play a soldier, but I'm the real deal."

Laughing, Nic left Kaden to his work and went back up to his office. The photos Lauren had taken in D.C. lay on his desk. As he sorted through the pile, his heart filled with pride. These were damn good. With her talent, she deserved to have her photos on the covers of all the major magazines. Someday people would be begging to work with her.

When he found the one of him wearing only a pair of camouflage pants, a grin spread across his face. Beth would love it. Kaden wouldn't. Perfect. Laughing, he signed the photo.

"I'm glad you're feeling better."

He turned to see Lauren. She handed him a tall glass of pop. "Kaden will be staying with us until Summer is found," he said.

"Good. You need all the protection you can get."

"He'll be protecting *us*. The doll was warning enough."

"Don't remind me." She pointed to his desk. "Were you going over the photos from the shoot?"

"I'm autographing one for Kaden's girlfriend. A thank you for monopolizing his time."

She pointed to the shot he'd signed. "That one's my favorite."

He pulled her onto his lap and chuckled when she blushed. "Tell me why."

As she traced a finger down his neck and into the open V of his shirt, she murmured, "When I see this photo, it makes me think of running my hands over all those muscles so I can feel them contracting and relaxing. Then I think of running my fingers over your chest and…"

He swallowed hard, aware of his rapidly increasing heart rate as she matched actions to words. "And then what?" His voice was gruff even to his own ears.

She unbuttoned his shirt in no particular hurry. "And then I think of kissing my way down your neck and your chest so I can do this." He inhaled sharply as her mouth closed around one nipple. All his attention lasered in on the touch of her lips, the swirl of her tongue.

"Oh yeah? Come to think of it, that's my favorite photo, too." He lifted his hips to push against Lauren's bottom. He was definitely rising to the occasion.

Nic heard a knock and reluctantly pulled his gaze away from Lauren to see Kaden lounging against the doorframe. The man had the worst timing.

"Sorry to interrupt." Kaden grinned. "A locksmith is coming in a few hours. I've changed the access codes on the security system. The new ones are on the kitchen table. I'm leaving to get my stuff. Call me if there's a problem."

"Sounds good. Thanks."

"Is that the photo for Beth?"

"Yeah. I hope she likes it." He handed the photo to Kaden.

Kaden glanced at Lauren. "If she likes it as much as Ms. James here, it might take me a bit more than an hour to get back."

Lauren blushed again, and Nic burst out laughing. "No worries man. Take your time. I'm in good hands."

"No doubt," Kaden said with a wink for Lauren. "By the way, everything's been tidied up in the master suite."

As Kaden's feet pounded down the stairs, Lauren playfully punched Nic in the arm. "You're incorrigible."

"No, just really, really happy you're here." He ran his hands along her thighs, pushing her skirt up, then turned her so she straddled his lap. "I haven't been able to think of anything but getting my hands on you since I first saw you in D.C."

"After all those kisses on the cheek, I thought you were feeling very brotherly."

"*Chérie*, there's nothing *brotherly* about what I want to do to you." He placed his hands under her ass and stood up. Wrapping her legs around his waist, she laughed in delight. While nibbling on her neck, he carried her to his room.

After laying her on his bed, he sat beside her and threaded his fingers through her wild hair. Blood rushed from his head to his cock as he imagined the soft strands slipping over his thighs as she.... Pushing the image aside for the moment, he brushed a stray curl behind her ear. "Are you sure about this? If you want to wait, we can."

She smiled. "I'm sure."

Okay then. Nic undid the top button of her blouse, then the second. When her eyebrows dipped in a small frown, his hands stilled. "Something wrong?"

"It's a little bright in here. Could we close the blinds?"

She averted her eyes. Ah. Lauren was uncomfortable letting him see her naked. "Whatever you want. But just so you know, I love your body. Someday, I hope you'll let me look at you in the light."

"I've seen the photos of the women you've dated. Actresses and supermodels. As close to perfect as a plastic surgery can get them. I'm nothing like them."

"Exactly."

Lauren narrowed her eyes. "I don't know how to take that. Are you saying I'm not beautiful? I know I'm not perfect, and frankly, I'm not sure what you see in me."

Hearing the anger and doubt in her voice, Nic's stomach did a slow, sickening roll. How could she have gotten everything so wrong? He took her hand, pressing it to the bulge between his legs. "I might be a good actor, but I can't fake this. You're beautiful. Inside *and* out."

She rolled her eyes. "Nice line, Nic. But have you ever slept with a woman who's had a child? Have you ever seen stretch marks or C-section scars? Believe me, they're not very attractive."

Lauren was right; he'd never slept with a mother before. How bad could her scars be to make her think they'd turn him off? He didn't think anything could do that. "My mother used to say scars and stretch marks are the badges of motherhood. You shouldn't be ashamed of that, Lauren."

He kissed her, then stood to close the blinds. Lauren grasped his arm. "Leave them."

"Don't do this for me."

After rising onto her knees, she rested her forehead against his. "I'm not. Don't you think I want to see you too?" She smiled shyly. "It's been a long time for me."

"How long?"

"Over five years." When his brows rose, she laughed. Five *years*? God, he couldn't imagine going five weeks. His dick would shrivel up and fall off.

He kissed the tip of her pert nose. "We'll take it slow and you can stop me anytime. Just say the word."

Chuckling, she wrapped her arms around his neck and pulled him onto the bed, twisting so he landed on his back. He was more than happy to let her take charge. It touched him that she was honoring him in this way. Straddling his lap, she removed her blouse, revealing the chain around her neck. Would she remove her husband's dog tags before they made love?

"I love your chest," she said, undoing the remaining buttons on his shirt. Her small hands sculpting his pecs made him groan with pleasure. When her nails traced the line of his hair down to the waistband of his pants, chills ran up his spine, and gooseflesh spread across his chest and stomach.

Unable to resist, he reached up to palm her smooth, supple breasts. As if reading his mind, she reached behind her back to unhook her lacy white bra. His hands were poised to catch her breasts when the cups of the bra fell away. "So beautiful."

Her gasps of pleasure as he rolled her nipples between his thumbs and forefingers drove him wild. He wanted more. Raising himself up, he twisted the chain around so the dog tags rested on her back, then he lifted her breasts in an offering to his mouth.

When his lips closed over both peaked nipples at the same time, she moaned. "That feels so good."

He agreed wholeheartedly. The taste of her as his tongue curled around her nipples was exotic and exhilarating. He wanted a lot more. She clasped his head against her breasts, rocking her hips in a rhythm like a slow dance. Reluctantly, he gave up his claim on her breasts and shrugged off his shirt. That first contact of hot flesh pressed against flesh was one of his favorite parts of sex, and he couldn't wait a moment longer to experience it with Lauren. As soon as the shirt was off, he lay back down and pulled her tightly against his chest. As if understanding what he wanted, she slid her hands over his biceps and wrapped her arms around his neck.

They were connected. Every inch of skin from their waists up, touching. Her softness molded against his hardness. He was burning out of control. And as he looked up into her beautiful flushed face, he gave in to the temptation of a mouth already swollen from their earlier kisses.

With his teeth, he tugged on her lower lip. She arched her back, crushing her breasts against his chest, and opened her lips. Never one to refuse such a charming invitation, he covered her mouth in a bold, decisive gesture. As her tongue wound around his, he imagined she was licking another part of his body. He growled deep in his throat.

Releasing her mouth, he eased her back up and slid his hands under her skirt, bunching the fabric at her waist. After a moment, he hesitated. "Are you certain, *chérie*?"

"Never more," she breathed, her voice husky and seductive as she reached for his zipper.

He shifted her down beside him and tugged her skirt off, then stopped to admire the sight of her in a lacy white thong that matched the bra on the floor. "Do all moms wear panties like this?"

"You like?"

"Oh, yeah. I like a lot." With a smile, he grabbed each side of the thong and pulled down as Lauren wiggled and lifted her bottom. He'd ask her to model these for him sometime. But not now. Twirling the panties on his fingertip, he caught her eye and let them fly across the room to land on the dresser.

With the twinkle of her laughter in his ears, he stood up and shucked his own pants and boxers. When he straightened, he was surprised to see she'd joined him. With a tentative touch, she reached out and circled him. His breath caught in his throat. As she stroked, he caressed her smooth shoulders and nuzzled her neck. "*Chérie*, that feels so incredibly good."

Before he knew what she intended, she slipped out of his embrace and knelt on the floor at his feet. One hand cupped his balls while the other gripped his cock. As her warm wet mouth closed around him and her tongue swirled around his swollen head, he wondered if she'd somehow read his mind. He ran his fingers through her curls, holding her in place. The silky slide of her hair on his thighs thrilled him more than he'd imagined. He reveled in the pleasure, reveled in the ecstasy. Reveled in the joy of what she was doing for him. The tightness of her mouth, coupled with her throaty moans, soon had him thrusting against her lips. He was losing control. Afraid to hurt her, he gripped her shoulders and lifted her up.

"Was I doing something wrong?"

"God, no. I loved it, too much."

With that, he picked her up by the waist and deposited her on the edge of the bed. Now it was his turn. After spreading her legs, he knelt in front of her and inhaled sharply at the view. Droplets of moisture glistened on her neatly trimmed curls and glowing pink flesh. The tantalizing scent of her arousal drew him closer, as he spread the delicate folds with his fingers. His eyes on hers, he swiped his tongue along her center in one long, slow lick. A shiver rippled through her as he closed his lips around her nub. His teeth scraped lightly, making her moan.

With a nudge on her stomach, he encouraged her to lie back on the bed. He flicked his tongue along the sensitive flesh of her feminine lips. Her hips shot off the bed when his tongue penetrated her, moving in and out, mimicking what he'd soon be doing with his cock. The musky taste of her hardened him almost to the point of pain. Taking his time, he inserted a finger into her tight opening, and after sliding in a second finger, he stroked her deep inside. Her body tightened and quivered. He returned his mouth to her, alternately nipping, licking, and sucking.

Within minutes, she was moaning and thrashing. Her fingers gripped the bedspread. As she lay before him, her body flushed and glowing with a sheen of sweat, her moans of pleasure ringing in his ears, she was the most beautiful woman he'd ever seen. Even if they stopped now, the experience would have still been worth it.

Extending one finger along the crease between her cheeks, he probed. She gave a startled groan and then her body bucked. Her inner muscles contracted against his fingers. He continued flicking his tongue on her nub to increase and prolong her pleasure. Ripple after ripple shook her body until she lay unmoving on the bed. Sated. After one last wet kiss on her thigh, he pulled himself up beside her. She opened her arms and he fell into her embrace.

As they lay in each other's arms, Lauren struggled to catch her breath. "That was amazing." Although she'd had some wild fantasies starring Nic The Lover, none had ever come close to bringing her this much pleasure.

"I'm glad you enjoyed it." He grinned. "I know I did."

But they weren't finished. Despite his words, Nic hadn't had all the enjoyment he could stand, and she wanted to make sure that by the time they were finished, he would have his own fantasies about her.

As though sharing her thoughts, he leaned over her and whispered, "But we aren't done yet." Opening the nightstand drawer, he pulled out a shiny square package. Thank God he'd remembered. She certainly wouldn't have. The last time she'd needed a condom was about nine years ago.

As Nic ripped open the package and slid the condom on, she wagged her eyebrows playfully. "Extra large, huh?" As bright flags of color appeared high on his cheeks, she had to laugh. "Come here, big boy."

No, they weren't even close to being done. Hands at his waist, she encouraged him to lie on her, to cover her fully. Then she wrapped her legs around him, loosely crossing her ankles at the small of his back. The weight of him pressing her into the mattress was pure heaven.

Placing his elbows on either side of her head, Nic rocked his hips, sliding his cock back and forth along her folds. A tingle began again where he was rubbing her, and she marveled at his expertise. In the past, she'd always had trouble achieving climax, but he'd brought her to that point easily.

As the tension mounted, she closed her eyes. He lowered his mouth to hers and after another deep kiss, slid his lips over to her ear and nibbled. Wave after wave of sensation flashed over her, through her. She'd die if he didn't bury himself inside her soon. Gathering her courage, she reached down between their bodies to palm him. He was hard steel encased in smooth silk. Chills ran up her spine in anticipation of being stretched to the limit, of having him fill her completely. Her toes curled and she purred with delight.

As if electrified by her reaction, he wrapped his hand around hers and guided his cock to her opening. She released him and wound her arms tightly around his neck, tilting her hips to ease his entry. He covered her mouth and slid his tongue between her lips even as he pushed himself home. She arched her back, moaning as the slow glide triggered every nerve ending in its path. Moisture blurred her vision. The moment she'd fantasized about for so long was finally happening.

Balancing on his elbows, he cradled her head in his hands while keeping his hips still. "Are you okay?" he whispered.

Lauren shivered as the husky tones of his voice washed over her. "Yes."

"You're so tight. I hope I didn't hurt you."

Smiling at his concern, she ran her hands down the ropes of muscle on his back until she could curl her fingers around the tight globes of his butt. The expression on his face as she pushed down with her hands and pushed up with her hips almost made her laugh. Nic The Lover was nothing like she'd imagined.

He was better.

She hadn't expected him to cherish her. Hadn't expected the tenderness in his touch. Hadn't expected the reverence in his eyes. On screen, his love scenes tended toward the hard and fast variety, and while they could try that another time, this time she rejoiced in the arms of this quieter, more loving Nic.

A tightening feeling began to build up in her core as he withdrew one inch at a time until only the head of his cock remained inside her. When she could stand it no more, he plunged. He repeated this over and over until she cried out. "Nic, please!"

With a knowing look, he grinned at her. "Tell me what you want, *chérie*."

"More!"

Lowering himself completely on her, he gripped her bottom, tilting her hips up, and began pounding into her with short hard strokes. With his face in the crook of her neck, he kissed and nipped at her shoulder. Suddenly she was desperate to feel his teeth on her breasts. She gripped his head and tried to push him lower. When he didn't understand, she made a mewling sound of displeasure. He lifted his head and she knew by the sexy look on his face that he was teasing. With a seemingly innate understanding of her needs, he raised himself to his knees, pulling her tightly against him so her bottom rested on his thighs.

Bending over her, he tugged one of her nipples between his teeth. The feeling, between a tweak and a pinch, along with the relentless pounding of his cock, sent her over the edge. As her world exploded into a kaleidoscope of color and sensation, she clutched his head against her and called out his name.

He released her nipple and pressed her down onto the bed. Pushing up on his hands, he thrust high and deep a few more times before achieving his own release and collapsing on top of her.

With the sound of his rapid breathing in her ear and the feel of his heart thumping against her chest, she lay in his arms and marveled at how happy she was to be here, with him. She'd missed this closeness to another person, to a man. Holding him in her arms, being held in his, sharing this basic, primal pleasure.

He lifted his head and pressed a tender kiss against her lips before rolling over and pulling her so she lay on his chest. With her finger, she traced the curves of his lips, his eyebrows, and the skin around his eyes.

"Maybe we shouldn't have done this."

Cracking open an eye, he shot her a penetrating stare. "Why not?"

"You just got out of the hospital. If I hurt Nic The Lover, women the world over will hate me." Something flashed across his face. Anger? Pain? Hurt? Whatever it was, she'd hit a nerve.

He smiled, but it didn't reach his eyes. "*Chérie*, I'm perfectly fine."

She rubbed the crease between his brows. "You're upset." When Nic averted his gaze, anxiety fluttered in her chest.

"Kaden will be back soon. I'd better hit the shower." He rolled her to his side and slid off the bed. "Are you hungry?"

"I'll get supper started, and then I'll have a shower. I saw some steaks in your freezer. Does that sound good?"

Shooting her a quick look over his shoulder, Nic acknowledged her words with a single nod. The bathroom door closed with a resounding thud. Lauren pressed a hand to her suddenly queasy stomach.

Their relationship had barely begun. Was this already the final curtain?

After the shower, Nic barricaded himself in his office. Kaden had returned, and he could hear him chatting with Lauren in the kitchen as she prepared supper. Sex with her had been everything he'd expected it to be, and more. The exquisite taste of her lingered on his tongue and her blissful moans echoed in his ears.

But her comment about sleeping with Nic The Lover pissed him off.

Had he been expecting—even hoping—she would see through the act? He scrubbed his face, hard. He was seriously messed up. So what if she thought of him as Nic The Lover? Maybe it was better that way.

And now that he thought about it… that she'd worn her dead husband's dog tags even while they'd had sex, that fucking pissed him off too. She'd seemed eager to get in bed with him, even leading the way at times, and for sure she'd enjoyed herself. It was his name that had echoed off the walls when she'd come. She certainly hadn't been thinking about Todd then.

Of course her husband had been important to her. But Todd had died five years ago. Her home was filled with photos of him and his clothes still hung in her closet. Wasn't that enough? Why did she need to keep a reminder of him around her neck, even when she was having sex with another man? It didn't take a degree in psychology to know something was off about that.

But hey, who was he to judge? They all had their crosses to bear. His was Rachel. And maybe Lauren's was Todd. If this relationship with her continued, they might find themselves in a position where they had to either share their secrets or….

Fuck. Enough of that. He turned on his computer to see how the press conference was being received. He checked a few mainstream entertainment sites. They'd kept their reporting close to the facts. Good. There were some mentions of a possible stalker, but thanks to Becker, he'd expected that. As he typed in the address of a high-profile blog site, trepidation stiffened his fingers. Bloggers were not held to the same standards as mainstream sites. Their *news* often held more fiction than fact.

Seconds later, he sat frozen, staring at the slander on the screen. The author of the celebrity gossip blog claimed Nic was a Rohypnol addict who regularly indulged in the drug for its disinhibiting effects, which apparently enabled him to act sexually with women. It went on to say he had drugged Summer so she would sleep with him and that he had paid Lauren to take the nude photos of him and Summer together all in an effort to cover up his homosexuality.

What kind of person would say shit like this about him? About Lauren?

Hollywood was fickle when it came to most aspects of filmmaking, but it was consistently conservative when it came to an actor's reputation. An actor could be on the A-list one day and on the blacklist the next.

If he didn't find Summer and clear up this mess soon, he'd be lucky to get a role as an extra in one of her porn flicks. And he wouldn't have enough money to continue funding the ranch for Rachel. He couldn't let that happen.

He picked up his desk phone and dialed Vivian. Seconds later, she answered.

"Hello darling. Is everything all right?"

"No. When I got home, Kaden found a message on my bathroom mirror, written in blood. We called the police. They'll probably want to question you."

"My God. You're sure it was blood?"

"The police tested it."

"Are you okay?"

"I managed not to pass out. So, I guess that's good."

She chuckled. "Don't be so hard on yourself. Everyone has their foibles."

"Speaking of foibles, have you seen what's being posted about me on the internet?"

"No. What are they saying?"

"Only that I'm a homosexual Rohypnol addict who uses the drug so I can have sex with women. If this ruins my career…." He paused and took a calming breath. "You know why I need this."

Silence.

"Vivian?"

"Yes, I'm here. Don't overreact. The police believe your version of the events. But maybe we need to step things up a bit to make sure the public believes it too. You need to show everyone that nothing has changed. You're still Nic The Lover, and you won't be intimidated by anyone."

"Any ideas on how to do that?"

"Do you trust me, darling?"

That was easy. "You know I do."

"Then take my advice. If we handle this right, it'll actually boost your career. Before this, you were a household name in America. After this, you'll be a household name around the world."

He sighed. She'd been saying stuff like this since the whole mess started, but instead of getting better, things were getting worse. "What's your advice?"

"First, send Lauren back to the hotel."

Not going to happen. "What else?"

"Stay in and rest for the next couple of days. I'll arrange for someone to accompany you to the Make-A-Wish fundraiser. You'll go as Nic The Lover, in full force. By the end of the evening, women will be falling at your feet, and anyone who ever doubted your virility will be proven wrong."

"I'm a good actor, Viv, but I don't think even Nic The Lover can make that happen."

Her chuckling came over the line, loud and clear. "Don't be silly, darling. All you need to do is be your usual sexy, charming self. Nature and pheromones will do the rest."

Nature and pheromones, huh? But there was one problem with her plan.

"I'm taking Lauren, not some silly starlet. And, of course, Kaden will need to come too."

"The bodyguard, yes. The department store photographer, no."

Letting out another sigh, he rested his head on the back of his chair. Hadn't they resolved this already? "Vivian. If I go, she goes."

"Have you considered how she'll feel when you start acting like Nic The Lover? If I recall correctly, it didn't end too well that time in D.C."

No, it hadn't. But, as long as he didn't pull a Paparazzi Kiss on her, she'd be more than happy to spend the evening with Nic The Lover.

After all, that's who she thought she was fucking.

CHAPTER 12

Nic was still upstairs brooding. How could they patch things up if he didn't come down, if they didn't talk about it? Lauren sighed as she tossed a Greek salad. She didn't even know what she'd done to upset him.

"Need help?"

Lauren jumped at the sound of Kaden's voice and pressed a hand to her pounding chest. He crossed the kitchen to stand beside her, peering at her face. "What's wrong?"

"N-nothing. I didn't hear you come in." She handed him the salad bowl. When he turned to take it to the table, she made her voice sound casual. "Have you been Nic's bodyguard long?"

His shoulders stiffened. "Why do you ask?"

"Just making conversation."

Shrugging, he set the bowl on the table. "On and off for the last year."

"Does he enjoy the fame and glamour?"

Kaden rubbed his chin. "He likes the fans but not the press so much." He sat on a barstool at the breakfast counter. "A few months ago we went to see a Kings game with some hockey friends of Nic's. The paparazzi caught up with us as we left and trailed us to the car. All the way, he kept up the banter, trying to charm them into leaving, but it didn't work, and some of his friends got pissed."

"Good thing they didn't have their hockey sticks."

"Yeah, I had to step in before all hell broke loose."

"What did you do?"

"I threatened to shoot them if they didn't back off."

She stared at Kaden, frozen for a full five seconds. "You pulled a gun?"

He laughed. "You should have seen the look on their faces. A lot like the one on your face right now." Then, his smile faded. "Nic kept it together, but when we got home, he punched a hole in the wall."

"So the keeping his cool part was an act?"

"Yeah, he hates having his privacy invaded. And this has to be really hard on him. He's had more people in his house today than in the whole time I've known him."

"You're a good friend." She patted his hand.

"Trying to steal my girl, Kaden? Isn't your lovely nurse enough?" Her back stiffened at the edge in Nic's voice. His mouth was stretched into a straight line, muscles working in his jaw. Not sure whether he was angry or jealous, she kept her mouth shut.

Kaden jumped off the stool. "No sir. Just sharing a few bodyguard stories with Ms. James here."

"Ah yes. I'm sure Ms. James loved hearing about the adventures of Nic The Lover."

Okay. They needed to talk. "Kaden, would you mind turning on the grill?"

"Right away, ma'am." He scurried out like a rat abandoning a sinking ship.

Linking her hand in Nic's, she led him to the living room and pulled him down beside her on the couch. The wary look he gave her spoke volumes. She ached to shield him from the rest of the world. But the feeling wasn't in the least bit maternal.

It was possessive.

Todd had never needed her the way Nic seemed to need her. And she delighted in the knowledge of that need. She pulled him into the circle of her arms. He tensed for a moment before accepting her embrace. When he sank against her and tightened his hold, relief flooded her. "I didn't understand. I never meant to hurt you."

He leaned back. His gorgeous blue eyes filled with something she couldn't quite identify—worry? Distrust? Hope? "What didn't you understand, *chérie*?"

Swallowing audibly, she took his hand in hers and pressed it to her chest before answering. "I understand now why you got upset when I called you Nic The Lover after we…." She trailed off. As his expression became carefully blank, her nerves jangled.

Voice flat, he pressed her. "What is it you think you understand?"

Oh God. For five years she'd been on her own, and she wasn't ready to let Nic go, didn't want to let him go. Her fingers tightened around his hand.

He grimaced. "Lauren, your nails…."

Immediately, she loosened her grip and brought his hand to her mouth. "You must think I'm crazy. I'm trying to apologize, and instead I end up clawing your hand."

Despite the heat that warmed her cheeks, and his stoic expression, she needed to finish what she'd begun. "For you, there are two Nics. There's the public one—Nic The Lover. He's outgoing and charming. Then there's the real Nic. He hates the media and craves privacy. Am I close?"

Jesus Christ. He wasn't ready to have this conversation with Lauren.

With his gaze fixed on the fireplace across from the couch, Nic let out a ragged, tired breath. "You make me sound like I have some sort of split personality disorder."

She chuckled. "I really do get it. Nic The Lover is an act. I'll admit I was confused at first. But can you blame me? You didn't win that Oscar for nothing."

No, he couldn't blame her. He'd been playing the part so long he'd forgotten how to be himself with a woman. Since meeting Lauren, he'd been delving into his Nic The Lover repertoire, trying to impress her. Maybe he and Nic The Lover weren't so different anymore. Maybe Nic The Lover was rubbing off on him.

And now that she knew about his act, she might accept his extreme need for privacy at face value. Maybe he could have Lauren and still keep his secrets. "To make it in Hollywood, I had to create this image, and now I'm stuck maintaining it."

With a flick of her wrist, she pushed her hair over her shoulder and gave him a saucy grin. "Well, do you know which Nic I want?"

Desire shot through him; his cock instantly hardened. He returned her grin with one of his own. "No, but please enlighten me."

Straddling his thigh, she wrapped her arms around his neck and whispered in his ear, "I want you. I want the real Nic. The same sweet, considerate Nic I knew in high school."

What the hell? "High school?"

Lauren jumped off his lap and slapped a hand over her mouth. Apparently she hadn't meant to let that nugget slip. "Come on, Lauren. We're being honest here, aren't we?" Yeah, yeah, he was a hypocrite. What's good for the goose is good for the gander and all that. But fuck it.

Red-faced, she turned away from him. "We went to the same high school."

Nic crossed his arms. He needed details. He'd remember a girl like Lauren. "What school?"

"Mundelein High School." No hesitation. When he continued to stare at her, she added weakly, "Go Mustangs!"

"Were we in the same grade?"

She nodded. "Eleventh." Again, no hesitation.

Images of everyone he could remember from high school flashed before his eyes. And that's when it hit him—Lauren was the cute school newspaper photographer he'd chased after his entire eleventh grade. He'd started to make the connection that day at the restaurant but had gotten sidetracked and hadn't asked her. After Rachel's accident, his memories of Chicago had blurred, but he hadn't forgotten the teenaged Lauren. She just looked nothing like the adult Lauren.

"Were we friends?"

"No… not really."

"What do you mean?"

Anger sparked in her eyes as she turned to meet his gaze, hands planted on her hips. "Well, we couldn't be friends when you never even noticed me, now could we?"

Nic wanted to laugh. He'd done more than notice her. He'd followed her around school and acted stupid, hoping she'd take his picture. Christ. Stupid didn't cover it; he'd been an utter moron. That night when he and his buddies had been drinking… he hated to think about what he'd done to try to get her attention. His crush on her had been of monumental proportions, but he'd never approached her directly. A stupid jock like him wouldn't have fit in with her friends.

She'd hung with the smart kids, the ones who were part of the photography club, the school newspaper, the math team. He'd loitered in the hall outside the darkroom after school to catch a glimpse of her when she walked out. But he couldn't let her know any of this.

"*Chérie*, believe me, I would have noticed you."

"Yeah well." She shrugged. "I looked a lot different then."

No kidding. She'd been skinny and shy in a quirky, oddly attractive way. "I'm sure you were beautiful." She smirked.

Time to change the topic. Taking her hand, he led her back through the kitchen to the patio. "We'd better check on Kaden before our steaks become charred lumps of coal."

"What? He told me he was the best steak griller around."

"Let's just say he has a very high opinion of his skills." The panic on her face made him laugh. She raced ahead and was soon engaged in a lively exchange with Kaden.

As Nic watched them bickering like brother and sister, he acknowledged his earlier jealousy had been unfounded but not surprising. Jealousy had consumed him each time he'd seen her with another guy at school. Late at night, he'd lain in bed imagining talking with her, touching her.

He wanted to confess everything. To tell her how beautiful she'd been. To erase the self-doubt he'd seen in her eyes. He wanted to tell her how madly in love he'd been. How much he'd wanted her, even then. He hated lying, but he couldn't risk her finding out about Rachel.

After pouring a glass of chardonnay for Lauren and grabbing two beers from the fridge, he walked out to the patio to join his friends. Because yeah, despite everything, these two people, who knew the real Nic, *were* his friends. And for the first time in his life, he was hosting a dinner party.

Lauren sat at the table sipping her wine, admiring Nic and Kaden's rearview as they stood at the grill. Kaden was a little taller than Nic and outweighed him by about thirty pounds of muscle. But for her at least, there was no contest. Nic won hands down. After his shower, he'd changed into a pair of faded jeans that were obviously old favorites. While he chatted with Kaden about the art of proper grilling, she philosophized to herself about the art of wearing denim and determined that Nic was indeed a master. Admiring the way the material molded his butt and cupped his package, she flashed back to what they'd done that afternoon.

Nic turned and caught her ogling his posterior. His knowing look caused heat to flood her cheeks, and she had to stifle an embarrassed laugh. After setting their plates on the table, he took a seat beside her. "A penny for your thoughts."

"Oh I think these thoughts are worth more than a penny." She loved the crooked smile he wore whenever she teased him.

He curled his hand around her nape. "Would you consider this appropriate payment?" His mouth descended on hers in a highly charged kiss, shooting her arousal from mild to extreme in a matter of seconds.

The kiss reverberated throughout her entire body, her inner walls clenching tightly. With his mouth he mimicked his earlier actions, but it wasn't enough. She wanted him again, deep inside. "More."

Kaden coughed, reminding them they weren't alone.

Abruptly she pulled away from Nic, her face flaming. She risked a glance in his direction and caught his cocky expression. "Does that meet your price, *chérie*?"

Rat fink.

But that kiss had definitely been worth more than a penny. With a saucy grin of her own, she teased him some more. "You've earned the right to my thoughts, but…"

"But what?"

"Can you handle them? I mean, I don't know if you can live up to your reputation…."

Nic pinned her with his eyes. "So, when you were screaming my name earlier, it was an act? Maybe you're the one who deserves an Oscar."

"Nic!"

"Yeah, something like that," he said, grinning from ear to ear.

"Now, now, children," Kaden interrupted them. "Settle down so Daddy can enjoy his dinner. If you behave, I'll let you go to bed early."

"Yes, Daddy."

"*Oui, papa*," Nic said, looking like a properly chastised little boy.

A moment later, they burst out laughing. Then Nic picked up his glass and raised it in a toast. "To my friends."

As the clinking of glass on glass echoed in the room, Lauren's heart swelled. Tears burned her eyes, but not with laughter this time. He considered her a friend, like Vivian. Even if their relationship were short-lived, she just hoped that when it was over, their friendship would endure.

Nic wiped away the moisture from the corners of her eyes, then gave her the sweetest, most tender kiss she'd ever had. It was the exact opposite of the one he'd given her earlier, but its effect was no less devastating. Her chest tightened almost painfully with an emotion she refused to name. She was going to enjoy this time she had with Nic, no strings attached.

The conversation flowed smoothly throughout the rest of the meal. When was the last time she'd felt so happy and relaxed? As she got up to clear the table and get dessert, Nic's phone rang. He excused himself to take the call in the living room. She turned to Kaden. "One of his hockey friends?"

"They're speaking French, so it must be Rémi Whitedeer, Nic's best friend back home."

"Does Rémi visit often?"

"No. He stays in Montréal to keep an eye on Nic's… uh… he stays in Montréal." Kaden averted his gaze.

Keep an eye on Nic's what? She'd never seen more than cursory information about Nic's past in any articles about him. It was as if his life started when he'd arrived in Hollywood at the age of twenty. Had the lockdown on his personal life been Vivian's idea or his?

He hadn't admitted to knowing her in high school, but it wasn't as if his name were John Smith. And she'd never mistake his smile or his deep blue eyes. He was hiding something—or someone—in Montréal. Something connected to the phone call he'd received during the photo shoot? He'd spoken French then too. And what about the emergency that had forced him to leave D.C. so quickly?

Nic wouldn't cheat on a wife or a girlfriend. Her mouth filled with the taste of acid, like she'd swallowed a vat of processing chemicals. God, she hoped she was right about that. But could he be hiding a child? Whatever it was, she had to know. He'd said she was a friend, but he didn't trust her fully yet.

To gain his trust, she'd have to break down his walls. Something she'd accomplish, even if it took a battering ram.

Installing cameras in Nic's loft had been a brilliant idea. She could monitor him anytime she wanted. And since she recorded everything, she could enjoy the show whenever it pleased her. And please her, he did.

Although watching Nic shower was usually the highlight of her day, watching his first day back at the loft had, in many ways, been even better. Using the remote control, she paused the video on an image of Nic and leaned back in the chair. She didn't have time right now to watch the entire footage, but what she had seen so far was a nice appetizer.

When the photographer followed Nic into the bathroom, fury had consumed her. How dare the bitch ruin Nic's homecoming? But then he'd seen her love note on the mirror and forgotten all about the whore.

The look on his face when he'd seen her blood vow—pure passion. Her heart stuttered just thinking about it. She couldn't wait to have all that passion focused on her.

Maybe using her own blood hadn't been the best idea, but she wasn't worried. By the time the police figured things out, she'd have Nic tucked away in their new home. She chuckled. He hadn't appreciated the blood as much as the words, but she'd had to do it. She needed to poke at his weaknesses every now and then. To toughen him up.

To let him know she was in charge.

He wouldn't be upset for long though. When he learned she'd taken care of the situation with Summer, he'd be thrilled. It was one more proof of her dedication, of her devotion. He truly had no idea of the extent of her love, how far she'd go to have him… her way.

Summer had dared to trick her and hurt Nic, but the lying bitch wouldn't be hurting anyone ever again. Once more, the cameras had come in handy. Watching the video of the night Summer had given him the Rohypnol, bile had burned her throat. But she'd forced herself to watch it all. Because she'd needed to know. And she'd been right. Even drugged, Nic had resisted Summer's pathetic attempts at seduction.

The idiot had thought that because she was young and had big boobs, Nic would be slobbering all over himself to have sex with her. But Nic wasn't interested in a child; he wanted a woman. And, a true woman, she'd taken care of her lover's little problem.

And it had been a pleasure.

She opened the journal resting on her desk and turned to the next free page. After jotting down the latest developments, she inserted the memory card from her camera into her laptop. Moments later, she was staring at the photo she'd taken of Summer this afternoon. She had big plans for this picture. It would serve as a warning to the other bitch who kept getting in her way. She printed off a copy and glued it into her journal.

After launching the photo editor, she pulled up her favorite wedding picture. Using the eraser function, she carefully removed her husband's neck, head, and hair. She opened her favorite shot of Nic, the one where he sported a black Armani suit and tie along with a silk shirt. Carefully, she selected his head and copied it. Returning to the wedding photo, she pasted it on top of the body.

When she was done, she examined the image from different angles. The differences in body shape were barely noticeable. This would be another photo to add to the collection in her journal. Anytime she felt sad or lonely, she'd flip through the pages. The images reminded her of her goal, of why she was working so hard, of what she was willing to do for Nic. Of how far she was willing to go to be with him.

Later, she'd review the video to see how the rest of his first day back home had gone. Watching him made her feel closer to him, less alone. She wanted to be with him, taking care of him. The photographer shouldn't have touched Nic, even to play nursemaid when he cut his hand on the mirror. The bitch shouldn't even be in his home. How she wished she'd had time to wire the first floor as well as the upstairs. She hated not knowing what they were saying or doing out of camera range.

As she flipped back to the photo of Nic lying on the ice, covered in blood like a gunshot victim, a smile tugged at her lips. If the photographer didn't get out of the picture soon, Nic would get another surprise. One guaranteed to make him seek her out. He'd need her like she needed him. He'd crave her like she craved him. He'd be hers like she was his.

Till death us do part.

CHAPTER 13

Nic parked his butt in the armchair facing the wall of windows and brought the phone to his ear. "Rémi. Is Rachel okay?"

"She's fine, now that you're out of the hospital. By the way, you owe Kaden. If he hadn't called in regular reports, Rachel would have dragged me out there to check on you."

Which would have been a fucking disaster. The last thing he needed was for Rachel to show up in L.A. "Sounds like I'll have to give the man a raise." How many was that today? Two? Lucky bastard.

"Rachel said you had some company."

"Yeah." He couldn't keep the grin out of his voice. She'd surprised him today. "Turns out I knew Lauren in high school."

"No way."

"Yeah way. But I told her I didn't remember her."

"Why hide it?"

"If I admit I'm that guy, she'll put two and two together. I don't want her to know what I did."

"No one forgets someone who looks like her."

"She looked a lot different."

"You had the hots for her even then, didn't you?"

"Fucking A. I trailed after her like Mary's little lamb."

Rémi chuckled. "I would have paid some serious cash to see that. So, what happened?"

"The girl never noticed me." Then he remembered her outburst. "Funny thing is, she says *I* never noticed *her*."

"Sounds like a case of stupid teenager-itis."

"Yep, but I've grown a brain since then." He wasn't going to blow things with her this time. After all, how many people got a second chance?

"You're Nic The Lover. If anyone can make this work, you can."

He'd do his damnedest. "I'll try."

"As the great Yoda once said: Do or do not. There is no try."

Nic smirked. "Your geek is showing."

Rémi barked out a laugh, but then his voice turned serious. "A lot of shit's been coming your way lately."

"And it just keeps on keeping on."

"Something new happen?"

Nic paused and rubbed his eyes. His pulse pounded behind the sockets every time he thought about it. "Bitch left a blood message on my bathroom mirror."

"Shit. How did she get in?"

"Same way she got in when she brought me home from the bar." He blew out a breath. "She got my key and the code to the security system. I'm going to find her, Rémi." Nic got up and started pacing. He usually thought better on his feet.

"What's your plan?"

"I was hoping you could help me with that." Rémi had gone to cop school, had even worked on the Montréal Police Force for a few years. "Got any pointers?"

"To catch a perp, you need to think like one. You need to understand her motivation."

Nic considered this for a moment. "So, to figure out where Summer might be hiding, I need to understand how drugging me benefited her?"

"Was there anything new or different going on in her life?"

"She said something about being offered the lead in *Alone No More*. Except that can't be right. They'd want an A-list actress for that role."

"Maybe not. Call the casting director." After a short pause, Rémi asked, "Are you involved in this movie?"

"I was offered the male lead." Maybe Rémi was onto something. He completed the circuit of the room and started in the opposite direction.

"Maybe she thought she'd have a better chance at getting the part if you two were an item."

"Could be, but Hollywood doesn't usually work like that. Couples change partners too often."

"Or maybe she wanted to blackmail you into helping her get the part."

Nic scratched his cheek and replayed that evening in his mind. "Summer made or received a call while I went to get our drinks."

"Did the police pull her phone records?"

"If they did, they didn't tell me. I'll talk to Kaden about it. He might have some contacts who can help."

"While they're doing that, ask them to find the last place her phone registered with the network."

"The last place it what?"

"Forgot you were a technophobe," Rémi said, the sarcasm in his voice as thick as his head.

"Cyborg," Nic shot back. How he missed slinging barbs with Rémi.

"Lame, my man. Very lame. I'll explain it so even a kindergartener could understand. But just in case, try to remember the words so you can repeat them to Kaden."

Nic laughed. "Asshole."

"Fuck, it feels good to jerk your chain. Here goes: a cell phone has to tell the network where it is so the network can find it when a call comes in. Every so often, it sends a message to the cell towers saying 'I'm here.' But if you know what carrier Summer used, they can probably look it up in their database. It'll at least give you a general location to start searching."

"Okay, that makes sense." *Sort of.*

A few minutes later, Nic flipped his phone closed and stared out the window. The sun was starting its descent into the ocean, bathing L.A. and his living room in a colored light. He'd finally get to share this view with Lauren. But not tonight. Tonight, they had to discuss *the plan.*

As usual, Rémi had come through for him. He had a rough plan now, well at least step one. He'd figure out the rest once they started getting some answers.

Feeling a hundred pounds lighter, he walked into the kitchen. A smile broke out on Lauren's face when she saw him. "Kaden's girlfriend sent these for dessert." She pointed to a plate of brown squares.

"I haven't had homemade brownies in years. Make sure you thank Beth for me," he said to Kaden.

"Want some coffee with them?" The tone of her voice caught his attention. When he turned to her, she wore a dazed expression, as if remembering something. Something that turned her on.

"I drink tea at night. There's some Earl Grey in the cupboard above the stove."

"Kaden? Coffee?"

"I'd love a cup of Earl Grey." When he saw her startled expression, he laughed. "What?"

She glanced at his hands, then at Nic's. "I'm picturing the two of you with your big paws trying to hold itty bitty teacups."

Nic laughed. "Don't worry *chérie*, I've got mugs."

"So Nic," Kaden said after Lauren put a kettle on to boil. "Want to discuss our plan for finding Summer?"

He nodded. "Rémi had some ideas that might help us. Do either of you know anyone who works for a phone company?"

"My ex-girlfriend works at AT&T. Why?" Kaden asked.

"Summer used her phone that night at the bar. If we get her records, we could find out who she spoke with." Nic pulled out his cell phone and gave

Kaden Summer's contact information.

"I'll call my ex tonight and see if she can help. At the very least, she should be able to tell us the carrier for this number."

"Rémi also said they could give us the location where the phone last registered."

"If it's an AT&T number, she should be able to get that information."

Nic bit back a sigh of relief that he wouldn't have to go through Rémi's explanation and sound like a fool.

The sound of the kettle's whistle startled them all. Lauren jumped up to prepare the tea. When she stretched to reach the cups on the second shelf, her shirt rose, giving Nic a peek of her smooth belly. Memories of kissing that silky flesh—the feel of it against his lips, the taste of it on his tongue—suddenly made his jeans a whole lot tighter.

She piled cups and plates on a tray and brought it to the table. After pouring the tea, she bit into her brownie and moaned, "Oh God, Kaden." Nic barely held back a snarl. Those were not words he ever wanted to hear coming out of her mouth. "These are delicious."

Nic tasted the brownies to see what all the fuss was about. Rich chocolaty sweetness hit his tongue as soon as he sank his teeth into the chewy square. All he could manage to do was mumble, "Wow," before taking another large bite. "I'm saving a few of these for breakfast. The thought of these along with a good cup of strong coffee makes me—"

Lauren interrupted him with a strange choking sound. "*Chérie*? Are you okay?"

"I'm fine," she croaked, then covered her mouth with a napkin, and cleared her throat. "I'll put some of these aside for you." She turned her face away, but he could see the color blooming on her cheeks. He'd give more than a penny to know what was going on it that beautiful, creative mind of hers. He looked at Kaden and arched a brow in question. His response was an eye roll and a head shake. But the grin that split across Kaden's face ruined the effect.

Shit. Time to get them all back on track. "Any other ideas?"

"Women usually go out in groups, and if Summer goes to this bar often, the bartender might know her friends. And one of them might know where she is," Lauren said.

A smile broke out on his face. "You're brilliant. She told me she has a roommate."

"So tomorrow we go talk to the roommate. You know where she lives, right?"

"Yeah." He turned away from Lauren only to come eyeball to eyeball with Kaden's how-you-going-to-explain-that look. Christ, he probably had *busted* stamped across his fucking forehead.

Then like only a true buddy would, Kaden spoke up and saved his ass. "I drove her home after the footprint ceremony." Nic blinked his eyes in silent thanks. By the time this was all finished, he wouldn't just owe the man a few raises; he'd owe him a freaking promotion.

"O-*kay*." Lauren's gaze shifted between the two of them. "We'll head over there right after breakfast."

As Nic gazed at the woman by his side, his thoughts turned to enjoying a breakfast of brownies and coffee with her. Their eyes locked.

Then he thought about enjoying *her* for breakfast. And grinned.

After their dessert and tea, Nic and Lauren excused themselves to get ready for bed. Nic had been unable to cover up some jaw-cracking yawns. Between dealing with the residual weakness from the drugs, finding the bloody message, having sex with her, and working through a plan to find Summer, it had been a hell of a day for him. Nic's normally tan face was pale and drawn with fatigue. But he still looked delicious enough to eat in the black silk boxers he wore instead of pajamas.

Lauren pulled back the covers and patted the mattress. "Come on, sweetie. Climb in. I won't try to jump your bones tonight." Nic looked crestfallen. "Hey, what's wrong?"

"I was kind of counting on a little breakfast."

"What are you talking about, Nic? We just finished supper." She reached up to touch his forehead. Maybe he had a fever or was having some sort of hallucination. But before she could touch him, Nic grabbed her wrist and brought it to his lips.

"A midnight snack then?"

"Nic." She was starting to get worried.

He released her wrist and fell onto the bed. "I'm kidding. When I saw you bite into the brownies, the face you made, all I could think about was having—" He cut himself off. "Never mind. It's stupid."

Lauren stilled. When he'd talked about brownies and coffee, her thoughts had definitely headed south. Had he been thinking the same thing? "Having what?" she whispered hoarsely.

He looked away and swallowed hard. "All I could think about was waking up and having *you* for breakfast. But I can't wait that long."

"Oh God." She practically threw herself on top of him. "I was sure after everything you'd been through today, sex would be the last thing on your mind. I didn't want you to feel pressured." She shook her head and buried her face against his chest. It sounded so stupid when she said it out loud.

He cocked an eyebrow at her. "Do you doubt my stamina?"

"After this afternoon? How could I?"

"Okay, then." She cracked up at the look on his face. "First you doubt my endurance and now you're laughing at me? What is this, pick on Nic day?"

"I'm not laughing at you." She grinned widely. "You just looked so cute, like a disgruntled little boy."

In one swift move, he flipped her onto her back and leaned over her, covering her. With deliberate movements, he laced their fingers and locked her hands above her head. Slowly, he lowered his face to hers. "Do I still look *cute*?"

God, no. He looked devastatingly dark and dangerous, like in his camo pictures. He'd gone from cute little boy to deadly stranger in a matter of seconds. She didn't know where the real Nic was in all of this, but she didn't care. Todd had been nothing but gentle with her, and she'd never dared to tell him she wanted something a little rougher, a little harder. Instead, she'd explored all those feelings, all that excitement in her fantasies. Fantasies that featured Nic in the starring role. And here he was, in the flesh, in her hands. A shiver ran up her spine and seeing it, one corner of his mouth rose in a snarl.

"Like this, do you?"

Oh, yeah. Unable to resist the lure of his mouth so close to hers, she arched up to try to kiss him. He shook his head. "Uh-uh. Tonight, I'm in charge." After letting go of her hands to tear off the long T-shirt she'd worn to bed, he reached down to remove her panties. When they got tangled in her legs, he ripped them apart and threw them over his shoulder. "I'll get you a new pair. Hell, I'll get you a dozen."

Heat flared in his eyes as he grabbed her hands again and held them above her head. She gulped, but not in fear. Somehow he'd been handed the screenplay to one of her more hardcore fantasies—the one where he held her captive and at his mercy. Thrilled, she moaned and writhed on the smooth sheets. Every change in his eyes, every variation in his voice, had her catapulting through a myriad of emotions. How could she ever give him up at the end of the week?

He claimed her mouth in a deep, soul-searing kiss. This afternoon, she'd wanted to possess him, but now he was possessing her. And she was giving him everything she had, everything she was. An ache began deep inside her and soon she was begging him to be filled, claimed. "Nic! Please… take me."

"No."

Her brows popped. He couldn't deny her now. His long hard erection pressed against her stomach, evidence he wanted her as much as she wanted him. "No?"

"No."

"Have sex with me?"

"No."

Sometimes Todd had liked dirty talk in bed. Maybe Nic wanted that? She met his piercing gaze and in her most seductive voice said, "Fuck me."

He bared his teeth. "I will *never* fuck you."

What the heck did he want her to say? "I'm dying here. I need you inside me." His dark, lust-filled expression turned soft as his eyes lingered on hers. What did he see there? He didn't want to fuck her, and he didn't want to have sex. A lightbulb flickered on in her head. Pushing past the emotions strangling her, she whispered, "Make love to me."

"Yes."

Thank God.

Screwing up her courage, she told him what she'd never dared say to Todd. "Hard and fast."

Without a word, he flipped her over onto her stomach and pulled her hips up until she was on her knees, spread wide.

She watched out of the corner of her eye as he pulled out a condom and covered himself. His large hand pressed on her back until her face met the pillow that smelled of his cologne. She inhaled deeply, the scent flooding her with moisture. A shudder roared through her as his warm tongue took a long, slow swipe.

"Better than brownies," he groaned, before gripping her hips tightly and plunging his cock into her. They moaned in unison. After holding still long enough for her to adjust to his size, he began to move. He pulled out so only the tip of his cock remained inside her, and then he pushed slowly until he was all the way inside, as far as he could go. His fingers on her hips held her in place, keeping her from pushing back and accelerating the rhythm. Then he began alternating long slow glides with short fast ones. Nine long, one short, eight long, two short....

She caught onto the pattern. In only a few more cycles, he'd be pounding into her. With each deep stroke, the sensations intensified and her anticipation ratcheted up a few notches. Oh God. She wasn't sure she'd make it to the ten short, fast strokes.

Nic was giving her everything she wanted, what Todd had never given her. Gritting her teeth, she braced her arms and held on for the ride.

"Oh God, oh God, oh God!" As he pistoned into her, his fingers tightly gripping her hips, the meaning of the expression *balls deep* became perfectly, exquisitely clear. It didn't matter that she couldn't catch her breath; she'd already died and gone to heaven.

His strokes changed, deepening, filling her. "Feel me inside you. Feel how deep I am."

"More."

"Your wish is my command." She gasped. Those words—they were straight out of her bar fantasy. Was she dreaming? A stinging smack on her butt brought her back to reality. At the same instant, he plunged deep inside her, deeper than ever before. The momentary flash of heat and the full-body pleasure of his penetration flung her over the edge, into a level of bliss she'd never before known.

As wave after wave of sensation reverberated throughout her entire body, he continued to hold her tight, pounding into her, never letting up on the speed or power of his strokes. Even before the contractions inside her completely subsided, his balls slapping against her swollen lips sent her over the edge again. This time he joined her. With a loud groan and a final tremendous push that sent her sprawling, he came too, collapsing on top of her, his lips pressed against her neck.

Without a doubt, this experience surpassed even her best Nic fantasy. As a smile curved her lips, she thought he'd be surprised to learn that he'd outdone himself.

Nic awoke to bright sun on his face, a warm body in his arms, silky hair tickling his chin, and the beautiful sound of Lauren's soft snores in his ears. A slight twist of his body placed his nose in the crook of her neck, where the aroma of her apple-scented perfume caused him to harden. It had been clear from the start that Lauren was dangerous for him. But until last night, it had been only the danger of her discovering the secrets of his past. Now the danger was her discovering the secrets of his heart, where she was beginning to take more and more space.

His hand drifted over her waist, gently tugging her closer into the curve of his body. She had the best butt he'd ever seen, all round and tight. The sight of it made him want to… well, do exactly what he'd done last night. A wicked grin curved his lips. His hand moved higher until he was cupping one generous breast, the already hard nipple pressing against his palm as if begging to be squeezed. No problem. A gentle tweak had her wiggling, pushing her ass hard against his groin. His cock soon found a cozy spot between her butt cheeks. The heart-shaped birthmark below her ear was calling out to him. His lips surrounded it and his tongue was about to touch its goal when Lauren's cell phone rang.

One sleepy eye opened and a smile spread across her face. "Are you going to answer your phone?" she asked him, her voice husky.

"It's not mine, it's yours."

"Oh! I better get it. It might be Jason or my parents." He reluctantly let her go but enjoyed the view as she got out of bed and bent over to retrieve the cell phone from her purse. Man, could he possibly get any harder? This had better be a short conversation, or he might die before she came back to bed.

"Vivian." He arched a brow and she shrugged. "Did you like the photos?"

He couldn't stand hearing only one side of the conversation so he motioned to her to come closer so he could listen in too. After climbing back onto the bed, she held the phone slightly away from her ear.

"I'm releasing your photos," Vivian said. "The contest organizers want three for publicity and the festival people want one. You can choose which ones to give them."

"I'll do it today." Nic smiled at the way Lauren's eyes glittered.

"The rest are yours to sell. But, I think I should help you with that." She paused. "I'd hate to see these end up in some paparazzi rag."

"I'd appreciate that."

"I'll send the proofs out to the editors of a few high-end magazines. I'm still not sold on the arena shots, but maybe Sports Illustrated or Men's World will like them."

"Thank you, Vivian. Do you want to talk to Nic?"

"Is he there?"

Taking the phone from Lauren, Nic brought it to his ear. "Thanks for helping Lauren."

"Were you having breakfast?"

"No."

"I see." Her voice sounded flat.

"Vivian, what exactly do you see?"

"You're involved with her."

"Do you have a problem with that?"

"Of course not. If she makes you happy… that's what matters. Just be careful. It's better for your image if women think you're still available."

"Will do." *Fuck my image.*

"Are you still determined to bring her to the fundraiser?"

"Yep." Of course, he'd have to ask her first….

"Make sure she gets a gown. Dog tags and cargo pants won't do."

Shit. Vivian was right. "I'll take care of it." After meeting with Summer's roommate, he'd take her shopping.

A flick of his thumb ended the call. At this point, having women think he was still available was the least of his worries.

"Everything okay?" Lauren's big, beautiful blue-green eyes watched him with concern. Something tugged at his heart. He didn't care anymore what Hollywood thought of him. The only person who mattered was lying next to him, her curls spread out on the pillow and her eyes round with worry.

After placing the phone on the nightstand, he stretched out beside her, circling her waist with his arms and laying his head on her chest. The regular beat of her heart and the gentle rise and fall of her breathing soothed him. "Everything's okay, now," he said as he feathered a kiss on her slightly curved stomach.

"I'll say," she answered and although he couldn't see her smile, he could hear it in her voice. If he lived through the mess he'd made of his life, he'd do whatever he could to keep this woman who made him happier than anyone else ever had. Even in high school, he'd known she was the one for him, but he hadn't known how to make it happen. All these years later, he still didn't know how, but he'd be damned if he didn't figure it out.

Lauren craned her neck toward his clock-radio. "What time is it, anyways?"

"Time for breakfast." Peals of laughter filled the air as he nibbled her stomach, her ribs, the sensitive undersides of her breasts....

Oh yeah. Nothing like a little breakfast in bed to start the day right.

CHAPTER 14

Lauren watched with avid interest as Nic ate his breakfast of champions—brownies and coffee made with freshly ground Starbucks beans. The rapturous expression on his face had her wanting to drag him back to the bedroom. She could definitely get used to waking up with him.

He wiped his mouth with a napkin. "After we drop by Summer's apartment, what do you say we go shopping?"

"Sure. What do you need?"

"I don't need anything. But you need a dress."

She glanced down at her mid-thigh navy shorts and matching blue and white tank top. "What's wrong with this?" But as she asked the question, she smacked her forehead in the universal sign for *Duh!* "Oh, right. This is way too casual." How could she have been so stupid? Of course Nic didn't want to run around town with her dressed like a soccer mom.

Nic's eyes widened. "Too casual to talk to Summer's roommate?"

"To be seen with you." She averted her eyes. "I should stay here and you go with Kaden." After the flight to L.A., she didn't have any money left to buy new clothes.

"There's nothing wrong with what you're wearing." His eyes lingered on her breasts. "In fact, I *really* like that tank top."

She took a moment to feast her eyes on the man sitting in front of her. "I have to admit, I'm a big fan of your jeans."

"These old things?" he said in a high-pitched voice.

She chuckled. "So, *why* do I need a dress?"

Nic sipped his coffee, then took her hand. "*Chérie*, I'm attending a fundraiser for the Make-A-Wish Foundation tomorrow night, and I'd like you to be my date."

She pulled her hand out of his grasp. "An occasion like that would require a formal gown. But I can't afford one right now."

His mouth curved into a sexy lopsided smile. "You're so freaking sweet. Don't worry, it's my treat."

"I can't let you do that."

"Why not? You wouldn't even need an evening gown if it weren't for me." He pulled her hand to his mouth and kissed the inside of her wrist, making her pulse rage. "Say yes. Say you'll go with me."

The thought of being seen in public with him, schmoozing with the who's who of Hollywood, had her practically shaking in her sandals. But this was part of being with someone like Nic, wasn't it?

"Think of it as an investment in your career. You'll get to meet a lot of potential clients."

He was right. But even more than that, he really seemed to want her to go with him. "I'll go. And I'll let you buy me a dress, but that's it."

Before she'd even finished speaking, Nic bounded out of his chair and scooped her up in his arms. As she laughed, he twirled her around, grinning from ear to ear.

When he set her down on the counter, their gazes locked. The dancing lights in his eyes and the tiny laugh lines that surrounded them mesmerized her. He looked happy, really happy. Who would believe someone like him could be so easily pleased? Her heart full, she leaned into him, feathering small butterfly kisses along the seam of his lips. He hugged her close and deepened the kiss.

"Are you two at it again?" Kaden asked from the doorway to the kitchen.

Nic leaned his forehead against hers and grinned. "We probably should get going."

"Yeah." But the only place she wanted to go was to bed. With him.

Nic helped her off the counter. As they walked through the living room, she grabbed her purse. Earlier, she'd put her smaller point-and-shoot camera in it, along with a spare battery pack, and she had a couple extra flash cards in the pockets of her shorts. She smiled up at Nic; she was ready for anything.

Hand in hand they walked out while Kaden set the alarm and locked the door. They took the elevator to the garage. When they stepped out, she saw a Nissan convertible sports car and an Audi SUV. Neither was something she'd imagined Nic owning.

"We'll take the SUV." Nic unlocked the doors and helped her into the passenger seat while Kaden took the back.

"I expected your garage to be full of toys." As soon as the words were out of her mouth, heat rose to her cheeks. She adjusted the air conditioning vent to hit her full in the face.

Nic laughed. "I have better things to spend my money on."

While Nic backed the car out and exited the garage, she wondered where he *did* spend all his money. It wasn't on his home or his cars. They were nice, but not millions-of-dollars nice.

As they drove through Nic's blue-collar neighborhood, she saw trucks double-parked as men with arms the size of her legs unloaded crates and ran them into the shops lining the streets. The sidewalks were crammed with harried moms and their small children rushing in and out of stores, arms loaded with purchases of meat, milk, and bread. Not a Gucci or Louis Vuitton in sight.

Within minutes, Nic parked the car in front of a low-rise building, and Lauren realized that he and Summer were practically neighbors. She put on a brave face and got out of the SUV.

Inside the lobby, Nic pressed the button to ring Summer's apartment. A moment later, they heard a buzz, and Kaden opened the security door. They climbed the stairs to the second floor, and Nic led the way to a door at the end of the hall and knocked. A tall brunette flung the door open, her squeals filling the hall. "Oh my God! It's really you."

Nic inclined his head. "You must be Tammy."

"Come in." With her hand, she indicated the living room.

Once they were all settled, Nic made the introductions. "I need to ask Summer a few questions, and I'm hoping you know where she is."

Tammy's hands went to her mouth and for a moment she looked stricken. "I heard what happened on TV. I can't believe Summer would do something like that."

"Have you spoken to her recently?"

"No. I've been out of town on a movie shoot. I just got back last night."

"Did she call you last Thursday night?"

She shook her head. "I haven't spoken to her in… hmm, let me see. It was a few days after the footprint ceremony. She told me she went with you and had a great time at the after party. Then the two of you—"

Nic cut her off. "Do you have any idea where she might be? At a friend's? Family? Her parents'?"

"The police asked me that, too." Tammy sighed and looked down at her hands. "I know she's not with her parents because the police already checked. And a couple of her friends have called me asking if I'd heard from her lately."

"Any boyfriends?" Kaden asked.

Amused, Lauren watched as Tammy became aware of Kaden. Her features brightened and her gaze traveled the length of him. "Nic's the only boyfriend she's ever mentioned."

Nic started coughing, and Lauren's head snapped back in his direction. "Are you okay?"

He nodded. Once he'd regained his breath, he asked in a strangled voice, "She said I was her *boyfriend?*"

"Yeah, after the ceremony, when we talked on the phone. She told me you two were dating."

Now it was Lauren's turn to experience some respiratory issues. Her chest felt like a boa constrictor was wrapped around it. Squeezing, preparing her for its next meal. With a finger, Nic turned her face until they were eye to eye. "I was *never* Summer's boyfriend."

She stared into his intense blue eyes. He held her gaze, unwavering. And she felt it. Deep in her heart, she knew he was telling the truth. But God, this whole situation was giving her the creeps. She nodded, and then flicked her eyes to the door, praying he'd get the hint.

"Listen, Tammy. We've got to run. If Summer contacts you, please let us know." He gave her Kaden's number, and they made a quick exit.

"I'm so sorry, Nic," Lauren said as they were getting back in the car. "I needed to get out of there. Hearing how Summer spoke about you…." She let her voice fade, unable to complete the thought.

Nic covered her knee with his hand, the warmth soothing her rattled nerves. "Tell me about it. The hair on the back of my neck is still standing up. The woman who jumped me at the footprint ceremony said the same thing."

"At least now we know Summer didn't call Tammy that night. Our best bet is getting her phone records."

Nic glanced at Kaden in the rearview mirror. "Any luck with that?"

"Not yet. I'm waiting for a text with the info."

"Okay, so for now, we concentrate on more enjoyable things."

Kaden leaned forward. "Oh, yeah? What's that?"

Lauren smiled at Kaden over her shoulder. "We're going dress shopping." If she hadn't been staring at him, she would have missed the tortured look in his eyes. As Jason would say, this was going to be *wicked* fun.

❧ ❧ ❧

As Nic drove along Wilshire Boulevard, he remembered the first time he'd come to Beverly Hills. The architecture, the vegetation, even the people had seemed so different from anything he'd known before. Like most tourists, he'd expected to see a star on every corner. People forgot that places like Beverly Hills and Hollywood weren't just cities on a movie set; they were real towns where real people lived their lives.

"Oh my God, Nic." Lauren pointed to the left. "That's the hotel in *Pretty Woman*."

"Yep."

"So, this is…" She trailed off when he turned right. "You're taking me shopping on Rodeo Drive?" Nic had to smile. She sounded excited and terrified at the same time.

"Where did you think I'd take you? You can't visit L.A. and not shop here." She shot him a small smile, her eyes as round as quarters.

After making another right, he headed into the parking garage underneath

Two Rodeo. As soon as he stopped the car beside a valet, Lauren opened her door and jumped out. Kaden laughed. "You chose the right place, Nic. She's already got her camera out." Nic grinned.

Lauren leaned in through the open door. "Are you guys going to sit here all day? Come on."

"We're coming." Outside the car, Nic said to Kaden in a low voice, "While we're here, Lauren's your top priority. Don't let anything happen to her, not even a catty comment from a salesperson. Got it?" Lauren's earlier comment about *Pretty Woman* had brought to mind some potentially uncomfortable scenarios.

"No one will get the chance to even look at her the wrong way."

Nic nodded, satisfied. In full bodyguard mode, Kaden was a force of nature. "Let's go before she starts bouncing off the walls."

They caught up with Lauren in front of the brass elevator that would take them up to street level. She shifted her weight from leg to leg until the door opened. She caught him with one hand and Kaden with the other and, like a tugboat pulling a cruise ship into port, dragged them into the small space. Immediately, she began jabbing buttons on the control panel. "Finally," she sighed when the doors began to close. Nic bit his lip to keep from laughing out loud.

Seconds later, the doors opened and she hurried out. Behind her back, he motioned to Kaden to get in front and tugged on her arm to slow her down. "Where do you want to start, *chérie*? Rodeo Drive proper or Via Rodeo?"

She looked at him blankly. "I have no idea."

He pointed up Via Rodeo. "This section is Two Rodeo. Versace and Tiffany are here. Over there," he said, pointing east, "is Rodeo Drive."

Her eyes widened. "Versace?"

"Do you prefer Valentino? That's just up the block."

Lauren grabbed his arm and spun her head around. "I need to sit down for a minute."

Worried, he led her to a bench in front of Tiffany's and knelt in front of her. "What's wrong? Do you need water or something?"

She took a deep breath. "A shopping spree for me is buying a pair of jeans at American Eagle instead of Kohl's." She offered him a shaky smile. "I'm a little overwhelmed."

He sat beside her. "Why don't we window shop for a while? If you see anything interesting, we'll go inside. Sound good?"

"Really good." She leaned forward to kiss him, but before their lips met, she pulled back.

"Why'd you stop?" he growled. Now that she had teased him with the promise of her lips, he couldn't think of anything else.

Lauren rolled her eyes. "Why don't you lay out the rules for me?"

"Rules?"

"You know, the rules about PDAs, what I should wear, what I should say. All that. Vivian would kill me if I did anything to tarnish your image."

His chest felt pinched. Their relationship was so new, so fragile. Maybe she wasn't ready for the pressure yet. He needed to make this as easy for her as possible. "*Chérie*, there are no rules. You can do whatever you want, say whatever you want, wear whatever you want. I like you just the way you are. If you don't want to buy a gown or if you don't want to come with me tomorrow night, that's okay."

Lauren smiled. "Really? I can go to this party in my cargo shorts and kiss you madly on top of a table?"

Nic considered the idea. It had definite possibilities. "Absolutely."

She laughed. "You're so full of it. But seriously, you don't mind if I kiss you right now, right here?"

He wrapped his hand around her neck, pulled her forward and whispered, "Not only don't I mind, I think I might die if you don't."

Her gaze fell to his lips. He tugged her the few remaining inches until their mouths met. He kept the kiss light even though he wanted to push her down on the bench and—

No, this was for her, to reassure her.

She raised her head and said softly, "Thank you. That meant a lot. You mean a lot."

"You mean a lot too." He took a deep breath, willing away the stiffness in his jeans. "Feeling better?"

She bounded off the bench. "Yep, let's go." Laughing, he steered her toward Rodeo Drive. If she agreed, he'd love to see her in a slinky Valentino gown and heels. And, of course, he owed her some new panties. *Christ*, could he get through seeing Lauren trying on sexy lingerie without backing her into a corner?

Kaden took point position as they strolled along the sidewalk. After many exclamations, questions and quick kisses, they ended up in front of Valentino, where Lauren studied the window display. She craned her neck to see past the mannequins to the back of the store. He took her hand and placed a soft kiss on her palm. "Do you want to go inside?"

She chewed her lip for a moment, then nodded. Kaden opened the door for Lauren, and Nic followed her inside. He held her back for a moment, giving Kaden time to make sure the store was secure. When Kaden nodded, Nic pointed to the men's section. "I'll wait over there."

As he watched Lauren wander toward a rack of dresses, a saleswoman approached him. She smiled and offered her hand. "Mr. Lamoureux, my name is Bridget. It would be my pleasure to assist you today. Are you interested in something for yourself?"

"For my girlfriend, actually. She needs a formal gown, shoes, handbag—the whole package."

Bridget peered behind him. "Is she the pretty brunette?"

"Yes, that's Lauren. And the big blond guy? He's her bodyguard."

She took one glance at Kaden and swallowed hard. "Okay. I'll make sure she finds everything she needs. Would you like to have a seat?" She indicated three plush chairs at the back, arranged around a low table.

Nic stretched out in one of the armchairs confident that Lauren was in good hands. While he waited, another associate brought him a cup of Starbucks. Did everyone know about his addiction? *Who cares*, he thought, taking a sip of the rich brew. After a few minutes, Lauren rushed over, followed closely by Bridget and Kaden. "This shop is fabulous. They have some wonderful gowns."

Nic eyed Bridget's empty arms. "Aren't you going to try anything on?"

Lauren lowered her voice to a whisper. "They're *really* expensive."

He struggled to hold back his grin and settled for a small smile. "*Chérie*, don't worry about the cost." Turning to Bridget, he said, "Please bring the gowns she liked."

As the woman was leaving, he asked Lauren, "What's your shoe size?"

"Seven, why?"

"Bridget, please also bring her some matching shoes in a size seven."

Lauren's eyes bulged. "Shoes too?"

"Come here," he said. "Might as well have some coffee and relax while you wait." With one arm, he pulled her down onto his lap, making her laugh.

"And here I was, all worried about showing you any signs of affection in public," she teased.

"Never be worried about that." He pulled her more tightly against his chest and crushed his mouth down on hers. He thrust a hand in her hair and let the strands flow through his fingers. Her tongue slid against his, making him groan deep in his chest. He loved the taste of her in his mouth and the feel of her in his arms. His cock was as hard as the fucking marble tabletop. Fucking? Tabletop? God, he wanted this woman.

Lauren whispered, "Bridget's back with the gowns."

Shit. As usual, Lauren had eclipsed the world for him. She stood up, grinning as if he'd muttered that out loud. Hell, maybe he had. He crossed his legs at the knee to camouflage the tenting action. "Go." He waved toward the changing room. Was it his imagination or was there more wiggle in her walk than usual? The little minx knew exactly what she did to him. And she loved it.

He took another sip of coffee, then looked up to see Kaden standing like a sentinel with his big arms folded across his chest. After scanning the room, he met Nic's gaze. "You have it bad, man."

"Is it that obvious?"

"As obvious as you winning another Oscar for *Bad Days*."

"Yeah, well." He grinned. "I don't care. I really like her."

Nic heard Lauren's soft laughter coming from the changing area. As he turned, she emerged, a vision in a flowing, curve-hugging black creation that fit like it had been made for her. Drawn by the mixture of joy and apprehension on her face, he rose and met her halfway. "You look outstanding," he said, his voice suddenly hoarse. He ran his fingers along the neckline of the gown until he encountered the dog tags. "But these don't go with this gown."

"What?" Then she looked down at his hand. "I… in all the excitement, I forgot I was wearing them."

He raised her chin until she met his eyes. "It's okay, *chérie*. I understand," he said, making his voice soft.

Her lip wobbled a little and her chest rose as she took a deep breath. "I'll take them off." She pulled the chain over her head and handed it to Bridget. "Could you put this in the changing room?"

"I'll set it on your purse."

Nic took Lauren's hand and twirled her around. "Let me see the b—"

Jesus Christ. The dress was cut low enough in the back to reveal the indentations at the base of her spine. He was torn between wanting to lick his way down to those adorable dimples and wanting to rip his shirt off and cover her up.

She shot him a knowing grin over her shoulder. "I knew you'd like it."

Fuck yeah. "It's beautiful. You're beautiful. And the shoes?" She lifted up the hem of the dress so he could see. The strappy silver three-inch heels made her legs look about a mile long, legs that would look awesome wrapped around his waist.

Bridget approached, holding out a small glittery handbag. "What do you think of this?"

"It's wonderful," Lauren said, reaching for it. Nic watched the women ooh and ahh over the ensemble and had to agree. Lauren looked stunning. She'd have nothing to worry about tomorrow night.

He shot Kaden a grin and joined him. "I have an errand to run, but I want you to stay with Lauren. I'll be right back."

"I'm not real comfortable with that idea."

He knew Kaden took his job seriously, but today, Lauren came first. "I'm just going down to Harry Winston's."

Kaden whistled low between his teeth. "Okay. But if you're not back in ten minutes, I'm grabbing Lauren and we're coming after you."

"Fair enough. But keep her busy. I don't want her to realize I'm gone."

He raced the half block down to the shop. Even though he didn't have the requisite appointment, as soon as he entered the quiet, classy interior, he was greeted enthusiastically by a smiling young man.

"I need something to go with a black gown."

"Diamonds, colored stones, pearls, or gold?"

"Her eyes are a bluish-green so I'm thinking emeralds."

The salesman peered into the display case and pointed to a necklace on his left. "Something like this emerald and diamond drop necklace? The setting is 18K yellow gold and platinum."

"Can I see it? And this one, too."

"You show a fine appreciation for jewelry, sir. Sunset by Harry Winston is a padparadscha sapphire and diamond necklace. The setting is also 18K yellow gold and platinum." He laid the two necklaces on a velvet-lined tray in front of Nic.

Nic eyed both pieces, imagining them around Lauren's neck in place of the dog tags. Either one would look fantastic on her, but which would go better with the dress? The emeralds would bring out the color of her eyes, but the pink sapphires would make her sparkle.

"I'll take the Sunset necklace. And matching earrings."

"Excellent choice, sir." The man artfully gift-wrapped the necklace and earrings. Nic checked his watch. He had to hurry; in about one minute Kaden would come after him. After paying, he raced out of the shop.

He reached Valentino in time to see Lauren emerging from the changing room wearing her shorts and tank. "Got everything you need?" he asked, hiding the bag behind his back.

Lauren's face shone as she indicated her choices. "Yep. Dress, shoes, and handbag. I'm all set."

Nic leaned down to whisper in her ear. "Not quite. Next stop, La Perla?"

She gulped. "Are you kidding? Their lingerie makes mine look like Walmart specials." He nuzzled her neck. "Okay. But, I'm going in by myself."

No. Not okay.

"Hey, don't look so disappointed." She laughed. "I thought it would be more fun to model my purchases for you at home. Alone."

His mouth went dry as the tent in his pants made a comeback. He couldn't think of a more pleasurable way to spend an afternoon than watching a beautiful woman parade around in sexy lingerie. And if there was a bed nearby? Even better.

Excitement and anticipation warmed her blood as she settled onto the comfortable leather couch, a glass of cabernet sauvignon and a bowl of strawberries and whipped cream beside her. Finally, she had a few minutes to finish watching the video of Nic's first night home. With any luck, he'd taken a shower. Watching him soap up his perfect body made her wet. She closed her eyes and brought up the memory of him lathering up until his hands were covered in bubbles, and then using one large hand to stroke his cock, up and down.... That sight drove her wild every time.

After taking a deep breath to slow her speeding heart, she hit play.

Seconds later, the TV lit up, showing Nic going through a stack of photos. She leaned forward and saw he was looking at photos of himself. When he pulled a sexy shot out of the pile and signed it, she frowned. Who was he autographing it for? It had better not be for that bitch Lauren.

A woman appeared in the doorway carrying a glass of something for Nic. She stiffened when she recognized the photographer. "Well, at least she's taking care of him," she muttered. When she heard them chatting about Kaden staying to protect them, she laughed. The bitch might need protection, but not Nic. She was all the protection he needed.

Her laughter abruptly cut off when the hussy sat on Nic's lap and ran her hand down his neck and into his shirt, unbuttoning it. Enraged, she jumped off the couch and got closer to the TV. What the hell was the tramp doing now? She gasped when she saw the woman take his nipple into her mouth. "Bitch! Get your hands off him!" she shouted at the screen.

Nic's bodyguard interrupted them. "Good man," she said out loud. She watched as he took the autographed photo from Nic and left. Returning to the sofa, she took a sip of her wine and prayed the whore would leave too. She really had to do something to get rid of her.

When the woman pulled up her skirt to straddle Nic's lap, she choked on her wine, spewing the red liquid onto the white carpet. Nic rose, the bitch's legs wrapped around his waist, and carried her out of the office. Her heart started to pound, and not in a good way. For a few seconds, the television was blessedly blank, showing only Nic's empty office. Wiping her mouth on the back of her hand, she prayed this would be the end of it. Nic wouldn't do this to her. He *loved* her!

The image on the screen changed to show Nic laying the bitch down on his bed, the big king-size bed he was supposed to share only with *her*. Dread tiptoed up her spine. She had a brief moment of hope when Nic stood up. Maybe he'd changed his mind? But no. Her heart sank when he returned to the bed. They spoke softly, but she could still make out parts of their conversation.

The bitch said, "It's been a long time for me…."

"How long?" Nic asked.

"Over five years."

So the hag hadn't been laid in five years? Didn't surprise her one bit. The only thing that surprised her was that the bitch actually thought Nic was going to end her dry streak.

"Ahh, Nic. You bad boy," she chuckled, picking up the bowl of strawberries, and relaxed against the couch. She selected the biggest, ripest berry, coated it in whipped cream, then bit into it as she watched the bitch take Nic in her mouth. He was toying with the woman, using her the way any man would use a whore; it was clear as day. That's all the bitch was good for: getting him off and then getting out. She couldn't wait for Nic to toss her onto the street.

Oh, what was this? Nic was stopping her? Priceless! The bitch couldn't even give a decent blow job. No wonder she hadn't been fucked in the last five years. She laughed so hard, tears clouded her eyes, blurring the screen. Eager to see the look of horror on the woman's face, she wiped away the wetness.

"No!" she roared, disgusted by what she was seeing on the screen. The woman lay sprawled out on the bed and Nic was servicing her! This was all wrong. Nic was hers, he was supposed to pleasure her, not some no-talent bitch. He *had* to be playing her. *Come on.* The man could have any number of beautiful women. Why would he settle for an overweight loser with stretch marks?

He wouldn't. Nic was her destiny. He was just slaking his needs with the bitch until everything was ready for them to start their future together.

With growing horror, she saw him roll a condom down his ready cock. Her gut clenched as he pushed himself between the bitch's thighs. Her eyes welled as his beautiful body undulated, muscles bunching and stretching. Her tears spilled as his back arched in ecstasy. She hit the stop button.

Nic had betrayed her.

Which left her with a dilemma: She could hate Nic and throw away their future together, or she could forgive him and live the life she'd planned for them. Could she do it? Could she forgive his infidelity? Closing her eyes, she looked deep in her heart. Nic was young. He'd made a mistake. Yes, she could forgive him, but first she'd bring him to his knees. Then she'd make him crawl.

And the bitch photographer had to go.

She'd done some research, and the slut's father was a former Chicago cop who'd raise hell if his daughter disappeared or turned up dead. That wouldn't deter her though. She'd just have to be more cautious getting rid of her than she'd been with Summer. Resigned, she decided to watch the rest of the video. Maybe something they said or did would give her an idea. She'd get the bitch out of the picture and punish Nic at the same time. What was that expression again? Oh, right.

She'd kill two birds with one stone.

CHAPTER 15

Lauren stepped out of the shower and sighed contentedly as she wrapped herself in a huge bath towel she'd heated on the warming rack. She might never be able to afford Nic's shower with its multiple body jets, but she could definitely treat herself to a towel warmer. In two days, she'd already become addicted to that little luxury.

She'd also learned that if she didn't use the Frizz-Ease she'd brought along, the heat and humidity quickly turned her hair into a big humiliating fuzz-ball. After applying the product, she pulled out the hair dryer and began scrunching her curls. As she worked, her mind drifted to the wonderful day she'd spent with Nic.

Starting with shopping on Rodeo Drive, the whole day had been beyond her wildest dreams. Like when they'd driven to Santa Monica to have a late lunch. While Kaden kept watch from a distance, they'd run along the beach, splashing in the water like two teenagers. The sun, the waves, the company—everything had been perfect. She'd felt young and carefree, the world her oyster. Was Nic the pearl hidden inside? She was starting to think so.

Her skin a little dry from the heat and salt water, she opened her purse to get the tube of cream she always kept handy. Reaching inside, her fingers tangled with Todd's dog tags. After slipping them on, she slathered herself with the cream.

With a naughty grin, she opened the box from La Perla and pulled out a sheer lace babydoll. All day she'd imagined Nic's reaction to seeing the lavender wonder. After slipping on the top and panties, she stood in front of the newly installed mirror, twisting and turning to see herself from every angle.

The triangle cup bodice allowed a hint of nipple to show through the lace and the split front exposed her belly. The matching g-string covered the dark triangle between her legs but the skirt of the babydoll revealed more of her butt than it covered. She'd never looked so sultry or felt more sexy.

When she bent over to fluff her hair, the dog tags fell across her face. She flipped them onto her back to get them out of her way, and then straightened, draping all her hair over one shoulder. After a last check in the mirror, she took a deep breath, opened the bathroom door, and joined her lover.

Nic sat leaning against the headboard reading a script. When he saw her, he tossed it and seemed not to notice when the script landed on the floor instead of the nightstand. His gaze fixed on her and his features tightened with lust. She shivered at his hunger.

He launched himself off the bed, advancing on her like a jungle cat. He was naked, hard, and ready—his intensity intimidating. For each step he took forward, she took one back until she felt the cold wall behind her. With nowhere left to go, she lifted her chin and smiled sweetly. "Do you like my surprise?"

"Like it? Jesus, Lauren. You look good enough to eat." He threaded his fingers through her hair and leaned down to kiss her. Her lips parted and he pressed his tongue inside, sliding it along hers, along her teeth. When he took a slow swipe across the inside of her bottom lip, she felt her world tilt. If not for Nic's strong arms holding her up, she would have fallen.

His hands skimmed down her sides and around to the backs of her thighs. He raised her knee, anchoring it on his hip, his fingers tracing up her leg. When he groaned, his hands cupping her butt cheeks, she knew he'd discovered the g-string panties. In a swift move, he lifted her up, pushing her back against the wall.

"Wrap your legs around my waist." His voice was husky with arousal. He thrust his hips, rubbing his cock against her core. She plunged her fingers in his silky hair and moaned as wetness soaked her panties.

He trailed soft kisses from her ear down her neck but then drew back. His face hard, he lowered her until her feet hit the floor. Why had he stopped? "What's wrong?"

Without saying a word, he put his hand against her neck and ran a finger under the chain she wore. He tugged, twisting it until Todd's dog tags fell forward to land in the palm of his hands. "You put them back on."

She raised her gaze to his face. What was going on? "I always wear them."

Sighing, he let them drop against her chest and sat on the bed. He leaned forward and held his head in his hands.

"What's the problem?"

He looked up at her, his eyes sad. "I know you loved your husband, *chérie*. But when we're making love, I don't want him in the bed with us."

Her eyes widened. "I had no idea you felt that way."

"Would you like *me* wearing a gift from a previous girlfriend?"

She'd hate that. She could barely stand his friendship with Vivian. Kneeling in front of him, she took his hand in hers and brought it to her lips. "I'm so sorry."

"You're still hanging on to him. Why?" His gaze was tender, filled with concern.

She sat down on the bed beside him. "I'll tell you, but it isn't pretty."

"*Chérie*, you of all people know my life is anything but pretty. Nothing you say will change how I feel about you."

She palmed Todd's dog tags. "The photo shoot in D.C. when I had you wear them was the only time I've ever taken these off, except to shower."

"It meant a lot to me." He placed his hand on her knee.

She let the dog tags slide through her fingers. "But I'm not wearing them for the reason you think." He furrowed his brow, and before he could ask the obvious question, she said, "To explain this properly, I have to start at the beginning."

He nodded. "Take your time."

Hugging her knees to her chest, she took a deep breath. "I'd known that Todd going to Afghanistan was dangerous, but I never imagined he'd be killed. The day I opened my front door and saw two uniformed men standing there, I couldn't believe he was dead."

Nic ran a hand along her cheek. "It was the same when my mother died." As he said this, she realized how little she really knew about him.

"The first week was terrible, but it wasn't the worst. I barely remember his funeral. But when the shock wore off…" She paused as her eyes welled. "I felt like my heart had been ripped out of my chest, leaving all this emptiness." Tears slid down her cheeks and she looked away, pressing her face against her knees. All the old feelings of helplessness and defeat flooded back.

"*Chérie*, I'm so sorry." Nic raised her chin with gentle fingers. When their gazes met, she saw the sheen in his eyes. "I shouldn't have brought it up. We don't have to talk about this now." When he wiped her cheeks with his thumbs, she leaned into his touch.

She smiled weakly, chest compressed, emotions raw. "No. You were right. I *need* to talk about it."

He wrapped a stray curl around her ear. Taking his hand in hers, she pressed it tightly against her chest. "I cried nonstop until one day, I had no tears left. All that remained was sadness. Sadness for myself and Jason. Sadness for Todd's parents. Sadness for the future Todd and I would never have together. I was sinking in quicksand, and the more I fought, the deeper I sank. I still shake just thinking about it."

She let go of his hand and held hers out to show him the tremors. After a moment, he cupped her hands in his, and brought her fingers to his lips. She gave him a shaky smile. "Only Jason kept me from plunging into depression. I had to pull myself together for him; I was the only parent he had left."

Nic looked away and stared at the wall. "My father suffered from depression. Unlike you though, he couldn't pull himself out."

"It's the anger that did it." She dried the last of the wetness from her cheeks. "I began asking myself questions. What had Todd done to deserve dying alone? What had I done to deserve being widowed so young? What had Jason done to deserve being left fatherless? Why would God hurt us this way?"

"None of you deserved it." Pain and understanding shimmered in his eyes. *Something had happened to him too.*

"I know that now, but at the time, I was so pissed." She jumped off the bed and began to pace. "And do you know what the worst part is?" she asked, shooting him a glance. "Todd wasn't even supposed to be in Afghanistan. Without even *discussing* it with me, he re-upped. He was such an adrenaline junkie that he chose the military over us. I bet Jason and I never even crossed his mind when he was signing those papers."

Nic's eyes widened. "Do you really think that?"

Her shoulders slumped. "I did. I even started thinking that I could have kept Todd home if I'd been a better wife, been more exciting, more adventurous—more like him."

"*Chérie.*" He shook his head. "You're perfect the way you are. If you were my wife, you'd always come first."

She stopped in front of him. "That's the sweetest thing anyone's ever said to me." He pulled her onto his lap and held her as if he'd never let her go. Nic would love the way he did everything—intensely.

After a few moments, he raised his head from her shoulder and frowned. "If you feel this way, why wear his dog tags?"

"Because I am—was—ashamed."

"Of what?"

"I was so angry and hurt that I started to hate Todd, to hate the man I'd loved for so long. It took some time for the wrongness of that to finally sink in. But when it did, I hated myself for feeling that way. I vowed to wear Todd's dog tags as a sign of my devotion to him, of our love for each other."

Nic rubbed lazy circles on her back. "Wherever he is, Todd knows you loved him."

Lowering her gaze, she once again reached down to take the dog tags in her hand. "The first couple of years were hard. I had no husband, no job, and no way to support myself and my three-year-old son, except for a small military widow's pension that didn't even cover the rent."

"What about your photography? Didn't you tell me you went to some fancy college in Seattle?"

"The Art Institute of Seattle." She smiled, pleased he remembered. "I did study photography there, but I'd never worked as a photographer, never worked at all, actually. Since Todd was away so much, we'd decided I'd stay home with Jason."

"So what did you do?"

"I got a job at a local department store taking photographs. The pay isn't great, but the hours are flexible."

Nic tugged one of her curls. "You're one of the bravest women I know. You took a terrible situation and made a life for yourself and Jason. It takes guts to do that, real guts."

"I was pretty gutless on the social side though. My friends, Julie and Sandra, kept asking me to go out with them, to meet new people, but I wasn't ready." Looking at Nic, she grinned. "One day, I saw you in a movie and realized that I wasn't dead, that I could still feel, that I could be happy again."

"You got all that from watching one of my movies?" he asked, arching a brow.

She burst out laughing. "When you walked on screen, all big muscles, killer abs, and to-die-for smile, I thought *I could kiss this man, I could—*" She cut herself off and grinned. "You get the picture. I went on a few dates, but they didn't work out. I wasn't ready to move on to other men. So I focused on Jason and on my photography."

"A wise choice." His words made her smile. *A touch of jealousy wasn't a bad thing.*

She paused, collecting her thoughts. "Looking back on it, I wasn't ready because I hadn't completely accepted Todd's death, and my reaction to it. I loved him, but God knows he wasn't the perfect man I'd made him out to be. I needed to remember who he really was—a young, adventurous, brave, loving husband and father proud to serve his country as a rescue medic." She offered him a small smile. "You helped me realize that, actually."

Nic eyebrows rose in a "who me?" way, making her chuckle. "Yes, you. I spent years comparing every man I met to you, well, at least, what I thought I knew about you."

"You compared other men to me?"

"Is that so hard to believe? You're a great guy. Todd was a good man, but we were young, and we made stupid mistakes."

Nic got a distant look in his eyes that she couldn't read. "Didn't we all?" He shrugged and dropped his eyes to the chain around her neck, fingering it. "What about now? Are you ready to move on?"

She nodded. "I probably should have done this a long time ago, but until now, I didn't have a compelling reason." She breathed deeply once, twice, and pulled the chain over her head.

"*Chérie,*" he said, his voice thick. "Todd was a lucky man to have you."

She pulled him close. "Maybe so. But now, I'm all yours." Her lips touched his and she kissed him, channeling all the emotions swamping her heart. Desire rose, different this time, stronger, deeper, truer. Nic returned her embrace with a fervor and fierceness she hadn't felt from him before.

Nic pulled back and lifted her hand that still held the dog tags. "What do you plan to do with these?"

She rested her forehead against his and sighed. "I'll give them to Jason. They'll mean a lot to him, and I think Todd would be pleased."

He rose from the bed and brought her a small box from the dresser. "If you want, we can put them in here for safekeeping." She held them out, and he slipped them into the box and put it back in the drawer.

As he came up beside her, she spun him around, tumbling them onto the bed in a heap. She smiled, happy in her favorite place—lying full length on her man. But after the long confession, her emotions were running close to the surface. "Make love to me, Nic. I need you," she whispered.

He held her gaze for several long moments, his eyes solemn. As he searched her face, she held her breath, the beating of their hearts the only sound in the room. Finally, a small smile curved his lips. "My pleasure." Threading his fingers through her hair, he pulled her down for a deep, thrilling kiss that stoked the fire burning inside her.

Did she love Nic? She drew back far enough to see his eyes. Eyes that said she was beautiful, sexy, and smart. Eyes that swirled with passion and desire. Eyes that devoured her. She'd loved Todd, but in all their years together, he'd never made her feel the way Nic did. The way he always had. It didn't matter what danger he was in, she couldn't deny her feelings anymore.

Nothing—not even her fears—would get between her and the man she loved.

Nic set a plate of crepes in front of Lauren and smiled at her surprised expression.

"You made me breakfast?"

"It was my turn." He shrugged. "Dig in."

Her cheeks colored slightly and she tugged on her bottom lip with her teeth. He squirmed in his seat and wondered if he'd ever learn not to wear tight jeans around her. "Need something?"

"I'm not sure how to eat a crepe."

"I'll show you." He forked one off the stack and dropped it onto his plate. "Do you like things sweet or really sweet?" he asked, wagging his eyebrows.

"Uh… really sweet."

"Great. That's how I like them too." He picked up the bowl of brown sugar and spooned some onto his crepe in a line down the center. After handing her the bowl, he waited while she did the same. "Fold it in half along the sugar. Now roll it."

Her lips puckered into a pout. "Yours is rolled up all nice and tight. Mine's a sloppy mess."

He laughed. "You'll get the hang of it. Now for the best part." He picked up the syrup and poured a generous amount, then handed her the bottle.

She scooped up a drop that was sliding down the neck of the bottle. As he watched her pink tongue dart out and curl around her finger, licking up the stray drop, Nic's blood pressure spiked. His eyes glazed over as he recalled the feeling of that same tongue curled around his….

Lauren's brows shot up. "This is the good stuff, isn't it?"

Nic blinked, then blinked again, trying to clear the image from his mind so he could focus on her question. "Yep, pure maple syrup from Québec," he said, his voice much raspier than the topic warranted.

"This is so much better than the grocery store crap I have at home." Her mention of home dampened his ardor, reminding him her vacation would be over in just a few short days. He had to find a way to keep her in L.A. Maybe he'd be lucky, and she'd get a call about her photos soon.

"Nic?"

Shrugging away his thoughts, he focused on Lauren. "Sorry, where were we? Oh right. The moment of truth. Cut a piece from the end, but be careful not to let it unroll or all the sugar will fall out." He waited for her to follow his instructions so they could have their first bite together. "Now eat."

As she chewed, her mouth curved into a slow smile. "These are awesome."

Awesomely sweet. He grinned and handed her a glass. "Here have some milk before you go into insulin shock."

He turned as he heard steps behind him. Kaden entered the kitchen, rolled up papers in his hand. "What's that wonderful smell?"

"Nic made breakfast."

Kaden arched a brow but said nothing as he took a seat across the table.

"What?" Nic asked, his tone defensive even to his own ears. Just because Kaden had never seen him do more than crack a beer and open a pizza box didn't mean he *couldn't* cook. It only meant that he *didn't*.

The asshole didn't take the bait though. Kaden just laughed and served himself. Nic ignored him and changed the subject. "So, I spoke with Detective Anderson this morning. They don't have any leads on Summer, but they've decided to go through all my old fan mail."

Lauren froze, the fork midway to her mouth. "Your fan mail? Why?"

"I think they're reaching, trying anything and everything to find clues." She put down her fork, the bite still on it, and took a sip of milk.

"Speaking of clues." Kaden pointed to the papers he'd brought in. "My ex emailed me Summer's cell phone records."

Nic looked up, smiling. This was good news. "Did she figure out where Summer's phone is?"

"Yep. But that part's not so great. Her phone last registered here in L.A. on the day you got out of the hospital, at three ten in the afternoon."

"After we got home," Lauren said. "So, she could have been the one to leave the note on the mirror."

"The records also show that Summer made a call Thursday night at ten forty." A spark of hope ignited in Nic's chest. It fit with the timeline the police put together from the witness statements. Kaden finished preparing his crepe and took a bite. His eyes opened wide and he pointed to his plate. "This is good."

"Thanks. Anyone want coffee?" Nic grabbed three mugs out of the cabinet and the carafe of coffee, then returned to the table. It would take him more than milk to get through this conversation.

Closing his eyes, he inhaled the rich scent, then took a sip. Delicious. When he opened his eyes, Lauren was staring at him, lips parted, a drop of syrup trickling from the corner of her mouth. Unable to resist, he leaned to the side and licked it with his tongue, continuing until his mouth met hers. The taste of crepes on her lips was intoxicating, and he couldn't help tugging on her bottom lip with his own teeth this time. She made a small sound of pleasure that had him hard in an instant.

When he heard a snort, he let go of Lauren's lip and flicked his eyes in Kaden's direction. The man was shaking his head and grinning from ear to ear. He gave Lauren another small kiss, then sat back.

Her cheeks flushed pink and her eyes stayed glued to her plate as she ate her breakfast. She looked so innocent sitting there, flustered from his kiss. There'd been nothing remotely innocent about that babydoll she'd worn last night. He had to stifle a groan. *Christ.* She'd known exactly what it would do to him. He was worse than a horny teenager. Men his age were supposed to have some self-control. But with her, he didn't have an ounce.

"Do you want to call it?" Kaden asked.

"Call what?" He glanced at Lauren, and she wore the same confused look he was sure was on his own face.

Kaden, the bastard, laughed again. "The number Summer called from the bar is in the report. Do you want to try it?"

Nic took a sip of coffee to clear his head. "Yeah." He pulled his phone out of his pocket.

Kaden stopped him. "Let's use mine. The fewer people who have your number, the better." He took out his phone, flipped through his papers, then punched in a number. "I'll put it on speaker."

Within moments, they heard a recorded message. "The number you dialed is not a working number. Please check the number and dial again." They sat in disappointed silence, staring at the phone.

Nic recovered first. "What the fuck does that mean? How can it not be working when we got it from the phone company records?" Seeing Lauren wince, he muttered a quick, "Sorry."

Christ, if she knew how much he swore in his head, she'd probably make him wash his brain out with soap. To keep from digging a deeper hole, he grabbed another crepe, dumped brown sugar on it, rolled it, smothered it with maple syrup, and stuffed a huge piece in his mouth.

Kaden started applauding. "Man, preparing that crepe took you all of twenty seconds. Must be some kind of record."

Lauren who'd been drinking her coffee, snorted. Nic paused in his chewing as her eyes grew wide and she ran, arms flailing, to grab some paper towels off the counter. "Oh God!" she said, laughing. "It went up my nose."

Nic resumed his chewing and swallowed his mouthful as he got up to check on her. "You okay?"

"Yeah, I'll be fine."

"That'll teach you to laugh at your boyfriend," he teased, joining her at the counter.

She coughed not so delicately into a wad of paper towels and then looked up at him. "My *boyfriend?*"

He practically growled at her. "What else would I be? You're my girlfriend, so I'm your boyfriend."

Light danced in her eyes. "Your girlfriend. My boyfriend. I *really* like the sound of that."

"You seem surprised."

"I hadn't thought of us that way."

"Why not?"

She averted her eyes. "You're… who you are, and I'm who I am."

"Exactly." He turned her chin so she had to face him. "You're Lauren James and I'm Nicolas Lamoureux. You're my girlfriend and I'm your boyfriend."

"Well, when you say it like that…." She grinned. "It sounds right."

His hands cupped her cheeks. "It is." He kissed her soft, warm lips.

"Okay, kids. Now that you both know who you are, can we get back to work?" Laughing, they returned to their seats.

"So, what do we know about this number? What's the area code?" Nic asked.

Kaden picked up the report. "305. It says here, that's Miami."

"Do you think your ex can find out which carrier owns that number?" Lauren asked. "Maybe they can tell us if it was a phone with a regular service contract or if it was one of those prepaid throw away phones. We might even be able to figure out where it was purchased."

Nic turned to Kaden and grinned. "You see why I like her?"

"Absolutely," he said, helping himself to another crepe. "While we're on the subject of numbers, did the police trace any of the messages you got from the stalker?"

Nic shook his head. "Not yet."

"Do you still have the second one?"

"You bet. I'm keeping everything."

"Can you forward it to me?"

"Are you thinking that the messages were sent from the number in the records?"

"They might be. We need to cover all our bases."

Nic picked up his phone and forwarded the message to Kaden without opening it. He didn't need to. The words would be etched in his brain forever. *You've been naughty. Lose the bitch.*

"Can you forward it to me too?" Lauren asked. "I'd like to analyze the photo using my editing software. I might see something useful."

He didn't want her seeing it again, but she was right. At this point, they had to follow every lead. "One thing I haven't figured out is how NicsBitch always knows where I am."

Kaden looked up, his mouth full. After chewing vigorously and downing the bite with half a glass of milk, he said, "It's got to be more than simply a case of being in the right place at the right time."

Lauren sat up straight and her eyes widened. "I just thought of something. When Jason started first grade, I got him a GPS-enabled cell phone and put an application on it that lets me know where he is."

"How can I know if there's a tracking tool on my phone?"

Lauren held out her hand and he gave her the phone. "If it's an authorized tool, it'll be in your applications folder or even on your home screen. But if it's real spyware, it won't show up anywhere." She expertly navigated through the menus. "You do have a couple location-based applications including Family Map. I can uninstall them, if you want. Doesn't mean there's nothing stealth though."

Nic caught the glum expression on his friends' faces. "Hey, you two. Don't look so disappointed." He forced optimism into his tone. "This might be a good thing. If there is a spy app on my phone, it's a direct link to the stalker. The detectives can use it to hunt the stalker down. And maybe your ex will come through with some useful information that will make all the pieces of the puzzle fit."

"Right. And let's not forget your fan mail." A grin broke out on Kaden's face. "There's always the off-chance the cops will find *something* interesting in one of those letters."

Nic's fan mail! Oh God. If the police found the letter Lauren had written to Nic a couple years ago, she'd die. He was in his office talking on the phone with Vivian about the location shoot for his upcoming movie, *At Last.* She had the living room to herself, to pace. She cringed. Her letter had described, in graphic detail, one of her Nic The Lover fantasies. What had she been thinking sending him that? With any luck, the police wouldn't go back more than a year, and her guilty secret would stay hidden.

The trill of her cell phone interrupted her self-flagellation.

"Ms. James? This is Helen Combs. I'm the assistant to the editor at *Vanity Fair* magazine. Vivian Carmichael sent us some photos you took of Nic The Lover. We're very interested in your work."

Lauren sucked in big gulps of air and sat down on the couch before she fell down. "You are? I mean, that's great." *Pull yourself together. This is the chance of a lifetime.*

Helen chuckled. "Your style is fresh, and that's what we need. We're relaunching the magazine with a new look in a couple of months, and we think your photographs will suit our new approach."

Lauren could barely believe her ears. Forcing herself to speak in a calm voice, she said, "A relaunch? That sounds exciting."

"We think it would be even more exciting with you on board. But first we'd like to see more of your work. Do you have a portfolio you could send over?"

"Digital or hard copy?"

"Digital's good. Our executive committee will review it and make a decision." Helen gave Lauren her email address and promised to get back to her in a couple of days.

Lauren's heart threatened to pound through the walls of her chest. This was it! Her career was finally taking off, and she owed it all to Nic. She couldn't wait for him to finish his work so she could tell him *Vanity Fair* wanted to buy some photos from their photo shoot. While she was waiting for him, she'd send off her portfolio. She flew up the stairs to the bedroom, grabbed her laptop, and flopped onto the bed.

Lauren James, freelance photographer. It had a certain ring to it, if she did say so herself. Lauren Lamoureux freelance photographer, well, that sounded even better. *No.* She scolded herself for acting like a lovesick teenager. *Don't go there.*

After rummaging through the side pockets of her shorts, she pulled out the paper where she'd written Ms. Combs email address. She addressed the email, attached her portfolio, and added what she hoped was a professional sounding note. Holding her breath, she positioned the mouse over the send button, squeezed her eyes shut, and said a prayer before she clicked. Then she opened her eyes and let out her breath in a puff of air. She'd done it.

Relaxing against the mountain of pillows on Nic's bed, she imagined what her life could be like if this worked out. She'd splurge a little and get better equipment. Jason would get a new bike, and they could get rid of the rusted one they'd bought at a yard sale last year. And maybe, she could finally afford to rent a better apartment or even buy a small house.

The notes of a beautiful song intruded into her thoughts. She turned her head toward the music. It was coming from Nic's cell phone lying on his nightstand. The singer's voice was gruff, mournful. Straining, she made out a few of the lyrics; something about the heavens falling. Curious, she crawled over to Nic's side of the bed and picked up the phone to check the caller ID. The display showed: Rachel Cell.

Who was Rachel? The lyrics weren't familiar but maybe if she had the full song.... Reaching for her laptop, she pulled up the search engine and typed in what she remembered. She read the first hit. Rachel's ringtone was *Sister* by Dave Matthews Band. Thinking back to their year together in high school, she tried to recall if she'd ever heard any mention of Nic having a sister.

When she shifted into a more comfortable position, she landed on something hard. She pulled out the offending object only to discover she'd sat on Nic's phone. Footsteps in the hall warned her that someone was coming. Quickly, she leaned over to put it back on the nightstand.

"Now that's a sight I'll never get enough of," a rough voice said behind her. She flipped her hair out of her eyes and glanced at the door. Nic stood, arms crossed, studiously examining her prominently displayed butt.

Images of their first night together flashed in her mind, making her blush. It had felt so good having him pound into her from behind. Like a cat, she arched her back, hoping to entice him. If she'd had a tail, she'd have waved it, high in the air.

He closed the distance between them with big steps. Within moments he was kneeling behind her on the bed. His hands, warm and firm, cupped her butt. She purred. He groaned, and skimmed his fingers to her hips, yanking her against him. When her butt met his groin, she moaned and clawed the bedspread. The phone clattered onto the wood floor. "What was that?" he asked.

"Your phone," she answered without thinking, her concentration fully on the feel of his hot, hard cock sliding between her butt cheeks. Only a few miserable layers of clothing separated her from heaven.

"Did I get a call?"

Resigned, she let herself fall face first on the bed. The wildcat sex was going to have to wait. Besides, she had news to tell him. "Yeah, it rang. I was going to bring it to you." Sliding off the bed, she picked up the phone and handed it to him. He checked the display and then slipped it into his pocket. "You're not going to call her back?"

"Her?"

Uh-oh. So much for subtlety. Before she could chicken out, she blurted the question she really wanted answered. "Nic, who's Rachel?"

CHAPTER 16

Lauren could actually see the blood draining from Nic's face. His features tightened and all trace of desire left his eyes. His reaction scared her. Maybe she'd been all wrong about Nic. Maybe there was no sister. If he wasn't the man she thought he was, she had to know.

"Come on, Nic. Last night I shared something very private with you. Trust is a two-way street."

Something flashed in the depths of his eyes and he dropped his head. "Rachel's my little sister."

So, she'd been right about that. Thank God. A sister was the least worrisome of all the possibilities that had run through her mind. "I didn't know you had any siblings. Does she live with your mother?"

He shook his head. "Our mother died two years ago."

"Oh, right. I'm sorry." Last night, he'd told her his father suffered from depression. Maybe Rachel was their father's caretaker? That would explain the guilt emanating from him in waves. "She takes care of your father?"

"He's dead too. He died ten years ago."

Lauren's eyes widened. "I'm so sorry. You're so young to have already lost both your parents. It's just the two of you, then?" He nodded, making the reasons for his protectiveness clear. But not why he kept her so secret. "How come I've never heard of her before?"

Nic sat down on the edge of the bed and let out a heavy sigh. His eyes shimmered with tears. Whatever he was going to say wouldn't be good. She sat down and put an arm around his shoulders. "You can trust me."

He cleared his throat, but his voice was still rough when he answered. "Rachel was partially paralyzed in an accident. The only way she can walk is with leg braces and crutches." Nic turned his ravaged face toward her. "Do you understand why I don't want the paparazzi anywhere near her?"

Lauren swallowed and rested her head on his shoulder. "Of course, I do." If the entertainment rags got a hold of this information, they'd stake out Rachel's home to get shots of *Nic The Lover's Paralyzed Sister.* They'd dredge up every detail of what was no doubt a very sad story.

He gave her a quick kiss, more of a peck really, then stood up. His back to her, he said, "We'll need to leave for the fundraiser in about two hours."

For several moments after he left the room, she remained on the edge of the bed. He hadn't told her the whole story. Too much pain and guilt lingered in his eyes.

Retrieving her laptop, she opened up the folder containing scans of photos she'd taken in high school. Most were of Nic, but she'd also captured some of the crowd at various sporting events. Maybe one of the pictures showed Nic's family.

After going through several photos, she found one of Nic carrying a pretty young girl on his shoulders. The girl shared Nic's coloring and bone structure. Sporting a pink tutu, she appeared to be about eight or nine. When their father died, she would have been twelve. No wonder Nic acted so protective of her; he'd practically raised her.

The accident had probably happened sometime between when she'd taken the photo and when Nic's family had left Chicago. She did a quick search on Google of accidents with injuries in the Northwest suburbs between those dates. Bingo. An article in the Daily Herald noted that a car had skidded off the road in bad weather and plowed into a bank of trees. A badly injured child had been rushed to the hospital. No names were printed in the article, which probably meant the occupants were minors.

She searched some more but learned nothing new. Her father might be able to help. Even if he didn't remember, maybe some of his buddies did. She grabbed her phone and punched in her parents' number. Seconds later, her father greeted her in his familiar deep voice. "How're you doing, Baby Girl?"

"Dad," she whined playfully. He'd been calling her Baby Girl since the day she'd gotten her first boyfriend, and the whine had become a part of their ritual.

He laughed. "Seriously, how are you?"

"I'm fine, Dad. How's Jason behaving?"

"He's doing good. No broken bones or furniture."

Hearing the smile in his voice, she joked, "Give it a few more days. I wanted to ask you something. When I was in eleventh grade, do you remember any of my classmates being involved in a car accident? At least one of the passengers would have been seriously injured."

"Can't say that I do."

"I found an article about it in the Daily Herald, but the details were sketchy. Could you ask your buddies on the force?"

"What's this about, Lauren?"

"Nic told me his sister was injured, but he didn't tell me how. I think it has something to do with why his family left town before the end of the school year. Anyways, I want to know what happened."

"Did you ask him?"

"We talked," she said, hesitating.

"I'll check, but I won't tell you anything that isn't public record."

"That's fair. Is Jason around?"

"Sure, he's right here." She heard the scuffling sound of the phone being passed to him.

"Mom?"

At the sound of her son's voice, she felt a pang in her heart. They'd spoken every day, but still she missed him. "Sweetheart, how was the Brookfield Zoo?"

"The stingrays were awesome, but the meerkats were even awesomer. Can I get a one?"

She laughed. "I'll have to think about that."

"Mom?" he asked, his voice suddenly small. "Is Nic really doing okay?"

His question surprised her. "I told you yesterday he was fine, remember?"

"I wanted to be sure. Sometimes people look like they're getting better, then they get sick again. Like last year when I got that ear infection."

"That does happen, but not this time. When I call you tomorrow, I'll make sure Nic's with me so you can talk to him."

"Why? We already talk every day."

Her brows shot up. "You do?"

"Nic gave me his number in case I needed to talk to him. When he got out of the hospital, I called him. Now he calls me."

She leaned against the headboard for support, not sure how she felt about this relationship between her son and her boyfriend. What if things didn't work out with Nic? Jason would be hurt. He'd lose a friend and he wouldn't understand why.

And what would happen to her if things didn't work out with Nic? She'd be hurt and she *would* know why. The wall between them was as thick as ever. This torn, confused man she'd fallen in love with didn't trust her enough to share Rachel's story. Even after she'd bared her soul to him last night.

She'd chinked the wall, but if she couldn't break it down by the end of her vacation, Jason wouldn't be the only one left devastated.

"Remember," Nic said, going over security details for the gala with Kaden. "Lauren's safety is your top priority tonight."

Kaden's brow creased. "Understood, but I don't like it. You have your gun, right?"

Nic patted the bulge under his arm. "Got it right here." When Kaden was hired, he'd insisted Nic get a gun and learn to use it.

Not wanting Lauren to worry, he'd gotten dressed and put on the shoulder holster while she'd been taking a shower. This baptism by fire into his world was going to be stressful enough for her. No need to add to it.

Nic watched his bodyguard's eyes drift over to the Harry Winston bag sitting on the desk. "You giving that to her tonight?"

"That's the plan. Why?"

"Lauren's pretty down-to-earth."

When he didn't continue, Nic prompted, "And?"

"And," Kaden said, averting his eyes, "it's none of my business, but I'll say it anyways. A woman like Lauren might have second thoughts about wearing a necklace that costs roughly the GDP of a small country."

The man was right, but… "How would she even know how much I paid? It's not like the price is on the box."

Kaden rolled his eyes and modulated his voice into a perfect imitation of Vivian at her snootiest. "Nic, darling," he drawled. "Everyone *knows* that Harry Winston is the jeweler to the stars. And that most stars *rent* his jewels because even *they* can't afford to buy them."

Nic had to laugh. "Fuck, that's creepy."

"Creepy but true."

"You're right, I need to downplay it." He'd get rid of the packaging.

After Kaden left to get ready, Nic turned his attention to the speech he needed to finalize for tonight's event. As Wish Ambassador and host, it was his responsibility to encourage attendees to open their wallets beyond the thousands of dollars they'd already spent for their tables, so that more children with life-threatening illnesses could see their dreams come true. He'd bought three tables himself so some of the children could attend. Since the gala was at the California Science Center, the kids were sure to have a blast.

Despite his desire to concentrate on the speech, his thoughts drifted to Lauren and their brief talk. She'd shared so much with him last night. He'd wanted to tell her about Rachel, about the accident. But his mouth had refused to form the words. She thought he was a "great guy." And he didn't want that to change.

His chest ached as he imagined the hurt and disgust he'd see in her eyes when she found out the truth. *Christ.* He was no better than Todd when he re-upped without consulting her; he was deceiving her too. Lauren had flat-out asked him about Rachel, about what had happened. But instead of owning up to the truth, he'd chickened out and told her only part of the story. The part that didn't make him look like a total shit. Tossing tonight's speech aside, he scrubbed his face.

I was so angry and hurt that I started to hate Todd, to hate the man I'd loved for so long.

He couldn't get her words out of his head. How long would it take for her to start hating him? Nic groaned. He didn't stand a chance.

I spent years comparing every man I met to you.

How could she not feel betrayed when he finally revealed the truth? She'd put him on a very high pedestal, and the fall when she booted him off might kill him. And if the panic in his chest at the thought of losing Lauren was any indication, he had to accept the truth: he had fallen in love with her. In fact, he'd fallen in love with the same woman twice.

Lauren shimmied into her new gown and stepped into the matching heels. The style of the dress demanded an up-do. She pulled a few pins from her makeup kit and twisted her hair into a loose bun, leaving a few wispy curls on either side of her face. Looking into the mirror, she sighed. The material draped her body perfectly, making her feel almost beautiful. She'd been raised middle-class and had never lacked for anything, but this outfit was a step beyond, almost magical in the way it transformed her from Miss Nobody to Miss Nic The Lover's Date.

Her hand rose to rest on her chest. Seeing the emptiness where the dog tags had lain for the last five years left an odd feeling in the pit of her stomach. Had she done the right thing? She'd broken her vow for Nic, a man who didn't trust her fully. And if he didn't trust her, could she trust him?

Hearing Nic enter the room, she turned away from the mirror. The sight of him stopped her mid-step. It was incredibly bad manners to stare, but she did it anyways. The impeccably tailored black tuxedo molded his chest and broad shoulders, while the white dress shirt contrasted beautifully with his dark hair and tanned complexion. A gray silk waistcoat and matching bow tie completed the outfit, adding a fashionable twist. *This was definitely not her father's tux*. Closing her eyes, she pictured herself smoothing her hands over his chest, the feel of the expensive material, the hardness of his muscles….

"Lauren." Nic cleared his throat. "Why'd you close your eyes? Do I look that bad?"

Her eyes popped open. Was he frickin' kidding? His lopsided smile answered her question. But then she had a question of her own. Why imagine, when Nic was standing right in front of her? With a slow sway to her hips, she approached him and let her hands run wild.

His heart pounded rapidly and his chest muscles bunched beneath her palms. Relieved, she smiled. He might be upset with her for pushing him about Rachel, but at least he wasn't turning away from her.

He gripped her wrists. "Uh-uh-uh." Her heart plummeted. Maybe she'd been wrong after all. But then he grinned and his eyes held a promise. "There'll be time for that later."

Still grinning, he tugged on her wrist and positioned himself behind her in front of the mirror. "I have something for you. Close your eyes." His words whispered against her skin, making her shiver. She squeezed her lids tight as he draped something warm around her neck. "You can look now."

"Oh my God," she breathed, her hand instantly going to the necklace of beautiful pink and orange crystals. "It's beautiful." Having worn only stainless steel for so long, she'd forgotten what it was like to wear actual jewelry. Her cheeks flushed when she saw her reflection in the mirror. "I feel like a princess."

"And you look like one, *chérie*. But something's missing." His hands reached up and an earring appeared at each ear. He smiled. "Do you think these will match?"

Her eyes rounded until she feared they might actually pop out of her head. Then they welled up. "They're perfect," she whispered past the lump in her throat. Tears spilled over onto her cheeks as she put the earrings on. Thank God she'd bought waterproof make-up.

When she was done, he turned her around and kissed away the tears, and brushed his mouth across hers. "Not nearly as perfect as you are." Taking advantage of her parted lips, he deepened the kiss. Her heart overflowing with emotion, she leaned into him and sighed. God, how she loved this man. Maybe she'd been in love with him since the eleventh grade. Maybe she'd been in love with him always.

All too soon, he pulled back. "I could kiss you forever," he said, and she knew exactly how he felt. "But we've got to get going. I'll wait for you downstairs." Then, seeming unable to resist, he cupped her cheeks and gave her one last kiss before leaving.

As soon as he was out of the room, her knees gave way. Grasping the dresser, she sucked air deep into her lungs, trying to slow the thundering in her chest. Did it mean something that Nic had given her the beautiful necklace and earrings? Or was he dressing her up so she wouldn't embarrass him at the gala? She ran the tip of her finger along the polished stones and shook her head. He'd called her *chérie,* and the heat in his eyes, the emotion in his voice.... No, it meant something to him, too.

Straightening, she dried her wet cheeks, grabbed her glittery handbag, and started for the door. The handbag began to vibrate. Pulling her phone out, she checked the caller ID. "Hi Dad."

"Hey, Baby Girl. I've got some news for you."

Thinking she might need to sit down for this, she perched on the edge of the bed, careful not to wrinkle her gown. "Okay, shoot."

"Joe, you remember Joe, right?"

"He was on your squad."

"That's right. He confirmed your friend and his younger sister were involved in a car accident when you were in the eleventh grade."

"Was she injured?"

"Actually, that's why I was able to get the info so quickly. Joe was working the night of the accident. He said he'll never forget the girl. He kept referring to her as the little broken angel."

Lauren's palms went damp. "Any idea why?"

"The whole time the team was working to free her from the wreck, she kept encouraging them, telling them everything would be all right. He says that by the time they finished, there wasn't a dry eye to be found."

Her breath hitched. This didn't sound good at all. If Rachel had brought hardened rescue workers to tears, she could only imagine how a seventeen-year-old Nic would have felt. "Was Nic driving?"

Her father tsked. "Lauren, that's his story to tell."

"He's so close-mouthed where his sister's concerned."

"Give him time. If you mean something to him, he'll open up."

"And if he doesn't?"

"Then he isn't the one for you." Hearing her father spell things out so bluntly made her chest ache. He was right, even if she didn't want to admit it.

But was she expecting too much too soon? After all, Nic had admitted having a sister today and that she was paralyzed. He'd taken a very big step, a leap of faith even, in telling her. If she gave him enough time, maybe he'd tell her about the accident, too. But how long was enough?

She couldn't stand to be shut out forever. It would be just like with Todd, all over again. Her heart wouldn't survive another round.

❧ ❧

As they exited the highway, Nic draped his arm across Lauren's shoulders. He'd always thought her beautiful, but tonight she was stunning. The sight of her exposed neck made him crazy. Every time he caught a whiff of her apple-blossom perfume, he wanted to bury his nose behind her ear and stay there. If he lived to be a hundred, he'd still never get enough of her.

Kaden turned the limo into the California Science Center, and the roar of the amassed crowd grew louder the closer they got to the red carpet. Some enterprising young girls ran along the row of limos, trying to peek in at the occupants. When they cupped their eyes, hoping to see past the darkened window, he tapped on the glass and rolled it down a bit. "Good evening, ladies."

The ensuing shrieks almost pierced his eardrums, and he felt Lauren jerk beside him. He turned to reassure her they were safe. Fans often lined up outside these events to greet him. But instead of laughing it off, she gasped and shielded her eyes. "What's wrong?"

"Oh God! I hope I was never that out of control."

Nic frowned, knowing full well she was exactly that out of control every time they made love. What was her problem? "They're just a little excited."

"No," she said, laughing now, but her hands still firmly covered her eyes. "Turn around and look."

He did, and had to smother the laugh bubbling in his chest. The girls had all lifted their shirts, baring their breasts like a scene from *Girls Gone Wild.* As they danced, they called out lyrics from his unofficial theme song. He cringed, hearing them sing about the man that made them moist and wet.

Forcing himself to act the way Nic The Lover would, he winked at the girls. "I'd love to invite you all into my caravan of love, but I'm already spoken for tonight."

He closed the window, but their encouraging shouts for him to keep his woman rocking continued to filter into the car. Nic leaned against the seat and pinched the bridge of his nose. "Jesus Christ, Lauren. I'm really sorry."

Lauren peered at him between her open fingers. As she let her hands fall, he saw her mouth curve into a big grin, and she laughed. "So, Mr. Lover, are you going to keep me rockin'?"

He stared at her, incredulous. She thought it was funny. Laughter erupted from the front of the limo. Apparently, she wasn't the only one. He let out a relieved breath. "Believe me, that's never happened before."

"Uh-huh," she said, her tone full of disbelief. When he didn't join in the laughter, she laid her hand on his thigh. "You're not responsible for what your fans do."

"Let's just hope there's no more breast-baring inside," he muttered.

"Speak for yourself," Kaden said, stopping the limo in front of the entrance.

While waiting for Kaden to come around and open the door, Nic smiled at Lauren and took her hand. "Ready?"

"As I'll ever be."

They walked inside. Nic was pleased to see that the reception area was already filling up. He placed his hand at the small of Lauren's back to escort her through the crowd. When his flesh met hers, electricity tingled across his fingertips.

Oblivious to the people surrounding them, he pulled her close and kissed the sweet spot where Lauren's neck met her shoulder as his hand skimmed her bare skin. Her face flushed and she flashed him a knowing smile. If it weren't for the kids, he'd throw her over his shoulder and whisk her away for a little rockin'.

After traversing the room and stopping many times to shake hands and make introductions, Nic grabbed two champagne glasses from a passing waiter and handed one to Lauren. She smiled and took a sip, holding his gaze. Her wet lips glistened, and all he could think of was kissing away the champagne. But children were present. They needed to keep things PG.

"Nic, darling," Vivian called as she approached. "My, don't you look wonderful. Ralph Lauren always looks good on you." She glanced at Lauren and her eyebrows shot up. "You bought her Harry Winston jewelry?"

Shit. His teeth clamped so tightly his molars ached. "Vivian."

"Oh, dear. Did I say something wrong?"

Couldn't she have kept her mouth shut for once? His eyes shot to Lauren, and seeing the dismay on her pretty face, he groaned. Oh, yeah. She knew all about Harry Winston. She gave him a tight smile, then turned to speak with Kaden, the surrounding chatter drowning out their words.

Nic grabbed Vivian's elbow and pulled her aside. "What's your problem?"

"I was just surprised, darling. Lorna doesn't seem the type to wear diamonds and padparadscha sapphires." She chuckled. "I bet the poor girl thought they were crystals."

Nic fingers clamped around the stem of his glass, almost snapping it. If Vivian insulted Lauren one more time or even said her name wrong, he was going to strangle the woman.

"Why can't a guy buy jewelry for his girlfriend without everyone second-guessing him?" he snapped.

"Girlfriend?" she sputtered.

"That's right." The urge to get in her face was strong, but as his mother always told him, you catch more flies with honey than with vinegar. He brightened his fake smile. "Can you be nice to her tonight, please? It would mean a lot to me."

"Of course. You're celebrating," she said, her lips pursed.

His brow arched. "Celebrating?" What was she getting at now?

"Didn't she tell you? *Vanity Fair* called. They like her photos."

Instantly, her smug tone put him on alert. He had no idea what she was talking about, but if he played along, maybe she'd go away. He'd ask Lauren about it later. "Yes, we're celebrating Lauren's good news. So don't ruin it."

"I wouldn't dream of it." She patted his arm and disappeared into the crowd.

Nic downed the rest of his champagne and let out a long breath. *Christ.* The evening had barely started and already he was exhausted.

Kaden sidled up to him. "Everything okay, sir?"

"Yeah. I'm just wondering what else can go wrong tonight." Several feet away, Lauren chatted with a group of women. She looked up and smiled at him, melting away the growing tension in his gut.

Moments later, she returned to his side. "This place is great. The children must be having a blast."

"Speaking of kids, let's go find them. They're more interesting than the adults anyways."

Threading his fingers through hers, he kissed their joined knuckles and led her to the Ecosystems exhibit, where the younger attendees and several of the older ones were being entertained.

Nic paused as they entered the gallery, taking in the sight of the children—all in varying stages of illness. Lauren turned so that his body shielded her and rummaged through her handbag, pulling out a tissue. "I'm sorry," she said, her voice tear-stained. "Give me a minute to pull myself together."

Nic rubbed her back. The same bittersweet emotions were twisting his own heart. But this night wasn't about him. It was about the children, whether they were in wheelchairs pushed by parents or on crutches, whether they were weak and balding, or whether they were dependent on an oxygen tank. All these children had one thing in common tonight—joy, expressed in a multitude of ways, ranging from shouts of laughter to a sparkle in a bright eye.

Pulling her close, he whispered, "It's all right, *chérie*. It's difficult to watch but even harder to live it. We need to be strong, be happy for them. Tonight, many are seeing their dreams come true."

She nodded, then wiped her eyes and gave him a shaky smile. After kissing her lips softly, he took her hand, and they strolled through the exhibit. They spoke to each child and their parents, welcoming them to the gala.

Too soon, it was time for everyone to move to the banquet hall for the dinner and speeches. Nic gave piggyback rides to some of the children, depositing them in their seats, while Lauren walked with some of the younger children, holding hands.

When everyone was seated, Lauren turned to Nic, her eyes bright. "You're a good man, Nic." He looked around the table, then at the other two tables filled with children and their families. Conversation flowed and everyone seemed happy. He wasn't the man he wanted to be, but he was trying.

As Nic was finishing his meal, the president of the organizing committee, Fred Sanders, walked up to the mike and began the formal part of the evening. Ten minutes later, Nic stepped onto the stage, the audience clapping and cheering. At the podium, he pulled the notes for his speech out of an inner pocket of his jacket, careful not to flash his gun.

His eyes searched the audience. Summer or NicsBitch, whoever the stalker was, could be here right now. He shot a quick glance in Lauren's direction to make sure Kaden was seated beside her.

Satisfied that Lauren was safe, he began speaking. "Ladies and gentlemen, the children, the Make-A-Wish Foundation, and I thank you for joining us this evening. With your generosity, the Foundation grants wishes to thousands of sick children each year, allowing them for a short time to push aside their struggles and enjoy simply being children."

He explained how the donations were managed, how wish recipients were selected, and how wish grantors were found. In the end, he thanked everyone for the honor of being Wish Ambassador and host of the gala. "We have some wonderful entertainment coming up and the exhibits will be open throughout the rest of the night. Enjoy the evening," he concluded.

As he went to step off the stage, Fred stopped him and whispered, "I hate to spring this on you at the last minute, but one of the children has taken a turn for the worse and we've had to move her up the list. We can grant her wish tonight, if you agree. It involves you."

"Of course."

At Fred's signal, a young girl was wheeled onto the stage followed by a man and woman. "Nic," Fred said, introducing them. "This is Claire and her parents, Jim and Linda."

Based on her face, Claire appeared to be about twelve, but her body was so frail and emaciated, she looked much younger. Although she was in the final stages of a terminal illness, her eyes glowed with an inner peace and confidence that was humbling. She smiled up at him.

Nic crouched in front of her so she wouldn't have to crane her neck to talk to him. "What's your wish, sweetheart?"

"I want to dance with you. To the *Luv Me Luv Me* song."

Nic looked up at Fred and the girl's parents and arched a brow. Shaggy's lyrics were better suited to a night club than a gala.

Fred grinned. "We have a cleaned-up version."

Nic met Claire's eyes and smiled. "Do you want to dance in your chair?"

She shook her head. "In your arms."

Bracing himself, he slid one hand under her knees and another behind her back, lifted her out of the chair and cradled her against his chest. Christ, he barely felt her weight in his arms. Swallowing hard, he asked, "All right like this?"

"Perfect," she whispered, looping her thin arms around his neck.

The first notes of the song started and he began to swing his hips in time with the beat. This was not going to be the same dance he'd danced last week at Taylors. Was it only last week? Felt like a lifetime ago.

"Sing it, please," Claire said. He focused on her face. Although she was a little out of breath, her eyes sparkled. This was her wish, her moment. All she wanted was a dance with him. He'd make it the best dance of her life, and his.

For her ears only, he began singing the lyrics. With each twirl and dip, her face became more animated and her shrieks louder. God, he couldn't believe he was making her so happy. This girl, in the too-big dress that drowned her shrinking body.

As the song neared its end, her laughter started to fade and her breathing became labored. He slowed his steps, turning his back to the audience. "Is everything okay? Should I stop now?"

Her eyes widened. "No!" she breathed, and although he could barely hear her, the desperation in her eyes told him she'd meant to scream it. Panting raggedly, she whispered, "I don't want this dance to ever end." Tears pooled in her eyes. As he watched, a single drop escaped and slipped down her cheek. He couldn't breathe. His chest ached and his heart broke. If keeping her in his arms would save her life, he'd do it. He'd hold this little girl forever.

The music ended and Claire's parents stepped closer with the wheelchair.

He eased her into it. When his arm slid out from under her knees, she grabbed it, pulling him to her. Knowing what she wanted, what she needed, he wrapped his arms around her and hugged her tight. "I love you, Nic," she said, her voice soft next to his ear.

Forcing himself to speak past the tightness in his throat, he said, "I love you too, sweet Claire. Be well, be at peace." She nodded. Pasting a bright Nic The Lover smile on his face, he kissed her cheek and stepped back.

As Fred introduced the first musical guest, Nic stumbled off the stage, blinded by the tears in his eyes. That had been one of the hardest things he'd ever done. Knowing he couldn't keep up the act much longer, he searched for an escape. When he spotted Lauren standing at the bottom of the stairs, waiting for him, the tears started to spill.

She held open her arms and he stepped into her embrace. Her warmth enveloped him as she gathered him to her and pressed his head into the crook of her neck, shielding his face from prying eyes.

The band started into their first song and music surrounded them. She swayed her hips, rocking him, comforting him. "Let it out, Nic. No one can see you."

"She's dying, Lauren." His voice broke. "I held a dying girl in my arms, and all I could do was dance with her."

Her arms tightened around him as his tears wet her neck. "I know this is hard, Nic. But it's not your fault. You did what you could for her."

He shook his head. "I can't fix it. And I can't stop it. It's happening all over again." Rachel hadn't died, but her legs had. Adrift in the tangle of his emotions, drowning in memories, he clung to Lauren, wanting to lose himself in her.

"What's happening again, Nic?" she asked, her voice gentle.

He wanted to tell her, to unburden his overwhelmed heart. But to do that, he'd have to admit to almost killing Rachel. "I wish I could have saved her," he admitted. "I wish I could save Claire. Save them all." But he couldn't, and soon Claire would be gone.

If he didn't want to lose Lauren too, he had to keep the truth about Rachel hidden. What he'd done was unforgivable.

Lauren pushed Nic's head up with her hands and cupped his wet cheeks. "Even you can't save everyone. What you're doing is helping, though. I see their faces. You're making a big difference to these kids."

"It's not enough."

The agony in his voice was breaking her heart. She wanted to hold him in her arms forever and take away all his pain. Instead, all she could do was try to comfort him. "I know," she said, resting her forehead on his and smiling through her own tears, "but it's all you can do, it's all any of us can do."

Although he hadn't said Rachel's name, he'd been talking about his sister. Lauren wanted to prod him, get him to open up some more about Rachel, but out of the corner of her eye, she spotted Kaden blocking Vivian's approach. This wasn't the time or place for confessions.

For several long minutes, they stayed as they were, arms wrapped around each other, swaying in time to the music. She hoped her presence soothed him as much as his soothed her. Her fingers were idly stroking the hair at his neck, when he jerked his head up. "Everything okay?" she asked, her voice tight with worry.

"Your purse zapped me."

"Zapped you? Oh, Jason must have sent me a text. I'll get it later." Nic dropped his arms and stepped back, leaving her bereft of warmth. Suppressing a shiver, she wiped at the wetness under her eyes. "I should clean up a little before we head back to our table."

Nic scrubbed a hand along his jaw, his smile wry. "I could probably use a good face dunk myself. If the kids see me like this, they'll wonder who's trying to impersonate Nic The Lover." Chuckling, she took his arm and they headed to the restrooms. After arranging to meet in the passageway, they parted.

On entering the ladies' room, Lauren was pleased to find she was alone, but someone came in and took the stall next to hers. So much for repairing the damage in private. At the sink, she washed her hands, then leaned over the counter to discover what needed fixing. She laughed at the disarray reflected in the mirror. While Nic's hands had felt good in her hair, they certainly hadn't been good *for* her hair. No problem. It was nothing her little comb/brush combo couldn't take care of. Opening her purse, she saw her phone and remembered to check the message she'd received.

When she saw the number was unknown, a shiver ran through her. Had Nic's stalker somehow obtained her number? "Calm down, Lauren. It's probably just spam." Her voice echoed off the walls of the restroom. Great. Now the woman in the stall would think she was crazy. With a laugh, she navigated to the message and opened it.

Horror freezing her in place, she could do nothing but stare at the photo she'd been sent. A woman lay on the floor, a knife protruding from her chest. Blood splatters covered her body and large pools of red marred the whiteness of the carpet beneath her. Summer wouldn't be contacting them ever again—Summer was dead.

Lauren scrolled down to read the caption below the picture.

Who'll be next?

The door to the occupied stall opened, and Lauren learned just how loud she could scream.

CHAPTER 17

Lauren's screams filled the restroom as she dropped the phone and jumped back from the woman, who gave a loud gasp. It was hard to tell which one of them was more scared.

Seconds later, the restroom door slammed open. Kaden appeared first, then Nic, both with guns drawn. With her mouth hanging open, she stared as Nic quickly moved to cover her while Kaden checked the stalls. She hadn't even known Nic owned a gun, much less carried one.

The woman took one look at the guns and ran shrieking into the hall.

"What happened?" Nic asked.

"My… my phone. I got a message." She wrapped her arms around her waist and shuddered. "Oh God, Nic. She's dead."

"Who's dead, *chérie?*"

"All clear," Kaden said. "What's going on?"

"Summer's dead. The stalker killed her."

Nic holstered his gun and picked up her phone. At the same time, she reached under the sink to retrieve the back and battery that had come off as the phone hit the floor. When they both stood up, face to face, Nic kissed her softly, then held out his hand. "Let me see."

He put the phone back together and powered it on, navigated his way to the message and swore. Handing the phone to Kaden, Nic said, "We have to get Lauren out of here. Right fucking now."

"I'll alert security."

"Do it on your way to the car. We'll meet you out front in two minutes."

Kaden glanced at his watch, nodded and left.

Nic pulled her against his chest and caressed her cheek. "You're safe, *chérie*."

She shook her head. "The stalker's coming after me now."

"No one's going to hurt you. Ever." She met his gaze and bit her lip to keep it from trembling. The intensity in his eyes told her he meant every word. But could he really protect her from a homicidal maniac? And what about Jason? She'd never forgive herself if something happened to him, and neither would Nic.

"I'm serious. No one's getting near you. Come on, we need to get out of here." He took her hand and pulled her behind him. After quickly checking the hallway, he motioned for her to follow. Luckily, the restrooms were located near the main entrance so they wouldn't need to re-enter the banquet hall. They edged along the walls, keeping to the shadows, and had almost reached the exit door when Nic came to a dead stop and pressed her against the wall with his arm. "Damn," he muttered under his breath. Peeking over his shoulder, she spotted Vivian.

"Nic, darling. You're not leaving already, are you?" Vivian asked, advancing on them.

"Yeah. We are."

Why didn't he tell her about the message? She was his best friend, his confidante, wasn't she? Vivian peered at them, her eyes darting from Lauren to Nic. Vivian wouldn't let them go until they gave a plausible excuse for their early departure. Lauren nudged Nic's arm out of the way and stepped forward. "I'm not feeling well. Must be something I ate."

Vivian chuckled. "Poor dear, it was probably the champagne. Was this your first time trying it, Lorna? Champagne is much more subtle than beer, and the effects can sneak up on you."

Lauren could only stare at the woman, unable to respond. Fortunately, Nic didn't seem to be experiencing the same lack of vocal ability.

"For Christ's sake Vivian, Lauren's fucking had champagne before. We're going home. End of story." Nic took Lauren's hand. "Let's go, *chérie*."

As he shouldered past Vivian, Lauren caught a glimpse of the woman's face. Her features hardened and cold eyes bore into Lauren's soul. Ice crystallized along Lauren's spine. She glanced away then back again. Vivian smiled, no trace of animosity on her face. *Jeez*. The message had her so rattled she was seeing things. Her trembling hand held firmly in the melting warmth of his, Lauren let Nic lead her away from Vivian, away from the crowds, and possibly away from the stalker too.

After seeing her settled on the back seat of the limo, Nic slammed the door closed, and with tires squealing, Kaden took off. As they turned onto the freeway, Lauren's thoughts returned to the photo she'd received. Summer had been stabbed. A bullet killed quick and clean—a knife killed slow and messy. Todd had always told her a knife was an up-close-and-personal weapon. Whoever had killed Summer had done so passionately, looking in her eyes. Enjoying it.

Who'll be next?

She shuddered, and Nic's arm tightened around her. He ran a finger along her jaw. "I'll keep you safe, Lauren. I promise."

When she didn't reply, he tilted her chin up, forcing her to meet his gaze. Lights from passing vehicles illuminated one side of his face while the other remained in shadows. But she could see his eyes, darkened by emotions. She opened her mouth to speak but words failed her. This situation was so foreign to her world.

Nic brushed her lips with his. "I don't know if this is the best time to say this, but I'm going to burst if I don't tell you what I'm feeling." He paused and held her gaze. "I love you, *chérie*."

As he spoke, Lauren's eyes welled. Nic loved *her*. He stroked her cheek and lowered his voice. "When you look at me, the world disappears, and I feel like I'm falling into your eyes, into a safe, happy place where only the two of us exist."

Lauren smiled through her tears and trailed a finger along his bottom lip. He had exactly the same effect on her. When they were together, everything else faded away. "And when we touch." He slid his hand down her neck to her bare back. "God, when I touch your skin, I feel alive, like I'm on fire."

She inhaled sharply as Nic's fingers trailed a path down to the base of her spine, igniting flames deep in her core. No man had ever uttered more beautiful words and certainly not about her. Could any of this be real?

He reached for her hand, placing an open kiss on her palm. A small flick of his tongue sent her temperature soaring. "I've shared things with you, things I haven't shared with anyone, not even Rémi or Vivian. I feel connected to you in a way I never have with any other woman. Ever."

Oh my God. If he didn't stop talking soon, her heart would explode. She saw love in his eyes, heard it in the warm tones of his voice, felt it in the strength of his arms wrapped around her. "I love you too, Nic," she said, then closed her eyes and laid her head on his chest, the steady beat of his heart calming her.

Nic meant what he said. He loved her and he'd do everything in his power to keep her from harm. So, why did she feel like a tightrope walker about to take a tumble?

Because he still hadn't told her about Rachel's accident.

Back at the loft, Nic snapped his phone shut and looked up to see Lauren and Kaden watching him, worry etching their faces. "The detectives should be here in about fifteen minutes. Maybe they can figure out where the photo of Summer was taken."

"That reminds me," Lauren said. "Earlier this afternoon, I got a chance to examine the photo from the arena using my editing software. There's flash glare in the Plexiglas on top of the boards. So it was taken from above, probably in the bleachers."

"Flash glare?" Kaden asked.

"Bright white spots made when the light from the flash hits a reflective surface." When Kaden nodded, she went on. "With my software, I reduced the glare and played with the colors to take away some of the shadows. The Plexiglas reflected the image of the person taking the picture."

Nic's gaze shot to Lauren. "You could see who took the picture?"

"No," she said, her voice heavy with disappointment. "I tried every trick I know, but all I could make out was the shape of a person, no identifying characteristics. While we're waiting for the detectives, I can take a look at the photo of Summer." She gave him a wry smile. "Maybe we'll get lucky and find a perfect reflection of the killer."

Nic took a seat beside her on the couch and tugged on one of the loose curls hanging below her ear. "*Chérie*, that photo's pretty gruesome. I'm sure the police have people who can examine it."

"I know, but I'll feel better if I'm doing something."

"Then why don't you go change and get set up here? I'll make some tea."

Lauren nodded and headed up the stairs to their bedroom. As soon as she was out of sight, he motioned to Kaden to follow him into the kitchen. Kaden sat on one of the stools at the breakfast counter.

"I've had stalkers before," Nic said as he filled the kettle with water and set it on the stove to boil. "They're a nuisance, but this time it's different." He leaned against the counter and crossed his arms. "This one is willing to kill to get to me."

Kaden rested his chin in his hands. "I've done a little research on this. Statistically, most victims of non-celebrity stalking know their stalkers personally or have at least met them once before. Maybe that's the case here."

"That's just fucking great." Nic scrubbed his jaw and sighed. "So, she could be anyone from a hair stylist I met on a movie set to someone I see regularly."

Kaden held his gaze. "There's only one option: trust no one."

"Christ. Things are getting *way* out of hand." Nic looked at his feet and took a deep breath before continuing. "I thought we could protect Lauren if she was with us, but now, I'm not so sure."

"I hate to say it, but at this point, she's probably safest away from you."

He lifted his head, meeting Kaden's gaze. "I know." Whatever the cost, he'd protect Lauren and Jason. Even if the price was his heart.

When the tea was ready, he piled everything onto a tray and carried it into the living room. Kaden followed with a plate of cookies. Hearing footsteps on the stairs, Nic set the tray on the table and turned to watch Lauren bouncing down the stairs with her laptop in hand. Despite the gravity of the situation, he grinned. She'd reverted to her comfort clothes, cargo pants and a T-shirt, and she looked cute as hell. Giving her up was going to kill him.

Lauren sat beside him on the couch and he pulled the coffee table closer so she could place her laptop on it. She smiled at him and held up a memory card. "I've already copied the photo from the message. After I upload it to the computer, we can examine it with my editing software." As she spoke, she pushed the card into a slot on the side of the computer and opened her program.

"Fuck," he muttered when the awful picture of Summer flashed onto the screen.

"Try to concentrate on the shadows."

"You seem pretty matter-of-fact about this."

"Sometimes I helped my dad analyze crime scene photos, searching for clues that weren't always obvious to the naked eye."

Pride warmed his chest. Lauren was an amazing woman.

"Oh!" She pointed to the upper-left corner of the picture. "Here's something interesting. This photo and the one of us kissing at the arena were taken with the same camera."

"How can you tell?" Kaden asked, moving from the chair to sit on Lauren's other side.

She pulled up the arena photo and placed the two shots side by side. Pointing to each picture, she asked, "See the white lines here and here? The camera that took this photo has a mark or a scratch on the lens."

Nic tilted his head to see the lines better. "Can you tell what kind of camera was used?"

"Not the brand but the type, yes. I'd say these shots were taken with a common point-and-shoot camera rather than a D-SLR."

"A D-SLR?"

"A digital single lens reflex camera, the kind professionals use."

"What makes you think that?" Kaden asked.

"A couple reasons." She pointed to the arena shot. "What's the first thing you notice about the photo?"

Nic ventured a guess. "It's grainy, like a video game with bad graphics."

Lauren beamed at him. "Exactly. To pack a high number of megapixels on a small sensor, point-and-shoot cameras use smaller pixels than D-SLRs, which have larger, more expensive, sensors. Smaller pixels make grainy photos, especially in low-light conditions. Do you notice anything else that's different than what you would see in, say, a shot of a player circling the ice with the Stanley cup?"

Nic eyed the photo carefully and thought back to the photos Lauren had taken of him carrying Jason above his head. "Everything is in focus."

"That's right." Her eyes twinkled with excitement as she launched into an explanation. "It has to do with depth of field and focal length. Narrowing the depth of field allows photographers to highlight an object by—"

Kaden held up a hand to stop her. "I don't want to be rude, but Nic's eyes are glazing over."

Nic snorted, but let the jab pass. She'd lost him at *depth of field*. "Could it have been taken with a camera phone?"

"Camera phone technology isn't powerful enough to create a shot this good, given the distance and lighting conditions. It had to have been a point and shoot camera."

She minimized the arena photo and returned her attention to the one of Summer. "Damn. No reflective surfaces. I'll increase the contrast to see if it brings out anything in the shadows." A few clicks later, objects appeared along the edges that hadn't been visible before.

"Isn't that the stalker's foot?" Nic pointed to the bottom middle of the screen.

Lauren magnified that area of the photo. "Yep, and she's wearing a black high-heeled shoe with a red sole."

"Looks like a Christian Louboutin to me," Kaden said. When they turned to him, eyebrows raised, he grinned. "What? Can't a straight guy be able to tell a Louboutin from a Jimmy Choo?"

"No," Nic said at the same time as Lauren.

"Well, I must be special then."

"That's one word for it," Nic joked.

Kaden laughed. Then he sobered. "Seriously though. I bought my ex a pair of these last Christmas. Louboutin shoes all have a red sole, like this one."

Lauren zoomed on the shoe some more. "This is a distinctive style. If I crop the photo to show only the shoe, a shoe store might confirm the brand and tell us where this kind of shoe is sold. I think it's worth a try."

"I agree, *chérie*. We can start first thing in the—." The buzz of the security intercom interrupted him.

Kaden rose from his chair. "That must be the detectives."

As they waited, Lauren started to fill the mugs with tea. Her hands shook. Nic took the pot from her and finished pouring. "How are you holding up?"

"When I'm focusing on something else, I'm not thinking about it. But as soon as I stop, it all comes back. Until tonight, it all seemed a little unreal. I guess that makes me selfish."

"Selfish how?"

"I mean, even before we knew the stalker had killed Summer, things were pretty serious. You'd been drugged and could have died. It should have felt real to me all along."

He pulled her into the circle of his arms. "You're not selfish. It's natural to downplay things that frighten you. I never thought it would go this far either."

She snuggled her head against his shoulder. "Still, I'm sorry. Maybe now that this is a murder investigation, the police will be more serious."

When the front door opened, he said, "We'll find out soon enough." They stood up to greet Anderson and Becker. Once everyone was settled, Nic told them what happened at the gala and what Lauren had found in the photo.

"Sounds like you've all had quite the evening. May we see the photo?" Anderson asked. Lauren turned the laptop toward the men, and they left their seats to crouch in front of the screen.

"It's a hotel room. Layout is standard but the carpet color indicates someplace high-end," Becker said.

"Ms. James, can you email me both the original and enhanced versions? Here's my address." Anderson handed her a card. "We'll check out the hotels in the area that have pale carpeting in the rooms and get back to you as soon as we have some news."

"I'll do it right now," Lauren said, already bringing up the email client on her laptop.

"Thanks. If the two of you don't mind, we'd like to keep your phones overnight. Have the techs check them out." Her concentration on the email she was writing, Lauren absently reached into the pocket of her cargo pants, extracted the phone, and handed it to Anderson.

Nic had to stifle a grin as an image of Lauren pulling a kitchen sink out of the large pocket popped into his mind. "Have them look for spyware. We think that's how the stalker always knows where I am."

Anderson accepted the phone Nic held out to him. "If we find any, we'll see if we can trace it to the stalker. We might get lucky."

"Should I get a new phone?"

"No," Becker said immediately. "The stalker communicates with you through this phone. You get rid of the phone, you destroy the link."

"Got it." Nic didn't like it, but he understood Becker's reasoning.

Becker stood up. "Unfortunately, we don't have the resources to put a man outside your door. The most we can do is ask for extra patrols in the area."

"We'll be okay with Kaden here." They shook hands and the detectives left.

"What now?" Lauren asked.

"Now we go to bed. No one can get to us here." Nic caught her hand and led her upstairs to the privacy of their bedroom. After the crowds and chaos of the day, it would feel good to be alone with Lauren, just the two of them, to hold her in his arms and enjoy sharing a bed with the woman he loved.

❧ ❧

The next morning, Lauren sat at the kitchen table, enjoying the sight of Nic savoring his cup of coffee. The intercom buzzing startled her out of her reverie.

Mistaking her reaction for nerves, Nic patted her hand. "It's probably the detectives returning our phones. I'll be right back."

Lauren nodded and fixed her gaze on Nic's butt as he sauntered out the door. The man was a walking advertisement for Levi's. Nic had it all: looks, intelligence, and an incredible intensity that let a woman know she had his full, undivided attention. She shook her head in bemusement. And he loved *her*. He'd told her in the limo and then again about a million times while he'd made love to her. Each time, punctuating the words with a warm, wet kiss. On her mouth, her neck, her breasts, her stomach, her…

Lauren gulped and clapped her hands to her flushed cheeks as Nic returned with the detectives in tow. He peered at her face. "Something wrong?"

"N-no," she stammered. "The coffee's hot and I burnt my tongue." Embarrassed by her lame excuse, she turned to greet the detectives. "Good morning, gentlemen."

"Good morning, Ms. James. Here's your phone," Anderson said, handing it to her. "We got all the info we could from the message you received last night. And you'll be happy to hear that your phone is clean—no spyware."

Then he turned his attention to Nic. "And here's yours, Mr. Lamoureux. As you suspected, a spyware tool has been loaded on it. The techs are working on accessing the website used to track your location information. If needed, we'll get a subpoena to force the host company to give us the account holder information."

Becker stepped forward. "In the meantime, we've cloned your phone. That means we'll get any messages sent to you at the same time you do." Although he was addressing Nic, Becker shot her a loaded look, then turned back to Nic. "We'll also be receiving and recording any conversations. Please keep that in mind."

Lauren narrowed her eyes at him. Did Becker think she and Nic engaged in phone sex or something like that? What a jerk. Then a bomb went off in her head. The fan letter! Had Becker found the letter she'd written to Nic two years ago? Head lowered, she rubbed her temples with her palms. Nic could *never* see that letter. She had to get it from Becker.

Anderson gestured to the chair beside her. "May I?" he asked. Lauren nodded, liking his old-fashioned politeness. Maybe Anderson would help her get the letter back.

"Using indicators from the photograph you sent us yesterday," he began, "we've found Ms. Rayne's body. Initial analysis puts time of death last Saturday. Once the autopsy is done, we'll be able to pinpoint the time frame to a four-hour window."

"So either Summer or the stalker could have written the message on my mirror. We know how Summer could have gotten the key and the security system code, but how would the stalker have gotten it?"

"Mr. Lamoureux, you need to consider all the women you interact with.

This person is intelligent and determined. She has strong feelings of attachment, even ownership, where you're concerned. She wears expensive designer shoes, always knows your general whereabouts, and has obtained access to your loft. Can you think of anyone who fits this profile?"

Summer herself had fit this description. But there had to be someone else. Who? Only one woman came to Lauren's mind. Could it be her? She'd need a lot more proof before she said anything to Nic. If she accused his best friend and she was wrong, she'd look jealous. But if she was right and she didn't say anything, she'd look dead.

After sitting down beside her, Nic raked a hand through his hair and sighed. "It could be any one of a number of women, except for the access to my loft. But then, if they were working with Summer, she might have given them the key and code."

"What about your agent?" Anderson asked.

Hearing the detective's question, Nic's face blanched and tension radiated from his body. Lauren put her hand on his thigh and gently squeezed. Even considering Vivian had to feel like a betrayal to him. Nic shook his head. "It can't be her."

After a brief pause, Anderson said, "Just think about it."

"We also determined the message from last night was sent using a prepaid phone purchased at a Walmart in New York," Becker said.

"Were all the messages sent from the same phone?" Lauren asked.

"The first and second messages were. That phone was activated in Chicago."

"Was it also bought at a Walmart?"

"We're still working to determine that."

Kaden leaned forward. "When was each phone activated?"

Becker pulled out a notebook from his jacket pocket. "The Chicago phone was activated on January tenth and the New York phone was activated on March twenty-first."

"The third one was also prepaid and probably activated in Miami, based on the number," Kaden said.

Anderson's eyebrows shot up. "The third one? I take it you've been investigating on your own?" The detective's face hardened.

Kaden scratched his jaw and averted his eyes. "A friend at the phone company pulled Summer's records. She called a Miami number when she was at Taylors with Nic."

Nic's brow creased. "In January, I did a promotional appearance on a talk show in Chicago. And in March, I attended an awards ceremony in New York."

"It's too bad we don't know when the Miami phone was activated," Lauren said.

"Well, I was on set in Miami in February." Nic took a deep breath and sighed. "So, if the phone was activated then, that means whoever bought the phones probably either went to each location with me or followed me there."

Lauren shuddered, and Nic put his arm around her shoulders. She shot him a faint smile even as her heart broke for him. Vivian was looking more and more like a viable suspect.

"Did anyone besides your agent attend all three of these events with you?" Anderson asked.

Nic pinched the bridge of his nose, and she could see the frustration in his eyes. "I couldn't say. A lot of fans attend all my events."

Anderson's gaze sharpened. "But no one you know personally?"

"No."

Becker put his notepad away. "We'll confirm the purchase location of the third phone, and we'll see if we can identify the store where the killer's shoes were bought." He shifted his gaze, including Kaden and Lauren in his hard stare. "Is there anything else you haven't told us? Now would be a good time to share."

Nic shook his head. "You know everything we do."

"Good. And from now on?" He paused until he had everyone's attention. "Leave the detecting to the detectives. The last thing we need is the three of you running around contaminating evidence. We need to catch the killer before she goes after Ms. James."

When Lauren gasped, Nic scowled at the detective.

"Sorry ma'am."

She inclined her head but remained silent. Of course Becker was right but, jeez, was a little sensitivity too much to ask for? Minutes later, they wrapped things up and the detectives left. She rubbed her temples as a massive stress headache pounded behind her eyes.

"Are you okay, *chérie*?"

She shot him a small smile. Nothing got past the man. "Just a headache."

"Why don't you take some Advil and have a nap?"

Great idea. She kissed him and went up to their bedroom. As she crossed the room, she took in the sight of her purse on the dresser next to Nic's keys, her book on top of his script on the nightstand. In the closet, she saw her gown hanging next to Nic's tux, her shoes next to his. She entered the bathroom to get the Advil from her cosmetics bag. Her eyes fell to the toothbrush holder where her brush stood next to his.

Her chest constricted painfully. Everything around them was so wrong, but this? This felt *right*, so unbelievably right. She wanted to see her toothbrush next to Nic's for the rest of her life.

Tomorrow, she had to go back to Seattle, back to work, back to reality. The roller coaster ride was over. She'd loved Todd, she really had. But losing Nic was going to hurt worse. So much worse. Tears welled up in her eyes at the thought of never holding him again.

Despite the emotions running high and the adrenaline rush they'd both been feeling last night, Nic had meant every word he'd said. He loved her. When she looked into his eyes, when they made love, when he held her close, she felt his love for her. *So why not stay? Why not make a life with him?*

Because sometimes love wasn't enough.

The faint sound of her phone ringing interrupted her thoughts. Crossing to the dresser, she got her phone out of her purse and answered it.

"Ms. James? This is Helen Combs from *Vanity Fair*."

"Ms. Combs. How are you?"

"I have some good news. Your talent and unique vision impressed the executive committee. *Vanity Fair* would like to offer you a position."

"A position?" Weren't they just talking about the purchase of a few photos?

"Yes, we have three photographers on staff, with you we'd have four. Each would provide shots for the cover and a headline article for three issues a year in addition to some smaller side projects."

Lauren began to hyperventilate and forced herself to take several deep breaths. When her throat relaxed enough for speech, she said in her most professional voice, "That sounds very interesting, Ms. Combs. Where is the job location?"

"Our headquarters and studios are in New York."

"Do I have to relocate?"

"No. You'll need to travel to our headquarters occasionally, and of course, we'll fly you to different locations for photo shoots." Lauren breathed a sigh of relief. So far so good. Travelling might be an issue, but her parents and her friends probably wouldn't mind helping her out from time to time.

"We would like to offer you a starting salary of fifty thousand dollars. We have a medical plan and a 401K program. Our HR department will provide you the details."

Holy crap! They wanted to pay her *fifty thousand dollars* to take pictures? That was twice what she made at the department store. Lauren inched her way back to the bed to sit down. "When…" She cleared her throat. "When would I start?"

"This is the part that might be difficult. We would need you in New York by Friday afternoon. We're having a four-day workshop with all the editorial staff and photographers to plan the next twelve issues. Because we're changing our format, we've had to throw out all our previous plans. We're starting with a clean slate, so this is the perfect time for you to be joining the team."

Lauren pressed a palm against her racing heart. Opportunity was knocking. Was she brave enough to open the door? It was a five-and-a-half-hour flight from LAX to JFK, plus the three-hour time difference. To be there by Friday afternoon, she'd have to either leave tomorrow morning or take a red-eye tomorrow night. Everything was happening so fast. Lauren rubbed her temples. A position at *Vanity Fair* would change her life and Jason's for the better. She swallowed hard and said, "I'd be delighted."

"Excellent. You can sign the contract and benefits documentation when you get here. Of course, we'll reimburse all your travel costs, so please keep your receipts."

Lauren thanked the woman again and ended the call. She fell back onto the bed and smothered her face in Nic's pillow, inhaling the faint scent of his Armani cologne deep into her lungs. It wouldn't take much to make her stay. Around Nic, everything was *more*. More exciting, more intense. He'd flash his brilliant movie star smile, peer into her soul with his baby blues and say, "Everything'll be all right, *chérie*," and she'd believe him.

No matter how much they might love each other, she had to be strong, had to resist him. Life with Nic was just too dangerous for her and Jason. The stalker's threat against her was clear. And terrifying.

Last night, when Nic had admitted that he loved her, she'd been bursting with joy. But even so, it would be irresponsible of her to put her son at risk for a man who wasn't honest about his past. If he loved her enough, he'd trust her with the truth.

She fought back a sob and hugged Nic's pillow more tightly against her chest. Maybe once things quieted down after the stalker was caught, they could see each other again and talk. They could find a way to make it work, if they loved each other enough, couldn't they? Maybe then he could trust her enough to be honest about Rachel. And if he couldn't? Her father had said it: he wasn't the one for her.

New York City and Vanity Fair's offer waited for her. A new chapter in her life was starting. This opportunity would better her life and Jason's. It would make her into the strong, independent woman she'd always wanted to be. And it was all thanks to Nic. Meeting him was the best thing to ever happen to her.

Leaving him would be the worst.

Nic paused in front of his office window and stared outside, unable to believe what he was hearing on the phone. Was Rémi yanking his chain? The man had pulled some pretty elaborate pranks in the past. As much as he'd be pissed at his friend for being such an asshole, he'd also be relieved. What Rémi had just said was his worst nightmare.

"Come on man. Stop fucking with me."

"I wish I were. When Rachel called me, I assumed she was misunderstanding something, overreacting, you know? But then she showed me the letter. There's no mistake."

His head was starting to spin, eerily reminiscent of his Rohypnol misadventure. On shaky legs, he stumbled to his chair and collapsed into it, putting his head between his knees before he passed out. "Tell me again what the letter said."

"It says:

Ms. Lamoureux, wire ten million to the following bank account within five days. If you do not produce the money, I'll hurt you, destroy the ranch, and kill your brother. I know what he did, and I'll tell the world the truth about the accident. Do not involve the police. I'm watching you."

Nic's stomach churned. Taking several deep breaths, he tried not to puke. "I can't fucking believe this. On top of the stalker, I'm being blackmailed. And the bastard is using Rachel to get to me." If anything happened to her, he'd never forgive himself.

"How does the blackmailer even know about Rachel?"

Good question. Only Vivian and Rémi knew the truth, only they knew he was responsible for what had happened to Rachel. He'd told Kaden he had a sister, although he suspected the bodyguard knew much more than he let on. But it couldn't be one of them. Someone else had dug into his life. "Except for my will, the only place our names are linked is in our medical files."

"So much for confidentiality."

He had two choices—pay the blackmailer the ten million dollars or come clean about his past, to everyone. Both options sucked, but the second was unthinkable. Lauren would hate him. His career would be destroyed. And without a movie star's income, he'd have no way to support Rachel and the ranch.

Nic's voice hoarsened. "I need to call Vivian to see if I even have that kind of money. One way or another, I'll take care of this, Rémi. Just please make sure Rachel is protected."

"Give me some credit, man. I haven't been off the force *that* long."

The corner of Nic's mouth kicked up. "Still, you can't watch her 24/7. Want Kaden to hire someone to help you out?"

"I was thinking of asking my cousin Tommy. You remember him, right?"

"He went to the police academy with you?"

"Yep. I'd trust him with my life."

"It's settled then. I'll call you back as soon as I know something more."

He ended the call and almost instantly his phone beeped, signaling an incoming message. *What now?* He opened the message and swore. He couldn't take much more of this shit.

You aren't taking me seriously, so I'm upping the ante. Talk to Rachel about the note she got. Get rid of the WHORE and pay the $10 million or she's DEAD and so are you.

Whoa. The stalker and the blackmailer were the *same* person. Below the text was a shot of him, lying on the ice covered in blood. The stalker must have taken it at the arena when he'd passed out. The caption read:

Bang! Bang! You're dead. ☺

A hard ball formed in the pit of his stomach. The stalker could have fucking shot him that day instead of taking a photo. *Christ.* The ball grew larger. She could have shot Lauren or Jason.

He continued to scroll the message. As a photo of Lauren going down on him appeared on the screen, his heart faltered. He recognized his room in the background. *How the fuck?* Had the picture been taken through the window? No, the angle was all wrong and he had privacy film on all the windows. He tried to scroll again, but the message ended with the photo. Dropping the phone, he smashed his fist on the desk.

The stalker had put a camera in his room.

Christ. This changed everything. Kaden was right, he had to get Lauren to leave. As another wave of nausea threatened him, Nic hung his head between his knees. Hearing a gasp, he looked up and saw Lauren at his office door. She ran to his side and rubbed his back. "Are you feeling sick again? Should I call the hospital?"

"I'll be okay. Give me a minute." After taking a few more deep breaths, he sat up.

"You're white as a ghost. Did you get another message?"

Nic looked away. What had he done to this woman that her first thought was about what new disaster was falling down on them?

"Tell me what happened."

He couldn't let this go on. He had to make a decision, before one was forced on him. He could protect Rachel, or he could protect Lauren. But not both. Nic rubbed the bridge of his nose and closed his eyes. What the fuck had he done to get them all in this situation? He'd never meant to hurt anyone, yet he was going to end up hurting everyone. This whole thing was going to blow up in his face.

Given that he probably didn't have the money to pay the blackmail, Lauren had to go. But first, he had to tell her the truth about Rachel. And if she ended up hating him? Maybe that was for the best. Pain stabbed deep in his chest. Before the day was out, maybe he would lose the woman he'd been waiting for his entire life.

Standing up, he took her hand. "I'll tell you, but this might take a while, so let's go downstairs where we'll be more comfortable." Kaden was working out in the exercise room, and since his workouts always lasted a couple hours, Nic would have plenty of time to talk with Lauren in private.

In the living room, he took a seat on the couch and patted the spot beside him. Once she settled down, he stared straight ahead at the fireplace, unable to meet her gaze. This was it. A shudder of apprehension slithered up his spine like a snake. Yeah, that's exactly how he felt—like a snake.

"You can tell me anything. It'll be okay."

He closed his eyes. Nothing would ever be okay again. Once Lauren learned the truth, she'd be out of his life faster than Gaborik on a breakaway in a tied Stanley Cup game. He opened his eyes but continued to stare at the fireplace.

"This is very hard for me to say, to admit. So I'm just going to start at the beginning." He cleared his throat before continuing. "My sister Rachel lives in Montréal where she runs a ranch for disabled children. They come and ride the horses and it helps them physically as well as emotionally. All the services are free."

"Where does the money to run the ranch come from?"

He raised his eyebrow. "Oh, I see," she finished quickly, her checks blooming prettily. His heart ached. How would he get through another day without her smiles, her laughter, the soft music of her voice?

Steeling his heart, he pressed on. "Today Rachel received a blackmail letter from the stalker. Either we pay her ten million dollars within the next five days or she will hurt Rachel and ruin me." Not the whole truth but close enough.

"Ten million dollars! Not exactly chump change, is it?"

"The thing is, I don't even know if I have that kind of money available. I'll need to check with Vivian. After expenses, everything I make goes to Rachel to fund the ranch and programs for the children."

Lauren sat up. "Vivian manages your money?"

He'd better explain. "Remember when I told you about meeting Vivian when I first came to L.A.?"

"You became a client of the agency she ran with her husband, David."

Nic felt his lips kick up at the corner. Lauren had definitely been paying attention. "They took me in hand, even going so far as to front me the money to buy this building. Anyways, as people began to take notice of me, it became clear Hollywood had certain expectations I needed to meet if I wanted to make it big. After much discussion between the three of us, Nic The Lover was hatched." He chuckled ruefully. How could you love and hate something so much at the same time?

"Hollywood wanted a charmer, a true ladies' man who'd be talked about in all the tabloids and on talk shows across America. I needed to be seen at all the right publicity events and in all the right clubs. The image needed to be fed." Sarcasm had started to lace his tone so he took a deep breath.

When Lauren stroked his back, he kissed her softly on the cheek. "Don't feel sorry for me, *chérie*. I chose this life, and it hasn't been bad. I've gotten more than I ever expected from it."

Taking her hand in his, he went back to his explanation. "Maintaining that kind of lifestyle is expensive, but I didn't want it to affect the amount of money I was sending home. Vivian and David had already proven to me they were savvy investors, so I agreed to let them manage all my money, which allowed me to focus all my energy on the business of making money."

"Vivian and David knew about the ranch and Rachel?"

"Yes. They understood why I needed to be a *big star*." Embarrassed by his youthful naiveté, his cheeks burned. "They even took me to a hippo-therapy ranch outside L.A. so I could see how this type of therapy could benefit Rachel. That's when the idea took root: with the money I made, I could build a ranch Rachel could run when she got older. Vivian and David helped me develop a business plan, and six years later, when Rachel turned eighteen, the ranch opened for business."

"Everything was going great. I was making loads of money, and with Vivian and David's help, my money was making even more money for the ranch. My image was exactly right, and I was firmly entrenched in the industry. Then David died, the economy tanked, and Hollywood tightened its greedy fists. To be able to send the same money home to Rachel, I now have to work nonstop. I make as many movies as I can, I go to all the publicity events, and I get all the sponsors possible just to make ends meet."

He glanced at Lauren and shook his head. "The more money I make, the more money I need to make. But whatever. I doubt that Vivian can put together ten million from my investments in five days."

Lauren peered intently at him. "There's something I don't get. Why would you even want to pay the blackmail? So what if your sister runs a camp for disabled children? That's a good thing. Not something to hide from."

"Yeah, well. That's the second part of what I wanted to tell you."

Lauren squeezed his hand. He took a deep breath. "When I was in eleventh grade, my parents had to go to an important dinner for my father's work on the same evening as Rachel's ballet recital. They left me in charge; all I needed to do was get her to the recital on time. A bunch of my friends came over, we ordered pizza and started playing video games. When the time came to take Rachel to her recital, I was winning a game and refused to stop. I told her, 'Give me five more minutes, then we'll go.'"

"Sounds like you were a typical teenage boy stuck babysitting his little sister."

He shook his head. "A half hour later, when I finally won the game, I went to get Rachel. She was huddled in the corner of her room, tears streaming down her cheeks. Feeling like the biggest shit ever, I promised her she wouldn't be late."

The support and compassion in Lauren's eyes had his stomach flipping and flopping so much he thought he might puke. She moved closer and put her arm around him as if sensing what he was about to say next. He allowed the embrace but turned his head to stare out the window before continuing.

"We jumped into my mom's old Taurus and took off. I had fifteen minutes to make a twenty-five minute drive in the rain and the dark. Two miles before reaching the auditorium, I took a turn too fast and skidded. The car hit the gravel on the shoulder of the road and flipped."

Lauren gasped and her arms tightened around him.

"We smashed into trees lining the road. My head hit the steering wheel. I heard Rachel calling me, but it took a few moments before I could turn my head. Then I saw the blood. Drops of it splattered on the beige leather seats." A shudder shook his body. "Big smears of it on her pink tutu, on her face, her arms, her legs.... Christ. She'd been thrown forward; her legs were crushed between the dash and her seat. Blood was *everywhere*." He sucked in a deep breath and squeezed his eyes shut against the Technicolor images that had been burned in his brain thirteen years ago.

"But do you know what was worse than the blood?" When she shook her head, he continued. "Her voice. She kept saying over and over again, in a pitiful, falsely cheerful voice that everything would be okay. But I knew. Christ, how could I not? I knew everything wasn't okay and never would be again. And sometimes, I still hear that voice saying, 'It's okay, Nic. Everything's going to be all right.'" He covered his ears with both hands and leaned over until his elbows rested on his knees. "Even when I turn the music up real loud, I still hear it."

Lowering his hands, he paused, taking several calming breaths. Lauren stroked his cheek. Taking her hand in his, he kissed her fingertips, tasting the saltiness of his own tears. "It took the fire department two hours to pry her out of the car. By that time, she'd lost a lot of blood and hypothermia had set in." Pulling out of Lauren's arms, he turned to face her. He had reached the moment of truth. Watching her carefully, he said the words that damned him.

"The doctors did some tests and discovered her spine had been injured. We'd hoped that once the swelling went down, she'd be okay, but she wasn't. Rachel was only nine years old, and she's been paralyzed ever since. She'll never dance or run again, because of me."

Lauren's eyes filled with the disgust he'd feared. Nic sat frozen, unable to blink, unable to turn away.

He'd been wrong about her. Oh God, he'd been *so* wrong.

CHAPTER 18

Lauren's eyes widened in horror at Nic's story of two young lives irreparably damaged. *Poor Nic. Poor Rachel.*

He jerked back as if he'd been tasered and looked away. "So there you have it—the ugly truth about Nic The Lover. I ruined my sister's life." His tone was hard when he turned to her, eyes narrowed. "Do you still think I'm a 'good' guy now?"

Her gut twisted at the naked pain clouding his gaze. Were Jason to be injured like that for any reason, guilt would tear her apart. Nic had been carrying his remorse for the last thirteen years.

"I'm so sorry this happened to you, to both of you." Lauren wrapped her arms around him and held him tight.

For several moments, he held himself stiff, but then he relaxed and hugged her back. "It still hurts so much."

"I remember every time Jason's been injured as if it were yesterday. But there's something I've learned after eight years of being a mother: I'm not responsible for every bad thing that happens to the people I love." She cupped his face and forced him to look at her. "And neither are you, Nic. It was a horrible, tragic accident, but an accident all the same."

He shook his head. "No. It *was* my fault. My selfishness and stupidity cost her everything. Christ. I didn't even think to make her to sit in the back."

"What about your parents?"

"They were devastated. And when the bills for the hospital care and surgeries began coming in, the arguing and fighting started. I could hear them from my room, and I knew they blamed me."

Lauren's throat tightened in sympathy for the boy he'd been. "I'm sure they blamed themselves, not you."

Nic leaned back against the couch and stared out the window. "My mother might have blamed herself, but my father blamed me."

"You don't know that."

When Nic met her gaze, his jaw was clenched tight, but his eyes were full of regret. "I do. He told me. Every fucking day."

She shook her head, still unable to believe what he was saying. "Could you have misunderstood?"

Nic rubbed his jaw. "He said I'd ruined everything, that I'd killed our family. And he was right. After the accident, everything started falling apart. He started drinking, and after a few months lost his job. By summer, we declared bankruptcy and moved back to Montréal. At least there we had medical coverage, and my sister could get the treatment she needed."

"Nic," she said gently. "He wasn't right. It's not your fault he started drinking. If he hadn't, he wouldn't have lost his job, and he would have kept his health insurance."

Nic rose from the couch and started pacing. He paused in front of the window, then shook his head. "You don't understand." His voice was rough, raw, and Lauren's chest ached at the sound of it. "What happened to Rachel devastated him. He drank to ease the pain, to get through each day. Every time he looked at Rachel, he cried. You have no idea how it feels to see your dad cry because of something you did. And every time he saw me, he got angry. Sometimes my mom tried to intervene, but I finally convinced her not to try. The last thing I wanted was for her to jump in and get hit."

"He hit you?"

His back still to her, Nic shrugged. "Can you blame him? I didn't."

Damn right she blamed his father. "No child deserves to be abused."

After letting out a long breath, he turned away from the window and crossed his arms. "Things didn't get much better in Montréal. We ended up on welfare, so I quit school and got a job at a fast food joint. When I brought my first pay home, my father laughed. He told me that the pittance I made didn't earn me more than a cot in the garage. That he didn't want a no-good high school drop-out living in his house. That all I did was eat and shit like a dog, and that I was lucky he didn't tie me to a post in the yard."

Bile rose in her throat. "How could a father be so cruel?"

Nic's eyes circled the room. "I deserved it." Before she could respond, his gaze landed on her face. "Two years later, I found him dead in the garage. He got his revenge; I still have nightmares about it."

Lauren recoiled in shock. "Oh, God. That's horrible." She reached out to him, but dropped her hand when he shot her a don't-touch-me look.

"It tore my mother apart. She kept telling me that my father was wrong, that she didn't blame me. But every night, she cried herself to sleep."

"She loved you."

"I know." Nic rolled his shoulders and began pacing again. "But now that she's gone too, Rachel is alone. Except for Rémi."

"No, Nic. She still has you." Injury or not, she was certain Rachel loved her big brother. No one in their right mind would blame him. What had happened to the Lamoureux family was tragic and sad, but it wasn't shameful. Nic had no reason to cave in to the stalker's demands. If done right, Nic could bring all of these secrets out into the open in a positive and effective manner that wouldn't be career-destroying.

Nic turned and braced his forearms against the window. Lauren rose and, pressing her body against his back, began to rock him in a soothing rhythm, hoping he'd understand there was no chance she'd hate him. If nothing else, he was her friend, and he always would be. "You're a good brother, Nic."

Nic scowled at her over his shoulder.

"I mean it. It was an *accident*." She took a step back when he turned, smirking. He started to say something, but she cut him off. "Okay, you used poor judgment, but what teenager doesn't? You were young, and you made a stupid mistake."

Nic shook his head. "You don't understand."

"I do understand, and you know it." The words came out more sharply than she'd intended. Softening her tone, she continued. "I wasted years of my life feeling guilty. Talk to Rachel, tell her how you feel, and get over it. Then thank God every day that she's still alive so you can be with her and enjoy your time together." Her eyes filled with tears. "That's something I'll never have the chance to do with Todd. So don't talk to me about guilt or remorse. I know *all* about it, and if I can move on, so can you."

Nic closed the distance between them and cupped her cheeks tenderly. "*Chérie*," he said, his voice soft. "I know you think this is like you and Todd. And in some ways, maybe it is. But Rachel isn't dead. She has to live with being paralyzed every single day of her life."

"That's the point. Rachel isn't dead. She's useful and productive, and together the two of you have built something wonderful. The ranch helps other kids with spinal injuries, and through the Make-A-Wish Foundation, you make a huge difference in the lives of hundreds of seriously ill children every year. There's honor in that. And if you doubt what I'm saying, remember the look on Claire's face when you danced with her."

"It's not enough." He dropped his hands.

"The way I see it, you accepted responsibility for your mistakes, and every day you work to make amends. Most people don't."

"I can try for the rest of my life, but it will never be enough. You're just not getting it." With rough movements, he scrubbed his face. "Because of me, my father drank himself to death, my sister is paralyzed for life, and my mother cried her way through the last ten years of her life. Because of my *stupid mistake*, as you call it, I wrecked the lives of my *entire* family. Nothing I can ever do will make up for that."

Lauren barely stifled a groan. How could she get him to understand?

"Your father blamed you, but he was wrong. Any time a parent leaves one child to care for another, they're taking a risk. And if something goes wrong, as it did that night, they have to share the blame. Your father drank himself to death because he knew the truth. He blamed you because it was easier than admitting his own guilt."

"Ah, Lauren, sweet Lauren." He wrapped a curl around her ear and smiled wryly. "I guess what they say about love being blind is true. When you have time to think about all this, your feelings for me will wear off, and then you'll see me for who I am." He leaned forward and pressed a gentle kiss to her lips. "And you'll leave me."

Lauren held herself as still as she could. Oh, God. How could she tell him about New York now? He'd automatically assume he was right, that she was leaving because of this. But she couldn't lie and say she'd never leave him, either. So she said the only thing she could say with all honesty. "You're wrong, Nic. My feelings for you will never change."

"I'm sure you believe that. But things are getting very dangerous. If you or Jason get hurt because of me, everything will change."

"Did something else happen?"

"The stalker's threats are escalating. She sent me a message with another photo to make sure I believed the blackmail letter was real."

"Can you send it to me?" Another photo meant the possibility of more clues.

Nic nodded.

"I'll do whatever I can to help the police catch her. This person knows everything about you." *Things no one knows besides Vivian.* But why would Vivian threaten to kill Nic? From the first time Lauren had met the woman at the photo shoot in D.C., it had been clear that Vivian had deep feelings for Nic, feelings he didn't reciprocate, at least not in a sexual way. Was Vivian trying to get Lauren out of the picture? Was Lauren the real target? Disturbed by that thought, she rubbed her arms to ward off the chill that suddenly gripped her.

She loved Nic, more than she ever thought she could love a man. But if she didn't want Jason to end up an orphan, she had to get away from him.

And away from Vivian.

Nic stood on the balcony taking in the view of L.A., relief and trepidation warring in his mind. Like Damocles sitting under the hanging sword, he knew it was only a matter of time before it fell. After his confession to Lauren, he'd given Kaden an abbreviated version. The man had concluded the whole blackmail thing was "bullshit."

Lauren's reaction had been more ambivalent. She hadn't exactly run screaming, but he'd seen fear flash in her green gaze when she'd told him: *this person knows everything about you.* She suspected Vivian, and some of the evidence did fit, but he couldn't bring himself to believe it.

Without Vivian, his mother would have died in the hovel they'd been renting. And Rachel? God knows what would have become of her. He owed Vivian everything.

The thought of her threatening to kill him, or anyone, was simply ludicrous. Besides, Vivian was an in-your-face kind of woman. She wouldn't hide behind anonymous messages. Pulling the phone out of his back pocket, he dialed her number.

She answered immediately. "Hello, darling. How is our dear Lorna today?"

"Vivian, you know that's not her name."

Nic heard silence on the line, then a long sigh. "You're right, and I'm sorry. Is Lauren feeling better today?"

"I have some bad news. Rachel received a blackmail notice. I'm to pay ten million dollars by Sunday or they'll kill me."

Vivian gasped but didn't say anything, so he continued. "The blackmail note also said they'd tell the press about Rachel's accident. Did you ever tell anyone?"

"Absolutely not."

"What about David?"

"He wasn't the sort to go spilling secrets. But, you never know. What are you going to do, darling?"

"Pay them. We need to discuss my finances and how we can get the money."

"I'll collect all your documents and be there in an hour."

"Thanks, Viv. You're a good friend."

He could hear the smile in her voice when she replied, "You make it easy, darling."

As he slipped the phone back in his pocket, Lauren stepped out onto the balcony. He turned and leaned against the railing, trying to catch a hint of what she was feeling. Her guarded expression gave him all the answer he needed.

She handed him a large glass of ice tea. "I thought you could use a cold drink."

He took the glass and planted a kiss on her pink lips. "I love you, you know that, right?"

She smiled, but it didn't reach her eyes. "I know. I love you, too."

What was he going to do? He felt like Romeo to her Juliet, lovers destined never to be together. Then he remembered something Vivian said at the Gala. "*Vanity Fair* contacted you?" Maybe talking about her career would bring the sparkle back into her eyes.

"The assistant editor called. They're interested in my work."

"This is just the beginning." He smiled brightly.

"Actually," Lauren said, her gaze focused on the view over his shoulder. "They're interested in more than a few photos. They offered me a position."

"A position? That's fantastic!" He pulled her into his arms and twirled her in circles, making her laugh. When he stopped, they were both breathless. "I knew everyone would love your work." Fingers threaded in her hair, he kissed her tenderly. "I'm so proud of you, *chérie*."

Lauren swallowed and pressed her face into his shoulder. "None of this would have been possible without you."

"That's not true. I may have helped, but it's your talent that made it happen." He looked down at the love of his life, hating what he had to do. When he spoke, his voice was rough. "So, you'll be returning to Seattle tomorrow? Kaden arranged for a bodyguard to go with you." Her head jerked up, her eyes wide. His words sounded like a brush-off, but it was better for her to be a little hurt than a lot dead.

"Ah," she cleared her throat. "Actually, I'm heading out to New York City."

What the fuck? "The job is in New York?"

"Yes." Then as he pinned her with his stare, she jammed her hands in the front pockets of her pants. "I start on Friday."

He frowned. "When did you find out?"

"This morning."

"Before or after I told you about the accident?"

"Before."

"And when did you decide to leave?"

"Why the inquisition, Nic?"

"Answer the question."

"When they called."

Nic whirled around, unable to bear the lie on her face. No way had Lauren decided to up and move clear across the country so quickly.

Unless she was trying to get as far away from him as possible.

"Nic." When he didn't respond, she tugged on his sleeve. "Look at me." Reluctantly, he turned and met her gaze. "What's going on?"

The concern in her voice had little effect on him. She could pretend all she wanted, but he knew the truth. He crossed his arms over his chest to keep from touching her, then leaned forward until his face was only inches from hers. "You're leaving because of Rachel."

"Oh," she gasped, her hand flying to her mouth. "Don't think that!"

"How can I not? I tell you, and less than an hour later, you say you're moving to the East Coast." He leaned his elbows on the railing and closed his eyes against the bitterness he heard in his voice.

"This has nothing to do with Rachel. It's about me. I want this job, and I need the money."

He sighed and opened his eyes. "There's more to this than just the job."

Pushing away from the railing, he stood in front of her. Giving in to the desire to feel her warmth, he cupped her shoulders with his hands. "Be honest with me. I've told you everything. You have the power to ruin me with one call to the paparazzi."

Tears welled in her eyes. She pressed her palm over his heart and leaned her forehead against his chest. He slid his hands down her arms and around her waist, holding her tight, and nuzzled her hair. Her body shook with the force of her sobs. *Shit.* "It's okay, *chérie*. I understand."

Lifting her head, she wiped her cheeks. "No, you don't." With her arms around his neck, she stared into his eyes and spoke a truth that shattered his soul. "I love you, Nic. I always will. But my son has to come first. The stalker killed Summer, and now she's coming after me. I know you'll try to protect me, but I can't take that kind of risk. I can't bring that kind of danger into Jason's life, not even for you."

Each word pierced his heart like a bullet. He'd known she'd dump him, but he'd hoped it wouldn't be so suddenly, and so completely. But she was right. Jason had to be her number one priority.

He caressed her cheek. "You'll both be safer if you have nothing to do with me. That's what the stalker wants." He pulled out of her arms and took a step back, thrusting his fists into his pockets. "I assume you'll want to leave for Seattle today."

She wiped her cheeks and nodded. "I think that's best," she said in a small voice.

Spinning around on his heel, he headed for the patio door. "I'll tell Kaden so he can alert your bodyguard to the change of plans." Inside the kitchen and out of sight of Lauren, he slammed his fist into the wall.

He'd wanted Lauren to leave. He just hadn't expected it to hurt so fucking much.

~

Nic paced the living room, listening to the small noises coming from his bedroom as Lauren packed up her things. It was probably a good thing she was leaving right away. Maybe it would be like pulling off a Band-Aid, the quicker you did it, the less it hurt. *Yeah, right.*

When the security intercom buzzed, he practically ran to the door, relieved to have something to take his mind off Lauren, if only for a few moments.

He let Vivian into the building and waited for her by the elevator door. As soon as they settled on the couch, Nic asked, "How much cash do I have?"

"Most of your money is tied up in investments I can't quickly liquidate. I might be able to pull together two million."

He ran his hands through his hair and leaned forward to rest his elbows on his knees. How could it be that even after ten years in the business with countless hit movies, he still had money problems like some struggling wannabe? The money he'd made last year had earned him the title of highest-paid actor. The numbers didn't add up.

"Where's all the money I made from *Darkness Rising*?" She started fidgeting with her purse strap and his anxiety shot up. Vivian never fidgeted. "Viv, whatever it is, you can tell me."

Tears flooded her eyes as she raised her gaze to meet his. He braced himself for some very bad news. The only time he'd ever seen Vivian cry was when David died. "I don't know how to tell you this. You're going to hate me."

He watched the tears stream down her cheeks, creating thin lines of mascara like scratches on her face. "Take a deep breath and start from the beginning. Whatever it is can't be as bad as you think."

"After David died, the hospital bills came in faster than I could pay them. I took out a loan, but when David's clients started leaving the agency, I started missing payments. After I missed the third one, they sent a collection agency after me. My lawyer managed to negotiate an extension to the loan but with a much higher interest rate." She arched a brow. "If I couldn't make the original payments, how on earth did they expect me to make the higher ones?"

Shock made his jaw drop. He'd known the agency was struggling, but he'd had no idea things had gotten this bad. She'd never seemed troubled by anything. "Why didn't you tell me?"

Her round, wet eyes implored him to understand. "I thought if you knew, you'd leave the agency like the others. Then I'd be alone. I'd have nothing and no one."

Unable to stand the shadows of fear swirling in his friend's eyes, this woman who had been his rock, he pulled her close as if to shelter her from the world. Rubbing her back, he whispered soothing words in her ear.

After several minutes, her sobbing subsided, and she pulled back. "I got your shirt all wet."

"Never mind. Just tell me the rest."

She bit her lower lip and continued to stare at his wet shirt for a moment. But then she nodded. "I know it was wrong, but...." She paused and turned half away. "I started borrowing money from you to make my payments. I was sure I could rebuild the agency and pay you back with interest, before you needed to know. Only..."

"Only..." he urged.

"Only things didn't work out that way. I couldn't get any other big-name artists to join the agency. And when the market crashed, I needed to borrow even more money from you to keep the agency afloat." Reluctantly, she met his gaze. "I'm so sorry."

Jesus Christ. What an absolute fucking disaster. Vivian knew that besides what he spent to maintain his image, every cent he made was used to support

Rachel and the ranch. He *needed* his money. "How much did you borrow?"

"Does it matter anymore, darling? The money's gone."

His fingers dug into the armrest. "How much?"

Swallowing visibly, she straightened her spine. "Forty million."

Nic's eyes rounded at the sheer magnitude of the number. "Forty fucking million? Even without insurance, David's hospital bills couldn't add up to that much. Did you fucking *burn* it?"

"You're angry." Her voice was flat, emotionless, like the Vivian he was used to.

"No shit, Sherlock." Jumping up from the couch, he began pacing the room. "How could you do this to me? I would have helped you if you'd asked. But to just take it?" He threw his hands up in the air. "God. I can't fucking believe this."

"Darling, please understand—"

He whirled around, interrupting her. "Understand what, Vivian? You haven't answered my question. What the *fuck* did you do. With. All. My. Money?"

"Besides the two million I borrowed for the hospital bills, David invested half of it in a land deal before he died. We were going to build a five hundred unit loft high-rise, right in downtown L.A. The projected returns were fantastic. Tripling your money. But then the real estate bubble burst and the deal fell through. We lost everything."

Nic was squeezing his fists so tightly, he drew blood. After a quick glance at his palms, he shoved his hands into his pockets. Blacking out was the last thing he needed right now. "What about the other half?"

"Carmichael Productions. Four years ago, David started a film production company. All our clients invested in it, including you."

"Nice of you to let me know. What happened to the company?" He sneered. "Let me guess, it went under too?"

Hands in her lap, she sat on the couch like a statue. Her lips barely moving, she said so softly, he almost didn't hear her, "I'll understand if you want to quit the agency."

He snorted. "Don't you realize I could have you arrested for fucking embezzlement?" But God, could he really do that to her? Vivian would never survive prison; she'd barely survived losing David. One thing was sure—she wouldn't be managing his goddamn money anymore.

"There is another way," she said.

"What are you talking about?"

"To get the money you need to pay the blackmailers. I'm selling my house. The deal should be going through in the next day or so."

Nic sat back down beside her. "You're moving?" Was another woman in his life leaving him?

Vivian smiled. "I'd never go anywhere without you. The house is too big and I don't need it anymore. The buyer agreed to pay six million for it, which with the two million from your investments leaves you only two million short."

"Any idea where I can get that kind of money?"

She grinned. "Lauren could sell her Harry Winston necklace."

He narrowed his eyes at her. "Never."

"I was kidding." She patted his knee. "But seriously, back when business was booming, David bought me some nice pieces. I'll take them to the jewelers and see what I can get."

He didn't want her to sell her home or the jewelry her dead husband had given her to pay him back. But what choice did he have? If he didn't pay the money, the stalker would still go after Lauren. "Why would you do this?"

"Because you mean the world to me, darling."

Just then, he heard a noise and looked over his shoulder to see Lauren coming down the stairs, struggling with her luggage. Vivian quickly pulled a tissue out of her purse and furtively wiped at the streaks on her cheeks. Nic raced up the steps and grabbed Lauren's bags, then set them on the floor near the door.

She stood frozen at the bottom of the stairs, staring at Vivian, saying nothing. Vivian broke the silence with one of her usual catty comments. "Leaving so soon, dear?"

Seeing Lauren's eyes narrow, Nic decided to intervene before things got uglier. "Vivian, thanks for dropping by." He hooked an arm around Vivian's shoulders and led her to the door. "Let me know when the deal goes through, okay?"

"You can count on it."

Closing the door behind her, Nic barely suppressed a sigh of relief. Both women had looked ready for a no-holds-barred cage fight. He plastered a blank expression on his face and turned around. "Ready?"

She nodded but didn't make a move to come closer.

"Is something wrong?"

"I... uh..." She stopped and swallowed, then licked her lips as if her mouth were dry. "I want you to keep an open mind about what I'm going to say."

"Okay." Her hesitation was making him nervous.

"Vivian wears designer shoes."

"What does that have to do with anything?"

Lauren closed her eyes for a moment and sighed. "Nic, open your eyes. Vivian fits the profile of the stalker perfectly."

Nic shook his head. Vivian had the means to do this and God knows she had the opportunity. But as far as he could tell, she had no motive. How would Vivian benefit from stalking him or trying to get money? Shit, the woman had already cleaned him out.

Lauren took a step toward him. "Promise me something."

"What's that?"

"Every time you see her from now on, look at her shoes. I know I've seen her wear red-soled shoes before."

Nic folded his arms across his chest. "Okay."

"Promise?"

When he nodded, she closed the distance separating them and rising on her toes, placed a tender kiss on his lips. "Be careful, Nic. I don't want to lose another man I love to violence."

He gazed into her sweet blue-green eyes, feeling like a dead man walking. "You already have, *chérie*. You already have."

Vivian stood silent, unmoving, after Nic closed the door behind her. The defeat on that moneygrubber's face as she plodded down the stairs with her luggage had been priceless. But before the celebration started, she had to be sure the leech was leaving for good.

She pressed her ear to the door. The cow was saying something, but she couldn't make out the words. Vivian eyed the handle. She did have the key.... Maybe she could open the door just a tad. As she was about to turn the knob, she caught sight of the security keypad and froze. *Shit.* Nic had changed the code and hadn't given her the new one.

Damn it, she had to know what they were saying. The gold digger had gotten the *Vanity Fair* job, what more did she want? Like Summer, she was using Nic as a launching-pad for her career. Why else had she entered that photography contest?

The sound of movement on the other side of the door captured her attention. After cupping her hand, she leaned her ear against it. *Lorna* was speaking. What was she saying?

"I don't want to lose..." Vivian's stomach fluttered. This could be it. God she was so close. The end of the sentence was garbled, but the missing word had to be "you."

Vivian waited breathless, for Nic's response. She couldn't stand much more of this. He had to tell the parasite to hit the road. She'd given him warning after warning, and he'd ignored them all. At least until receiving the blackmail notice. Oh, what genius that had been, if she did say so herself. Her poor darling was wonderfully protective and loyal to a fault. She'd never doubted the extremes to which he'd go to protect his sister, and himself, from the press. She chuckled softly at the thought. He was a bit of a diva that way.

"You already have," he said, and tingles raced up and down Vivian's spine, like the precursor to a supernova of an orgasm. Hallelujah! Nic had finally dumped his little piece of tail.

Vivian leaned her head against the door and breathed a sigh of relief. For a few days now, she'd been worried that he'd mess up her plan. And even though she really hadn't wanted to hurt him, she would have if he'd continued seeing the tramp.

But today, he'd manned up. Her chest warmed with pride at how he'd honored her love and friendship. The hurt in his eyes when he'd asked why she hadn't confided in him about the agency's troubles had broken her heart. But his expression of bemused love when he'd accepted her offer to loan him the cash to pay the *blackmailer*? Well, that look of love made this whole charade worthwhile. She felt a momentary pang of remorse for the necessary deception but shrugged it off.

Everything she'd done had been out of love.

She hadn't enjoyed killing Summer. Well… maybe just a bit. But that was beside the point. She'd killed her because she'd had to. The too-stupid-to-live idiot had deserved to die for what she'd done to Nic. And if that slut *Lorna* tried to ingratiate herself back into his bed, Vivian would have to take a more direct approach to getting rid of the vermin in Nic's life.

Vivian pushed away from the door. She'd heard enough. Her plan was coming together. Now that Nic had chosen her above all others, she could move on to the next step: resolving the blackmail issue. Tomorrow she'd call him and let him know that by some miracle, she'd managed to scrounge up the full ten million dollars. She grinned, thinking how pleased he'd be with her for saving him and Rachel from exposure. On Saturday, she'd join him at the ranch, and on Sunday, they'd meet the deadline and transfer the ransom to the *blackmailer's* account, together. And then, finally, her dream would come true.

A laugh bubbled in her chest as she imagined his reaction when she brought him to the island paradise she'd created for their mutual pleasure and showed him what his money had bought. After they were married, she'd gift him with the blackmail money. She couldn't wait to see the surprise on his face when she told him it was all in a joint account she'd set up for them in the Bahamas.

Just thinking about the appreciation he'd lavish on her sent a thrill of excitement rippling through her body. It would be nothing like what she'd seen him do with that cunt because Nic loved her. His actions today had proved it.

But how was she going to get him away from Kaden? A smile broke out across her face. Summer's idea of using Rohypnol had been brilliant, even though she'd had to die because of it. But unlike Summer, Vivian knew what she was doing.

She'd slip a tablet of Rohypnol to Kaden somehow and stash him somewhere no one would find him for a while. Then she'd suggest Nic take her to Starbucks. A little Rohypnol in his coffee, and *voilà*! They'd be off to the airport, and off to paradise. And if anyone commented on Nic's state, she'd laugh and say something like, "You know how these Hollywood types like to party…"

A chartered plane would be waiting to fly them from Montréal to the Caribbean, and from there it would be a short boat ride to their new home.

Behind her, the elevator made a noise. Shit, someone was coming. Turning, she spotted the emergency stairs. She'd stay there until the coast was clear. Soundlessly, she slipped into her hiding spot.

And rejoiced in her victory.

CHAPTER 19

The door shut behind Lauren with a finality that threatened to stop her heart and made her mind reel. How fast everything had changed. This morning she'd woken up in Nic's arms, and now she was leaving, never to see him again. Except in movies. Her life had come full circle. She was back in that lonely place she'd been before meeting Nic. Worse even, because she'd have to live with all the memories of what could have been. Tears filled her eyes.

The elevator opened, and she stumbled walking into it. Jake, her new bodyguard, gripped her elbow, steadying her. She murmured her thanks and turned away, trying to keep him from seeing the tears tracking down her cheeks.

"Thought you could use this ma'am," Jake said gruffly, handing her a handkerchief.

Embarrassed, she dried her eyes, then glanced at him. "I'm sorry, Jake."

"No need, ma'am. Partings are hard."

Lauren nodded. It would take a lifetime to get over losing Nic, a lifetime to ease the ache in her chest.

They arrived on the ground floor and Jake led her to a limo waiting by the curb. She turned to look up at Nic's windows. When a curtain fluttered, her stomach somersaulted. But then a breeze moved the curtain again. Her stomach plummeted. He wasn't there.

A barren emptiness grew in her chest, bending her like a leaf. Sobbing, she slumped against the side of the car, and wrapped her arms around her waist. It was just like when Todd died, when depression had gripped her in its fist. Oh God! She couldn't let that happen again. *Fight it, Lauren!*

Seconds later, Jake was at her side. "It'll be okay ma'am. You'll be safe with me." He helped her into the back seat of the car. When she just stared at him dumbly, he added, "I promise." Then he shut the door and climbed into the driver's seat.

As the car drove off, she forced herself not to glance back. She had to focus on her future. She'd lost Nic, but she hadn't lost everything. The job with *Vanity Fair* opened up new possibilities for her and Jason.

Jake wheeled the limo onto the freeway. Through the window, cars and buildings zoomed by. Life was like that. It zoomed by and if you didn't keep your eyes wide open, you'd miss it. That's how her relationship with Nic felt—over before it started.

What hurt the most was losing him even though he loved her, she loved him, and they were both alive. She hated this whole situation. Hated that a stalker was dictating their actions. Hated that violence was once again controlling her life.

She pounded her fist on the seat beside her. She'd get her revenge. If there was any evidence hidden in the photos they'd received from the stalker, she'd find it. Nic had sent her the latest one, and as soon as she got a chance, she'd examine it. Maybe something in the photo would prove her suspicions about Vivian right or wrong.

And if it was Vivian? *God help us, God help us all.*

Nic stood by the window and eased the curtain aside to watch Lauren leave. As if sensing his presence, she turned and looked up. He let the curtain drop back into place. After waiting a few seconds, he edged the curtain out of the way again. He didn't want to miss seeing her for what might be the last time.

Inch by agonizing inch, he leaned over until she came into view. The sight below iced his blood, freezing him in place. Lauren lurched and fell against the car, gripping her stomach. Was she hurt? *Jesus Christ!* Had the stalker shot her?

Shaking off the paralysis, he whirled and started running for the door. Kaden stepped in front of him, blocking his path. "Let her go, man."

Nic glared at his bodyguard. "She's hurt! I have to help her." He tried to shove his way past, but Kaden refused to budge. What the fuck was his problem? Anger roared through him. "If you don't get out of my fucking way right fucking now, this is going to get fucking ugly."

"It'll only make things worse if you go down there."

"What the fuck are you talking about? I can't leave her to bleed to death in the street like a dog. I love her!" He was shouting now, but he didn't give a shit. If Kaden wouldn't let him get to the door, he'd jump out the goddamn window.

Kaden gripped his shoulders. "Listen, man. Lauren's not hurt. At least not the way you think."

"But I saw her fall."

"Out of grief." Kaden patted his arms and released him. Nic reeled as understanding hit. He stumbled to the couch. How were they going to make it through this? Seeing her fall like that had nearly killed him. He shouldn't have pushed her to leave. But… she'd decided to leave even before he'd brought it up. So, why was leaving him hurting her so much? Why was it hurting her as much as it hurt him?

Because she hadn't *wanted* to leave.

He had to make this right. He had to get the stalker out of their lives. One way or another, by Sunday he'd end it.

Fired up, he raced to his bedroom, Kaden close on his heels. He considered the angle of the photo the bitch stalker had sent of Lauren and him. Eyes up, he examined the ceiling.

"What are you looking for?"

"The stalker hid a camera here."

Shock colored Kaden's features. "Really? How do you know?"

"The bitch sent me a photo. It was taken here."

"Can I see it?"

Nic's head flew around and he practically growled. "No fucking way."

Kaden held up his hands. "Okay, man. Just asking."

Christ. He was the world's biggest shithead. Of *course* Kaden would ask to see the photo. He had no way of knowing Nic would have to kill him if he ever saw Lauren that way. Nic shook his head and purposely softened his expression. "It's personal."

"Enough said."

"The camera should be positioned high on the wall or on the ceiling." Their eyes locked. Nic grinned, though it probably looked more like a grimace. "Let's tear this place apart."

"Wait," Kaden said. "Do you have a flashlight?"

Nic grabbed one from the nightstand drawer and handed it to Kaden.

"Perfect." Kaden hit the lights. "Get the blinds, will you?"

Nic lowered the blinds, plunging the room into darkness. "What now?"

Kaden aimed the beam at the ceiling light fixture. "We look for hiding spots. The camera lens will reflect the light."

Nic ran to his office and grabbed the extra flashlight he kept in his desk. When he returned, Kaden had finished with the ceiling light and was working his way along one wall. Nic started searching the opposite side of the room. He pulled down every picture and painting, examining every inch. Then he ran the light along the edge of the ceiling. That's when he spied a tiny glimmer, no more than a speck of light, at the junction of the wall and the crown molding. "I've got something!" He climbed onto the dresser to get a closer look.

Kaden pushed a nightstand against the wall and joined him. He leaned in with his flashlight. "Aye, thar she be," he said in an overblown pirate voice. Nic laughed. Kaden was going to get rich off him, but it wouldn't be for his acting skills.

After a moment, Nic's laughter died, and the truth of the discovery hit him. The stalker wasn't just sending him messages and tracking him through his phone. She was spying on him, in his home. This bitch, whoever she was, had watched him in the most private of places, doing the most private of things with Lauren. Nic barely held himself back from punching a hole in the wall to rip the fucking camera out.

Wordlessly, he signaled to Kaden to move into the hall and closed the door behind them. "You have no idea how much I want to destroy that thing, but after the comment Becker made about leaving the detecting to the detectives...."

"I feel you, man. But it's better this way. The LAPD has camera detectors. If there are more hidden around the loft, they'll find them."

"More? Christ, I hadn't even thought of that. The bitch has probably been getting her jollies watching me shower." Nic's cheeks heated, from anger or embarrassment, he wasn't sure. Kaden rubbed his mouth, trying to smother a smile.

Under other circumstances, Nic might have gotten a kick out of the situation, too. But Lauren had been in that fucking shower. And there was nothing funny about that. The stalker had video footage. What if she posted everything on the Internet? His hands itched with the desire to tear the place apart, until not a single wall remained untouched, until he'd located and destroyed every last camera.

Nic pulled out his cell phone and called Detective Anderson. "This is Nic Lamoureux. The stalker planted cameras in my loft."

"Did you touch anything?"

"No."

"We'll be right over with the tech crew."

Nic hung up. "They're on their way."

Kaden arched a brow. "And once they're done, then what? The safety and security of the loft has been compromised."

Nic nodded. He couldn't stay here and didn't want to. Lauren had stayed here with him only one short week, but he felt her presence in every room. Even worse, he now felt the stalker's presence in every dark corner, every shadow. A shudder flashed up his spine. He never wanted to set foot in this place again.

He had to get up to Montréal and make sure the ranch was still secure, that it hadn't also been violated by the stalker. And he had to talk to Rachel, let her know he might not be able to pay the blackmail, that their secret might be made public. She'd already suffered so much because of him, and now she might have to share in his humiliation. If she kicked him out of the house, he'd deserve it.

Rubbing his neck, he breathed out a long sigh. His whole fucking life was crumbling—Lauren gone, his career threatened, the sanctity of his home annihilated. The stalker had invaded every aspect of his world and destroyed it.

When Lauren left, she'd taken every hope of happiness with her. Maybe after spending some time on the ranch, the pain of losing Lauren would ease. It was the only place on earth he could breathe, where he could relax and be himself.

Nic's shoulders sagged. Who was he kidding? He'd never get over losing Lauren.

"What now?" Kaden asked again.

Nic met his bodyguard's solid, reassuring gaze. He might have lost the woman he would love for the rest of his life, but he would make sure she was safe, wherever she was.

A plan formed in his mind.

He squared his shoulders and thumped Kaden on the back. "Now, we go home."

Anxiety coiled in the pit of Nic's stomach as he wheeled the rented SUV onto the narrow country road. He took the next curve, passed a copse of trees, and halted under the large wooden arch engraved with the scripted letters R and H, proclaiming the ranch Rachel's Haven.

After keying in the security code to open the gates, Nic mentally kicked himself. Turning to Kaden, he grimaced. "If I'd been even half as smart as the stalker and installed a security camera here, we'd at least know who delivered the damn blackmail note."

Kaden peered over at the mailbox, then up at the arch and nodded. "Yep, but we'll catch her, anyways."

Nic drove through the gates and filled his lungs with a breath of clean ranch air, hoping to calm his nerves before facing Rachel. Since the mere mention of the accident brought to mind their father's rages and hate-filled words, they'd never really discussed what had happened that night thirteen years ago.

The few times the subject had been broached, Rachel had been quick to discount his part in it and changed the subject. If glossing over the truth helped her move on, so be it. Who was he to judge? Clearly, it was something she didn't want to talk about. But they had to discuss it. He had to tell her he didn't have the money to pay the blackmail.

After all these years, he was going to hear how she really felt about him, about his role in her injuries. His stomach cramped and bile rose in his throat. Everything he'd done since that day, he'd done for her. If he lost Rachel too, it would kill him. With slightly unsteady hands, he stopped the car in front of the main house and turned off the motor.

Before opening the door, he turned to observe Kaden's reaction. The house was small, tiny even, compared to Hollywood standards, but it suited them perfectly. Rachel and their mother had instantly fallen in love with the two-story house with its wrap-around veranda, while he'd been captivated by the acres of land surrounding it. Even though he didn't visit the ranch nearly as much as he'd like to, unlike anywhere else in the world, this was home. "So, what do you think?"

Kaden watched the ranch hands lead the horses out of the stable to frolic in the fields before the kids arrived for their therapy sessions. As the horses' whinnies reached them, his expression grew wistful, and Nic realized he didn't know much about his bodyguard beyond his exemplary military record and spotless reputation in the small world of personal security. Kaden glanced at him, then returned his attention to the horses. "I don't know how you do it."

"Do what?" Rachel had been running the ranch since she turned eighteen. He didn't do anything, except send money.

"Live in L.A., and put up with all the shit that goes on there. If I had a place like this"—Kaden indicated the ranch with a sweep of his hand—"I'd never leave."

Nic let his gaze wander, taking in the house, the land, the animals, and sighed. "I do it because I have to." He'd been planning to cut back on the number of movies he did, but now, that wouldn't be possible.

"Not that I want to stick my nose in your business, but I have heard the rumors. You earned millions from *Bad Days* alone. With that kind of money, you could quit Hollywood today and still live comfortably for the rest of your life."

Holding up his empty hands, Nic shook his head. "I'm broke."

Kaden's brows shot up. "What?"

"Apparently, before he died, David invested my money in several bad ventures. Then Vivian *borrowed* most of what was left." He made quotes in the air with his fingers. "It's pretty much all gone."

Fucking bitch. Kaden didn't say the words out loud, but Nic read them clearly in his expression. "What're you going to do?"

Nic gave a half shrug, trying to look casual as he opened the door. "The only thing I can do: keep working."

"Nic!" He heard Rachel calling him from the house's large front porch. A brilliant smile lit her face when he turned to her. Slightly in front of her, his stance protective, stood a large man, who by the resemblance to Rémi, had to be his cousin, Tommy. Nic slammed the door shut and raced up the wheelchair ramp. After briefly greeting the man, he bent down to give Rachel a hug. "It's so good to have you home again," she said against his shoulder.

He tightened his hold on her, then released her and crouched on his haunches. "How are you, Rachel?"

"I'm doing great." The optimism in her voice warmed him. "The doctor said the fracture is healing more quickly than he'd anticipated. If things keep going this way, I can start some light physical therapy on that leg too in a couple months."

Nic gripped her hands and bent to kiss her knuckles, hiding his face. He swallowed hard to push down the lump in his throat. "Thank God," he managed to murmur. He heard heavy footsteps on the ramp and stood up as Kaden joined them. "Rachel, Tommy, this is Kaden Christiansen, my bodyguard."

Kaden took Rachel's hand. "Pleased to meet you, Ms. Lamoureux."

"Please, call me Rachel."

Kaden nodded, then shook hands with Tommy. Nic placed his hand on Rachel's shoulder as he pinned Kaden with a sharp stare. "Rachel is your new number one priority."

"If I'm Kaden's *new* number one priority, who was his last?"

Nic absorbed the words like a punch in the gut—hard. He glanced at Kaden, but the fucker just shrugged. *Shit.* Nic really didn't want to talk about Lauren right now.

Kaden gave him a slight reprieve when he picked up the luggage and asked, "Why don't I take these inside?"

"Thanks, man," Nic said, barely suppressing his sarcasm. "Pick a room on the second floor for yourself. Mine's on the top floor." When they'd moved into the house, he'd had the attic converted into a suite for himself, and the first floor extended to include a suite for Rachel. Between her rooms on the ground floor and the three bedrooms on the second, there'd be plenty of room for Rachel's family, if she married someday. It pleased him to imagine the sound of her kids running up the stairs to his attic room to wake up their lazy uncle.

During all his years in L.A., he'd held on to this dream, but since meeting Lauren, the dream had altered. He could easily picture Jason running up the attic stairs and jumping on his bed where Lauren lay sleeping, curled in his arms, to wake them up for breakfast. Nic's breath caught in his chest. He wasn't ready—wasn't willing—to give up the dream. He *wanted* Lauren in his bed. He wanted to hear Jason's feet pounding up the wooden steps in the morning.

After this situation with the stalker was over, he'd go to Lauren and do whatever she wanted to move them beyond this impasse. If she was still worried about her and Jason's safety, he'd hire an entire army to guard them. If it took him the rest of their lives, he'd make her see they belonged together.

Rachel kept silent as Kaden threw his duffle bag over one shoulder and Nic's over the other. When the screen door banged shut behind him, she reached out for Nic's hand. The sight of her small hand in his much larger one sent his stomach plunging down into his shoes. Rachel was his little sister and he was supposed to *protect* her, dammit, not come here and turn her world upside down. Again.

"Tell me. Who was Kaden's first priority before me?"

"Lauren," he admitted, more gruffly than he'd intended.

"Where is she? Is she safe? Why didn't you bring her here?"

Nic scanned the area. The ranch was coming to life, and numerous workers were within hearing distance, not to mention Tommy, who had taken up a post at the edge of the porch. "Let's go inside where we can talk in private."

Rachel wheeled herself through the door he held open for her. "Living room, okay?"

"Sure. Want something to drink?" he asked, hoping to distract her.

"No. Let's talk before Rémi comes over and things get crazy."

Resigned, he settled into his favorite recliner and waited while she maneuvered herself to a spot in front of him. It was killing him not to jump up and help her, but the doctors insisted that fostering her independence was an important, even necessary, factor in her recovery.

"So, what's going on with Lauren?"

Nic forced his voice to sound casual, unaffected even. "She's on her way to New York City. *Vanity Fair* offered her a job."

"That's fantastic. She must be thrilled."

The memory of Lauren crumpling against the limo outside his loft materialized in his mind. He closed his eyes against the tightening in his chest. When Rachel rubbed his forearm, he lifted his lids and met her gaze. "What is it?"

"It's over." *At least for now.*

"Why?"

Nic rubbed his face with his hand. "She said it's too dangerous for her and her son to be with me." When Rachel opened her mouth to respond, he held up his hand to stop her. "Before you say anything, let me finish. The stalker killed Summer and threatened to kill Lauren, too. And this blackmail stuff, well, that's just icing on the cake."

"I can understand her being worried about the stalker, but I don't see how the blackmail has anything to do with it."

Lauren's words replayed in his mind: *Talk to Rachel, tell her how you feel, and get over it.* Lauren wouldn't steer him wrong, would she? No. The raw honesty in her voice had been clear. She truly believed Rachel didn't blame him. Well, there was only one way to know for sure: he had to grow some balls and say what needed to be said.

After pausing for a moment to gather his courage, he took Rachel's hand in his. "I couldn't keep Lauren because I can't protect both of you."

Rachel's eyes sought his. "Protect me from what? Between Rémi and Tommy, no one can get near me."

He held her gaze and made his voice as gentle as he could. "Protect you from the press, Rachel. If I didn't get rid of Lauren and pay the ten million dollars…." He stopped and took a deep breath. "The stalker knows everything about me, about what I did."

"So what?"

So what? "The paparazzi will feed on this story like coyotes on chickens. Don't you understand? They'll hound you every minute until you can't even step outside anymore."

"Oh I understand, all right." Her eyes narrowed, and she shook her hand free of his. "No one would care about this if you hadn't made such a big deal of hiding the truth."

Nic froze, taken aback by the hurt in her eyes and her hard tone. "I did it to protect you."

"No. You did it to protect *yourself.* At least be honest about that." Her voice broke and she turned her head, but not before he caught a glimpse of tears shining in her eyes.

Jesus Christ. Was she right? Lauren had said as much about his father: *He blamed you because it was easier than admitting his own guilt.* Nic sighed and shook his head. He was as bad as his old man.

Rachel turned back to him. Red-rimmed eyes glared at him as her chin edged up. "I'm sick of being treated like your dirty little secret."

CHAPTER 20

"My dirty little—!" Shocked, Nic slipped out of his seat and sank to his knees beside Rachel's wheelchair. Even in his mind, he couldn't complete the thought. With both hands, he raked his hair, tugging on the strands until his scalp hurt, eager to find a new home for the pain in his heart. Rachel brought his hands to her lap and held them. Lifting his head, he looked deep in her eyes. "Rachel, sweetheart. I never thought… I never meant…." His voice trailed off as the words got stuck in his throat.

"Maybe so, but that's how I feel, how I've always felt."

What kind of shit hides his sister from the world so he won't have to face what he's done, so he can escape judgment? "I'm so sorry. For the accident, for destroying our family, for ruining your life, for making you feel less than you are. I'm sorry about everything," he finished, his voice cracking.

Rachel stroked his hair as he'd often done to her when she'd been little. "I know you feel responsible for what happened, but it wasn't your fault. Don't you think I blamed myself, too?"

Nic jerked his head up. "Why would you blame yourself? You were just a child."

She squeezed his hands and smiled sadly. "You were just a child too. Maybe if I hadn't whined and pushed so much, you wouldn't have rushed. I've told you many times, the accident was just that, an accident. Before she died, *Maman* helped me understand that sometimes there isn't anyone to blame. We have to make the best of the hand we're dealt."

"*Maman* was usually right. But not in this case. I took away your future. You might have grown up to be a ballerina or something."

Rachel stared at him open-mouthed for several moments. Then she began to laugh. "A ballerina? *Mon chère frère*, is that why you've been making yourself so miserable all these years? Believe me, I can dance better on my horse than

I ever could on my own legs."

"But Rachel—"

"No, Nic," she said, the sharpness of her tone surprising him. "Stop feeling sorry for me. It's not like my life ended that night." A pang in his chest made him catch his breath.

Her eyes grew round. "My God. That's what you think, isn't it? In your mind, the little sister you knew and loved died in that accident."

Nic bowed his head. "No, Rachel. Never."

"You think that because I'm in a wheelchair, I'm completely dependent on you, that I can't fend for myself, that I can't be a contributing member of society. Jesus." She raised her fists, shaking them in the air. "I feel like I'm trapped in a bad movie where I play the poor crippled sister to your heroic self-sacrificing brother."

When he opened his mouth to speak, she stopped him. "I'm not finished." After a moment she let out a long breath. "I've made my peace with it, and now that I'm older, I realize that in some ways it's been a gift."

"A gift?" he sputtered.

She caressed his cheek. "Yes, a gift. Because of my paralysis, we created this ranch. We've helped hundreds of children. We've shown them how to be happy." Her eyes sparkled and she smiled widely. "I can't imagine a better life."

Nic could only stare at his sister, amazed by her words. Lauren had been right about this, too. Rachel *was* useful and productive. And they had built something wonderful together, beautiful even. Something that could be destroyed if people turned on him when all this went public. He sat back in his chair and gazed out the wide bay window. "We might lose the ranch."

"You're afraid this will destroy your career?"

Nic's jaw tightened. But he had to get it all out there. No more lies, no more secrets. "Yes, but I'm not just worried about my career. Most of my money is gone."

"Gone?" she asked, wide-eyed.

He swallowed and faced her. "Vivian and David made some bad investments. That won't be a problem if I can still work, but…." He shook his head.

Rachel narrowed her eyes. What had he said to set her off this time? "What do you think I've been doing with the money you put in the ranch account?"

"You spend it on the ranch and kids, of course."

Rachel tilted her head, a puzzled expression on her face. "I know you've been away most of the last ten years, but you do know I'm attending university, right? And that I'm majoring in business administration?"

"Yes, but what does that have to do with the ranch?"

She rolled her eyes and anger laced her voice. "I run the ranch. That's what this has to do with it."

"But the accountant takes care of all the money stuff."

She shook her head. "He was useless, so I fired him. Then I improved the budget by reducing the expenses. The money I saved, I put into a scholarship fund. A fund which I invested quite well if I do say so myself. Unlike your Vivian, I know how to handle money."

"Christ, I had no idea." Rachel was one surprise after another today.

"The fund now provides for twenty-five percent more children than when we started offering free services four years ago. So you can stop worrying about throwing money at the ranch. Even if you never provided another penny, we could probably keep the ranch going for a long time."

"How much is in this fund?"

"Over two million. My stocks did well."

Nic could only gape at her as he absorbed what she'd said. In the four years since the therapy part of the ranch had been up and running, she'd managed to accumulate millions in savings and investments. And how interesting that the amount in the fund was the same amount he still needed to pay the blackmail.

Using the money to shove all this ugliness under the rug wasn't the answer. He'd learned something in the last few weeks: he wanted a normal life, with a family, and he couldn't have that if he spent all his time protecting a secret, protecting himself. If he lost his career, so be it. He'd only started it to support Rachel and the ranch. As long as they were both safe, it didn't matter what happened to him.

"Do you forgive me?" he asked.

"There was never anything to forgive. A better question is: do you forgive yourself?"

Nic closed his eyes briefly. Lauren had called it a stupid mistake, one he'd accepted responsibility for. Maybe it was time he stopped punishing himself, and Rachel by extension. Because the guiltier he'd felt, the less often he'd visited the ranch. He let out a long breath and forced a small smile. "I'll work on it."

"That's good enough for me. Now, what are you going to do about Lauren?"

Nic rose and crossed his arms. "There's nothing to do, until this situation with the stalker is over."

Rachel smiled sweetly up at him. "Bullshit."

His brows shot up and he rocked back on his heels. "What did you say?"

She grinned. "I said bullshit. You love her, don't you?"

He uncrossed his arms and thrust his hands into the front pockets of his jeans. Looking at his feet, he said, "Yeah. But sometimes love isn't enough."

"Bullshit."

Nic jerked his head up and burst out laughing. "This new grown-up attitude of yours is going to take some getting used to."

Rachel pursed her lips. "Oh, get over it. I haven't been a child in a long time. Stop treating me like one.

"I don't—"

"Yes, you do. I'm a grown woman with a mind of my own. I'm sure I can relate to Lauren better than you can."

He held up his hands in a placating gesture. "You win." Smiling at her, he arched a brow. "So, Dr. Phil, what's your advice?"

"Fight for her. Prove to her that you're man enough to protect her and her son."

"Easier said than done."

"Isn't she worth it?"

She was. He'd do anything for Lauren. Even if it meant, as Rachel had said, he needed to stop protecting himself. "If I take our story to the press, the stalker will have nothing to blackmail me with, except for her threats against Lauren, of course. But I can hire as many bodyguards as it takes to keep her safe."

"That's it," Rachel said, excitement dancing in her eyes. "We can rip the rug out from under the stalker's feet. Let's invite the press here, show them the ranch, show them what we've built, let them see the children and how happy they are with the horses."

His heart beat a wild rhythm in his chest. This could work. By coming clean about his secrets, he'd prove to Lauren that he wasn't hiding anymore. He could put the past where it belonged and begin focusing on the future.

A future with Lauren and Jason.

Lauren glanced at her watch and sighed. The creative director had been droning on for three straight hours, and he wasn't losing steam. The first hour had been a fascinating overview of the new face of *Vanity Fair*, the intent of the redesign, and the new reporting focus. Her fear of failing had dissipated, replaced with a glowing hope, the knowledge that she could be successful in this world.

But then, he'd started in on a lengthy analysis of the financials and market research that had gone into defining the re-vamped look, and he'd lost her. A glance around the conference room confirmed she wasn't the only one. Many people fidgeted in their seats, several were surreptitiously checking email and messages on their cell phones, and one poor soul had fallen asleep, his face mashed against the folders they'd been handed. Surely the creative director could have condensed his million PowerPoint slides into a sixty-minute presentation?

Then again, not even the most scintillating slideshow could compete with the "best of Nic Lamoureux" reel unspooling through her mind. In the past couple hours, she'd gone over every conversation they'd had since meeting in D.C., every moment they'd shared, every kiss, every look. And her heart was breaking.

With mounting irritation, she reached into her pocket and pulled out a fresh tissue to dab at the moisture leaking from her eyes. Damn. She had no right to cry. It had been her choice, her decision. *She'd* left Nic, not the other way around. Now she had to suck it up and deal with the consequences. She was strong, she'd get over him. In ten years. Maybe.

The sound of rustling papers and chairs creaking as people stood up to gather their belongings forced her to leave her pity party. As she rose and stretched, Helen approached her. "I hope Mitch didn't bore you to death. The man is brilliant, but he can rattle on."

"Oh, no," she said, offering the woman a weak smile. "The first part was particularly interesting."

Helen grinned and patted her arm. "I know it's too early now for dinner, but what about in a couple hours, say around 6:00?"

Dinner? God, no. Her stomach churned. She needed to be alone. Go back to her hotel, sink into cool sheets and bawl. Bawl like a child who'd just thrown her favorite toy into a river and realized she can't get it back. Lauren smiled at the woman but let a touch of the pain she was feeling show in her eyes. "If you don't mind, I think I'll skip dinner tonight. I have a bit of a headache. Must be the jet-lag."

"I'm so sorry to hear that. Get some rest, and if you don't feel better, call me. You have my cell number, right?" Lauren nodded and thanked Helen for her kindness.

Minutes later, she headed across Times Square to her hotel. Before the door to her room finished closing behind her, she'd already dropped her purse and laptop bag on the floor and tumbled onto the king-size bed, a bed that was too large and too empty without Nic in it. A sob ripped through her as she clutched the T-shirt she'd slept in last night—Nic's T-shirt. Unable to leave the loft without at least one item that smelled like him, she'd grabbed the shirt off the dresser where he'd discarded it and stuffed it into her suitcase. Holding the rumpled material against her cheek, she cried, letting her emotions pour out until her throat was swollen and raw, until the pounding in her head left her drained of energy.

Weakly, she sat up and laid the now damp shirt out to dry. She needed something to do, something to get her mind off Nic. Her eyes found the computer bag on the floor. She hadn't analyzed the photo Nic had sent her, the one of him lying on the ice with blood on his chest. She shuddered. If the stalker had wanted it, the blood could have been from a bullet instead of Jason's nosebleed. She froze. *That's* what Nic had meant when he'd told her she'd already lost him to violence. Without even putting up a fight, she'd let the stalker win. She'd feared losing Nic and, like some self-fulfilling prophecy, had let him go.

How could she have been so irrational? Her mind accepted that under normal circumstances, Nic's life was not much more dangerous than anyone else's, certainly less than Todd's or her father's had been. But her heart? All her heart knew was that the constant fear, the constant worry would eat at her until paranoia took full control. God, how had her mother handled the stress of her father being a cop?

Lauren slipped off the bed and got the phone from her purse. Quickly, she dialed her parent's number before she chickened out. She wasn't sure whether to be relieved or scared when her mother answered.

"Hi, sweetie. How did your first day go?"

"I think I'm going to like it." They chatted about the people she'd met and how she was enjoying New York City. After a few minutes, Lauren couldn't keep up the pretense and stopped talking.

"What is it, dear?" The concern in her mother's voice brought fresh tears to Lauren's eyes.

"How did you do it, Mom? How did you deal with knowing each time you kissed Dad goodbye, it could be the last time you saw him?"

"Oh, honey. I did the only thing I could do and still do. I cherish every moment we have together, tell him every day that I love him, and I never let him leave the house or go to bed angry." As her mother spoke, Lauren could hear the emotion in her voice. "But most important of all, I make sure to leave nothing unsaid and nothing undone between us. That way, if the worst should happen, neither of us will have any regrets."

Lauren squeezed her eyes shut in a vain attempt to keep the tears from sliding down her cheeks. She'd done the exact opposite. There was a lifetime of words unsaid and things undone between her and Nic. "Oh God, Mom. What have I done?" she sobbed.

"Is this about Nic, sweetheart? Tell me what happened."

Lauren grabbed a tissue from her pocket and wiped her nose. "I left him."

"Why? You sounded so happy on the phone." The incredulity in her mother's tone reinforced the facts—she, Lauren James, was an idiot.

"That's just it, Mom. I don't know why."

"Start from the beginning."

Lauren sat in the chair by the window, staring out at Times Square. She'd always wanted to visit New York, but without Nic, everything seemed gray, lifeless. "The stalker threatened to kill me, like she did Summer, if I didn't leave Nic."

Her mother gasped. "Are you alright? Are you safe?"

She couldn't be any safer than with Jake guarding her door, shadowing her every move. The man took his job *very* seriously. "Nic hired a bodyguard to protect me."

"What's the problem then?"

"The woman wants to *kill* me."

"But you said you're safe. Or don't you really believe that?"

"Yes… no… maybe." Irritated with herself, she leapt off the bed and began pacing the length of the small room. "Oh, I don't know."

"I think I understand, honey."

Lauren held the phone away from her ear and stared at it. "You do?"

"If I put this together with your initial question regarding your father, I'd say, you think your body is safe with him, but not your heart." After a moment's hesitation, she asked, "What are you really afraid of, Lauren? I don't think it's this stalker at all. If it were, you might have stayed away for a while until she was caught, but you wouldn't have left Nic."

Lauren returned to her seat by the window and forced herself to sit calmly. "Mom, his life is dangerous. This isn't his first stalker and I'm sure there'll be more. How can I put Jason at risk like that?"

Soft laughter floated across the phone line. "He's an *actor,* for heaven's sake. And from what you've told me, Nic's ready and willing to do what it takes to keep you and Jason safe."

"But, he's a multi-millionaire movie star. Women fall at his feet. He can have whoever he wants. Why would he settle for me?"

"Isn't that his choice? It's clear to me that he's chosen you."

"But—"

"But nothing. These are just excuses, sweetie. What's really bothering you?"

That was the million dollar question, wasn't it?

"I don't know, Mom."

"You know the expression *it's better to have loved and lost than to have never loved at all?* Well, it's true. You can't protect your heart by pushing him away. In fact, you're hurting yourself more now because you're denying your heart what it so clearly wants. You've already fallen in love with him."

Lauren groaned. "Why couldn't I have fallen in love with a boring tax accountant or an engineer? Someone whose biggest risk is getting a paper cut?"

"You already answered that question, honey." Lauren could hear the smile in her mother's voice. "A man like that would be *boring.* Like all the women in our family, you need a warrior, a man who leads an exciting, vibrant life. After being married to Todd, I thought you'd have known this about yourself."

Was her mother right? Was she attracted to Nic for the very reasons she'd left him? God, that was so messed up. "But what can I do about it, Mom? This whole thing scares me."

"Look deep in your heart and ask yourself why you're so scared. I don't think it's the danger at all. You dealt with that just fine while you were married."

Had she? Or had her constant fear driven Todd away?

"Honey?" Her mother asked when the silence dragged on a little too long. "Are you worried Nic might shut you out of parts of his life the way Todd did? Is that what this is really about?"

Lauren leaned her head back against the chair and closed her eyes. "He already has. Nic has lots of secrets and he's kept some things from me."

"But you've only been together a short time. It took your father years to open up to me. Have you told him all your secrets already?"

Lauren remembered the fan letter and groaned. "Not everything."

"Well, there you go. Relationships take time to build. If you reveal everything at the beginning, the mystery is gone too soon."

She sighed. "You make hiding things sound so romantic, Mom. But Nic's very protective. What's to say he doesn't start treating me like the little woman who can't handle the big bad things in life?"

"Worse than having a homicidal maniac after him and you?"

Lauren laughed. "When you put it that way..." And she had to be honest—Nic *had* told her everything. And if he didn't want the whole world to know about it, that was okay. She certainly wouldn't want her fan letter posted on the Internet.

"I guess I'm just scared. Nic seems to like me well enough now, but what about in a few years? In ten?" Her voice was rising. She took a deep breath, then said what she feared most. "It took Todd only five years to lose interest in me, and we were on an even playing field."

"I wish I could give you a big hug. Based on what you and Jason have told me, Nic sounds like a genuinely nice guy. He's not into all that sex, drugs, and rock and roll, is he?"

Her mother sounded more curious than anything and that made Lauren laugh. "He's not." Although... he was definitely into the sex.

"Are you worried he wouldn't be good for Jason?"

Lauren thought back to the weekend they'd shared in her little apartment. "Nic's like a big kid. He and Jason get along great."

"Why do I hear a 'but' at the end of that?"

"Well, he's a great friend to Jason, but would he be a good father? Todd was never around even when he was alive, so Jason's never had the type of father figure he needs." Nic had helped support his sister, but it was clear he hadn't been around for the day-to-day task of raising her. "Now that Jason is getting older, I'm worried I can't be both mother and father to him. I don't think I can enforce the discipline that's required to manage a teenage boy."

"A boy does need a father. But if Nic had tried to father Jason too soon, how would Jason have reacted? Nic's approach was the right one. They need to build a rapport so that when Nic does need to discipline him, Jason will understand it's coming from a position of love."

Lauren mulled that for a moment. The few times Todd had scolded Jason, their lack of a relationship had been apparent; Jason had invariably ended up crying alone in his room. She couldn't picture that happening with Nic. "That makes sense, but what if Nic's so busy making movies that like Todd, he's never around? I think that would be worse for Jason, and me, than how we are now."

"Honey, you two can work that out. But I don't think you have to worry. Since getting out of the hospital, Nic and Jason have taken turns calling each other, and Nic hasn't missed a single day."

"Even now?" *Wow.* She'd dumped him, yet he hadn't dumped Jason. Most men would have.

"Nic called this afternoon." Unless it was her imagination, her mom's tone sounded oddly triumphant.

"No one's perfect, Mom." But Nic *was* pretty darn close. Maybe she wasn't giving him enough credit.

"You have to trust what's in your heart."

Lauren stood up and leaned her forehead against the window. Her hand trembled as she held the phone to her ear. "But how do I know things won't turn out the way they did with Todd?"

"You can't, honey. No one can."

Lauren squeezed her eyes shut, trying to control the fear rising in her chest. "I just don't know, Mom."

"I know you're scared, sweetheart. You've spent the last five years alone. So ask yourself this: how's that working for you?"

Unbidden, a burst of laughter escaped her. "Been watching a lot of daytime T.V., Mom?"

"You know me. I've got to get my daily fix of Dr. Phil." She chuckled. "What's your answer?"

"I've been miserable. Being with Nic these last few weeks made me realize how empty and bland my life has been. I love Jason, but I need something more." *I need Nic.*

"Take it slow, sweetie. It's not like you're getting married tomorrow, are you?" she teased.

"He did give me some very nice jewelry. But no ring."

"Don't be scared by what-ifs. When the time is right, you'll know if Nic's the one."

Lauren smiled. She could do that—live one day at a time and see where things went. As soon as the stalker was caught, she'd go to Nic and talk things out. Before ending the call, she decided to follow another piece of her mother's advice. "I love you, Mom." She injected as much meaning into the words as she could.

"I love you too, Lauren. Be happy."

She slipped her phone back in her purse, then grabbed the laptop bag beside it. The sooner they caught the stalker, the sooner she could get on with the business of winning Nic back.

After booting up her laptop, she opened the photo and shuddered. Then she tilted her head to view it from a different angle. It was darker than the shot of her and Nic kissing since it had been taken after the lights had gone out. But, it also had flash glare in the Plexiglas.

Lauren's heart began to pump faster. She'd seen the outline of the photographer in the last photo, maybe this time… After smoothing out the flash glare, she tried manipulating the brightness and contrast to sharpen the image. And groaned in frustration. The reflection of the photographer was only slightly clearer than in the first shot. Still not enough to identify the stalker.

Time for caffeine. She pushed back from the desk and prepared the coffee machine to boil some water. She opened the door to her room and leaned out. "Hey, Jake. I'm making tea. Want some?"

"Don't usually drink the stuff, but I think tonight I'll make an exception," he said, smothering a yawn. Lauren had to laugh at the sight of him speaking through clenched teeth.

She opened the door wider. "Come in and relax for a while."

"Thanks, ma'am. Don't mind if I do."

Jake followed her into the room and dropped into the chair by the window. It was a large wingback that easily accommodated his size. He indicated the laptop. "They got you doing overtime already?"

She shook her head and sat on the bed instead of at the desk where she'd have her back to him. "I'm going over a photo the stalker sent to Nic, looking for clues. I was hoping to catch a reflection of her."

"Since you aren't jumping for joy, I guess you didn't find one?"

"No, I see one. But I can't make the image clear enough to see much of anything beyond a vague outline." Lauren glanced over at the laptop. Hmm… maybe if she…. Hopping to her feet, she pointed to where she'd been sitting. "Can you sit there?"

Jake perked up and made it to the bed in one big stride. True, the room was small. But still. "Okay, what do I do now?" he asked, his enthusiasm making Lauren grin.

"Watch the screen and let me know if the image is getting clearer or blurrier. I'm thinking you might actually see it better from the bed." Leaning over to get her head out of the way, she began slowly adjusting the zoom to demagnify the picture.

"Getting clearer," he said. She reduced the zoom a bit more and each time he confirmed that the image was getting sharper. When she tweaked it once again, he shook his head. "Uh-uh. Go back one increment."

Lauren twisted around. "What do you see?"

"A figure. Looks like a woman, but it's too dark to make out any features."

"Let me try something else." She adjusted the contrast, lightening the image. "Good?"

"A little more… okay. But now everything is kind of… flat."

"Flat?"

"I can see a face, but I can't tell the chin from the neck."

"I'll try to adjust the color." After adding some red, she mixed in some blue and a touch of green. "How's that?"

"Getting better."

Lauren walked over to the bed. After several seconds, she snapped her fingers and returned to the desk. Moments later, she glanced at Jake over her shoulder and asked, "Now?"

He smiled. "Your head's in the way."

"Oh, sorry." Heat rose to her cheeks. Ducking, she turned away from him, then heard him suck in a breath of air.

"You got it. She's a real looker."

Lauren's eyes shot to the screen but from so close, she couldn't make much out. She lunged for the bed, nearly knocking Jake over in her haste. "Whoa." He chuckled as he steadied her. "The photo isn't going anywhere."

Her eyes snapped to the image on the screen as she let him guide her to a spot beside him. The blood drained from her face and her whole body went numb. Oh God, it *was* Vivian.

CHAPTER 21

"Ms. James. You know that woman?"

Lauren averted her gaze from the photo and met Jake's eyes. She cleared her throat. "Vivian Carmichael, Nic's agent."

His eyes widened. "Mr. Lamoureux's agent is the stalker?" He scrubbed his jaw. "Shit. Uh… sorry." He shot her a quick glance before turning away. "I need to call Kaden."

As he reached into his back pocket, she put her hand on his arm. "No. We can't risk her finding out. She's already put a tracking device on Nic's phone. Who knows what else she's done? For all we know, Kaden's phone is bugged too. We have to go to Montréal tonight and show this to Nic."

"Okay. Pack up while I make the flight reservations."

Lauren released his arm and started collecting her things while he placed a few calls. "Okay," he said, glancing at his watch. "It'll be tight, but we can make it if we hurry."

She zipped her suitcase shut and smacked her hand on it. "I'm done." All the important stuff was in the pockets of her cargo pants, anyways.

As they waited their turn at airport security an hour later, Lauren took a deep breath. Two days ago, she'd run from Nic as fast as her legs could carry her and yet, here she was beating all kinds of speed records to get *to* him. Had she gone mad? And what happened to waiting until the stalker was caught? What would she do if Vivian had already joined Nic at the ranch? She was no actress. Could she pretend she didn't know, or would Vivian see right through her? Her stomach lurched and she clutched her waist. The woman was a *killer*. Maybe she'd been too rash in suggesting they jump on a plane. They could have called Kaden and asked him to call back on Rémi's phone or something like that.

The line advanced, and it was her turn to remove her shoes and take her laptop out of its case. As she stepped through the metal detector, she almost hoped that the guards detained her long enough to miss their flight. But nothing happened. No alarms, bells or whistles. Nothing. Surely that was a sign she was doing the right thing?

At the gate, her mother's words came back to her. No one got guarantees. The boring tax accountant she'd hoped to meet? He could die from an infected paper cut. Vivian's betrayal would hit Nic hard. He'd need someone to love and support him. And that someone was her, Lauren James. Single mom. Professional photographer. Reformed scaredy-cat. Hopefully, he'd still talk to her. But if his feelings had changed—

No, she wouldn't think about that. One day at a time, that's what her mother had said. Get to the ranch, tell Nic about Vivian, and help the guys come up with a plan to catch her. Then she could worry about having a future with Nic.

But damn, after everything they'd already been through, they both deserved a chance to have a happily ever after. Together.

"Thought you could use this," Rémi said, handing Nic a bottle of beer before perching himself on the veranda railing.

Nic thanked him absently and took a long swallow. The beer was surprisingly good. He glanced at the label and had to laugh. "*La fin du monde.* The End of the World. How appropriate."

"Just showing the love, man."

Nic snorted. "Asshole."

Relaxing on the porch, his gaze drifted to the giant ball of fire hovering above the tree line and the pink, purple and orange streaks painting the sky. He met his friend's eyes. "I've missed being here."

Rémi's expression sobered as he leaned forward, picking at the label on his bottle. "We've got to end this, brother. Did you hear from the LAPD?"

"Anderson called. Because the stalking has crossed state and now international lines, they've called in the FBI. All the phones used to send the messages were disposables bought at Walmarts across the U.S. The FBI is running the security tapes through their face-recognition system."

Rémi nodded. "That's good. If the same face shows up at all locations, then they've got their suspect."

Nic ran his thumb through the condensation accumulating along the bottle and remembered countless summer evenings spent exactly like this: talking things over with Rémi while sitting on the wide veranda drinking a good beer. He'd always been honest with Rémi. There was no reason for that to change. "Lauren thinks Vivian's the stalker."

After taking a slug from his bottle, Rémi arched a brow. "And you?"

"I don't want her to be right."

"But you think she might be."

Nic blew out a long breath. "Yeah." He balanced the chair onto its back legs and leaned his head against the wall. "The thing I don't get is why. I keep asking myself: what's Vivian's motive? And I keep coming up blank."

"I'm no expert, but from what I understand, stalkers often have relationship fantasies. In her mind, you could be her boyfriend, even her husband."

"Which could explain killing Summer and threatening Lauren."

Rémi nodded. "She would see that as cheating."

"But why the blackmail? It doesn't make any sense."

"Consider this: where're you getting the money to pay?"

Nic's eyes widened. "From Vivian. This way, she looks like a hero. Like she's saving me, my career, and the ranch."

"And at the same time, makes you even more dependent on her because now you owe her."

"Jesus Christ. Talk about showing the love."

Rémi laughed. The screen door slammed against the wall as Kaden stepped onto the veranda. "Incoming," he said. "I just buzzed Jake in at the gate."

Nic let his chair fall forward with a thud. "Jake? He's supposed to be in New York with Lauren." His gut plummeted as fear for her washed over him. "Is she here too?"

Kaden nodded.

"Shit." Lauren had been so adamant about staying away from him, only something serious could have brought her here. Why hadn't she called?

The gate opened and a car passed under the arch, triggering the security lights along the driveway. Nic took off down the wheelchair ramp, running faster as the car's headlights bobbed closer. His heart seized when the passenger door opened and a small figure jumped out of the slow-moving car. The person stumbled a bit but didn't slow down. Seconds later, Lauren was in his arms. "Nic, I'm so sorry."

"*Chérie*." He took her face in his hands and felt the wet warmth of her tears. His chest tightened and he cocooned her with his body, ready to protect her from everything and anything. "Are you okay? Tell me what's wrong."

"I… I…," she started, but then another sob cut off her words.

Nic lifted her up and cradled her against his chest. "Shh. Whatever it is, we'll handle it," he murmured, carrying her up the ramp. Rémi held the door for him. Nic slipped through, nodding his thanks, and sat on the couch with Lauren on his lap.

She blushed and wiped the tears off her cheeks when Rémi took a seat across from them. "God, this is so embarrassing."

"Oh, I don't know. I quite enjoyed it," Rémi teased.

When Lauren laughed, Nic smiled, glad his friend had defused the situation. "Lauren, meet Rémi—"

"The best friend," Rémi interjected.

"—and this is Lauren."

"The girlfriend… if he'll still have me." When she turned and angled her chin up, he saw love and longing in her eyes, and his heart swelled.

He threaded his fingers through her long curls and pulled her to him. "I will," he whispered as his lips met hers. When his tongue slid between her teeth and curled around hers in a gentle caress, she moaned and threw her arms around his neck, pressing her breasts against his chest.

With half an ear, he heard Rémi mutter, "And that's my cue to leave." The screen door slammed as he went outside to join the two bodyguards.

The sound startled Lauren. She wrenched her mouth away from his and put a restraining hand against his chest.

"What is it?"

"I forgot to ask, is Vivian here?"

He shook his head. "She's coming tomorrow."

Lauren breathed a sigh of relief. "I got so caught up with seeing you again and…." She trailed off, waving her hand between the two of them.

Nic grinned in understanding. He'd gotten pretty carried away, too. "Let's get your things. You can freshen up and then we'll talk. Okay?"

Someone had brought in Lauren's bags. He handed her the purse, then grabbed her suitcase and laptop bag. They climbed the two flights of stairs to his suite. "The attic's pretty large, so I have a bedroom, a full bath, and a den up here."

He deposited her belongings next to the bed. She surprised him by taking his hand and leading him to the pair of wingback chairs beside the windows. He sat in one and when she moved to sit in the other, he tugged her down onto his lap. "Here's better," he said when she raised her brows. He loved the feel of her ass against his thighs.

Lauren swallowed, then lowered her head. "I want you to know that my running off had nothing to do with anything you told me about your past."

Nic tilted her chin, forcing her to look at him. "Then why?"

She averted her eyes. "I was scared."

"That's understandable. The stalker did threaten you."

She stared at her hands clasped in her lap. "It wasn't just the stalker. I was afraid to commit to our relationship."

He stroked a hand through her hair and wrapped a curl around her ear. "Why?" he asked, his voice low. "Were things moving too fast?" After she'd joined him in L.A., their relationship had gone from zero to sixty, and he'd been helpless to slow it down.

Lauren shook her head. "That was part of it, but deep down, I was afraid to commit to someone I could lose." She shifted on his lap so that they were face to face. When she ran a hand along his jaw, Nic leaned into her palm. "You're gorgeous—" She laughed when he grinned and wiggled his eyebrows. "And rich and smart and funny. And I'm none of those things."

As soon as he opened his mouth to object, she pressed her fingers to his lips, shushing him. "I was scared that things would turn out the same way they did with Todd."

"I'm not going to die, Lauren. We're going to grow old together."

Lauren smiled, but he could still see a trace of disbelief in her expression. "Things with Todd went bad before he died. He'd already grown bored with me. The re-upping was just one sign."

So *that* was the real problem. Why couldn't he have been a poet? Then he could weave a web of words to convince her she was his world. Instead, he had to settle for raw honesty.

"Lauren, I love you. I always have and I always will. I had such a mad crush on that cute photographer in high school. On *you*. When we met again, I didn't recognize you. But my heart did." He smiled and slid his fingers through her curls. "My heart never forgot you."

The uncertainly in her eyes disappeared, replaced with a glow that sent his blood pressure through the stratosphere. "My heart never forgot you either." She kissed him, and when she drew back, tears glittered in her eyes. "I want to be with you, Nic. I want to grow old with you. Can you ever forgive me?"

A strange warmth erupted in his chest, growing until he thought he would burst. Lauren had come back to him, and not just for a while. They'd have their entire lives to get to know each other, and he'd have forever to prove he'd never tire of her. Nic cupped her cheeks with his hands and traced the softness of her lips with his thumbs. "There's nothing to forgive, *chérie*," he whispered.

She hooked her arms around his neck, pressing her mouth against his. He could feel relief and love in her kiss. Hope for the future filled him as his hands skimmed down her back to her ass. She squirmed, pressing against the growing bulge in his lap. Her soft moan made him harden even more. She raised her head and abruptly drew back.

"What?" he asked, as best he could given where he'd thought the kiss was going.

She blinked a few times. "Stars."

Nic glanced over his shoulder to see what had captured her attention. Behind him was an entire wall of windows through which they could see a vast array of constellations against the clear night sky.

Lauren went to the windows. "They're real." When he said nothing, she turned to him and the tinkling sound of her laughter cascaded over him. How he'd missed that sound. "For a moment, I thought I was seeing stars… from your kisses."

Nic stood up, grinning. If she gave him a few minutes, she would be seeing stars, and they wouldn't be the ones outside. Hell, she might even see some fireworks.

As he took the few steps to join her at the window, she turned slowly and looked around. "This room is amazing."

He had to agree. It was his refuge in the wilderness. The entire western wall consisted of bare six foot windows, covered with the same one-way privacy film he had at the loft. A fireplace sat across from the king bed, and above it hung a large flat-screen TV. Open beams stained to match the hardwood floor traversed the vaulted ceiling.

"I'm glad you like it." His eyes fell to the bed and the mountain of multicolored cushions covering it. Ever since Lauren had shown up at the hospital, he'd been imagining her laying all pink, spread-eagle on this very bed, her brown hair fanned out on his cream colored sheets, her hips propped up by one of his many multi-hued pillows. His groin tightened at the image and a light sheen of sweat broke out on his forehead. Need clawed at him, making its demands known. He wanted to take her here, in his room, in his bed, in the moonlight, then again in the sunlight, over and over, until his was the only face she saw, until his was the only name she remembered.

She must have sensed the change in his mood, because her smile faded, and her darkened eyes and flushed cheeks reflected his own heat. Hard nipples jutted through the thin material of her T-shirt, beckoning him, begging him to relieve their tightness.

Slowly, they moved toward each other, closing the distance until they stood toe to toe. As if by mutual agreement, they kept their arms tightly by their sides. Eyes locked on hers, Nic leaned forward. His lips hovering above hers, he breathed in her scent. A tremor shook her body and her tongue darted out to swipe his lips. Nic moaned and pressed his forehead to hers, breathing hard.

"We need to go downstairs," she panted.

"Why?"

A shadow darkened her eyes. "I have something to show you and Kaden. Rachel and Rémi should see it too. It can't wait."

"Shit."

Her breath feathered his lips, and he couldn't hold back a groan.

"Later," he growled.

"Later," she purred.

When Lauren entered the living room with Nic, Kaden and Jake were sprawled on one couch, while Rémi sat in an armchair beside a woman in a wheelchair. She had both feet on the footrests, one leg in a sort of open cast. The woman had to be Rachel, but hadn't Nic said she could walk with a brace and crutches? And why was her leg in a cast? A glance at Nic's face showed only his own excitement. Okay, so this wasn't a new development. Thank God. One less thing to deal with today.

When they took note of her, all three men stood up. Lauren deposited her laptop bag beside the empty couch and let Nic lead her over to the woman. Nic beamed at her then said, "Rachel, I'd like to introduce you to someone very special to me. This is Lauren James."

"Lauren. I'm so happy to finally meet you." Rachel held out her hand. Lauren had no idea if she was supposed to shake it or kiss Rachel on the cheeks.

But she needn't have feared. Rachel tugged Lauren down so she could hug and kiss her. "The pleasure is mine," Lauren said, smiling.

"Everyone, have a seat. Would you care for anything to drink? Tea, coffee, beer?" offered Rachel. Lauren shot a teasing glance at Kaden, wondering if he'd once again choose tea over coffee or beer.

"I'll have tea, Earl Grey if you have it," he said, eyes on Lauren, as if daring her to say something. When Jake smothered a laugh, Kaden pinned him with a look. "Jake, too. We're on the clock."

A slight widening of her eyes was the only sign of Rachel's surprise. "*O*-kay. Rémi, I imagine you want another beer?" When he nodded, she turned to Nic and Lauren.

"I'll have a beer as well. But not a *Fin du monde* this time." He grinned widely.

Rémi and Rachel both laughed, and Lauren vowed that first thing Monday, she'd purchase one of those Berlitz DVD sets to learn French.

"I'll have tea as well," Lauren said. "But, please, let me help."

Kaden elbowed Jake and said, "Lauren, stay here. Jake will help Miss Lamoureux." Jake looked startled for a moment, but rose from his seat and waited for Rachel to lead the way.

"Thank you, Jake. We'll be back in a few minutes." As she prepared to roll herself into the kitchen, Jake stepped behind the chair.

"May I?"

Nic stiffened at the question but relaxed when Rachel nodded. Jake took hold of the handles and wheeled her out to the kitchen.

While they waited for Rachel and Jake to return, the conversation turned to sports. Lauren laughed as Nic and Rémi exchanged good natured barbs. With his tall lanky build, copper skin and high cheekbones, Rémi looked typically Native American. But the brilliant emerald eyes that caught her gaze screamed of a mixed heritage.

Rémi wagged his eyebrows. When she blushed, he grinned. "I hear you're working for *Vanity Fair* now."

Nic sat up, looking startled. "Shit. Weren't you attending a four-day workshop?"

Lauren shrugged. "You were more important."

Nic flashed her a grin before sobering again. "You didn't quit, did you?"

Rachel rolled back into the living room with Jake close behind in time to catch Nic's question. "Please say you didn't. *Vanity Fair* is such a great opportunity."

"No, I didn't even tell them I was leaving. I have to call Ms. Combs later." The concern on Nic's face warmed her heart. "It's okay, Nic. I'll tell them I had an emergency, and if they let me go, then so be it."

Nic shook his head. "You'd give up your dream job for me?"

She took his hand and smiled. "I'd do anything for you."

Kaden sighed loudly and Rémi burst out laughing. Rachel shook her finger at them. "You guys are just jealous." Then she turned to Lauren and said, "Nic is lucky to have you."

Lauren blushed as everyone stared at her. For a moment, she'd forgotten she and Nic weren't alone. "I'm the lucky one."

Nic took her hand and kissed her fingers. His warm lips on her skin sent a sizzle up her spine. A slow sexy grin spread on his face. He knew exactly how his kisses affected her. She busied herself with handing everyone beverages from the tray Jake had placed on the table. The sooner they got on with the business at hand, the sooner she and Nic could go upstairs and—

Stop right there.

She swallowed a sip of tea, then looked up at the assembled group. "Jake and I came here tonight because we found something in one of the photos the stalker sent Nic. We didn't call first because I was concerned our phones had been tampered with."

Turning to Nic to ask him a question, she was transfixed by the sight of his throat working as he swallowed a sip of his beer. She lifted her gaze to his lips now glistening from the drink, and that was almost worse. "I assume you've told everyone what we know so far?"

Nic nodded. "Yes. There's been a new development. The LAPD called in the FBI to search security footage from the Walmarts where the phones were purchased."

Setting her cup on the table, she reached for her laptop. "That's good news. The FBI will confirm what I've found." Nic regarded her, his expression closed. She turned the laptop so everyone could see the image she'd modified. "Tell me who you see."

Rachel inhaled sharply.

Rémi cursed.

Kaden sucked in a breath.

Nic remained silent, his eyes glued to the screen. She placed her hand on his arm. After a few moments, he turned and met her gaze. The misery in his eyes would be forever burned into her brain. As long as she lived, she never wanted to see that again.

"Fuck!" He closed his eyes, and dropped his head into his hands. "I can't believe she'd do this to me." Lauren scooted closer and rubbed his back.

Several long minutes passed, during which no one dared even take a breath. Nic raised his head and scrubbed his face. "I have to talk to her." He shook his head, as if trying to shake off a nightmare. "Before I turn her in to the police, I need to hear her admit it."

"That's too dangerous," Kaden said, his tone curt.

Yes, it was. But Vivian was Nic's friend, his mentor. They'd supported each other through the worst and the best life had to offer. The photo wasn't absolutely clear. There was an outside possibility that the woman reflected in the Plexiglas was someone who resembled Vivian. Nic needed to be sure.

Over Nic's head, Lauren met everyone's gaze, one by one. "Nic wants to do this. So, let's come up with a plan to get the evidence and keep him safe." She kept her voice firm. This wasn't up for negotiation.

Nic blew out a long breath and leaned back against the couch. After taking her hand in his, he cast her a brilliant smile. Rémi grabbed a pad and pen from a side table. "Let's brainstorm. Anyone have an idea?"

Rachel took a sip of her tea. "Well, before we start, I think we need to have clear goals."

"Spoken like a true business major," Nic said. She flushed when he smiled proudly at her.

"She needs to confess to stalking you," Rachel said to Nic.

"And to killing Summer," he added. Lauren shivered, and Nic pulled her against his side. His warmth helped her forget that she was next on Vivian's hit list.

"We want the confession on tape, preferably video," Kaden said. "It may or may not be admissible in court, but it will definitely be useful to the police."

"I'll borrow some video equipment from the guys in my old unit," Rémi said.

"I can help set it up," Lauren volunteered. Nic squeezed her arm and smiled.

Rémi looked up from his notes. "Great. Now location. Where do we want the big confession to happen?"

Everyone mulled that over. Rachel sat up straighter. "In the stable. Lauren can hide the video cameras and set up some photography equipment as a decoy. If Vivian asks, Nic can tell her it's picture week for the kids."

Lauren nodded. "That could work. But how will Nic get her there?"

Jake set his untouched cup of tea on the side table and piped up for the first time. "Ask her to go for a ride."

Nic shook his head. "She doesn't like horses."

"So we have to think of something she wants enough that she'd go into the stables to get it," Rachel said.

Out of the corner of her eye, Lauren saw Rémi exchange a look with Nic.

Nic inclined his head and said, "Me."

Lauren's eyes widened. "You?"

"It makes sense," Rémi said. "We've been talking about it. What better bait could we have? She's stalking Nic because she wants him."

"Sure. But it's not like he can wave a red flag at her and shout 'I'm here. Come get me.'"

His expression serious, Kaden finished off his tea then leaned forward to put the cup on the coffee table. "Vivian's not stupid." Lauren waited as he rested his elbows on his knees, and steepled his fingers. "Whatever you do, Nic, it has to be something believable."

Nic shot Lauren a nervous glance. "I'll come on to Vivian and ask her to meet me in the stables so we can have some private time."

Lauren wanted to jump up and shout, "Are you crazy?" But she forced herself to remain seated, to appear calm. "So… uh, you'll be acting, right?"

Nic's gaze bore into her. "Yes, but she'll believe every minute of it." A lump formed in her throat. Of course Vivian would believe it. The danger was that Lauren might fall for his act, too.

She tore her eyes away from Nic when Kaden addressed her. "Lauren, you and Jake need to stay hidden. If Vivian finds out you're here, she'll know something's wrong. Things could get very dangerous."

She gulped. "I understand."

"I'll take your rental to my place," Rémi added.

"Anything we forgot?" Rachel asked.

"The shoes." Rémi and Rachel stared at her with identical puzzled expressions. "The stalker, Vivian, caught her foot in the photo she sent of Summer. She was wearing Christian Louboutin shoes. None of this is conclusive, but if Vivian's got a pair of Louboutin's with her, it's one more piece of evidence."

Nic nodded. "If she isn't wearing them, one of us will need to check her room."

"I'll take care of that," Kaden said. "We need to talk scenarios now. What happens when she confesses?"

"*If* she confesses," Nic said.

"Okay, what happens if she confesses? She'll probably be pretty pissed at that point. Do you want us to come in and restrain her?"

Rémi looked up, his smile a little too bright. "I've got zip ties."

Kaden tapped his holster and grinned. "But I've got a gun."

Rémi's smile turned into a frown, making Lauren laugh despite the seriousness of the discussion.

Nic scrubbed his jaw, looking suddenly tired. "About that. Even if Vivian killed Summer…." He hesitated.

Lauren was pretty sure she knew what Nic was trying to say. "You don't want her to be hurt."

He nodded. "I want her to get the help she needs. I owe her that much. Without her, I'd probably still be flipping burgers."

"You love her."

"And I feel guilty. What if something I said or did set her off?" He averted his eyes. "Maybe I led her on somehow."

"Don't even go there," Rachel said. "None of this is your fault." The sternness of her tone surprised Lauren, but she completely agreed. Nic's gaze fixed on his sister. After a few seconds of silent discussion, he nodded.

"Now that that's out of the way, let's summarize. After Vivian confesses, I get to tie her down with my zip ties." Rémi's eyes held a mischievous glint in them.

"Second scenario. She killed Summer with a knife. What if she pulls one on you, Nic?" Kaden asked.

"Unless my life is in danger, do nothing."

Kaden bristled. "You hired me to protect you. If she pulls a knife, you're in danger."

"We could use a signal," Jake suggested. When everyone turned to him, his voice lowered to a mumble. "It was just a thought...."

"That's a good idea," Kaden said. Jake smiled. They discussed various suggestions and finally decided that if Nic wanted the cavalry to charge in, he would say *slap shot.*

"But whatever you do, don't come in with your guns," Nic added.

Jake looked confused. "Why not?"

"In hostage situations, the bad guy always makes the cops give him their weapons. And the last thing I want is for Vivian to get one of your guns."

Kaden eyed Nic. His jaw tight, he said, "Then we'll have to shoot from outside the room."

"But only on my signal."

Rémi tapped the pencil on the pad. "When do you want this to go down?"

"Tomorrow evening. Sunday's the blackmail deadline, so this has to end before then. Vivian's plane lands at four. I'll have a limo waiting, so she'll probably get here around five."

Rachel breathed a sigh of relief. "Phew, at least the kids will be gone by then."

Everyone sat back.

"Shit," Nic said, his tone exasperated. "I hadn't even thought about that."

"As they say," Jake said. "Thank God for small favors."

Rémi shook his head sadly as he met Rachel's gaze. "Not another one." They burst out laughing while Kaden and Jake eyed them as if they'd lost their minds.

"Hey!" Nic laughed as he reached for his beer.

"Another one what?" Lauren asked.

"On his last trip here, Nic was crowned the King of Fortune Cookie Crap, but Jake here might be able to challenge him for the title."

Laughter rang out across the room. Even Jake smiled. Before the laughter had completely died down, Nic stood up and reached for Lauren's hand and led her to the stairs. "I think we're done here. Goodnight everyone."

Lauren looked over her shoulder at the group in the living room. A flush crept across her cheeks. Everyone knew why Nic was so eager to get her upstairs. But when he ran his thumb over her palm, the heat in his eyes melted away any lingering embarrassment. She grabbed his shirt, intending to tug it out of his pants. But he stopped her and whispered, "Catch me if you can," then turned and ran up the stairs.

Laughing, she took off after him. She'd already caught him.

And she'd never let him go.

CHAPTER 22

As Nic reached the steps leading up to his attic suite, he pretended to stumble. He landed with his butt on the steps and waited. Lauren careened around the corner and flew into his arms. "Gotcha." He grinned.

She wrinkled her nose at him. "I thought I was supposed to catch you."

"Does it matter?"

Laughing, she looped her arms around his neck. "Not one bit."

"I missed you so much," he whispered in her ear and groaned at the feel of her stomach pressing against his cock. As if they had a mind of their own, his hands slid under her shirt. Nic wanted to shout out with relief when he felt the softness of her breasts against his palms. Several times over the past few days, he thought he'd never feel her silky skin again or hear her sexy moans. But here she was.

Where she belonged.

But the clothes had to go. He grabbed the hem of her shirt and pulled it up over her head. Her bra soon followed. With his hands on her waist, he lifted her higher so he could taste her ripe nipples. Hearing the sounds of pleasure she made at the back of her throat, his hips jerked against hers. But when he reached for the snap of her cargo pants, she stopped him. "Nic, we're on the stairs."

Christ, he'd done it again. "Everything disappears when I'm with you."

She smiled. "Let's go to your room."

Nic had all the best intentions in the world, but after kicking the door to his suite shut, he didn't want to take another step. Naked from the waist up, she was beautiful. Turning, he backed her against the wall. He wanted her. And he couldn't wait until they got to the bed.

Kneeling before her, he undid the snap and zipper on her pants and tugged them off. Tonight, she wore a lacy green thong. It was the color of her eyes and sexy as hell. He nuzzled her through the thin material, relishing her moans of delight.

Her breathing hitched as she speared her fingers through his hair, pulling him tighter against her. Inch by inch, he lowered her panties, his tongue trailing a wet path in their wake. She writhed as if anticipating the pleasure he would soon give her. He'd wanted to drag things out, to tease her a little. But where she was concerned, he was a weak man.

Desperate for the taste of her, he yanked off the tiny scrap of material, nudged her legs apart and brought his mouth to her pink flesh. *Oh man.* She tasted even better than he remembered. He'd been crazy to give in to the stalker's demands, even for one minute.

As he thrust his tongue into her opening, she tugged on his hair. He resisted. She tugged a little harder. "I need you inside. Now." He raised his eyes to her and she groaned. "Seeing you like that… you're killing me. Come here," she insisted, again.

The sight of her so aroused and demanding made him grin. It would be his pleasure to satisfy her tonight and for the rest of their lives. In one smooth movement, he stood up, lifting her at the same time. Her legs wrapped around his hips, while her hands worked to undo the fly of his jeans. When her hand closed around his cock and started stroking him, he stopped breathing. And like some hormonally challenged teenager, he had to fight not to come in her hand. "Condom… wallet," he said, praying she'd understand.

While she fiddled with his wallet, searching for a condom, he pressed his cock against her core in a rhythmic grind. Each small bump elicited a soft "Ah" from her that ratcheted up his desire. It was pure torture, but he couldn't stop. Didn't want to stop. After what felt like years, she dropped the wallet on the floor and waved a shiny wrapper in front of his face. "Got it!"

Moments later, with his cock enclosed in latex, he pressed her back against the wall and slammed home, making them both gasp.

When she wiggled her bottom, he gripped it and began to move. She was hot and tight, and he wouldn't last long. The smooth column of her neck drew his attention and he raked the pale skin gently with his teeth. Her moans almost pushed him over the edge. Trailing his lips along her jaw, he took little nips along the way. She worked her fingers through his hair and pressed her mouth against his.

Her lips opened, and he deepened the kiss, sucking her tongue into his mouth. Each time he nibbled the tip or stroked his tongue against hers, she made one of her wonderful sweet sounds that were like music to him. Her muscles contracted, heat bathed his cock. The pressure sent him reeling. But she was close and he wanted her to come before him.

Resting one hand on the wall beside her head for balance, he lifted her a little higher with the other. When he thrust into her from this new angle, her eyes shot open. "Oh!"

Oh, was right. A tingle began at the base of his spine and he knew the end was near. Slowly, he withdrew until only the tip of his cock remained inside her. "Look down," he said. When she did, he pressed into her, watching as she swallowed him into her body. Her muscles tightened around him, gripping him like a warm wet fist. He felt her legs tremble.

"Do it again," she whispered.

He pulled out of her, letting her see his cock lengthen. But this time, as his cock disappeared inside her core, he pressed a finger against the small opening in her rear. Her eyes flew to his face. "I'm coming."

He caught her words with his lips and thrust hard. Her body clenched, her muscles clamping down on him, a velvet vise. She spasmed around him. His own pleasure spiraling out of control, he pressed his face into the crook of her neck and inhaled her sweet apple scent. His hips jerked and he released inside of her.

As they drifted back to their senses, he tugged on one of her curls. "*Je t'aime,* Lauren." If he hadn't known it before, he knew it now: he couldn't live without her. And what was more, he didn't *want* to live without her. She was his love, his life. His soul. Without her, there was nothing.

After rezipping his jeans, he took her hand. "Come, I have something to show you."

She grinned. "I think you've already shown me everything."

As they passed the bathroom, Nic reached in to grab the bathrobe off the hook and handed it to her. "Wouldn't want you catch a chill. I have lots of plans for you, *chérie*."

Once he got her bundled up and seated on the bed, he stepped into the walk-in closet. With butterflies in his stomach, he reached into the red hatbox on the top shelf and pulled out a small box. He ran his thumb over the velvet material before stuffing the box in his pocket.

His heart started pounding like a jackhammer and his mouth felt dry. Was it too soon? Maybe, but it didn't matter. She owned a piece of his soul, and he needed to know what she meant to do with it.

After running through a few breathing exercises to settle his pulse, he walked back to Lauren. She stared, eyes wide as he knelt in front of her and wrapped his arms around her waist, putting them at eye level. With a slightly unsteady hand, he reached into his pocket to pull out the small jeweler's box. "Will you marry me, *chérie*?"

Eyes locked on her face, he held his breath. Her answer would determine his future. Either he'd spend it living on a cloud or in the pits of hell. When she smiled, he started to breathe again. Capturing his face in her hands, she whispered against his lips, "Yes. I'd love to be your wife."

His eyes burned as he held her in his arms. Lauren had agreed to be his, to spend the rest of her life with him. He wanted to open the windows and shout it out to the world. But first, he had to put a ring on her finger.

He opened the box and held it so she could see the antique diamond ring. "We can have it fitted." When she raised her gaze, her eyes glistened with unshed tears. He removed the ring and slipped it onto the third finger of her left hand. It was a perfect fit.

She threw her arms around him. "It's beautiful."

Losing his balance, he tumbled backwards onto the floor, his fiancée on his chest. "It's a family ring, handed down through the generations from father to son. When my mother died, she left it to me in her will with the admonishment that I carefully choose its next owner."

Lauren pressed her face against his chest. "I don't know what to say, except maybe, thank you. I wish I'd known her."

Nic glanced out the windows at the twinkling stars. His hand stroked Lauren's wild curls and he smiled. "She would have liked you. In many ways, you remind me of her."

"How so?"

"She was smart, determined and fiercely loyal. And she was a wonderful mother."

"I hope Jason feels that way about me some day."

Nic laughed. "He will. And so will all our other children."

A slight frown creased her forehead. "*All* our other children? Exactly how many kids do you want?"

"Enough to have our own hockey team," he teased.

She grinned and socked him in the shoulder. After a moment, her expression grew serious. "You've made me happy again. And that's only one of the many, many reasons why I love you."

"I love you too," he said, letting all his emotions for her show in his eyes. Love, desire, and just plain liking. He liked being with her and talking with her, hearing her opinions and seeing humor light up her face. He wanted to spend every day learning about her until he knew her better than himself. He wanted to spend every night exploring her body and hearing her sounds of pleasure.

He smiled. There was no time like the present to further his explorations.

Rolling them over, he brought his lips to hers in a heated kiss. His body was on fire. Blood roared through his veins. Every cell rejoiced and his heart pounded in the knowledge that they would have a lifetime together.

But first, they had to survive tomorrow.

Lauren woke up in heaven. Nic's broad chest pillowed her head and his strong arm circled her waist as if to ensure she didn't go far. She smiled as she rubbed her cheek against the patch of fuzzy curls that hid a small flat nipple, enjoying the sensation. Her tongue darted out to lick the small bit of flesh while she massaged his smooth skin.

Out of the corner of her eye, she saw a reflection bounce off something on her hand. Her heart stuttered as the memories of last night flooded back. Had it all been just a dream, another fantasy? With a gasp, she bolted up in the bed and stared at her left hand. No. With the sunlight reflecting off it, the antique ring was even more spectacular than she remembered.

Had she been wrong to accept Nic's proposal? She'd promised herself to take things slowly, and mere hours later, she was engaged. Maybe she'd gone crazy. *Jesus.* What if it was just the excitement and danger of the last few weeks that had brought them together? Would he change his mind when life got back to normal?

"Good morning, *chérie*."

At the sound of Nic's voice, thick with sleep, she looked up from the ring she'd been contemplating. He looked so good laying there, his skin burnished gold by the sun. Like a Greek god awaiting his pleasure.

She licked her dry lips and watched his eyes track the motion. Something twitched next to her thigh, catching her attention. She grinned. On second thought, maybe he was more like the Energizer Bunny. "Good morning to you, too."

Feeling deliciously naughty, she leaned forward and traced Nic's hard muscles with a single finger. His eyes darkened and his skin broke out in gooseflesh. Desire swept through her. "I love your chest," she said, reaching with both hands to massage the wide expanse of warm skin.

"Feel free to wake me up like this anytime you want." His husky voice stirred something deep inside her. A feeling of tenderness, a need to pleasure, to cherish.

"Anytime?" she asked, feigning surprise. He chuckled and the sound wrapped around her heart. Enjoying his laughter, she tweaked his nipple, making him growl.

He arched a brow and made snapping jaw motions with his fingers, inching closer and closer to her breast. When his fingers reached their destination and tugged at her tender flesh, she moaned. His slow cocky smile made her laugh.

Her hands slid up to his shoulders and she pushed forward to take his nipple between her teeth. Carefully, she bit down. He made a rumbling sound deep in his chest and his fingers gripped her hips. Against her lips, his heart raced. Her breathing increased to match the wild tempo.

Desperate to taste and touch all of him, she threw her leg over his hips and lay on him, covering him like a human blanket. He was hard where she was soft, rough where she was smooth. She arched her back, pressing her belly against Nic's erection. He made a sound deep in his throat.

The stubble on his face rasped against her cheek when she stretched up to run her tongue along the rim of his ear. But she didn't mind. Her pleasure spiraled to new heights as she imagined the slight abrasion on an even more sensitive part of her body.

Taking advantage of her position, Nic used his thighs to spread her legs wide and press his cock against her core. But instead of entering her, he used his feet to close her legs, trapping himself between them.

Then Mr. Lover started a rockin'.

With slow, steady thrusts of his hips, he eased his cock through her folds, repeatedly hitting her sweet spot. Moisture flowed from her, bathing them both in warm wetness. Her cheeks heated as the scent of her arousal rose between them.

Nic inhaled sharply. Flames danced in the blue depths of his eyes. He wanted her as much as she wanted him. One big hand clamped onto her butt cheek and pressed her down, increasing the pressure. Increasing the pleasure. The fingers of his other hand trailed along her spine, to the base of her neck, leaving behind a path of fire. Her skin burned and she wanted more.

Shamelessly, she writhed against him, arching and twisting until he groaned loudly. His hips bucked, and she found herself tossed in the air. With a thump, she landed half on his chest, half off. When she lifted her head, he was watching her with a sheepish expression that had her laughing. Sex with Todd had always been so serious, but with Nic each time was different. Slow and sweet. Fast and hard. Playful.

As if to prove her point, he opened his eyes wide and said in a haughty British tone, "I daresay, my dear, there's nothing quite like a morning romp to start off the day."

"Oh, I don't know," she said, infusing her voice with a healthy shot of Texas twang. "I think I prefer to ride."

"You want me to play horse to your cowgirl? Just call me Black Stallion."

After taking a shower and working her hair into some semblance of order, Lauren bounded down the stairs, drawn by the aroma of fresh coffee brewing. No way was she going to miss the chance to watch Nic drink his first cup of the day.

Nic and Rachel were already seated at the kitchen table, talking in low voices. Spotting Nic's empty hands, Lauren smiled. "Good morning."

When she reached his side, he cupped her neck and tugged her down until their lips brushed against each other. His lips curved into a smile, and she enjoyed the feel of it against her mouth.

"Coffee's ready," Rachel called out, chuckling.

With a last quick kiss, Nic released Lauren and they both turned to take the steaming cups of coffee Rachel handed them.

"Mmm… this smells so good." Smiling at his sister, he added, "There's nothing in the world like Rachel's coffee. I don't know how she does it, but if she could bring it to market, she'd blow the competition out of the water."

Lauren watched Nic take a sip and grinned. He'd worn the same look in bed that morning. Bliss. She loved how wonderfully expressive his face was. It hit her then. She was seeing the real Nic. This was his home, a place where he felt safe, and he didn't have to hide his emotions or his reactions. She lifted her cup to her mouth, and after inhaling deeply, took a sip.

"You're engaged?" Rachel screamed, pointing to the ring on her finger.

Lauren choked. And Nic grinned like a loon.

Rachel took her hand and smoothed her thumb over the ring. Was she upset that Nic had given Lauren the ring? Lauren studied her face but couldn't find even a trace of jealousy. "I'm so happy for you. For both of you." Her voice was warm and rich with excitement. "Have you set a date?"

Lauren shook her head. "We haven't talked about that yet."

Nic took her hand from Rachel and kissed her wrist. The moist warmth sent a small shiver coursing from her hand to belly. Hooboy! She met his gaze. His eyes were dark, reflecting her own desire. He smiled and said softly, "We're taking things slow. When Lauren's ready, she'll let me know."

Warmth filled her heart and she grinned. "I knew I loved you for a reason."

"Okay, I see who wears the pants." Rachel laughed.

Nic rubbed a palm over Lauren's butt. "I do have a thing for these cargo pants."

Rachel pointed to a plate of muffins and biscuits and shot them a knowing grin. "Eat. You two need to keep your strength up."

They ate, drank coffee and chatted. It all felt so normal, so good. Except Jason wasn't here. And that wasn't normal. She'd never gone more than a few days without seeing him, and now it had already been over a week.

Nic tilted her chin up and frowned. "You got quiet all of a sudden. What's wrong?"

"I miss Jason." She sighed heavily.

"I miss him too. As soon as this is all over, we'll bring him out here."

Like her mom said, he was darn near perfect. "I'd love that."

"What about your job? You haven't called Helen yet, have you?"

Her eyes widened. "I forgot all about it."

Rachel laughed again. "Who could blame you?"

"I'll call her now."

As she started to push away from the table, Nic laid a restraining hand on her arm. "Before you do that, there's something else I need to tell you." He glanced at Rachel and she nodded.

Lauren stomach rolled. *Please God, don't let it be something bad.* Taking a deep breath to steady her nerves, she resettled in her seat.

"Yesterday, Rachel and I cleared the air about a lot of things, and we've come to an understanding of sorts."

Rachel leaned forward. "We understand that Nic's a big twit and I'm the perfect sister."

Nic shook his head in mock dismay. "See what I have to put up with?" Lauren smiled. She loved seeing this side of him. "I realized I wasn't keeping the accident a secret to protect her but rather to protect myself." His gaze drifted to the window. "It was a hard truth to accept."

Lauren's chest tightened with a bittersweet mix of sympathy and pride. "It takes a big man to own up to his mistakes. And an even bigger one to forgive himself."

"I'm going public with it. Rachel agrees. We'll invite the press, explain about the hippo therapy, everything."

Her breath caught in her lungs. It was a huge risk. If people reacted as he expected, he'd be devastated, not to mention that his career would be trashed. But given the right spin....

"With everything out in the open," Rachel added, "we take away the ammunition for any further blackmail."

Nic watched her for a moment. "Do you think *Vanity Fair* would be interested in an exclusive?"

Lauren's eyes widened. "I'm sure they'd jump at the chance. It would be a great cover story. Do you want me to ask Helen?"

He nodded. "Yes, and she can pick the reporter. But you're the photographer."

"Are you doing this to save my job?"

Nic chuckled. "No, but if it helps...."

Lauren shook her head. "You know they won't turn down an opportunity like this. When do you want to do the interview?"

"Next week." His face darkened. "I have to take care of Vivian first."

"I'll call Helen now."

"Wait." A smile broke out across his face. "I have a surprise for you."

Lauren had to laugh. Jason wore the same expression whenever he had a gift for her, as if giving her a present were more exciting than receiving one. "A surprise? Where?"

"In the stables." Nic leaned back in his chair, and she wanted to shake him. Why was he just sitting here when he had a surprise to show her?

She pushed her chair back and jumped up. "I'm ready."

"Now I know what to do whenever I need to get you moving in a hurry," he teased.

"Come on. Let's go," she urged him as she grabbed her coffee mug.

Nic laughed as he followed her out of the house. They crossed the field hand in hand. She was so excited she would have been skipping had she not been holding the coffee mug.

"Is it a horse?"

"No."

"A new cowboy hat?" Nic arched a brow and she huffed. "I'm just trying to think of things that might be in the stables."

He led her to a door on the side and opened it, ushering her inside with a wide sweep of his arm. "*Après vous, Madame.*"

Lauren stepped inside and froze. The spacious room had two large windows on the west facing wall and had been set up like a studio. "This is where you'll bring Vivian?" she asked, uncertain what to say.

He nodded. "Yes. But I didn't stage this for her. I ordered the equipment after our weekend at your place. This studio is for you."

"But you couldn't know that I'd come here."

He smiled. "A guy can dream."

Lauren returned his smile. She knew all about dreams.

Her eyes bounced around the room. Nic hadn't missed a thing. On the back wall was a desk on which sat a large widescreen LCD monitor connected to a state of the art desktop computer. But what immediately caught her attention and got her feet moving again was the brand new Nikon D3S that rested next to it. She picked it up as if it were a newborn child and with much the same awe. "How did you know I wanted this one?"

"You told me when you showed me how to use your camera."

"You remembered?"

"I remember every minute I spend with you."

"Thank you so much," she said before carefully setting the camera on the desk and wrapping her arms around him. "But why?"

"Because I'd do anything for you, *ma bien aimée.*"

"*Ma bien aimée.* What does that mean?"

"My beloved."

Her heart bursting, she swallowed past the lump in her throat. "You should have a pet name too."

"How about master? That has a nice ring to it." She smiled and shook her head. "No? Maybe stud then?"

"I see where you're going with this." She laughed. Then she spotted something hidden in the umbrellas. "Oh! You got me a wireless flash system." After examining her find, she pressed his hand to her heart. "I can't believe you did all this for me. Everything I could ever imagine needing is right here."

With a feather-light brush of his thumb, he stroked her cheek. "Do you have any idea how talented I think you are? I want to support you as a photographer in any way I can."

"In any way, huh?" She flashed him a naughty look. "In that case, I think we should take some sexy shots of you. You know, to test out all this wonderful new equipment."

"Your wish is my command." He whipped off his T-shirt. "Where do you want me?"

Her gaze trailed over the length of him and she lingered on the sculpted muscles of his chest. “Anywhere, everywhere.”

“Right here, right now?”

“God, yes,” she agreed, falling into his arms.

CHAPTER 23

Kaden snapped his phone shut. "That was the limo driver. They're about ten minutes away."

Flanked by Kaden and Rémi, Nic had been watching the horses in the field as he awaited Vivian's arrival and mentally readied himself for what he had to do.

"Rémi, I want Tommy to stay with Rachel at all times."

"I'll make sure of it."

"Kaden." Nic waited until the man half turned, then held his gaze, injecting as much meaning as he could into his next words. "Make sure Jake knows, no matter what happens, he has to keep Lauren out of it."

"Understood."

"And," Nic added, "unless you have absolutely no choice, Vivian is not to be hurt."

Kaden exchanged a look with Rémi, and both men nodded.

They weren't happy with his decision, but he held firm. Vivian needed medical help, not a bullet in the head.

Rémi held his hand in front of Nic and opened it. In his palm sat a device similar to a Bluetooth earpiece. "Kaden and I will each be wearing one of these. We'll hear everything that's said in the studio. Anytime you need us, just say the word."

Nic clapped him on the shoulder. "Thanks, man. It helps knowing you guys have my back." Pushing off from the wooden fence he'd been leaning on, he thumped it with his fists, and turned away from the horses. "Okay, then. Game on."

"Game on," they echoed.

After a round of knuckle bumps, Rémi and Kaden walked back to the house, leaving Nic to his thoughts. He rubbed his neck and glanced toward the stables. Earlier, Lauren and Rémi had set up the borrowed video equipment, effectively hiding it among the camera equipment he'd bought for her. Rémi's cop friend had also lent him a system that would allow Lauren and Jake to see and hear everything from the room above the studio. He hated that she'd be upstairs watching, but she'd have found some way to see what was going on. A way that might have put her in danger. This was definitely the safer solution.

Nic checked his watch. Five minutes to showtime.

He shook out his legs and arms, rolled his shoulders, and stretched his neck. Then he filled his lungs until he felt a slight burn, and let the air out slowly. With his eyes closed, he repeated the breathing exercise a few more times, imagining himself in his role. He would be charming like Nic The Lover, but not so smooth that Vivian would get suspicious.

Tonight he was playing the part of a man whose entire life has turned to shit. He's lost most of his money and is on the verge of losing his career because he doesn't have enough money to pay the stalker who's blackmailing him. His past is rearing its ugly head, and he's about to lose everyone and everything that's ever meant anything to him. Except *her*—the leading lady of this little farce. He'll see that she's the only one who has stood by him, the only one who really loves him. And he'll realize he loves her, not as a friend, but as a woman. He'll invite her to a night of seduction and ply her secrets from her, pressing her to prove her love.

It would work. It *had* to work.

Behind him, he heard the gate open and the low purr of the limo's engine as it drove down the lane. He arranged his face into a slightly desperate expression before turning to face her. She needed to see a man on the brink whose only hope for salvation had just arrived.

Taking large steps but maintaining an unhurried pace, he approached the car now parked in front of the house. When he was still several steps away, the driver got out and opened the passenger door. Nic stepped closer to help Vivian out of the car but paused to admire the long leg encased in silk hose that appeared. His eyes trailed down to her toes and his expression slipped. On her foot was a shoe—with a fucking red sole. He had to hand it to the woman; she was absolutely fearless.

Vivian extended a hand out of the car for him to take. He dove back into character. Damn, he couldn't fuck up like that again.

Summoning all the grace he could, he handed her out of the limo, then raised her fingers to his lips, kissing them with reverence. "Vivian, you have no idea how happy I am to see you."

She leaned forward, kissing him on the cheek. Her breast pressing against his arm was obviously not unintended. "Darling," she said, stoking his cheek, "have things been so terrible?"

He rubbed his face in the palm of her hand and looked deep into her eyes.

He lowered his voice and said, "Everything's falling apart, Viv. And I've been so lonely without you."

Tilting her head, she smiled slightly. "Well, I'm here now. And I have a surprise for you."

"Really?" His eyes widened without any acting on his part.

She chuckled. The deep sound, so different from Lauren's light laughter, grated on his nerves. "Should I tell you now or keep it for later?"

"Now, please," he said, making puppy dog eyes at her. Excitement rolled off her in waves. Whatever this news was, it was big.

"I managed to get another two million." She gripped his arm and made little hops in her three-inch red-soled heels. "You have enough money now to pay off the blackmailers."

Acting appropriately happy, he wrapped his arms around her waist and twirled her around. "Thank you! Thank you." He made one last circle, then set her down but didn't release his hold. He stared into her eyes as if opening up his soul to her. "I don't know what to say."

"Then don't say anything." Her voice was low, husky with arousal. Her hard nipples poked into his chest. Nic knew what he had to do.

He let desire cloud his eyes. While maintaining eye contact, he lowered his head until only an inch separated their lips. Then he hesitated, and pulled back, dropping his arms. "God, Viv. I'm so sorry."

Vivian blinked, looking a little dazed. "What are you sorry about?"

"I hope I didn't offend you." He stepped back. "Having you as my agent means a lot to me. I'd hate myself if I ruined that."

Her eyebrows shot up. "It's never been just business between us."

He remained silent, but gave her a skeptical look.

"Why do you think you never settled down with anyone in all these years?" Her eyes flashed with irritation. "All the women you've been with were using you. Even that no-talent department store photographer."

Nic clamped his jaw shut. *Play along.*

She touched his chest. "Darling," she said, her tone soft. "I know it hurts to admit it. But you know I'm right."

He blew out a long breath and dropped his head. "As soon as she got that offer from *Vanity Fair*, she dumped me."

"She wasn't good enough for you. None of them were." Her hand smoothed over his chest, and he had to grit his teeth to keep from shuddering.

Instead, he raised his head and frowned, as if considering her words. Then he nodded. "You know, Viv, even when I had no money and no prospects, you saw something in me. You made me who I am, and you never expected anything from me in return."

She smiled and squeezed his arm. "Even then I knew you were special."

"I got the impression you saw me as a kid."

"Hardly." Her fingers ran up his arm to caress his shoulder. "You're all man."

Nic swallowed and met her gaze. "Since the day we met, I've had feelings for you, Vivian."

"Good," she said, pressing against him, "because there's something I've wanted to do for a long time."

When her mouth touched his, Vivian made a small sound, like a sigh, and tightened her arms around his neck. Closing his eyes, he imagined Lauren's sweet face while Vivian nibbled his bottom lip and smoothed over the tiny bites with her tongue. Could he do this? Vivian was beautiful, but he'd always thought of her as a mother, or a favorite aunt.

It's just another acting job.

Except it wasn't. This time, his life—and Vivian's—depended on his skills. She had to believe every word, every look. Every touch.

"You make me so hot," he said, his voice low. With his hands on her face, he inched back so she wouldn't notice his lack of response, and took control of the kiss. He kissed her deeply, then ran his lips over her jaw and buried his face in her hair. "I want you. But not here. You deserve better."

Pretending to breathe hard, he drew back. Her eyes gleamed with desire. *So far, so good.* Without giving her time to say anything, he took her by the elbow and led her up the ramp. "Let's get you settled in."

He opened the door to the house and had to bite back a smile. As planned, Rémi and Kaden were in the kitchen, engaged in a rather loud argument concerning the relative merits of the Montréal Canadiens and the L.A. Kings.

Rachel and her nurse, Marie-Soleil, had set up a physical therapy session in the living area. Nickleback belted out one of Rachel's favorite rock anthems from the speakers scattered around the room. Tommy jumped on the couch playing air-guitar while both ladies sang along loudly—and off-key.

Vivian halted abruptly in the entrance as the noise registered. Nic plastered a resigned expression on his face. She arched an auburn brow. "I thought you said you were lonely."

"I am." He shook his head. "They go about their day being *happy* while my life falls apart."

Vivian frowned and caressed his face. "My poor, darling. They don't deserve you." She stretched up on her toes and brushed her lips against his. Out of the corner of his eye, he caught Rachel grimacing and had to glance away.

When she settled back on her heels, Nic rubbed a thumb along her lips. "You know what, Viv?" He flashed one of his practiced movie star smiles guaranteed to make women melt. "I think we deserve each other."

"How right you are, my darling. I'm going to make you happier than you've ever been in your life."

Leaning down, he gave her another quick kiss and moaned as if he wanted to take it much further but couldn't. With an exaggerated sigh, he picked up her luggage and took her hand, pulling her up the stairs. He opened the door to the remaining empty room. "I'll put your things in here."

Her gaze swept the room, stopping on the single bed. She turned to him but a loud noise on the stairs saved him. Wide-eyed, they watched as Kaden and Rémi thundered past, playing an athletic game of catch in the hall. Nic barely had time to kick the door shut before the football slammed into it. Seconds later, the door crashed open and Rémi fell into the room.

Vivian's mouth hung open, seeing the man lying on the floor at her feet.

"Damn, almost caught that one." Rémi grinned like a fool.

Nic coughed to cover a surprised laugh. But like some looky-loo at the scene of an accident, he couldn't look away.

With perfect slapstick precision, Rémi tripped over the ball as he scrambled to stand up. His hand shot out, grabbing Vivian's arm. She lost her balance and grabbed Nic, sending the three of them to the floor in an inglorious pile. Nic scrambled to his feet, while from his position on the bottom of the pile, Rémi roared with laughter.

"Nic, man. You should've told me your new squeeze liked sandwiches," Rémi said, as he winked at Vivian and pinched her ass. "I'm up for it if you are, sweetheart."

Her lips curled into a nasty excuse for a smile, and Nic could see her nails digging into his friend's chest as she shoved away from him. "I wouldn't let you touch me if you were the last dick on earth."

Nic intervened before things got even uglier. He smacked Rémi's hands off Vivian's butt and lifted her up. Her mouth was set in a thin line, and her eyes flashed with anger. Running his thumb along her chin, he cupped her cheek. "I'm so sorry, Vivian. Give me a minute to take care of this."

A slight movement of her head brought her lips into contact with his palm. Her tongue darted out and swirled against his skin. Nic bit his tongue to suppress the shudder that started at the top of his spine. Her mood seemed mercurial. Volatile. So different from the cool professional woman he thought he knew. Had she been this way before, and he just hadn't seen it? Or was this something new? As her friend, he should have noticed, should have tried to help her through whatever problems she was having.

Vivian shot a death glare in Rémi's direction. Nic touched her arm to draw her attention. Cold, hard eyes met his, chilling him to the bone. His remaining doubts evaporated.

Hers were the eyes of a killer.

Nic made a show of grabbing Rémi by the front of his shirt and hauling him out into the hall. "Don't you ever go near her again, you asshole," he shouted. "She's mine, you got that? I'll never share her, not even with you."

Rémi held up his hands in surrender. "I was just having a little fun."

"Get out of here, both of you." Nic shoved him toward Kaden, who'd remained near the top of the stairs. Rémi glanced behind Nic, then his expression turned serious and he mouthed, "Be careful."

Nic nodded and returned to Vivian's room. She was sitting on the edge of the bed, legs crossed at the knees, cool and calm as ever. "Interesting friends you've got, darling," she said with a smirk.

After forcing his face into a pout, he went to sit beside her. "It's like living in a frat house. All they think about is having fun and partying."

"Sounds to me like they're using you, too. They can't get their own women, so they hang around you, waiting to grab up your leftovers."

Jaw set, eyes blazing, he turned to her. "But Rémi will never get you."

"Of course he won't." She pressed a kiss to his mouth. "I *never* share."

On the surface, her words sounded like a promise, but the underlying threat was clear. Nic brightened his expression and smiled. He'd give her what she wanted. Or at least the illusion of it.

He brought her hand to his mouth and trailed little kisses down her arm. He lowered his voice. "I need you. Right now."

Tunneling her fingers through his hair, she whispered, "Darling, I've waited so long to hear you say that."

Stay in character. He pushed aside his revulsion and kissed her deeply, curling his tongue against hers. When she tried to make him fall back onto the bed, he wrenched his mouth away. "*Chérie.*" The word would catch her attention.

Tears shone in her eyes. His subconscious started to niggle at him. How could she look at him with such love after everything she'd done to him, to Lauren, and to Summer? Either she was a fabulous actress, or she believed her own press. He needed to hear her confession.

"*Chérie*, we can't make love here. The last thing I want is someone banging down the door and ruining our first time together. I want it to be as special as you are."

"Do you have some place in mind?"

Nic thought for a moment, then snapped his fingers. "I've got the perfect place." Rising to his feet, he added, "Unpack and freshen up. I'll come get you when I've got everything ready."

"I do love surprises."

Bending down, he whispered against her lips. "I promise I have plenty of surprises in store for you tonight."

As he headed into the hall, Nic offered up a silent prayer to St. Genesius, patron saint of actors. His performance had better be Oscar caliber.

Or one of them could end up dead.

CHAPTER 24

As soon as she heard Nic's footsteps going down the stairs, Vivian shut the door. If that half-breed friend of Nic's saw it open, he'd probably try mauling her again. And then she'd have to kill him.

Nic wouldn't like that, though.

None of it mattered, because tomorrow she and Nic would pay off the *blackmailer,* and then she'd whisk him away to their new home.

She spread her suitcase on the bed. Her cosmetic bag where she'd stashed the Rohypnol lay on top of the clothing. Would she need it tomorrow when she took Nic away from here? She'd planned to kidnap Nic to bring him to the island. But today, everything had changed. From what he'd said, he was ready to start a new life with her.

Vivian's hand trembled as she touched her lips, reliving the feel of Nic's mouth on hers. Although he hadn't said he loved her, the way he'd touched her and tasted her, the way he'd stood up for her, had said it for him.

Sliding her hand along the edge of the suitcase, she retrieved the switchblade. With a flick of her thumb, the long blade extended. She brought the strip of shiny metal to her lips and kissed it. The knife's twin had served her well when Summer had tried to hurt Nic. And it would serve her well again if anyone tried to keep them apart.

No one would get in the way of her happiness tonight.

She slipped the knife into her purse, and then threw in the packet of Rohypnol. As she dropped her purse on the dresser at the foot of the bed, she caught her reflection in the mirror. Her business suit was elegant, but it was hardly ideal for tonight. This evening would be their first time together. Whatever she wore had to be spectacular. Spectacularly sexy.

Rummaging through the various outfits she'd brought along, she spotted the light blue teddy she'd picked out with him in mind. She'd been keeping it for when they got to the island. Should she wear it tonight instead? It was certainly sexy enough.

An idea came to her; the tailored black skirt with the slit along the side would be perfect. Carefully, she pulled on the threads, lengthening the slit so it ended high enough that the teddy would be visible. As for the top, any blouse would do, as long as it was mostly unbuttoned. Her pulse sped up as she imagined Nic's face when he saw her. She'd finally get to hold his hard cock and work it as she'd watched him do in the shower. And if he was a very good boy, she'd give him a blow job he'd never forget.

Of course, she'd wear the Louboutins. A guy hadn't been born who didn't like seeing his woman in fuck-me heels and a teddy. Maybe he'd even want her to keep them on when he got down on his knees and sucked her pussy. If he made her come that way, she'd forgive him for pleasuring that slut *Lorna*, for forgetting that like the rest of him, his mouth belonged to her.

Vivian couldn't keep the smile off her face as she changed her clothes. Nic was hers now. Of course, he always had been; he just hadn't known it. But now he did. Her heart contracted as his shout echoed in her mind. *She's mine.*

That shout said it all: she was special, he wanted her, she was his.

There would be no more interfering women.

No more interfering friends.

It would be just the two of them. Alone. Forever.

❧ ❧

Click, click. Click, click.

Lauren's fingernails tapped the coffee mug cradled in her hands. Because Nic had insisted, she'd agreed to remain in this room, above the studio, where she'd be safe. But the wait was killing her.

Careful not to give away her location, she'd watched Vivian's arrival through a small window facing the house and even though she hadn't been able to hear anything, she'd seen more than enough. And she sure as heck had seen the Louboutins Vivian had been wearing.

The way Vivian had slithered up Nic's body and kissed him made her stomach churn. Although she'd known Nic was acting, Vivian *wasn't.* Jealousy had flared in her heart, and poor Jake had practically had to restrain her to prevent her from storming out into the lane and physically pulling Vivian off Nic.

Lauren took another sip of coffee.

Click, click. Click, click. Her nails tinged against the ceramic.

A hand wrapped around the cup, trapping her fingers. "Ma'am, I know you're worried, but, please… stop."

"Sorry."

Jake released her hand and smiled. "You don't have to be nervous. When we were in Afghanistan, Kaden took a bullet with my name on it. Trust me, your fiancé is safe. And I'm right here if either of them needs backup."

"Thanks for telling me." And strangely, she did feel reassured. Surely nothing too terrible could happen with Kaden, Jake, Tommy, and Rémi keeping watch. Except… they'd interfere only if his life were in danger.

But what about his heart? What about hers? How far would Nic have to go to get Vivian to confess? Could he live with himself if he had to do more than kiss Vivian? Could she live with herself? Yes. Even if Nic had to have sex with Vivian, she'd deal with it. Vivian wasn't going to win, no matter what. Lauren wouldn't let her.

Beside her, Jake straightened in his chair and pulled on a pair of headphones. "Someone's coming."

Lauren adjusted her own headphones and watched the monitor as Nic entered the studio. He made a thumbs-up sign in the direction of the camera and proceeded to lay out the props he'd need for tonight's seduction: several thick blankets and cushions, candles, champagne, and a picnic basket. When he was done, he lit the candles and pressed the button to lower the window blinds. She was relieved to see he stopped the blinds a few inches short of the frame, as they'd agreed, so Kaden and Rémi could keep watch from outside. A CD player sat on the desk next to her new computer along with a selection of music. Nic picked a CD and inserted it into the machine, setting the volume low so the video camera could still capture anything that was said in the room.

Maybe they should have involved the police. Even with Kaden, Rémi, and Jake standing by, any help they could give was after the fact. Nic would still be alone with Vivian. Alone with a killer.

Downstairs, Nic pulled out his cell phone. Her gut contracted painfully when she heard him say, "Hello, *chérie*." That was his name for *her*.

Breathe, Lauren. He's acting.

He invited Vivian to join him in the stables. It took a little cajoling but in the end, she agreed. When Nic laid on the charm, no woman, Vivian included, could resist him.

Before hanging up, he looked straight at the camera. "I promise, *chérie*. This will be a night to remember, for both of us." Lauren's eyes welled up. Nic meant this promise for her. Tonight, the nightmare would end.

While Nic waited for Vivian, he went through some sort of warm-up routine, shaking out his arms and legs, rolling his neck and breathing deeply. When he raised his head, the changes to his appearance shocked Lauren.

Gone was Nic Lamoureux and in his place was Nic The Lover. He'd relaxed his jaw, and his mouth appeared softer. His eyes became heavy-lidded and had a slight sheen to them. Even his skin seemed darker, flushed somehow. He drifted over to the champagne and poured the liquid into two flutes, his movements more languid and fluid than usual. Each change was small, subtle. But put together, the effect was dramatic.

Nic turned as Vivian entered the studio. Smiling, he held up the flutes. "I thought we could start with a celebratory toast."

Vivian returned his smile and sauntered into the room. Lauren scowled when she noticed the slit on Vivian's skirt and her undone blouse. Why had the woman bothered to wear anything at all?

Nic handed her one of the flutes. "To the future," he said, raising his glass.

"To the future," she echoed.

Vivian drained her glass and held it out for more. Nic laughed and refilled it. She arched a perfectly shaped brow. "To our love?"

Even to Lauren, it sounded more like a question than a toast. She steeled herself for Nic's response.

He ran his tongue along his bottom lip, and clinked their flutes together. "To our love." Lauren gagged. Did his voice have to be so low and sound exactly like it did when he had sex on his mind?

"Easy there, ma'am," Jake murmured.

Lauren nodded. She *knew* he was acting even if she couldn't help reacting like he wasn't.

When she returned her attention to the monitor, Vivian was looking around, squinting to see better in the dim lighting. "What is this place?"

"It's usually for storage. But Rachel wanted to get photos of the kids on their favorite horses. Since it'll take about a week to get all the photos taken, I'm letting the photographer use this room."

She sniffed the air. "Have any horses been in here?"

Nic laughed. "Not yet. They're starting on Monday." He took her hand and led her over to the makeshift bed. "Are you hungry?" he asked, pointing to the picnic basket.

When she sat down, she managed to expose even more of her legs through the slit in her skirt. "Maybe a little."

"Some strawberries and whipped cream to go along with the champagne?" He pulled two containers out of the basket.

Vivian's eyes widened. "You remembered?"

He chuckled. "I told you. Since the beginning, it's always been you." He selected a strawberry and dipped it in the whipped cream before bringing it to her lips. She opened her mouth and bit. A drop of juice dripped to her chin. Nic leaned over and licked it. "Mmm… delicious."

Amazed, Lauren watched Nic begin his seduction. Not a hint of his true feelings showed in his face. If this were a movie, she'd totally buy his sexual interest in Vivian.

Nic lay down on his side, tugging a cushion under his arm. "This feels so right. Why did it take us so long to admit our feelings for each other?"

Vivian's lips twitched. "Well, you did have all those other women." Lauren fought the twinge of jealousy that stirred in her gut.

"It's a good thing they're gone, then." When Vivian grinned but didn't say anything, Nic cocked his head and smiled like he knew a secret. "You didn't have anything to do with that, did you, *chérie*?"

Hearing Nic's question, Lauren tensed and gripped the arms of her chair. This was the first step. If Vivian admitted to stalking him, maybe she'd admit to killing Summer, too.

Vivian's eyes opened wide and she put a hand to her chest. *"Moi?"*

"I know how you are." He trailed a finger along her arm. "You can be a real lioness when you want something." He met her gaze. "And you want me."

She opened her mouth as if to say something, then clamped it shut.

"Come on, Viv. I won't be mad." He inched closer to her. "They were using me. If you helped get rid of them, you did me a huge favor."

Vivian averted her gaze. "I might have sent a few messages."

"And photos?" When she nodded, Nic picked up another strawberry and coated it in whipped cream. As he placed it in her mouth, he smiled. "Sweet, Vivian. I owe you for that."

"You aren't even a little angry I got rid of *Lorna*?"

Lauren resisted shouting her name at the monitor. Good thing too, because Vivian would probably have heard her through the floor.

Nic shook his head. "Did you send her the curly haired Barbie too?"

"It looked a lot like her, didn't it?"

"The dog tags clinched it."

Vivian threw her head back and laughed.

"You should have seen her face when I opened the box." He laughed along with her. "As they say in that credit card commercial: priceless."

Lauren leaned forward to see the screen more clearly. Nic's eyes shone with what looked like genuine happiness. To all appearances, he was having a grand old time at her expense. She took a deep breath. *It isn't real.*

"What about the woman at the footprint ceremony? Was she part of this?"

"I looked into it. She was just a crazy fan."

Lauren shuddered, thinking how close the woman had come to being killed.

Nic pushed himself into a sitting position and leaned forward so only a few inches separated him from Vivian. "You have no idea how cherished I feel knowing you did all this for me."

"I have gone, and will continue to go, to great lengths to protect you."

Grinning, Nic pretended to roar like a lion while Vivian purred in return. Lauren was seriously starting to feel sick.

"And NicsBitch. Did you get rid of her, too? She knew exactly where I was all the time."

Vivian laughed. "How innocent you are, my sweet Nic. *I* was NicsBitch."

Nic drew back a little, his brow furrowed in confusion. "It was you?"

"I put a tracking app on your phone that let me keep tabs on you. That way, if you needed me, I could intervene quickly."

"But why did you post my location on the Internet?"

She lowered her chin and lifted her eyes up to his, a slight smile playing with her lips. "I only did that when you needed a little reminder."

"Of?"

"Of who you belong to."

Lauren's mind reeled. Vivian had used the internet postings to punish Nic whenever she'd felt he was getting out of line.

Nic put his hand behind Vivian's head and lowered her to the blanket. "I don't need any reminders now. I belong to you." His mouth descended on hers. She moaned and arched into him. Nic's expression turned fierce as he tore her blouse open, sending the few remaining buttons flying across the room. His hand slid up her stomach and cupped her breast, massaging it.

"I knew you'd understand my message."

His eyes heavy with desire, he said, "*You're mine, only mine.* Even now, thinking about it makes me hot."

"You didn't mind the blood?"

"You know what the sight of it does to me." His gaze locked with hers, penetrating. "But I understand now. It was a promise, wasn't it?"

"A blood oath," she murmured. A chill ran up Lauren's spine.

Nic took Vivian's mouth again. To Lauren, Vivian looked like she had eight arms. Within seconds, she'd ripped off Nic's shirt and her hands were on the snap of his jeans.

How far would Nic have to go?

Lauren sighed in relief when Nic pulled back onto his knees. "I want to see you in that teddy. All of you." He pulled her skirt down her legs. "But keep the heels," he added as he kissed her ankle.

Vivian inhaled sharply as he rained little bites up her calf and kissed behind her knee.

"You're so beautiful. I don't know how I survived without you."

She made little sounds of pleasure as his kisses moved further up her leg. "You never had to, Nic. Since you met me, you've never been alone."

What did Vivian mean? Lauren turned to Jake and raised her brows in question.

"Kaden told me she planted cameras in the loft. They discovered them the day we left."

Her stomach dropped as though she were on a roller coaster. "Where… where were they?"

"The cops found some in Nic's bedroom and bathroom. There may have been others. I'm not sure."

Lauren swallowed, fighting back waves of nausea. Vivian had watched as

Nic showered. As she showered. As they'd showered *together*. Her cheeks flamed. Even worse, Vivian had been in Nic's bed with them. She'd heard and seen everything they'd said, everything they'd done. Even her confession about her guilt over Todd's death. "That fucking crazy *bitch*." Lauren understood exactly how violated Nic felt. Because she felt the same way.

When she returned her attention to what was going on in the room below, she wished she hadn't. Nic's face was dangerously close to Vivian's crotch. Lauren's stomach heaved and she slapped a hand over her mouth, certain she was going to puke. How could Nic stand doing this when she could barely stand to watch? She wrenched off her headphones and pushed her chair back to get up, but Jake clamped his hand down on her arm. "Stay." When she made no move to sit, he reminded her, "You promised him."

He was right. She had promised. Against her better judgment, she plopped back into her seat and settled the headphones over her ears.

As she watched, Nic sat back on his heels, shoulders sagging. "Before we go any further, there's something I have to tell you."

Eyes wide and breathing in small pants, Vivian propped herself on her elbows. "What is it, darling?"

"It's about Summer." He let his head hang. "I went to her place once."

"I know." She smiled like a benevolent parent.

Nic shook his head and continued. "I let her do things to me." Then he rushed to add, "But then I thought of you and you called. Thank God you called. And then I left."

Her smile widened. "I was very proud of you that day."

He blinked as if surprised. "You aren't angry with me."

"I was a little angry at her though. She knew better."

"And when she drugged me? You must have been more than a little angry then."

Lauren glanced at Jake and saw that he too was waiting on tenterhooks for Vivian's reply. This could be it: the big confession.

When Vivian didn't answer, Nic kissed her stomach, his tongue swirling around her navel through the holes in her lace teddy. "You can tell me anything."

Beneath him, Vivian writhed and gripped his hair but still she remained silent.

"Do you know the worst part of what happened with Summer?" Nic asked. "I don't know what she did to me while I was out of it." He kissed his way up her stomach, and laved one of her nipples through the thin material.

"You're right. That is the worst part." Vivian pressed Nic's head against her breast and arched her back. He sucked a nipple into his mouth but she pushed him away, and started tugging at her teddy. "Get this off me."

Nic chuckled as if her impatience amused him. Slowly he undid one button then paused. "Why the hurry, sweetheart?" he teased.

"You know what I want, darling," Vivian said. When she opened her legs wide, Lauren had to turn away.

"Tell you what," she heard Nic say. The lightness in his tone brought her eyes back to the monitor. What was he up to? He picked up the bowl of whipped cream. "I'll give you what you want, if…" He paused.

"If?"

Nic scooped some whipped cream on his finger and positioned it directly above Vivian's crotch but didn't touch her. "If you answer a question for me."

Vivian's eyes were glued to his finger. Slowly, he brought it to his lips. Her gaze followed. His tongue slipped out and cleaned all the cream off in languorous licks. He sucked his finger into his mouth, then pulled it out with a popping sound. Vivian's gaze locked on his. "Question?" she managed, although her voice sounded like she'd swallowed some cat fur.

"Did you have anything to do with Summer drugging me?"

Vivian looked genuinely shocked. "No! Of course not. I even tried to stop her."

"How's that?" he asked, his voice light as if he were making casual conversation. But it didn't work.

Vivian eyed his finger pointedly. "You got your one question." Nic sighed. "What's the matter, darling? Did I upset you?"

"No." He smiled ruefully. "I thought you'd want to tell me about all the things you did to protect me. Kind of like foreplay, you know?"

"Hearing this stuff turns you on?"

Nic flashed her a cocky smile. "Like nothing else."

In seconds, Vivian was on her knees. "Let me see," she urged, tugging on Nic's zipper.

Nic laughed as he pretended to fall back, pulling Vivian on top of him. But that didn't stop her. Her hand snaked down between them. Before she reached his groin, he rolled over, pinning her under him.

Lauren pushed back her chair, dropped the headphones, and glared at Jake when he tried to restrain her. "I have to stop this."

"Why? He's finally getting somewhere."

She scowled at her bodyguard and shook his hand off her arm. "No, Jake. Vivian's the only one getting somewhere and where she wants to get is in Nic's pants."

If Vivian saw her, maybe the shock would get her to talk. At least it would save Nic the humiliation of having to go further with this sick charade. But first, she had to get past Jake.

In a flash, she grabbed her mug of cold coffee and threw it in Jake's face. Before he had a chance to react, she ran for the stairs.

CHAPTER 25

The woman had a one-track mind.

Nic lay on top of Vivian, pinning her hands above her head so she'd stop trying to grab his dick. Since he couldn't fake an erection, one touch and it would be game over.

A loud noise from above caught his attention and he pulled back.

"What's that?" Vivian asked. "I hope it's not that crazy friend of yours."

"I'll go see," he said, pulling one of the blankets around her. "Put this on so you don't get cold."

"This is why I love you."

Seeing her bright eyes, his heart twisted painfully. For the first time since she'd arrived at the ranch, he was seeing *Vivian*, the woman who'd been his mentor, his confidante, and his friend for the past decade. What had happened to her that she'd lost herself? He dropped a tiny kiss on her lips and rose to his feet.

When he was still a couple steps away from the door, Lauren rounded the corner and ran into his chest. Automatically his arms went around her. She looked at him with pity in her eyes. His fiancée had apparently decided he needed rescuing. He dropped his arms as Vivian approached.

"My, my. Look what the cat dragged in," she hissed. "Aren't you supposed to be in New York?"

Lauren's eyes darted between Nic and Vivian as if she didn't know how to answer. Nic bit back a groan. How the hell was he going to get her out of here?

Ignoring Lauren, he put his arm at the small of Vivian's back and led her to their makeshift bed. If he stayed between the two of them, Vivian wouldn't be able to hurt Lauren. And right now, keeping Lauren safe was the only thing that mattered.

Vivian pulled the blanket more tightly around her shoulders, all trace of desire gone. Hatred flashed in her eyes and rang in her voice. "Why is she here?"

"I don't know."

"Well, get rid of her. Before I do."

Fuck. Vivian wouldn't buy his act unless he was hard on Lauren. Hell, he was so pissed, it wouldn't be much of a stretch. He turned to face her. "What the fuck are you doing here? I told you when you left, that we were done. That I never wanted to see your lying face again."

Lauren flinched. But when she straightened her spine, Nic knew he was in trouble. "I… I couldn't stay away. I quit my job for you."

Vivian's mouth gaped.

"You shouldn't have." Nic shrugged and threw his arm around Vivian, pulling her against his side. "Viv and I belong together. You lost your chance."

"I'd do anything for you." She bit her lip. "I'm even willing to share."

Vivian turned to Nic. "You see? I was right. She's nothing but a whore."

Lauren eyed Vivian up and down, and grimaced. "Come on, Vivian. You know you can't handle a guy like Nic. You need someone like me to pick up the slack."

All his blood dropped and pooled in his feet. She was playing a very dangerous game.

"Someone like you?" sputtered Vivian.

"Someone *young*," Lauren said, emphasizing the word.

Vivian lunged at her. "You little bitch!"

Lauren chuckled and jumped out of the way. "See?"

Nic tried to get between them. "Ladies. Let's all calm down."

Vivian shrugged and turned away. Nic felt a moment of relief when she picked up her skirt and slipped it on. He'd seen more than enough of her teddy. She jammed her arms into the sleeves of her blouse, tying it in a knot below her breasts. Finally she picked up her purse.

"Leaving so soon, dear?" Lauren asked, echoing Vivian's mocking words.

Without answering, Vivian headed for the door and Nic wondered if this would be the end of it. He'd managed to get her to admit to the stalking but not to murdering Summer. Would it be enough?

As she came even with Lauren, Vivian pivoted and Nic knew he'd made a deadly error. Before he could reach them, Vivian grabbed Lauren from behind and put a strangle hold on her. Nic's heart stopped beating when he saw the blade against Lauren's throat.

"Drop it!" shouted Jake as he threw himself into the room.

Jesus *fucking* Christ. Vivian had Lauren by the throat and now he had to worry about Jake, too. At least he hadn't come barging in with his gun drawn.

"Well, well, well. What have we here?" Vivian asked, her light and flirty tone at odds with the situation.

"Release Ms. James. No one needs to get hurt, ma'am."

The intensity of Jake's expression and the tightness of his body clearly said to Nic that he was set to make a move. Nic chanced a glance to the side window and caught a reflection. Kaden's gun was pointed at Vivian. And Lauren was in the way. The panic etched on her features jump-started his stopped heart, which began thundering in his chest. As she stared at him wide-eyed, his mind raced with a thousand possibilities, each more gruesome than the last. "Get out," he said to Jake. The bodyguard's presence only added to the confusion.

"Darling, I'm not stupid," Vivian said, shaking her head. "If he leaves, he'll tell that delicious bodyguard of yours."

Jake held up his hands. "No, ma'am. I won't."

"Such a good boy." She smiled, then her expression hardened. "Hit him."

Nic blinked. "What?"

"I said hit him." When he hesitated, she added, "Knock him out. Now."

This wasn't good. But maybe they could trick Vivian? He locked gazes with Jake, trying silently to convey his plan. "Sorry, man," he said, right before punching Jake in the side of the head. Jake's eyes rolled back and he crumpled to the ground. Nic had to admit that under the circumstances, the bodyguard's acting was pretty damn good. He actually wasn't certain whether Jake had passed out or not. Breathing hard, he turned back to Vivian. "Let her go, Vivian. I love you, not her."

"No. Since the cow is here, I might as well use her as a test."

"A test?" he repeated stupidly.

"Of your love." Smiling, she lowered her head and licked Lauren's neck. "If you truly love me, you'll let me kill her."

He didn't want Vivian dead, but if she hurt Lauren, all bets were off. Before he could say anything, Vivian pressed the blade, piercing Lauren's pale skin. Lauren whimpered, a sound that tore at his heart. He was going to kill Vivian with his bare fucking hands.

Vivian cackled as blood began to drip down Lauren's throat. "So pretty," she mused. When the stream of blood reached Lauren's white T-shirt, he flashed back to the accident, to Rachel's blood splattered on the front seat of the car, the stark contrast of red on white turning his stomach. He started to drift. Fighting back, he tore his eyes away from Lauren's neck. He was *not* going to pass out.

"What's the matter, darling? Is the blood making you woozy?"

Ignoring the jibe, Nic forced himself to focus on Vivian's face and not on the blood dripping down Lauren's neck. He swallowed hard. He had to get the knife. But how? As he searched the room, he again saw the glint in the window. His mouth went dry.

If Kaden fired now, he'd hit Lauren.

In one long leap, he jumped on the women, knocking Vivian back. Grabbing her knife hand, he pulled it away from Lauren. But Vivian kept her other arm around Lauren's throat in a death grip. The three of them fell to the floor in a tangle of arms and legs.

White hot pain shot through him as something sharp pierced his side. But Vivian still held the knife. With a cold emptiness in her eyes, she slammed the hilt down toward the side of his head. He raised his arm, deflecting the worst of it, but the momentum sent him sprawling on his back.

Vivian shoved him with her foot and scrambled upright, using Lauren as a shield. Nic caught his breath. The knife was once again pressed against Lauren's throat. Vivian peered down at him. "Tsk, tsk, darling. You've cut yourself."

What? He brought his hand to his temple but Lauren shook her head and pointed to his side. "Vivian, he's bleeding. Let me help him," she begged.

With his gaze locked on Vivian, he sat up and slid a hand over his side. The area was wet. He raised the hand to his face and sucked in a breath. The bitch had stabbed him. Unable to resist, he glanced down at the wound. And began to sway.

No! Fuck no!

He had to get Lauren out of here. His gaze snapped back to Vivian and he swallowed repeatedly to force back the nausea.

"Are you angry, darling?" She was enjoying all the commotion. Or was it the blood that excited her?

Fighting down the bile that rose in his throat, he flashed her a grin as if he too were in on the joke. He needed to get back into character. "What's a little blood sport between lovers?"

Lauren twisted her head so she could see Vivian's face. "Is that what happened with Summer? Did your sex play get out of hand?"

Vivian jerked back; her eyes filled with disgust. "That bitch was trailer-park trash who couldn't follow simple instructions. She deserved everything she got."

The knife jabbed Lauren again as Vivian's arms tightened around her neck. The cut was deeper this time and more blood flowed. He could see the tears in Lauren's eyes, but she didn't make a sound. When she shook her head slightly, his chest contracted. He understood. Vivian hadn't quite confessed yet.

Nic let his eyes fill with love and adoration as he met Vivian's gaze. "Did you do that for me? Did you kill Summer because she tried to hurt me?"

As he held her gaze, a smile tugged at her lips, and when she spoke, her voice was low, husky. "She wanted to take you away from me. I couldn't let her do that."

"So." He paused and cleared his throat. "You killed her?"

"Yes. I had to stop her."

Nic shot her a lopsided grin and pushed to his feet. "Thank you, *chérie*. Thank you so much." He said the words to Vivian, but they were meant for Lauren. She'd managed what he hadn't been able to do: she'd gotten Vivian to confess.

"I'd do anything for you." Vivian yanked her arm, choking Lauren. Nic felt his own breath leave his body. He took a step closer, but Lauren opened her eyes wide, warning him not to. He hesitated.

"I'll take care of this little rodent problem now," Vivian said in a high-pitched singsong voice that told him everything he needed to know about her sanity. "You don't need her anymore."

He nodded. "I have you now."

"We can be together like we always wanted. You know you're mine."

"I know," he said. "But you need to let Lauren go. If you kill her, the police will be after us. We won't have the future you planned."

Vivian shook her head. "I can't do that."

As Nic took another step to close the distance between them, Vivian yelled at him to stop. He froze but not before his arm hit one of Lauren's umbrellas. His hand shot out to steady it before the wireless flash unit could dislodge and fall to the floor. When he lowered his gaze to the women in front of him, he caught a glimmer of hope in Lauren's eyes.

Careful not to show any reaction, he watched her tap the pocket of her cargo pants with her left hand. Did she have the flash controller in her pocket? Warmth flooded his chest and he wanted to smile. This was so Lauren: prepared for anything.

It was dark enough that if they could trigger the flash units, the light would temporarily blind Vivian and she'd let go of Lauren. It was definitely worth a try. He needed to distract Vivian so Lauren could get the controller out.

His eyes on Vivian, he twisted his mouth into a pout. "Let me get my shirt so I can staunch this bleeding, okay? Then we can figure this out." He backed up to the blankets, picked up his shirt and pressed it firmly against his side. He winced when the material touched his wound.

"Does it hurt, darling?"

"What's a little pain?" he asked conversationally. From this position, he faced Vivian but he could also keep an eye on Jake, who lay on the floor slightly behind and to Vivian's right. "Pain adds to the pleasure, don't you think?"

If he kept her talking, he could edge close enough to make another grab for the knife when the flashes went off.

"I'm glad you think so." Vivian smiled.

"Promise you'll punish me when I'm bad?" he said, winking.

Lauren unbuttoned the pocket of her cargo pants. Jake's fingers twitched.

When Vivian laughed, he smiled. "You've always been there when I needed you, and you always knew exactly what to do to make things better." And he wished he'd been there for her when she needed him. Maybe none of this would have happened. He actually meant every word, and let it show in his eyes. Careful to stay between Lauren and the window, he closed half the distance between them, as Vivian focused on his expression. "Can you tell me, how are we going to get away from here?"

"We weren't supposed to leave until tomorrow, but I suppose I can adjust the plan. After we take care of our little problem"—she yanked on Lauren's hair and Nic had to put all his skills to use to cover up his flinch—"we'll take my car and drive to the airport. A plane will take us to a private island in the Caribbean."

An island? How the hell had she bought an island? "That sounds wonderful." Lauren held up five fingers. He took a step and she put one down. "Will we be alone on this island?" Out of the corner of his eye, he saw Jake's hand move.

"Yes, except for the natives I've hired."

One step. Three fingers.

"How will we pay them? All my money is gone."

Jake inched his hand along his leg. What the hell was he doing? Nic's fist clenched. Jake was probably wearing a backup weapon at his ankle. Now he had two guns to worry about.

One step. Two fingers.

"That's the beauty of my plan." Vivian grinned as if about to reveal a big secret. "Your money's not gone."

"It's not?" No need to fake surprise. "But what about the blackmailer? We have to pay her tomorrow."

Vivian tipped her head back and laughed. Lauren edged the controller out of her pocket. "There's no blackmailer. That was all me. We have enough money to live on the island for the rest of our lives, just you and me."

"I can't imagine anything more romantic." *Horrific.*

"It will be, darling. I've waited so long for this. To have you all to myself."

One step. One finger.

With only one step to go, Nic pretended to cough so he could glance in Jake's direction. Did he understand their plan? As long as there was a hope to end this without killing Vivian, he wouldn't give the signal to shoot. "Just you and me, as it always should have been."

As he took the last step, Lauren pressed the top button on the wireless controller. Prepared, Nic squinted against the bright lights that flashed around the room.

Vivian screeched and covered her eyes with the back of her knife hand as the lights blinded her. Lauren twisted and swung her arms locked together, clocking Vivian in the head. Reeling from the impact, Vivian's hold on Lauren loosened, and she struggled out of her grasp.

Nic threw himself on Vivian, grabbing the hand that held the knife. "Jake! Get Lauren out of here," he shouted without taking his eyes off Vivian.

Snarling, Vivian clawed at Nic's face with her sharp nails and tried to knee him in the groin. He twisted his hips just in time to avoid serious injury. "I've never hit a woman, but for you, I think I could make an exception."

Vivian laughed. "Go ahead. I like it rough."

Despite everything she'd done, seeing the madness in her eyes broke his heart. "It didn't have to be like this," he said, pinning her knife hand to the ground.

"This was all about your little whore, wasn't it?" she spat.

Jake appeared to his left. His gun trained on Vivian, he said, "I've got her, sir."

"Where's Lauren?"

Jake indicated the direction of the door with a slight jerk of his head. Nic released his hold on Vivian. When she didn't make a move to attack him again, he stood up and took a couple steps back. Jake bent down to secure Vivian's hands with zip ties.

Nic turned away from the sight of Vivian lying on the ground. He should hate her, but he couldn't. At least maybe now he could get her the help she needed.

Lauren rushed to his side. "Are you okay?" Her hands flew to his temple and then to the cut in his side. He hissed. "Oh God, I'm sorry," she said, her face turning white.

"It's just a scratch," he said, pulling her into his arms and hugging her tight. She was safe and the nightmare was finally over. But he needed to make sure Vivian hadn't done any serious damage. "Let me see your neck."

When he brushed her hair back to examine the spot where the knife had cut her, she pressed her head against her hunched shoulder so he couldn't see the wound. "Don't," she said.

"It's okay—"

"Hey, that was supposed to be my job," said a very disgruntled Rémi.

Jake looked up and grinned. A grimace of pain spread across his features as Vivian took advantage of the moment of distraction, kicking him in the groin with the heel of her Louboutins.

Vivian picked up the fallen knife and rushed at Nic and Lauren.

Lauren screamed.

"Slap shot!" he yelled, giving Kaden and Jake the signal to shoot. Nic pushed Lauren to the floor and threw himself on top of her. If anyone was going to get hurt, it would be him. Rémi landed on Nic's back. Shocked and surprised, he could do no more than brace himself on his elbows to keep some of the weight off Lauren.

Jake pointed his gun at Vivian and fired. A window shattered as a second shot rang out. Vivian screamed.

Nic covered Lauren's head with his hands to protect her as shards of glass rained down. Guilt swamped him when he felt Rémi's hands cover his own head and heard him grunt as pieces embedded in his back.

As the echo of the shots died out, silence fell. Rémi eased off him and Nic glanced over at Vivian. She lay sprawled on her back, unmoving. Blood leaked from a hole in her forehead. A red stain bloomed on her chest.

Lauren whispered, "Don't look."

He kissed her cheek and rolled off her. "I won't pass out."

Kaden ran into the room, skidding to a stop beside Rémi. He took one look around, then grabbed Rémi's arm. "Let's go call the cops."

Climbing to his feet, Nic helped Lauren up and into his arms where he held her, his face buried in her hair. "I was so scared to lose you."

Her arms tightened around him. After a moment, she pulled his head up and peered at him, her eyes round with concern. "Are you okay?"

Nic shook his head. "I have to see her."

Lauren nodded and stepped out of his arms. He didn't like letting go of her so soon, but he had to do this. He had to say goodbye. As he approached Vivian's body, Jake went to stand at Lauren's side.

Nic knelt beside Vivian and brushed a lock of hair off her cheek. His chest constricted painfully as he studied her face. The face of the woman who'd nurtured him, listened to him, helped him become the man he was today. The woman who'd loved him as a mother. Until something had gone terribly wrong.

Bringing her hand to his lips, he kissed her fingers and vowed to remember her as the strong, loving, professional woman she'd been before all this happened. His eyes burned as he placed her hand on her stomach. Tears rolled down his face and splashed onto hers when he leaned forward to kiss her cheek. "Goodbye, Vivian," he whispered. After one last caress, he stood up, turned away, and stepped into Lauren's open arms.

For several minutes, she just held him, rubbing soothing circles on his back. "I'm so sorry you had to lose her this way, Nic," she murmured next to his ear.

He straightened his back and wiped away her tears even as she wiped his. When she offered him a tremulous smile, he inclined his head and brushed his lips against hers. "I couldn't let her kill you."

"I should have listened to you. I only made things worse."

Nic stared into her eyes, this woman who was his whole world. This woman he'd almost lost. "No," he said, his voice rough. "I couldn't have done it without you." Tenderly, he pressed his lips to hers, letting her feel every emotion that was in his heart. Admiration for her bravery. Relief that she was safe. But most of all love.

When their lips parted, she touched her nose to his. "We're quite a team."

He kissed the tip of it and smiled. "Always."

CHAPTER 26

Lauren dried her hands on a dish towel, then ran upstairs to get Nic's surprise. With trembling hands, she grabbed the package. Because Anderson had come through for her, she could present Nic with her last secret.

Determined, nervous, happy, she made her way downstairs and, after stopping to retrieve the tray of lemonade she'd prepared, joined Nic on the veranda.

"Hey, gorgeous. A penny for your thoughts." Nic patted the spot next to him on the swing. "Or are these thoughts worth more?" he teased.

Lauren placed the tray on a low table and sat beside Nic, relaxing against his chest. "I was thinking how happy I am."

Nic's arm tightened around her shoulders and he kissed her head. "We never discussed where you want to live. Seattle? Chicago? Wherever it is, just say the word."

Surprised, she looked up at him. "I assumed you'd want to live in L.A., or here."

"L.A. is great for adults, but I'd think the ranch would be a better environment for Jason to grow up in." He hesitated, arching a brow. "Would Jason want to live here?"

"He'd be happy anywhere you are."

"You know I'm going to have to travel to film on location. But whenever I'm not working, I'll be here with both of you."

Her mom had been right. Nic would spend time with them because he wanted to, not because he had to. And she'd meet him halfway. "And we can join you whenever Jason isn't in school. We'll make this work."

"You and Jason come first in my life, and if making movies gets in the way of our being a family, I'll make changes."

"Really?" Her heart contracted as a warm feeling grew in her chest. He was nothing like Jason's father. Whereas Todd had chosen to give up his family, Nic was putting them first.

"Yes, really." Nic grinned at her. "I'll only take work based in New York City."

Her lip quivered. To cover it up, she kissed his cheek. "I don't think it'll come to that."

He shifted uncomfortably on the swing.

"Am I hurting you? I shouldn't be leaning on you until your wound is completely healed."

"No, no." Was it the light or was her fiancé blushing like a school boy caught spying on the girls' locker room?

"What is it then?"

"I have something to tell you. It's about Chicago." He looked away from her.

Concerned, she twisted around to face him. "After everything we've been through, I can't imagine there's anything you can say that will shock me."

"This isn't bad, just embarrassing… for me." She raised her brows but didn't dare say anything to delay the confession.

"One night, me and some guys were at a friend's house drinking and watching some R-rated movies. We got to talking about girls. I told them about you, and how no matter what I did, I couldn't get you to notice me. That's when one of the guys had an idea guaranteed to catch your attention."

"Oh my." She laughed. "A bunch of drunk teenage boys. It must have been truly brilliant."

He nodded. "This was definitely one of the most *brilliant* things I did as a kid. And it's the reason I never have more than two drinks. Anyways, we all pooled our money and called a taxi because we'd need a getaway car."

A getaway car? Lauren pressed her fingers to her mouth to keep from laughing out loud.

"The taxi driver drove us to your house."

"You came to my house?"

"Yeah. While my friends sang Elton John's *Can You Feel the Love Tonight*, I threw rocks at your bedroom window. My aim was a little off though, and I hit your parents' window instead. Within moments of the window breaking, I saw your father and mother looking out at us on the front lawn. Your father started yelling. We must have woken you up because your window opened. For once, I had your undivided attention. I had to do what I'd gone there to do. So, I…" He glanced at her before continuing. "Pulled down my pants and mooned you and your parents."

Lauren convulsed with laughter. "I had no idea that was you."

"The next thing I knew, your father was waving around a rifle and yelling at me to get the hell off his property or he'd put a bullet in my ass. We dove into the taxi and hauled it out of there."

Tears streamed down her face as she recalled the incident. "You know, for years I wondered if the whole thing had been an insult or a compliment."

Nic's eyes widened. "Believe me, *chérie*. It was meant as the highest of compliments."

Try as she might, she simply couldn't keep a straight face. "This will definitely be one of those how-we-met stories we tell our kids."

He groaned and covered his face. "Please don't say that."

Lauren laughed. After a quick glance to make sure they were alone, she picked up the box she'd brought out. "I got you something." She licked her dry lips. Would Nic be upset? Should she be this honest with him? Yes. If there was one lesson she'd learned from her marriage to Todd, it was *begin as you mean to go.*

Nic slowly untied the big red bow that held the box closed, his face glowing with anticipation like a child at Christmas. When he lifted the lid, his brow creased. "What's this?"

She took the cover away but didn't say anything.

Nic pulled out the four silk scarves, revealing a long feather, a can of whipped cream and a bottle of chocolate sauce. His brows tipped into a frown as he pulled out the letter she'd written. "You wrote me a letter?"

"A fantasy actually."

Nic pushed everything back in the box, and slammed the cover on. He grabbed her hand and began pulling her inside.

"Where are we going?"

He stopped abruptly, enclosing her in his arms. "We're going upstairs so you can tell me, in detail, about this fantasy of yours."

Lowering his head, his lips met hers in a passionate kiss. When he grabbed her hips and yanked her against his groin, there was no doubt. He meant business. Her heart filled to bursting for this man who accepted her as she was, and who wanted to make her happy, whatever it took. "I love you, Nicolas Lamoureux."

"And I love you Lauren James, soon to be Lauren Lamoureux." Her legs grew weak. Nic's accent was so sexy when he said her new name in French. "But right now? You'd better start running."

She gaped at him. He hadn't had time to read it yet. He couldn't possibly know. "Why?"

"It's time to begin your fantasy."

Suddenly, she understood. "You knew about my fan letter? All along you knew?"

"Lauren, *ma bien aimée*, I personally read all the letters from my fans." He grinned, adding, "Yours was very edu… uh… entertaining." Turning her around, he slapped her butt. "Now go."

She squeaked and took off, running up the stairs to their attic bedroom with Nic right on her heels. And when he caught her, Lauren knew she was the luckiest woman in the world.

Because the reality of Nic Lamoureux was a million times more exciting than any fantasy.

Continue reading for a special preview of

Kristine Cayne's second Deadly Vices novel

Deadly Addiction

Available March 2012

A proud people. A nation divided.

Rémi Whitedeer, police officer turned substance-abuse counselor, dreams of restoring order to his tribe. Violence and crime are rampant throughout the unpoliced Iroquois reserve, and a civil war is brewing between the Guardians, a militant traditionalist group, and other tribal factions. As the mixed-race cousin of the Guardians' leader, Rémi is caught in a no-man's land—several groups lay claim to him, but all want him to deny his white blood.

A maverick cop on an anti-drug crusade.

When she infiltrated the Vipers to take down the leader of the outlaw biker gang responsible for her brother's death, police sergeant Alyssa Morgan got her man. But her superiors think she went too far. Her disregard for protocol and her ends-justify-the-means ethics have branded her an unreliable maverick. To salvage her career, she accepts an assignment to set up a squad of native provincial officers on a reserve.

A radical sovereigntist bent on freeing a nation.

Decades of government oppression threaten the existence of the Iroquois Nation. But one man, Chaz Whitedeer, is determined to save his people no matter what the price, even if it means delving into the shadowy world of organized crime.

When Rémi and Alyssa uncover the Guardians' drug-fueled scheme to fund their fight for true autonomy—a scheme involving the Vipers—Rémi must choose between loyalty to family and tribe or his growing love for Alyssa.

Can Rémi and Alyssa leave everything behind—even their very identities—for a future together?

An excerpt from ***Deadly Addiction***

Eyes closed, Alyssa pressed the glass of water to her neck. "I can do the talking if that makes you feel any better."

Although Rémi heard the words, it would have taken an act of Parliament to get him to respond.

The heat of her skin caused the condensation on the glass to liquefy. Like a tractor-beam, his eyes followed a drop of water as it slid down the long pale column of her neck, followed the curve of her right breast and slipped under the collar of her blue cotton T-shirt into the V of her cleavage. *Oh fuck*. He wanted to be that drop of water. He wanted to be snuggled between her warm ripe breasts. His cock swelled and lengthened, letting him know that it wanted to be there too.

He squeezed his eyes shut and willed his hard-on away. This wasn't the time and certainly not the place for Mr. Happy to make an appearance. But the more he tried not to think about where the drop had gone, the more he did. He'd thought he was a leg man, but he knew the truth now. It had slapped him in the face. He was a breast man. An "Alyssa's breasts" man, and he fucking wanted to see them, to feel them, to taste them. Right now.

Continue reading for a special preview of

Dana Delamar's first Blood and Honor novel

Revenge

Available January 2012

A woman on the run

Kate Andretti is married to the Mob—but doesn't know it. When her husband uproots them to Italy, Kate leaves everything she knows behind. Alone in a foreign land, she finds herself locked in a battle for her life against a husband and a family that will "silence" her if she will not do as they wish. When her husband tries to kill her, she accepts the protection offered by a wealthy businessman with Mafia ties. He's not a mobster, he claims. Or is he?

A damaged Mafia don

Enrico Lucchesi never wanted to be a Mafia don, and now he's caught in the middle of a blood feud with the Andretti family. His decision to help Kate brings the feud between the families to a boil. When Enrico is betrayed by someone in his own family, the two of them must sort out enemies from friends—and rely on each other or die alone. The only problem? Enrico cannot reveal his identity to Kate, or she'll bolt from his protection, and he'll be duty-bound to kill her to safeguard his family's secret.

A rival bent on revenge…

Attacks from without and within push them both to the breaking point, and soon Enrico is forced to choose between protecting the only world he knows and saving the woman he loves.

An excerpt from *Revenge*

Enrico raised a hand in greeting to Kate, and she returned his wave and started descending the steps.

She headed straight for him, her auburn hair gleaming in the sun, a few strands of it blowing across her pale cheek and into her green eyes. With a delicate hand, she brushed the hair out of her face. Enrico's fingers twitched with the desire to touch her cheek like that, to feel the slide of her silky hair. A small, almost secretive smile crossed her features, and he swallowed hard. *Dio mio.* He felt that smile down to his toes.

She stopped a couple feet from him. "Signor Lucchesi, it's good to see you, as always."

He bowed his head slightly. "And you, Signora Andretti." He paused, a grin spreading across his face. "Since when did we get so formal, Kate?"

She half-turned and motioned to the doorway behind her. And that was when he noticed it—a bruise on her right cheek. *Merda! Had someone hit her?* Tearing his eyes off the mark, he followed her gesture. A tall, sandy-haired man, well-muscled and handsome, leaned in the doorway, his arms crossed. "My husband, Vincenzo, is here."

Enrico's smile receded. He looked back to Kate. "I'd like to meet him." *And if he did this to her, he's going to pay.*

Made in the USA
Charleston, SC
12 September 2012